# THE SECRET LIFE OF MRS. LONDON

# THE SECRET LIFE OF MRS. LONDON

REBECCA ROSENBERG

LAKE UNION PUBLISHING

This is a work of fiction. Names, characters, organizations, places, events, and incidents are either products of the author's imagination or are used fictitiously.



Published by Lake Union Publishing, Seattle

www.apub.com



ISBN-13: 9781542048736
ISBN-10: 1542048737

Cover design by PEPE *nymi*

Printed in the United States of America

*To my own muse, Gary.*

*Who else would listen to my scenes in bed?*

*What is drama but life with the*
*dull bits cut out.*

*—Hitchcock*

# *Part I*

## California

*"I would rather be ashes than dust! I would rather that my spark should burn out in a brilliant blaze than it should be stifled by dry-rot. I would rather be a superb meteor, every atom of me in magnificent glow, than a sleepy and permanent planet. The function of man is to live, not to exist. I shall not waste my days trying to prolong them. I shall use my time."*

—*Jack London,* Jack London's Tales of Adventure

# 1

## Beauty Ranch, Glen Ellen, California
## September 1915

*For her I accomplished Odysseys, scaled mountains, crossed deserts; for her I led the hunt and was forward in battle; and for her and to her I sang my songs of the things I had done. All ecstasies of life and rhapsodies of delight have been mine because of her. And here, at the end, I can say that I have known no sweeter, deeper madness of being than to drown in the fragrant glory and forgetfulness of her hair.*

—*Jack London,* The Star Rover

Nothing breathes vigor into a marriage like a boxing match. And it helps to have a stupefied audience to witness the fight. If I can get Jack boxing this morning, with his drinking buddies cheering him on, he'll be revved up for a good writing session followed by a "grand lolly" that will linger in our loins for days.

So I pull on muslin bloomers and leather boxing boots from my wardrobe, twist my hair into a topknot, daub on lavender oil for luck. Our fox terrier raises his head from my bed, ears perked. I stroke his chest and lift him down, his little heart beating in my palm. "Come on, Possum, he can't say no to you."

Slinging boy-sized boxing gloves over my neck, I cross the hallway to Jack's own sleeping porch, where he sleeps it off after our houseguests plied him with martinis at the Glen Ellen saloon until the wee hours. Possum romps at my heels. Jack still reeks of gin, and his snoring drowns out the jeering blue jays.

"Rise and shine." I whisk off the plaid blanket, exposing fine muscled legs in red flannel shorts.

Jack's not moving. So I lift Possum up and let him lick Jack's face. "Time for our match."

"Charmian, no. It can't be morning." He pulls a feather pillow over his head, and Possum nuzzles underneath.

"Oh, but it is." I throw the pillow to the floor, and Possum laps at his cheeks. "And a deal is a deal."

Jack groans and lifts up onto one elbow, holding the dog off with his other hand. "I can't do this after last night."

"You can. I know you can." I take Possum in my arms.

Jack's valet, Nakata, enters with a cup of coffee balanced on his upturned palm, dressed as usual in a haori jacket and skirted trousers. "*Kishi kaisei*, Mr. Jack."

Jack sits up and takes the coffee. "My head's too fuzzy for Japanese this morning."

Nakata smiles with teeth straight as piano keys. "Wake from death and return to life."

Jack grimaces. "That supposed to make me feel better?"

Nakata bows and leaves, Possum following him for breakfast. The Socialists criticize Jack for employing servants, but Nakata is essential to his well-being. He starts Jack's day with platitudes and strong coffee, grants his wildest wishes, manages our household staff so we can focus on writing, and, in the evening, prepares Jack's cot with philosophy books and farming journals, small and large writing pads, sharpened pencils, and a thermos of martinis (equal splashes of vermouth and olive juice). Together, Nakata and I handle Jack's needs, and I pray he will never leave us.

I lace on Jack's boxing boots while he slurps his coffee, his ankles swollen. Drinking always kicks up his gout.

"I was kidding about the boxing," he says. "A joke for the Crowd . . ." His nickname for the Bohemian-Socialist-literary folks who worship at his feet. Come to think of it, that's exactly where I happen to be at the moment.

"Oh no. You're not getting away with it this time." I knot his laces tighter. "'Bring me the boxing gloves if I'm not up by eight,' you said. 'Best thing in the world for a hangover,' you said. 'We'll do the drop-and-grind drill,' you said."

Jack smirks. "I love it when you talk dirty."

"Come on, champ. Let's give it a go. Our audience awaits." I hoist his arm over my shoulders, staggering under the weight he's gained of late.

He limps to the back door.

Nakata and some of the staff have gathered to watch on the back stoop between our separate sleeping porches, Jack's remedy for my chronic insomnia and his late hours.

In an apron and calico dress, Jack's sister, Eliza, washes the windowpanes, doughy underarm flesh swinging with each swipe of her dish towel. "Boxing is no good for Jack." She clucks her tongue at me. "Just brings out the poison in his system all over again."

"Better out than in," I answer.

Lawrence Godfrey-Smith, the Australian concert pianist turned eucalyptus broker, and George Sterling, poet king of the Bohemians, follow us out to the porch with coffee mugs.

"What's all the ballyhoo?" Lawrence nudges me in the overfamiliar way he's adopted since that time on the beach in Australia . . .

I step down to the garden. "Don't you remember Jack's promise when you stumbled in last night? He wanted to box this morning to get his blood flowing for writing."

"Who's he going to wallop?"

I thrust up my gloved hand. "Me, of course."

Lawrence turns to Sterling. "Do all American couples fight?"

"Of course," Sterling says, stroking his goatee. "They just don't usually wear gloves."

It's nine o'clock already, and the sun just cleared the top of the redwoods, illuminating the garden like an arena. Our boots crush the creeping thyme, melding with the herbaceous smell of ripening chardonnay grapes.

Jack bounces forward on his left foot, then weaves back, shifting his weight to the right, then back again. Red shorts hug his waist and skim his well-built thighs. He looks fitter than he is, from a past regimen of boxing, swimming, horseback riding. It's not fair how men look better than us as they age. Not fair at all.

"Come on, pretty boy." I hold my fists up in front of my face. "Let's see what you're made of."

"The legs of a Roman goddess." Sterling whistles.

"Mind your p's and q's, Greek," Jack says. "Those are my wife's gams you're looking at." He throws the first punch, which lands square to my glove.

"I'm talking about *your* legs, Wolf." Sterling combs long fingernails through his goatee, making my skin crawl. The disheveled poet could use a comb and nail scissors . . . and a bath, come to think of it.

Jack camps a pose and spins his white satin boxing sash around like Jack Johnson at the world championship.

After I take a playful poke at his ribs to get his attention, suddenly he's jumping around me like Possum dancing for a scrap of meat.

For a while, Jack and I practice our drill, throwing rhythmic punches, gaining confidence and speed. We must look hilarious with Jack so much taller and broader and me, his "small woman," holding my own.

"Hey, Wolf," Lawrence says. "If you win, I'll take a hundred dollars off your eucalyptus starts."

Jack thumbs his nose in jest, though I know it eats at him to owe Lawrence for the seedlings, with no way to pay yet. Our Aussie friend convinced Jack eucalyptus would make him a fortune, but the seedlings have only added to our growing debt.

A mighty punch whizzes past me. Jack huffs and rolls his eyes. "You've got the advantage today, Mate-Woman. I have the willies."

"Excuses, excuses." I make a right jab at his chest, and he takes it, his shoulder swinging back. Abdomen, chest, or shoulders are fair game, but anything below Jack's belt isn't allowed—his kidneys and liver have taken all the abuse they can handle.

Eliza shoos the staff inside. "Don't you people have work to do this morning? The ranch doesn't run itself." Her nostrils flare at me. "Though some folks seem to think so."

Nine years married to her brother, and Eliza still sees me as a nuisance to endure.

"Stay in the match or I'll knock your block off." Jack takes a swipe.

We go at it for another quarter hour. Jack's chest swells out, his breath labors. I prance and punch to give him a fight, but not too much to tire him out or bruise his ego.

Lawrence watches my antics with palpable pleasure, which Jack pretends not to notice. Now for the tricky part, how to end this thing. In an effort to go down fighting, I swing in the air, but my glove catches his jaw. I lose my footing and fall on the flagstones, hitting my tailbone with a searing pain. Lawrence runs and lifts me up. "Are you all right?" Jack asks, blood trickling from his mouth onto his chin.

"You won. You won, Wolf." Sterling claps long hands together in mockery. "You beat the stuffing out of the little lady."

"Did I hurt you, Lady-Boy?" Jack holds his jaw, jiggles it side to side.

Breaking free of Lawrence's grasp, I run to wipe the blood from Jack's chin with my shirttail. "Now if you'll excuse us, gentlemen, we have a novel to write." Jack's golden rule: write a thousand words a day. And my job is to keep him to it.

I take Jack's hand and pull him up the steps, feeling Lawrence's eyes on my backside, tingling despite my good intentions. Damn eucalyptus. Damn blue-eyed, blond Aussies.

"I feel like a new man." Jack pats my rear and makes me jump. "You know just what I need, don't you, Mate?"

"What you need is a shower." I hold open the screen door. "After we finish the story, we'll figure out what else you need."

Jack and I met Lawrence in Sydney six years ago when we sailed there on our forty-three-foot ketch, the *Snark*. Jack invited him to Beauty Ranch. Lawrence has been in and out of our lives ever since.

The three of us prove great companions. Jack loves stimulating company, and Lawrence is young, handsome, witty, downright seductive. Of course, I'm an old lady compared to him, thirteen years older, five older than Jack.

Jack always loves a full house, as long as I keep guests busy with horseback riding, hikes, fishing, swimming. So when he is preoccupied with building Wolf House or off to Hollywood or New York, Lawrence fills my days with piano, singing duets, creekside picnics. We never stop talking.

But over the last few weeks, our babbling current has turned perilous, like a rushing river carving deep into the bedrock of my marriage. Lawrence's eager touch makes me feel like . . . a woman. A cherished woman. A feeling as delectable and addictive as wild raspberries or icy champagne.

Jack noticed the change in me, but instead of throwing a jealous fit, he slipped a note under my sleeping porch door at bedtime.

"I am filled with the joy of your voice when you sing for Lawrence and me," he wrote. "The fiber-sounds in your throat tell me I love you as madly as I have always loved you. Meet me in my den after everyone retires."

The specter of adultery spurred Jack's love that night. He took me on the floor of his studio, violent and unrelenting, rubbing my backbone raw on the Oriental rug.

A carnal lesson about Jack I'd half forgotten, something that fascinates me and frightens me. The key to his passion is his jealous streak.

After that night, Jack begs us for duets on the Steinway. Lawrence sits close to me on the bench, shoulders and arms rubbing as our four hands create ecstasy and heartbreak on the black-and-whites. Jack watches us, knuckles pressed to his mouth, his fertile mind churning.

One morning, after our writing session, Jack sits in his studio, making notes for the next day, while I occupy Lawrence with some lark or another. We are picking figs in the garden outside Jack's window when Lawrence holds one out for me to eat. Jack watches from his desk, a lock of hair over his eyes. Daring myself, I bite into the luscious fruit. Lawrence's fingers linger at my lips, pushing a piece of fig into my mouth. I look up to Jack. He smiles and writes on his notepad.

I send Lawrence to gather eggs from the henhouse while I check in on Jack.

"What are you working on?" I move behind him to look at his notes, but he covers them with his hand.

"A new novel, *The Little Lady of the Big House*," he says. "A love triangle between husband and wife and the dashing guest at their ranch. But each of the three is good. Each of the three is big. No weaklings or moralists. They are cultured, modern, and at the same time profoundly primitive. All sex from start to finish."

"So now we're puppets to your puppeteer? I've had enough." I turn to leave.

"But have you, Lady-Boy? Have you really?" He smirks like the devil who relishes my temptations.

I pick up a book to throw at him, and he shields himself with both hands, grinning all the more.

"You're too good a writer to resort to sex in your novels." I slam the book down on the pile. "Is it more money you're after? We'll find the money to build Wolf House some other way."

"Don't be afraid, Charmian. This will be a winner. And we need a winner."

I sit on the arm of his chair and stroke his hair. "How does the novel end?"

He peers up at me through his eyebrows. "That all depends on my heroine. She's very much her own woman."

I scoff. "Am I? I thought I was a figment of your imagination."

He hunches over to make another note, inspired by a new idea.

I kiss his neck. "We're going to make a fig tart in the kitchen. Want to help?"

"Braving the kitchen without Manyoungi? You're taking your life in your hands." He scribbles a note.

"Come, Jack. It will be fun."

"I can't leave this now." He lowers his head to his notes. "You and Lawrence have your fun."

Like he's giving us his blessing.

Two can play this game. Over the following week, I challenge myself to see where this dalliance leads. Where does writer Jack London draw the line and husband Jack London claim me as his own? All for the sake of his novel, of course. The more I play into Lawrence's flirtation, the more attention Jack pays me. After nine years of marriage, I need all the help I can get to keep him interested, especially with his ready supply of lady friends: Blanche Bates, the two-bit actress, and that New York journalist Sophie Loeb. And his first love, Anna Strunsky. How does an old lady like me fight with unrequited loves like them? Fire with fire.

During those lazy September afternoons at the duck pond, warming our bodies on the raft, Lawrence counts each new freckle on my nose. Does a man, any man, really do that? Since I've been married to Jack, it's been about building his dreams. Most people think that's writing the great American novel, but no. It's building an agrarian utopia of Beauty Ranch, with Wolf House as the monument to his success. His writing fuels the dream, just as I fuel the writing. A noble cause in light of his brilliance.

But this summer, it's Lawrence who infuses my days with laughter and joy. He touches the nape of my neck, telling me how downy and lovely it is.

Most seductive of all, Lawrence reads my first published story, "The Wheel," and praises me for my poetic language and depth of thought. Granted, he is no literary genius, but his words soothe the gnawing in my gut that I'll never be the writer Jack is.

This morning, in our cozy cottage under ancient redwoods and valley oaks, Jack is finishing up *The Star Rover*, a poignant reminder of what it is about Jack that gets under my skin. Even more than his genius, it's the eagerness in his voice, as if he's writing the story just for me.

A golden thread spins from Jack's tongue to my fingers working my Remington typewriter like a loom weaving an intricate tapestry.

*The Star Rover* is not an adventure book like *Call of the Wild* or *White Fang*, but more akin to his social/political novels *Martin Eden* and *Iron Heel*. But *The Star Rover* has its own mesmerizing prose and reflects Jack's search for meaning in the universe.

As long as the keys of my typewriter descend and rise, I am his muse, his instrument, the witness to the outpouring of his soul.

"Oh, make no mistake, I am no callow, ardent youth." Jack circles me, reciting like an actor. "I am an elderly man, broken in health and body, and soon to die."

My fingers spasm, but I don't dare stop typing. He props his hand against the paned window of his study, early sun streaming on his brow. Tilting his head, he listens to the gray vireos warbling from the fig tree in the garden, a wave of chestnut hair glints bronze in the sunlight, and though he's already thirty-nine, his boyish beauty still catches me beneath my breastbone.

My fingers follow his confession, knowing full well his stories are autobiographical one way or another.

"Always has woman crouched close to earth like a partridge hen mothering her young." His voice breaks and noble cheeks sag.

Is he thinking of our baby, Joy, or his own little girls who his ex-wife forbids at Beauty Ranch? Either way, I'm to blame.

Moving behind me now, Jack plucks a tendril from my topknot and sends a thrill down my neck.

"Always has my wantonness of roving led me out on the shining ways, and always have my star paths returned me to her."

Jack always comes home to me. That's something, isn't it? Women love Jack and die for love of him. They send him long letters, which he keeps in a locked box under his bed. Once I asked why he keeps in touch with old sweethearts. He said, "One must be kind, you know."

"The figure everlasting . . ." Jack lights an Imperial cigarette while his sailor-blue eyes bathe my face with fondness. I lower my chin to hide my forty-three-year-old neck, which looks more like a rooster's than his beloved's. I've taken to wearing high necklines.

"The woman, the one woman, for whose arms I had such need, that clasped in them, I have forgotten the stars." He sucks a long drag. "Getting all this, Mate-Woman?"

I raise an eyebrow, hands hovering over the keys, not about to let him break our hard-won concentration.

We need to finish *The Star Rover* to fund the construction of Wolf House. A yawning pit of log and stone gobbling up as much money as Jack can feed it. Fifteen thousand square feet with four stories, twenty-six rooms, nine fireplaces, a reflecting pool in the center atrium that runs from one end to the other. Modern electricity, central heat, hot water, indoor plumbing, even a vacuum cleaning system and refrigeration. All the conveniences our cottage lacks, he says.

I love our cozy cottage.

Jack starts to dictate again, and my hands jump to keep up. "After the dark, I shall live again, and there will be women."

Always women. My bottom tingles in his wooden captain's chair, and I shift around in my skirts, struggling to set down his words. Live again . . . what does he mean? Ah yes. Reincarnation. But is it clear? I must remember to rework that.

Jack never shies from difficult subjects, no matter how taboo. Rather, he slogs through the muck of life: infidelity, terror, failure, suicide. Even if my own writing falls short, at least I have a hand in his genius.

"The future holds the little women for me in the lives I am yet to live." Jack pops a Formamint into his mouth. "And though the stars drift and the heavens lie, ever remains woman, resplendent, eternal, the one woman, as I, under all my masquerades and misadventures, am the one man, her mate."

My fingers linger on the keys, savoring the resonance of his words. Then I tear the page off the carriage and place it upside down in the box.

Jack traces my cheekbone with his finger. "I never tire of watching how you keep up with me. It's like you are thinking the story before I speak it and humoring me to imagine you are typing my creation."

I take advantage of his mood. "Did you have a chance to ask Macmillan if they'll publish my *Log of the Snark*?"

"Sorry, Mate." He avoids my eyes. "The Great War has made the market soft for travelogues. Macmillan asked me to write my autobiography, but I have no feeling for it."

"That book took me nine years to write, they can't turn it down." I swallow the rock in my throat. "You said it was good. The cannibals, the fire dances, the great sea fishing . . . Didn't I capture the feeling of the islands?"

He winces and covers his cheek with his hand, and I see it's swollen. "Good descriptions."

"That's all?"

He nods, then shakes his head. "Very good descriptions, indeed."

His scant praise cuts my spirit like a blade. "What's wrong with your mouth?"

Jack's valet enters with a package wrapped in brown paper. "Sorry to interrupt, but Mr. Jack asked me to bring him mail from post office."

"Can you take a look at this front tooth, Nakata? It hurts." Jack opens wide and points.

Maybe his lackluster appraisal has more to do with his teeth than my writing.

Nakata's eyebrows slope together as his delicate fingers prod Jack's gums. *"Yuruidesu,"* Nakata says. Too loose.

"Oh, Jack, I'm sorry." He needs every tooth he has, after losing several to scurvy in the Yukon.

Jack's hand cups his swollen jaw. "Charmian, you should quit writing and take up prizefighting." He looks at Nakata. "Can you take care of this before I leave for the Bohemian Club?"

Nakata rubs his palms together. "If one does not enter the tiger's cave, one will not catch its cub."

Jack tilts his head. "Does that mean you'll do it?"

*"Mochiron."* Of course. Nakata opens Jack's first aid kit: rattlesnake oil for rheumatism, Dr. Bonker's Egyptian Oil for stomach cramps, heroin for asthma, morphine granules for pain, cocaine for toothaches. "Mr. Jack, meet me in the kitchen, and I fix you up." Nakata leaves with a couple of vials.

"Let me call the dentist." I pick up the candlestick receiver of the telephone and jiggle the cradle, a bitter taste in my mouth. "I should have been more careful."

"Put the telephone down. I don't need the operator gossiping about how you knocked out my tooth." Jack studies the postmark of the package. "Besides, Nakata is studying to be a dentist."

*"Honto?"* I slip into the Japanese Nakata's been teaching me for ten years, since he came back with Jack from the Russo-Japanese War. "Really? Since when?" I put the telephone down.

"I found him a correspondence course." He winces. "Least I can do for the fellow who saved my life in Japan."

Walking behind Jack, I massage his taut shoulders. "You're so munificent."

"Translation?" He raises a bushy brow.

"You don't know the meaning of *munificent*?"

One shoulder shrugs. "You're my dictionary."

"*Munificent* means generous to a fault." I laugh, happy to find a new word for his digestion. "What will Nakata do for your tooth?"

"Pull the damn thing." He smiles crookedly, and my own mouth aches in sympathy. "He's got to have his first patient sometime. Besides, I don't have time for a dentist."

He rips the brown wrapping from the package and traces his name engraved on the cover. "Hey, hey. *The Scarlet Plague*. Wondered when they'd send my copies." He slaps his knee, and I come around and sit on it, our ritual when a new book arrives fresh from the publisher. He lifts the red cloth-bound volume between us, and we lean in to hear him crack open the pages. Then he brings it to my nose for a whiff of fresh-milled paper and tang of ink.

Today it smells a little like defeat. Almost forty books and fifteen years of typing and editing for Jack, and I've yet to see my own name engraved in gold on a book cover.

Jack takes his Waterman fountain pen and reads aloud as he inscribes the book. "Dearest Mate-Woman, whose efficient hands I love—the hands that have worked for me long hours and made me music on her piano. The hands that have steered the *Snark* through rough seas, do not tremble on a trigger, that are sure and strong as a Marquesan stallion, the hands that are so sweet with love as they pass through my hair, firm with comradeship as they grip mine, and that soothe as only they, of all hands in the world, can soothe. Your Man and Lover."

I hug him, his chest warm against my bosom. Smells of tobacco and eucalyptus flood my body with desire. "Let's try again, Jack. I know how much you want a son," I whisper into his neck.

After Baby Joy's birth two years ago, the doctor said I needed surgery to repair severe internal damage. In other words, he'd butchered my insides in the delivery. After surgery, he announced,

"I saved your uterus, such as it is." Ever since, my periods vary from spotty to torrential.

Aunt Netta lays the blame on the first signs of menopause, but I still hope I can produce a son for Jack and appease the raging alcoholic he depicted in *John Barleycorn*. A son is the one thing that can tame that beast once and for all and let us live in peace.

Jack blows on the book inscription, waiting for the ink to dry.

I move behind him, circling my arms around his shoulders, leaning down to kiss his neck. What keeps him away from my bedroom? I miss his hands on my breasts. I miss the pure weight of him anchoring me to the bed. I miss his triumphant shudder in my ear. "Let's go to my room before you leave for the Bohemian Club. The doctor says I'm fine now."

He searches through piles of papers. "The Greek and I have to leave at noon, and I have no idea where my speech is."

My mouth goes dry. "What about Lawrence? You're taking him along, aren't you?" Jack must see how he tracks me like a dingo hunts a rabbit. I don't trust him, don't trust myself.

"He doesn't want to go." Jack mimics his down-under accent. "He said, 'Why would I want to hear you spewing Socialist propaganda when I can stay here at Beauty Ranch with your darling wife?' Can't say I blame him." He takes my palm and kisses it, like Lawrence did on our hike. Oxygen whooshes from my lungs.

"Then take me with you." I clutch Jack's arm.

"Don't be silly, the Bohemian Club is men only." He shakes me off. "Besides, I need you to keep an eye on Wolf House construction if we have a prayer of moving in next month. They're supposed to be staining the woodwork and sealing the rock before the winter rains start."

"Don't go, Jack." I hide my hot cheek on his chest like a begging schoolgirl, petrified what will happen if he goes. "I need you here. Please."

His body stiffens. "Hysterics don't become you, Charmian. You should know that sort of thing gets less than nothing from me."

My chest prickles. Jack expects a comrade, not a sniveling woman. "You're using the revolution speech, right? Let me make you a mimeograph."

I find the original speech in my files and guide the pages through the mimeograph. Turning the crank, I hope the damn machine works this time. The copies come out the other side, rippled with wet ink but readable.

"Here you go, Mate." I hand him the speech with a hearty smile to mask my chagrin. "Set a fire under those Bohemians."

# 2

## Beauty Ranch, Glen Ellen, California
## September 1915

*It was what should have been a bright summer day, but the smoke from the burning world filled the sky, through which the sun shone murkily, a dull and lifeless orb, blood-red and ominous.*

—*Jack London,* The Scarlet Plague

Three more days until Jack and the Greek come back from the Bohemian Club. Lawrence perches on a Tahitian barstool, sipping one of Nakata's rickeys, watching me play the Steinway grand piano. His blond hair is slicked straight back from his sun-kissed forehead, and he looks as enticing as he did on the beach in Sydney six years ago.

"You're so gay and full of life." His Australian lilt always strikes a chord in me.

"That's the ragtime." I force a laugh.

His cerulean eyes meet mine. "That's you, Charmian."

Lavender oil heats on my pulsing wrist. "It's Joplin, trust me." I start to play again, determined to keep it casual between us.

Lawrence sets down his cocktail and sits next to me on the bench. I move to get up, but he touches my forearm, making my nerve endings dance the tango. How I miss that dance.

"Show me how to play ragtime."

I sit down again and play "Chinatown, My Chinatown."

His sprightly fingers are light on the piano keys, and soon Lawrence plays harmony to my melody as if we're performing on a stage.

My head feels dizzy with him so close. I've gone too long without Jack's touch. Our duet reaches the crescendo, and heat rushes up my neck, burning my ears.

"You are a marvel, Charmian," he says.

Wobbly as a newborn colt, I escape from the bench and move to the open window to cool myself. If this is Jack's idea of testing my fidelity or prowess as a hostess, I'm fearful I'll fail on both fronts.

"Wonder how Jack's speech is going at the Bohemian Club," I say.

His rosemary pomade tingles my nose a second before his hands enclose my waist, strong with desire.

I pull away and walk to the piano. "Damn this September heat." Snatching a sheet of music, I fan my face. "Not a breeze in Sonoma Valley."

My thoughts skitter like field mice. Of course, I won't succumb, but lately Jack's too preoccupied to visit my bedroom. And what about his lady friends in New York, Hollywood, and Carmel?

Aunt Netta's voice rumbles around in my head as it has since I was six: "What's good for the goose is good for the gander." Her voice became my conscience after Mother died. But what good has "free love" done her, living with my "uncles" Roscoe and Edward, like a queen bee with too many flowers to pollinate? Though I'd never admit it, Netta's liberated philosophy never rang true for me. Free love is never free.

Lawrence smiles slyly and sits back at the piano bench. "It's spring in Australia. Remember the magnolias?"

"I swear the aroma of those trees drugged me."

"You can't blame a tree for your naughty behavior."

"That was years ago, Lawrence. I've changed." My free-loving spirit drained from the colander of marriage.

"Not from where I sit."

His eyes rove my body, and I pull in my tummy under his scrutiny.

"Never met a girl who handles a horse like you, and you still beat me swimming to the raft this afternoon." He winces. "Keep that between us, will you? Wouldn't want it known a girl beat the Sydney swim champion."

"A girl? Really, Lawrence."

He strikes the piano keys with the jubilant sound of ragtime. How does he get such volume from my Steinway? Like a Magnavox foghorn amplifier . . .

Nakata shuffles in wearing tabi socks and sandals, holding a frosty pitcher of rickeys in one hand and his ear with the other. "There are even bugs that eat knotweed." He sets it on the bar, scrunches his nose at Lawrence, and leaves.

"Japanese proverb?" Lawrence continues playing.

"Nakata doesn't care for ragtime," I say, but I suspect it's Lawrence he doesn't like.

I hear the front screen door open. "I know you're in there, Charmian." In an instant, I recognize Aunt Netta's pretentious accent, the way she stresses the "Charm" and swallows the "ian" like a secret. "I certainly did not pour a fortune into piano lessons to have you play ragtag mumbo."

Netta breezes in, back from months in San Francisco. She's a vision in white batiste, smocked bodice, and puffed sleeves, white hair flowing from a center part and falling around her shoulders.

Whistler's *Symphony in White*. She dressed like the painting. I'm as sure of it as I'm sure her visit will siphon every ounce of my energy. It always does.

"Oh, that's not you playing." She walks around Lawrence at the piano, drinking him in.

"Mr. Lawrence Godfrey-Smith, this is my aunt Netta."

Lawrence stands up from the bench, tall and lean. "This can't be the aunt who raised you. She's too young."

His teasing tone makes me gnaw at my cuticles. He's just rascal enough to spill everything I told him about my aunt's ever-changing triad.

"Delightful accent," Netta says. "Great Britain?"

"Australia, madam."

Netta presses her palm to her cheek. "So you're *that* Lawrence. I should thank you for all you did for my niece in the hospital." She perches on the boar-hide settee and pats the seat next to her, and Lawrence sits beside her like a fly caught in tapioca. "Charmian, aren't you going to offer me a drink?"

Thinking of no excuse, I pour her a rickey in the smallest glass I can find.

Netta places a manicured hand on his knee. "You're the handsome Lawrence who brought Charmian an armful of violets when Baby Joy died."

"That's enough, Auntie." She hates when I call her that.

"And when Jack rushed off to Hollywood . . ." Her finger circles the rim of the glass. "The loyal Lawrence stayed by Charmian's side until she recovered."

"We almost lost her." His voice falters, and he swallows the rest of his drink.

He really is a dear.

Netta looks at me, then back at Lawrence. "And here you are again, two years later."

"Like a bad penny." He clinks her glass.

Netta laughs and flutters her eyelids, taking me back to childhood—the flirtatious tilt of her head, the way her fingers sift through her hair, how she bites her pinkie as if Lawrence fascinates beyond reason.

"Watch and learn," Netta used to instruct me. "Modern women don't have to choose. You can have it all."

Apparently, now she wants Lawrence.

"She was always the dreamer, my Charmian," Netta murmurs and sips her rickey.

"I see that when she plays piano," Lawrence says. "When did you start her lessons?"

"Right after she came to live with us." Netta preens her waves. "When my sister died, I found her only child, a poor little ragamuffin, singing and playing 'Chopsticks' on the piano in her father's saloon while he collected tips."

I clear my throat. "Let's not bore Lawrence with my childhood."

Netta pats my hand with a sympathetic expression I want to slap off her face, her sympathy a way to keep me beholden to her, as my guardian and savior.

"She had talent even then. Her tiny fingers moved so quickly. At first her father put up a fight when I wanted to raise her. But I gave him a hundred dollars, and he walked away." She flicks back her hair and laughs. "He never knew Charmian would inherit property from her mother's side."

Lawrence turns to me with raised eyebrows. "You're an heiress?"

My throat goes dry, and I cough. Lawrence hands me a rickey, and I take a sip, making a face. Can't stomach the smell of gin.

Netta turns to me. "I really came to talk to Jack, though."

"He's speaking at the Bohemian Club," I say. "Uncle Roscoe's a member, didn't he go?"

"Roscoe is enjoying the company of a French schoolmarm in San Francisco." The afternoon sun glaring through the window melts Aunt Netta's rouge into the fine crevices of her cheeks. She looks so sad I should comfort her, but it's hard when she brings this upon herself with her carousel of lovers.

"And now Jack has the audacity to dam our creek," Netta whines. "We won't get any water at the Wake Robin cabins, and that will destroy the value."

"Don't be so melodramatic, Auntie. He needs the water for the eucalyptus grove."

Netta nudges Lawrence. "Some shyster convinced Jack to plant eighty thousand eucalyptus trees."

"That shyster would be me." Lawrence flashes a smile. "The latest shipment will make half a million eucalyptus starts."

Netta sits upright. "You let Jack do this?"

"Since the 1906 earthquake, California's desperate for good building lumber." I defend Jack, though his gamble terrifies me. "Jack says the eucalyptus matures in seven years. We'll cut fifty thousand trees a year, and replant."

"They'll get a thousand dollars per tree for the lumber," Lawrence adds. "Then they can pay me for the seedlings."

"You won't have to wait seven years," I say. "We're expecting a check from the movie studio any day, and you can be on your way."

"But autumn is so beautiful here, and we have so much to amuse us, you and I." Lawrence pours Netta another rickey.

Her eyes roll side to side, calculating. "Firewood has risen to forty dollars a cord."

"Jack will be the lumber baron of the West," Lawrence says.

"But Wake Robin is all I have left, and he'll ruin it if he diverts the stream for eucalyptus." Netta's mouth twists into a knot, and she turns to Lawrence. "I suppose Charmian told you she supported us with her inheritance growing up."

"No, she didn't, but I'm not surprised. Charmian has always been generous with her affection." Lawrence squeezes my hand, and I pinch hard in the web between his thumb and forefinger.

"You'll have plenty of water in the creek," I tell Netta. "Besides, you don't own Wake Robin anymore. You transferred the deed to me when I bailed you out of debt, remember?"

Her eyes go round and woeful with something more than the creek at stake. "I think Roscoe has left me."

I should be kind, but Netta's whining and conniving have shriveled my sympathy. "Don't fret, Auntie. Maybe Edward will marry you now."

"When will Jack be home?" she says.

"We don't expect them until Sunday."

"Sunday?" She looks from Lawrence to me. "What will you do with yourselves for three days?"

Lawrence gives a wicked wink, and I follow his lead just to spoof her.

"Oh, you know me, Auntie." I set my glass on the bar. "We'll find some mischief to get into. Ready for that ride up to Wolf House, Lawrence? Jack told me to check on its progress."

I should be proud Jack left me in charge of construction, but did he notify the foreman and architect? What shall I do when they come to blows, as they do daily, with Jack as their referee?

People blame me for the extravagance of Wolf House, but it is truly Jack's own "House Beautiful," as he wrote about in an essay. Wolf House is his reason to write and sometimes, I think, his reason to live.

It started so innocently ten years back, when Jack bought the first 130 acres on Sonoma Mountain. We moved into the cottage above the old stone winery where we live now, simple, down-to-earth, and quiet enough to write. Jack hired his sister, Eliza, to manage the ranch, and we wrote prolifically during those first years: *The Game*, *White Fang*, *The Road*, among a dozen others. Good work. Meaningful work. Work we're proud of.

But Jack fixated on buying every adjoining parcel of land, until the money ran out. Still he kept buying.

Several years ago, I carefully constructed an argument to convince him not to expand the ranch any farther. Late one night, I found him on his sleeping porch, sitting up in bed, surrounded by books and periodicals, his Imperial cigarette dangling from his full lips. His face shone by a lamp fashioned from wildebeest horn, a gift from a Fijian chief (that guaranteed virility, but we know how that goes).

He held up his forefinger. "One minute, let me catch this thought." Scribbling a note, which he clipped with a clothespin onto the wire stretched above his bed, to keep his thoughts airborne for his dreams. "What is it, Charmian?"

"You've spent your life fighting for Socialism," I said, bolstering my conviction. "Your dream was that Beauty Ranch would be a utopian society where the workers share in the fruits of their labor."

He nodded, and I felt encouraged.

"Surely you see that continuing to expand the ranch is against Socialist principles. We don't need more land, and we don't have the money, besides."

Jack drank from a thermos radiating fumes of juniper and olives. "I've neglected your reading, Charmian. We are beyond those ideas now."

"Beyond Socialism?" My ebullience deflated like a sputtering balloon. "Where are we, then?"

He snuffed the butt of his cigarette into his brass Korean ashtray. "Jung says man must turn away from the uncaring void of the universe and live abundantly, be blinded by life, create his own truth from what is good here on earth."

Not saying I'm dense, but sometimes it takes a miracle to follow his ever-evolving philosophy.

"Let me explain this a different way," he said, lighting another Imperial. "If the universe is a random collection of atoms and chemicals, we must blind ourselves to that and buy into the 'vital lie' that there is meaning to our struggle against inevitable oblivion."

"So Wolf House is your fight against oblivion?" Not sure I got it right.

He nodded and released smoke in a whoosh. "My house will be standing for a thousand years . . . Ah God! You are so close to me right now, so dear, so dear. No matter what I do now, I want to share it with you. What I read, what I write, what I am building. At all times it is you, you, you." He opened his arms to me. "Come here, let me read to you and catch you up with the logic."

No matter what the cold universe had to do with the ranch, I longed for the warmth of his arms. I crawled close to him on his feather mattress and pulled the impala skin over us, laying my head on his beating chest, and he read me Jung.

After that, Jack mortgaged everything in sight, the barns, our cottage, and the new one he built for Eliza. In August, with just three hundred dollars in the bank, he negotiated a second mortgage to finish Wolf House before winter.

Why should I destroy his dream?

I shouldn't have brought Lawrence to Wolf House without Jack. Not now. Too quiet since the workmen went home.

As he swigs from a bottle of Kunde Zinfandel we're sharing, his boots scuff across the newly stained hardwood floors of Jack's spacious writing studio, almost eight hundred square feet on the second floor. He takes off his bush hat and runs his hand through his hair, damp and curling around his sunburned neck, looking out the window to the undulating Sonoma Valley hills, riotous with autumn color. "Some rarefied view you have from up here."

The wine, new paint, and smell of his shaving soap make my temples throb. Lawrence stares out at the vineyards, too long; something's brewing. I want to smooth those curls at his nape, that vulnerable spot I held in the pond while he floated on his back, eyes closed, chiseled abdomen simmering in the sun.

My little game with Jack has gone too far. But then, with a frisson of exhilaration, I know I wanted it to.

He gestures to boxes of books on the floor. "Want help shelving these?"

"Not until the linseed and turpentine dries on the bookcases." I blow sawdust off a book, and it lands on the oily rags and paint cans left in a pile. "They should clean this stuff up, it's a hazard."

He runs his hand over the new mahogany rolltop writing desk still in packing material. "Jack says he's broke, that he can't pay for the eucalyptus."

My chest clenches, protective of Jack. "The desk is a housewarming present from Macmillan."

"I heard workmen complaining they haven't been paid this month." He takes another swallow and hands the wine bottle to me.

"Look, if Jack said he'd pay you, he will. He's just a bit short right now." More wine numbs my brain. Don't think.

"He's got *you* buffaloed, that's for sure." He chucks me under my chin, and I pull away. "Where's the bedroom?"

"Up in the sleeping tower. Let's go back. Nakata will wonder why we didn't come for supper."

Lawrence takes the bottle, grabs my hand, and tugs me to the top of the spiral staircase. His mouth drops open. Circling the enormous tower surrounded by redwoods, he stops in the center and lays his arm around my shoulder.

"I have to admit, this is some glorious bedroom he built for the two of you."

His comment touches a sore spot. "Oh, this is Jack's sleeping tower. Mine is on the other side of the house."

He nods slowly. "Separate suites here, too?"

I start down the steps. "A beautiful suite. You'll see."

I show him my office, sitting room, and bedroom. The nursery that was supposed to be Baby Joy's. My hand lingers on the cradle I still hope to fill. "You *were* sweet to bring me those violets in the hospital," I tell him. Jack just wasn't raised with those delicate sensibilities, growing up on the Oakland docks.

"Do you still want a child?" He turns his head away and drinks the Zinfandel.

"If I can. Jack wants a son more than anything."

He reels around. "Jack, Jack, Jack. Why is it always Jack?" Grabbing a shoulder, he shakes me hard. "Wake up, Charmian. You deserve a life, too. What is it *you* want?"

"You are hurting me."

His hands throttle the wine bottle. "I'm sorry. I hate to see Jack get away with it." Tearing away from me, he starts down the staircase leading outside.

I run to the landing and yell, "Just what do you think Jack is getting away with?"

His face is red and contorted with emotion, and I realize for Lawrence this is more than a game.

"He's buying you, Charmian." His voice crackles. "Buying your talent. Buying your devotion, with this . . . this . . . monstrosity of a monument to himself." Pushing the door open, he walks out.

I look back at my quarters, impressive but solitary. Silence radiates through the void as cold and uncaring as the damn universe . . .

"Lawrence, wait." Running down the stairs and out the door, I call for him again, but there's no answer. The sun has dropped behind the mountain, leaving a dusty pink haze and shadows. I walk around the back of Wolf House, looking for him, odors of gasoline and raw lumber meld with the eternal scent of giant redwoods. A horse neighs somewhere off in the woods, doesn't sound like my Maid. Maybe Lawrence is riding back to the cottage. Then I hear a rustling around the scaffolding and footfalls on the stairs.

"Lawrence? Is that you?" A breeze rustles the oak leaves.

Finally, I find him brooding where we tied up the horses near the rock outcropping over the twilight valley below. I should leave now and return to the cottage, but something draws me to him. I touch his shoulder.

He turns and embraces me, kisses me fervently, his body trembling. His desperation digs a well of craving so deep in me I cannot resist any longer. Thoughts of Jack dissolve in the dusk, and we fall to the blanket of autumn leaves, allowing the desire fanned to a flame by Jack's imagination. He loosens my topknot and strokes my hair. Lawrence takes his time with me, as if nothing else matters. So different than Jack's waning passion. He teases out places that bring me the most pleasure: the white underside of my wrists and elbows, the insides of my thighs, the backs of my knees, the small of my back, the softness of my belly. Divining uncharted territory with his mouth and trembling fingers.

My hips rise and fall with the rhythm of crickets and hooting owls, harmonic as an exquisite piano duet . . .

Afterward, we lie back on the leaves, chests heaving, gazing up at the stars blinking through the redwoods. My body shivers with pleasure . . .

But moments later, a chill fog creeps into the night and congeals in my heart. I turn away and gather up my jodhpurs, shirt, and vest. I've gone too far.

"Don't leave." He grabs my hand. "I don't care if Jack pays me. Let him have his damn Wolf House. Let's just go back to Australia." He kisses my palm, but I can't look at him.

The ground pounds from hooves on the path. I pull on my clothes. My skin itches, and I realize the leaves we lay in are mixed with poison oak.

"We can't be seen together," I say. "Can you take care of the horses?"

"You'll never leave him, will you?"

Pulling my hand away, I walk through the woods to the cottage, not wanting to attract the attention of the staff. Lost in the brush, I can't tell deer trails from walking paths. I stumble and fall over an empty red-and-yellow Shell can, smelling of gasoline. I pick it up to take it back with me. Finally, I see a familiar path.

As I near the cottage, Nakata steps out to the porch and yanks the farm bell with such fury the rope breaks. Ranch hands pour out of the bunkhouses and mount horses, pelting me with gravel. Others run on foot, hooting and hollering. Men fill horse troughs of water at the well and load them on a wagon.

They all run past me toward Wolf House. Flames erupt from the redwood forest behind me and split the cobalt sky like molten lava, radiating a ghoulish halo.

Nakata stands on the porch, eyes pinched in mistrust. *"Kaden rika."* He nods at the gasoline can in my hand. "Avoid standing under the plum tree where you look suspicious."

"What?" I scratch my bottom, itching horribly. "The can was lying in the woods. I brought it back to put in the barn." Red welts rage on my back, thighs, and arms, and Nakata sees the swelling, proof of my sin.

George Sterling steps out onto the porch. Nakata takes the gasoline can and drops it behind the azalea bush.

"What's going on?" Sterling asks. "Did Wolf find you down there? He made us leave early, practically whipped the driver to a frenzy. Drank like a fiend the whole way back." He peers above my head into the forest. "Where did Lawrence go?"

"He's around somewhere," I say.

Sterling shakes his head. "His suitcase is gone. Like a rat fleeing a burning ship, that guy. Never trusted him."

An explosion jolts my body toward Wolf House.

"Hellfire and damnation!" Sterling says.

Fire spirals off in all directions like fireworks, electrifying the dead sky.

"Jack!" I run toward Wolf House, flames imprinting my retinas. "Jack!" Running as fast as I can, each new blast shatters my heart into a million tiny pieces.

Our vineyard manager and his crew beat the flames with brooms and rakes, as if their valiant efforts will not be worthless. Ranch hands attack the sand pile brought up by wagon for cement mixing, filling buckets with sand and throwing them on the flames. Nakata joins their ranks and Eliza, too, dressed in nightgown and cap.

Searching frantically for Jack in the chaos, I finally find him sitting on the rock outcropping. His face is mottled from the searing heat, his hooded eyes staring into the utter destruction, an empty Zinfandel bottle in his hands.

"Oh, Jack." I put my hand on his shoulder, but he doesn't respond. A confession claws at my throat, but I stuff it down, then go join the others at the sand pile.

Neighbors from Glen Ellen and Kenwood come to fight the fire, but after a few hours, it's clear there's nothing that can be done. They stand around shaking their heads, watching fire leap from log to rafter.

Massive redwood logs, which the architect and builder claimed would be fireproof unless ignited in a dozen places, burn like an inferno. In a deafening roar, the Spanish red-tile roof clatters down inside the rock and concrete walls.

“Why aren’t you doing anything, Wolf?” Sterling says. “You don’t seem to know what’s happening to you.”

“Wolf House was the only home I ever made for myself,” Jack says.

I pass through the crowd and thank them for their efforts. “It’s been a long night. Go home and get some sleep.”

Sterling, Nakata, and Eliza are the last to leave.

The first pink of dawn tints the sky above the Mayacamas mountain range. Taking the wine bottle from Jack’s hands, I throw it into the smoldering ruins, and it smashes on the volcanic rock. Then I sit beside him. He crumbles into my bosom and trembles like a child.

# 3

## Orpheum Theatre, San Francisco, California
## November 1915

*Love cannot in its very nature be peaceful or content. It is a restlessness, an unsatisfaction. I can grant a lasting love just as I can grant a lasting satisfaction; but the lasting love cannot be coupled with possession, for love is pain and desire, and possession is easement and fulfilment.*

—*Jack London,* The Kempton-Wace Letters

I know how magic works—all smoke and mirrors, suffocating doves, and defecating rabbits. Of course, Jack knows these things, too. He rails against the cruelty of using trained animals in vaudeville. But his adoring Crowd from Carmel (that whole arty, hashish-smoking Bohemian clan) insists Jack join them for the Great Houdini show. Front-row seats, they say. The most famous magician in the world, they say.

"We need a little magic in our lives," Jack says, and I can't argue with that.

The Orpheum is morbidly gaudy with flocked velvet walls, tooled woodwork, and gilt, lots of gilt. Jack sports his rumpled khakis du jour, while he asked me to dress like a heroine from

*Martin Eden*: chartreuse taffeta suit shimmering with purple undertones in the theater lights.

But this confounded waistline cuts into my expanding middle like a butcher pinching off sausage casing. I don't know why I haven't told Jack my good news when I've known for a while. That's a lie. I hold back because he'll count the months and wonder, like I do.

The Crowd blow kisses to each other in a cloud of pheromones and cigar smoke. They pass the silver flask of gin under my nose, and the odor stretches my brain like the taffy puller in the lobby.

George Sterling slides his lanky frame into the seat next to mine, reeking of patchouli and cannabis. "Looks like this is just what Jack needed to forget about Wolf House burning down."

"Nothing will make him forget that night." My head reels around to see Jack deep in conversation with Anna Strunsky. They only talk deep. That young actress Blanche hangs on his arm, pretending she understands. She doesn't.

"Wolf says Lawrence burned it down and ran off."

"You're such a liar," I say, but maybe it's true. I haven't seen or heard from Lawrence since I left him by Wolf House.

"You and Wolf should pick your friends more wisely." Sterling grins like Satan.

"Funny, I was thinking the very same thing. But unfortunately, Jack likes you." I make a face.

Thankfully, the sixteen-piece orchestra fires up below us in the pit, and Sterling slinks back to his seat. Brass trumpets glint in the crossing spotlights and raise my spirits with their triumphant sound.

Jack sits next to me, puffing his Imperial. I can't break his mood no matter how many times I tell him nothing happened with Lawrence.

Nothing I care to share, that is.

The Great Houdini appears in a spotlight and high-steps onto the stage, keeping time with the music, striking in his immaculate tuxedo and gleaming black hair. When the song ends, he marches right in front of the footlights and welcomes the audience, impossibly white teeth flashing, announcing his opening trick.

Women's mouths drop open. Men scoot to the edges of their seats. His voice, harmonic and commanding, vibrates through the charged air and holds them awestruck. Houdini's powerful arm points at Jack. Heavens.

"Mr. Jack London, ladies and gentlemen." Spotlights flood our faces.

How does he recognize Jack?

"Won't you join us on the stage, Mr. London?" Houdini calls, and the Crowd starts chanting: "Wolf, Wolf, Wolf . . ."

Jack holds up his palms in protest.

The magician persists. "If not you, how about your lovely wife? I promise to take great care of her."

The Crowd jeers for me to go up, already too much gin passed between them.

Jack leans over and whispers, "My feet are killing me. Take this one, will you?"

I see my redemption in his pleading eyes. But I feel like a bratwurst. I can't go up there.

"Buck up your courage, Mate." Jack pushes me to a stand. "The Crowd will get a kick out of it."

My heart sinks as I make my way to the stairs. He wants to entertain his worshipping Crowd at my expense. Blanche swoops into my vacant seat, snuggling his arm. I yank the pearl buttons choking my neck and one pops off, rolling into the orchestra pit. Lifting my stiff taffeta skirt and crinoline petticoat, I step up, but my foot slips off.

Two strong hands circle my waist and sweep me onto the stage with the grace of a waltz. Black eyelashes rim his eyes with mystery, but kindness crinkles at the edges.

"Trust me," Houdini whispers, smelling of wood-spice cologne. Then his voice booms out to the audience, "Let's give the brave Mrs. London a round of applause, shall we?"

A child enters from backstage dressed in tights and velvet knickers, a fluffy beret mushrooming over his jet-black pageboy.

Houdini smiles and holds out his arm. "And another hand for my beautiful wife and assistant, Bess Houdini."

My stomach hitches, and I look again. The elf bows with a flourish and lifts her face with a wide grin, dimples circled with rouge, throwing kisses to the audience. The miniature woman steals the show with her boyish figure in sequined tights, round eyes that flash and roll and wink and hold us spellbound no matter what Houdini is doing. I would have bought the ticket to watch her.

The magician steps into the spotlight, and the audience hushes. "And now, on this very stage, we will perform our most renowned illusion, the one and original, Metamorphosis! Pay close attention to catch any sleight of hand or cheat, for you will see none. With your very own eyes, you will witness myself, bound, handcuffed, and locked in a trunk, only to be magically transformed into my beautiful assistant, Bess."

The audience buzzes with excitement while Bess Houdini rolls a steamer trunk to center stage. "Mrs. London, tell the people in the *crematorium*, have we ever met before?" she asks in falsetto.

"Auditorium?" Confused and tongue-tied looking out from the stage to three hundred San Francisco elite . . . "No, we haven't met."

"And have you ever laid your eyes on this trunk before?"

Jack would say something witty, but my mind draws a blank. "No." The burning footlights blind me mercifully from seeing his disappointment in the front row.

"Will you examine the trunk for any tomfoolery?" She waves her birdlike limbs theatrically, reeking of gardenias.

I unbuckle the leather straps and peer inside the trunk. Feeling along the edges, banging the sides. "No trick doors, if that's what you mean."

"I understand you're an excellent sailor, Mrs. London." Houdini cocks an eyebrow. "And quite an expert with knots."

"How would you know that?" I shade my eyes to see Jack and damn if Blanche isn't canoodling his ear. "I won first place at the yacht club for my knots."

"Impressive, but can you tie a knot from which the Great Houdini cannot escape?"

"Absolutely." Jack says it's over with Blanche yet dangles my dalliance over my head like a noose.

Houdini takes off his jacket and rolls up his shirtsleeves, crossing his muscular wrists together.

Mrs. Houdini hands me the rope and whispers, "Tie a slipknot." She winks a blue eyelid. So that's their game.

Mutiny tingles in my fingers. Like hell, slipknot. I tie an anchor hitch that would secure a yacht in a typhoon.

Pulling the sack up over him, Mrs. Houdini leans to kiss him. My God, their mouths open and move like the French. His sensuous lips suck hers like she's a juicy plum. My belly clenches. How long has it been since Jack kissed me like that?

Mrs. Houdini pulls the feed sack over her husband's head and winks at me again. But I tie my strongest knot on the bag, a double bowline, tight and secure.

Bess Houdini's chirp pierces my eardrums. "Now, ladies and gentlemen, we'll place the Great Houdini in the steamer trunk for all *intensive* purposes and lock it up."

We padlock the trunk and wrap it profusely with rope. Feeling smug now, I tie yet another sailing knot: double square knot this time. No way can this trickster get out.

Mrs. Houdini closes heavy velvet curtains in front of the trunk. She smiles at the audience, and her theatrical makeup cracks around her eyes; she's no child herself. "Mrs. London, do you feel very certain the Great Houdini cannot *excape* your knots?"

Jack punches his fist in the air and calls out, "Her knots have secured sailing ships from here to Borneo!"

A pang riddles my gut. What if I truly bring down the Great Houdini? The kettle drum rumbles and spectators choose sides, placing bets, laughing nervously.

Mrs. Houdini lifts her arms over her head and claps her hands together three times, accentuated by a clash of cymbals that echoes through the cavernous theater. Spotlights crisscross the frescoed ceiling. The timpani stops abruptly and pandemonium ceases. The audience leans forward.

Spotlights swing to center stage, revealing the Great Houdini stepping through the velvet curtain, fists held high in triumph. The orchestra blares.

My every nerve ending is burning, screaming. No, no, no, no. It's impossible.

The magic man takes my hand and holds it high, a current charging from his grasp down my arm. The audience explodes with enthusiasm. He smiles intimately at me as his confidant. But I feel betrayed. He'd said, "Trust me," yet I haven't an inkling what just happened.

"You're a natural." Houdini bows and bows to the relentless applause. When it finally dies down, he looks around the stage.

"Mrs. London, where is my dear wife?"

I turn to where Mrs. Houdini was standing, but she's gone. "She was right here."

He taps his index finger on his cheek. "Oh, Mrs. Houdini? Are you back here?" He draws open the velvet curtain, which reveals only the steamer trunk with all my knots intact. How is that possible when Houdini stands beside me?

"Mrs. London, can you untie your knots?"

My chest crackles with curiosity as my fingers struggle with the rope, every knot as secure as I tied it. The oboe plays a sinister tune, which twists my insides.

When all the knots are finally undone, Houdini opens the trunk. Inside, the burlap sack bumps and moves.

"What have we here?" Houdini cuts the bag open with a shining saber, which appears from nowhere.

Bess Houdini pops out, all five feet of her, hands tied behind her back. She cackles like a maniac, then curtsies to the stunned audience.

The orchestra strikes up a rousing number, and the audience cheers and whistles.

The Houdinis take my trembling hands, and we bow together. They step aside, presenting me. My cheeks grow hopelessly hot as I force myself to raise my eyes to the frenzied theater and let the applause wash over me.

The Crowd chants my name from the front row. But Jack scribbles in his ever-present notebook, oblivious to their revelry. Oblivious to my moment in the spotlight.

Yet I'm gratified. I've given him a fresh topic to write about.

When I return, Jack's staring at the stage with half-closed eyes, and I know he'll retell this scene in a book.

Anna Strunsky kisses me on both cheeks. "Wolf told me about your book *The Log of the Snark*. He's so proud of you."

"Really? The manuscript's gathering dust on his desk as far as I know." I push past her and sit beside Jack, still focused on the stage.

My abdomen jolts. I should tell him about the baby, but he's been so mercurial since Baby Joy was born, I want to wait until I'm sure.

Mr. Houdini appears at our seats, pumping Jack's hand and clapping him on the back. "What a great honor to have you in the audience."

Jack's rumpled khakis look pitiful next to Houdini's tuxedo. Both men have unruly curly hair and barrel chests, but that's where the similarity ends. Jack is taller than Houdini by head and shoulders, but Houdini's disciplined physique is awe-inspiring. The two of them emanate masculinity in such different ways. Jack's street tough and adventuring, ever the underdog and fighter. Houdini radiates knowledge of things beyond knowing, a steely mastermind who influences people by controlling their thoughts.

Houdini reaches as if to shake my hand, but instead takes it to his mouth and kisses it.

"That trick has my mind racing," I say. "What did you call it again?"

"Metamorphosis." Houdini peers through thick lashes. "The inevitable transformation of all people, places, and things."

"Inevitable transformation." Jack writes down the words in his notebook. "Metamorphosis."

"Would you two like to join us for dinner?" Houdini glances at the Crowd.

My chest tightens. The Crowd's traveled all the way from Carmel to see Jack, but I'd much rather dine with Houdini.

"Ever been to Tadich Grill?" Jack says. "Great food."

"We'll join you as soon as Mrs. Houdini is dressed." He salutes two fingers to his broad forehead.

Jack begs off the Crowd, kissing Blanche on the side of her mouth (as if he never kisses the whole thing) and leaves the theater.

I follow, and despite his limp, I have to run to catch up.

"I can't stand this distance between us, Jack." I pull my cloche down over my ears against the evening chill. "We have to talk it out."

"Some things are better left unsaid." He limps on toward Tadich Grill.

"But you forced me to host Lawrence at the ranch while you and the Greek ran off to the Bohemian Club."

"I didn't expect you to fall for that pansy."

"Lawrence is not a pansy."

"You would know."

My mouth goes dry. "Please, Jack. I feel like such an idiot about Lawrence. We have to get past this."

He stops short and grabs my ruffled collar. "I thought we were happy, Charmian. I was building Wolf House for you."

"I didn't burn down Wolf House, if that's what you think."

His strides lengthen. "Save it, Charmian."

"You were toying with Lawrence and me for your novel." I hold my aching abdomen, proof of my transgression. "I just wanted to feel what it was like to be needed again."

He turns around and walks back to me. "Mate-Woman, I always suspected I had a heart, but now I know. When I was face-to-face with the possibility of losing you, my heart came right into my throat. I ate it, I'll tell you, and forced it down." His body moves against mine, his rising ardor strong and passionate. "You have no idea the power you hold over men, Charmian. A woman above all women, a mate men will fight for."

"It's always been you, Jack. Only you."

His mouth presses down on mine, bruising my lips with his denture plate, leaving me breathless. Then he pulls away and walks on.

If he still loves me, there's hope.

# 4

## Tadich Grill, San Francisco, California November 1915

*But I am I. And I won't subordinate my taste to the unanimous judgment of mankind.*

*—Jack London,* Martin Eden

The Houdinis are waiting outside Tadich Grill, and I can't imagine how they beat us here. Bess Houdini wears a scarlet suit trimmed in white fur, oddly reminiscent of a Santa costume. When Jack opens the door, delicious aromas of oregano, garlic, and olive oil waft over us, fighting with Bess's gardenia perfume.

Mr. Tadich, a balding man with a dark mustache, greets Jack with a bear hug and wet eyes. "Mr. London, it's been too long." He grabs menus and nods at me. "Good to see you again, Mrs. London. Right this way."

He leads us past enclosed booths, tables laden with bowls of lemon quarters, garlic braids hanging between ornate mirrors. I catch my pasty reflection, dark hollows under my eyes. Too much worry over Wolf House. Jack's obsessed with rebuilding when we can't afford it, fueling our discord of late. My hand brushes my pooching belly. This child will change all that.

Ahead of me, Jack claps Tadich on the shoulder. "How's the family?"

"Benny's doing better, Mr. London, thanks to you. God bless you, sir."

I can't hear Jack's answer, because right behind me, Mrs. Houdini pecks at her husband like the woodpecker. "Did you hear the audience roar when I came out of that sack? We'll be the Great Houdinis together again, like we used to be."

The after-theater crowd tracks us with their eyes, talking behind their hands, recognizing Houdini. Though most don't know Jack, he always commands attention with his manly presence, even with his dragging left foot.

Tadich seats us in Jack's favorite booth and hands us green leather menus.

"Double martini, three olives, right away, please." Jack smiles, and Tadich disappears.

I lean to him and whisper. "You need to eat something." This morning I was happy to find him writing in his studio until I saw the shaker of martinis by his coffee cup, his elixir to start the words flowing.

"I had a big breakfast." He lights a cigarette with the silver lighter Macmillan gave him to commemorate thirty novels.

Tadich returns with his drink, and Jack pulls him aside, then turns back to us. "I ordered a special treat." He rubs his hands together. "Houdini, what are you drinking?"

The magic man smiles with teeth white as quartz. "Seltzer with lots of lime." He turns to his wife and me. "And what may we get for you ladies?"

"Champagne, please," we say in unison.

Mrs. Houdini shrieks like an inept sword swallower. "*Jinx*. Personal *jinx*. We're sisters now." She giggles and squeezes my hand across the table, and I have no idea what she's jabbering about. "When two people say the same thing at the same time, they're bound together for life."

Jack questions her about the notion of jinx. Must be gathering wool for a character; otherwise he'd ignore her outburst. Jack hates giddy women.

A waiter brings Houdini his seltzer, and he squeezes lime into it. His cufflinks are shaped like handcuffs. Dark waves cascade from his center part, and I wonder if his hair feels soft or wiry. He glances up through thick lashes and smiles as if reading my thoughts.

Tadich sets down a dewy ice bucket and opens a bottle of Veuve Clicquot. "It's the last vintage we'll see for a while because of the Great War. We'll still have our own Buena Vista, of course."

As much as I like my bubbles, I hate to hear the Great War reduced to where I get my next vintage.

Tadich hands us sparkling coupes. "Enjoy, ladies."

"Down the hatch." Bess swishes champagne around her mouth like Listerine.

"Those ruthless Huns slaughtered a quarter million Frenchmen this year." Jack bites an olive off his toothpick. "When is the president going to stop hiding his head in the sand and join the Great War?"

"Mother always tells me, 'A bad peace is better than a good war.'" Houdini locks and unlocks his cufflinks. "We're helping the Allies more than you think, with weapons and strategy."

"We're a bunch of stinking cowards making the Allies do the dirty work," Jack says.

"I should have known you'd think that," Houdini says. "I attended your lecture at Carnegie Hall. You railed against the United States. How could we, the most prosperous country in the world, justify ten million citizens dying of starvation because they can't afford food?"

Goose bumps prickle my chest to hear our speech again.

"The entire audience jumped to their feet, shouting, 'Revolution! Revolution!'" Houdini says. "They would have stormed the White House at your command."

Jack lifts his chin and blows out smoke. "So you're a Socialist, too?"

"I'm a patriot." Houdini polishes his steak knife with his napkin.

Jack scoffs. "A patriot is a puppet who does whatever the president says without question."

"That's right, Mr. Houdini does whatever the president asks," Bess says.

Jack pokes his cigarette at Houdini. "Let me tell you something. Never has the ruling class relinquished a single privilege unless they're forced to. It's the things we fight for, bleed for, care most for."

"So you support war," Houdini says. "That must be why Hearst sends you to the front lines to write stories of hate and rebellion."

Jack's skin flares around his collar, and he stubs out his cigarette.

"It's that conviction that makes Jack a great war reporter." I pour chilled champagne in our empty coupes.

Bess gazes at the stamped-tin ceiling and hums "Hello, Frisco!" to herself.

"And now Hearst's sending you to Panama in the middle of the Great War," Houdini says. "Hearst would do anything to sell newspapers. Including sacrificing you."

"You're going to Panama?" I ask.

"The trip hasn't even been announced." Jack glares at Houdini. "What's your game?"

"This is no time to play soldier," Houdini says. "The Germans just sank an American cargo ship, along with the ocean liner

*Lusitania*, killing a thousand passengers. Germans are swarming our East Coast, attacking any weak entry point. You'll be an easy target in Panama."

"I don't take orders from Hearst," Jack says. "Or you, for that matter. I'll go to Panama because America needs to wake up to this war and I have the alarm clock." Jack pushes his chair back with a screech. "Get your things, Charmian."

Bess wakes from her daydream and grabs Jack's arm, tilting her doll face up to his. "Don't leave. My husband likes to *pontifiskate*. I tell him people don't like it, but he doesn't listen. No wonder we don't have friends." Her painted lips pout.

Houdini stands and folds his napkin by his plate. "Please, I overstepped. I'm obsessed with the war these days, it seems to infiltrate everything I do."

Jack's lips strain at the corners. He used to have such expressive lips, but his denture plate stretches them flat. I miss his soft, tender kisses.

"There's no escaping the mad dog of Germany." Jack rubs the back of his neck and sits down.

And just like that, they sheath their swords and their war is over. Men.

The waiter arrives with a heaping platter of Dungeness crab, rosy and fragrant with salty smells of the sea and melted butter.

Bess's eyes grow round. "Oh my goodness. Oh my goodness. I've only ever had horseshoe crabs at Coney Island, like creepy little spiders."

Houdini blanches. "I'm sorry, waiter. I don't eat crab. Do you have steak?"

"It's not just crab, it's Dungeness," Jack says. "Most heavenly taste in the world." He cracks the biggest claw in two, dips it in butter and offers it to Houdini.

The magic man holds his hand up. "Porterhouse, please, medium rare."

Jack's crab claw hangs midair, dripping butter on the checkered tablecloth.

"Mr. Houdini's father was a rabbi, *excetera*." Bess takes Jack's crab claw and nibbles with her tiny yellow teeth. "Oh my goodness."

I'm dying to ask more but don't want to risk bringing up any old prejudices that Jack's worked hard to conquer. "Will you have a chance to see the Panama-Pacific Exposition while you're in San Francisco?"

"Mr. Houdini's performing at the Palace of Fine Arts on Friday." Bess dips a piece of crab in melted butter and pops it in her mouth. "Why don't you come sit with me?" A strip of eyelashes dangles precariously off her eye.

"Waiter. Another martini," Jack calls, holding up a finger. "What kind of name is Houdini?"

"Houdini's my stage name, after Robert-Houdin, a French magician."

"So you're French?" I ask, relieved. Jack has nothing against the French.

He shakes his head. "Grew up in Appleton, Wisconsin."

"The newspaper said you were born in Germany," Jack says. "Is that why you don't use your real name?"

"Reporters always get it wrong, you know that," I say.

"I'm American." Houdini rearranges his water glass and utensils to precise positions, just in time for his steak to be delivered, sizzling and aromatic.

"The war must be bad for your ticket sales," I say, steering away from race and religion. "People don't have money to spare."

"Europe is closed to me, of course, but knock on wood"—a rap startles us from the table, but his hands are cutting his steak—"America is smitten with my escapes, the more dangerous, the better. And I'm booked solid with performances for our troops."

Jack lurches forward. "Egad, man. Our troops should be fighting, not watching magic shows." He pounds his glass down, spraying vermouth and olive juice over my taffeta suit.

Good. I hate this suit. I hate war. I especially hate the fury it ignites in Jack. And when was he going to tell me about his trip to Panama?

I excuse myself from the table and sit at the old upright piano in the corner. Nothing like my Steinway at the ranch, but any port in a storm. It's so dark I can barely make out the keys, so I feel for the ivories, smooth and soothing under my fingers. They almost start to move on their own, a poignant melody rising from the old upright and wending through the smoky air. For a few minutes, the bloodthirsty warmongers are disarmed and my personal skeletons are laid to rest.

When I finish the sonata, the diners applaud and I bob my head in acknowledgment, cheeks hot. Jack stands at our table, clapping loudest, eyes shining. The Houdinis are clapping, too, and suddenly I'm a bit embarrassed.

Houdini reaches for my hand, and electricity zings up my arm. "Haunting, Mrs. London. Lovely and haunting." His voice soothes me.

"Wait till you hear her ragtime," Jack says. "She'll really get this party started."

Dizzy now, I kiss Jack's cheek to ground myself. His eucalyptus scent and evening stubble excite me.

"Ooooh, ragtime." Mrs. Houdini pops a jazz finger in the air, bounces her hips in her chair.

Her silliness makes me smile. "I hate to break up the party," I say. "But we have a telephone call with Macmillan in New York in the morning."

George Brett's telegram had been specific: 9 AM PACIFIC TIME -stop- SUBJECT: JACK LONDON AUTOBIOGRAPHY -stop-

I'm sure Jack will refuse again. "Wasn't *John Barleycorn* enough?" he'd said. "My lust for gin, my pink elephant hallucinations, my duels with white logic? What more do they want from me?"

Houdini pulls a thin volume from his suit jacket and presents it to Jack. "Would you mind having Macmillan look at my book? I published it myself, but it would be a best seller with a real publisher."

Even the Great Houdini has the nerve to ask Jack for favors. Jack thumbs through the pages.

"Mr. Houdini sells it in the magician magazine called *M-U-M*," Bess says.

"For *magic*, *unity*, and *might*," Houdini clarifies.

Jack studies the cover of Houdini's book. "*The Right Way to Do Wrong*, sounds like a great movie serial."

"Like *fillum* movies?" Bess asks.

"Say, you're a pilot, aren't you, Houdini?" Jack says. "We could fly down to Hollywood and meet with my studio."

"Mr. Houdini doesn't fly anymore after his crash in Australia," Bess says. "Too dangerous."

"Yes, dear." He pats her hand.

"But isn't it danger that drives you as an escape artist?" I ask.

"Danger is dancing with death without succumbing to her charms." Houdini lifts his glass and Jack clinks it.

"Time to skedaddle, Jack." I tap my watch. "Morning meeting?"

But he's pushing salt and pepper shakers, sugar bowl, bread dishes, and glasses into strategic formations. "Show me where off the coast they've spotted Germans."

Houdini looks at me. "We won't be long, Mrs. London, I promise. We both have to be at our best tomorrow."

He doesn't know Jack. Once he gets wound this tight, he'll be up all night writing, thinking it's genius, but it will be drivel I'll struggle to save. Sometimes a lost day spirals to weeks if I can't set him right, and in the worst case, Jack falls into his "long sickness," with me as his only life preserver.

"Can't leave yet, Mate-Woman." Jack grins madly. "Houdini and I need to save the world." They've set up a battlefield of dishes and utensils, napkins representing submarines and U-boats.

I excuse myself to the ladies' room. Houdini is there in the hallway, leaning toward me, face tense. I look back at the table where I just left him. Bess is singing to Jack, who looks amused.

"Don't let Mr. London go to Panama," he says.

I scoff. "You overestimate the influence I have over my husband."

"The president can't afford to have him report on what he sees in Panama."

"So now you speak for the president?"

His back straightens, eyes harden, and I see he's dead serious.

A hysterical giggle escapes me. "Your imagination is running away with you. Panama is just a gateway for trade between the Atlantic and Pacific." I push the door, but Houdini clutches my wrist. His grip alarms me.

"Panama is the only thing that stands between us and war," he says. "The Germans have built bases on the Galápagos and Easter Island."

Sounds of clinking dinnerware and lively conversations from the dining room fall away, and all I hear is the thud of my heart against my clavicle. "That won't scare Jack. The bigger the stakes, the better the story."

He tightens his grip on my wrist. "He can't write about it."

"What's the big secret in Panama?" I pull my wrist from him, smarting from his grasp.

A woman leaves the restroom, glances at us, then walks on.

Houdini turns back to me, voice taut and low. "Eighteen forts, thousands of US soldiers, an entire navy fleet."

"But why keep it secret? Don't Americans have a right to know?"

"In due time."

"Why aren't you telling this to Jack?"

"What would he do if I tell him?"

The truth dawns on me. "He'd go to Panama."

"The Secret Service doesn't want Mr. London in Panama. A match on gasoline, they said. He's a muckraker, anarchist, a threat to national security. They keep a thick file on London's war reporting, Socialist speeches, his collusion with Clarence Darrow and Upton Sinclair, his radical books like *War of the Classes* and *The People of the Abyss*. They'll stop him, one way or another."

He takes my sore wrist and rubs it gently with his thumbs until the redness disappears. "You are an exceptional woman, Charmian." He kisses my wrist and glances up with a seductive smile. "Mr. London is very fortunate to have you." And the magic man leaves in a smoldering trail of smoke and mirrors.

Yanking open my high collar, I lean against the wall. My abdomen throbs like I'll miscarry right here. I have to sit down.

But Bess Houdini enters the hallway, fluttering her arms at her sides like a hummingbird.

"Don't let him get to you with all his cloak-and-dagger stuff." She retrieves a hand-rolled cigarette tucked in her fur cuff, lights it with flame-tipped fingernails, then inhales with a little cough.

"So he doesn't know the president?"

"Oh, he's thick with the president," she says, fanning the burning-hay fumes. "Want some?"

I shake my head, still reeling from Houdini.

"Live a little. That's what I tell my husband. What's the harm?" She giggles and holds out the cigarette, pink lipstick gumming up the end.

I hold up my hand. "I don't smoke."

"My husband doesn't smoke, doesn't drink, eats like a monk, doesn't expend energy before a show, and afterward he's too spent." Her pretty nose wrinkles. "If you take my meaning."

And I do. Jack's libido is like a faulty lamp. One night it shines bright; another night I'm alone in the dark. But what about the Houdinis' deep kiss during the performance? Just part of the act, I guess. Somehow that makes me feel better.

Bess sucks in her cheeks with another drag from the cigarette. "Us girls got to have fun, don't we?" She winks, blue eye shadow creasing in her eyelid.

I push open the ladies' room door.

"You go ahead," she says. "I was just sneaking off to the bar."

Alone at last, I recline on the pink tufted divan in the ladies' room and immediately drown in a leftover sea of perfume. I could tell Jack about the baby . . . that should keep him from going to Panama. But from experience, I know better.

Bess kicks open the door, holding martini glasses. "Thought you could use a pink lady." Mischief sparks her baby blues.

Gin. I sip the evil stuff anyway. Juniper sweeps the fog from my head.

Her eyes never leave my face. "So how do *you* live with a legend?"

My gut twists. Here we go. Everyone wants a piece of Jack London. I've learned the hard way. The friendlier the conversation, the more likely to end up as scandalous headlines in the newspaper.

Bess takes a long draw from her glass, imprinting lips on the rim. "Don't get me wrong, fame has got its rewards. Mr. Houdini built us a new brownstone off Central Park, very tony. And I buy all the clothes I want, the showier the better. We're in show *bidness* after all."

"Show business. *Bus*iness," I correct her.

Bess giggles. "That's my showgirl talk. It's second nature now, do you like it?" She leans on the other side of the divan, false eyelash still dangling, sucking her cherry. "You look so cool, like you don't *prespire*." She hiccups. "*Per*spire, you see? You must be a mother. Nothing rattles your cage."

"Jack has two daughters from his previous marriage." My mind rumbles back two years ago, the night Joy was born.

When Jack saw our precious girl for the first time, he punched me playfully in the arm. "Better luck next time, Mate." His heart was set on a boy. Sure, he made a big play of counting ten fingers and toes, but his loud laugh sounded hollow.

"I have to go to Hollywood," he said. "You don't mind, do you, Mate? You're in good hands here. Two studios are fighting over *Call of the Wild*. Be back before you know it." He ran out, all bluster and purpose.

After Jack left for Hollywood, the doctor sedated me. I awoke the next day with my breasts throbbing and swollen, prematurely hot with milk. I called for my baby but was told the doctor had her. Later that night, they brought me my sweet girl. Joy! A lifeless swaddled bundle, eyes mercifully closed and yellow as a lemon. She struggled valiantly, the doctor said. Unformed lungs, he said. These things happen.

Mrs. Houdini takes my empty martini glass. "You need another drink." She pushes the door open with her small behind and disappears.

I fall back against the divan, a raft adrift in the ocean.

But my peace is short-lived. The door slams open, her shoes tap across the floor—a bang of a stall, tight skirt ripping, the inevitable retching. I start to get up, leaving the hummingbird to pull herself together, but her whimper draws me.

"Mrs. Houdini, are you all right in there?"

Her moan turns into soft sobs. The stall door gapes with the woman-child resting her cheek on the toilet rim. Layers of melted mascara ring her eyes.

"The men will wonder where we went to," I say.

"Tell him I drowned." She drops her head into the bowl.

I pull her out, gardenia perfume gagging me. Her curls feel fine and sticky as cotton candy. "You don't mean that." I prop her up, and her head lolls about.

"There's only one woman for Mr. Houdini, and she's dead. He's never been the same since his mother died."

"I assumed she was alive the way he talked about her." I pat a linen towel about her face.

"Oh, Mr. Houdini talks to his mother every night, but she's buried in Queens. Since Mother passed, there's no reason for him to come home. He's always on tour or some mysterious mission."

"Let's get you up." I lift her, and she rambles on, touching my heart nonetheless.

"Once Mr. Houdini became the great *excape* artist, he threw me away like yesterday's newspaper. He only keeps me around for one trick." She sobs. "Metamorphosis."

I support her tiny waist and help her to the divan, her shoes tapping and slipping on the marble floor. "Why is that?"

She flings her head back and laughs. "Because I'm the only one that fits in his damn trunk."

I put my arm around her. "I'm sure that's not true. What about when you first met?"

"I was twenty, singing with the Floral Sisters on Coney Island." Bessie snuffles. "Mr. Houdini and his brother *preformed* the magic act after us. His brother couldn't fit in his magic trunk, but I did. The next week, Mr. Houdini dumped his brother and married me." Her curls are tangled, lips smeared, eye sockets dark as coal bins, dress ripped to her hip.

"Mrs. Houdini, let me take you back to your hotel, and we'll have a cup of tea. I'll tell our husbands and have the headwaiter hail us a cab."

"Call me Bess." She smiles. "No, call me Bessie, and I'll call you Charmie."

"Please don't."

"Oooo," she squeals. "Do you think they have *sassy-fracks* tea?"

"Sassafras? I'm sure they do."

In the taxicab, Bessie leans on my shoulder, blithering on about her vaudeville days. When she calls me Charmie, I don't correct her.

# 5

## The Palace Hotel, San Francisco, California
## November 1915

*Ever bike? Now that's something that makes life worth living! Oh, to just grip your handlebars and lay down to it, and go ripping and tearing through streets and road, over railroad tracks and bridges, threading crowds, avoiding collisions, at twenty miles or more an hour, and wondering all the time when you're going to smash up. Well, now, that's something!*

*—Jack London*

At the Palace, Bessie transforms herself in the ladies' room, washing away the black smudges under her eyes, stripping off the eyelashes, and combing her hair into waves that shine under the stained-glass ceiling. She looks less like a marionette without her stage makeup. Busboys are clearing the tables and resetting for breakfast, but we wrangle a pot of tea. A quick cup of tea with the ditsy, drunken wife of the Great Houdini, and I'll take a taxi back to the Nob Hill Hotel, be in bed with Jack by midnight. I'll tell him about the baby, and he won't go to Panama.

"Now you know enough about me to be dangerous." Bessie slurps her sassafras tea, three sugar cubes. "Your turn, Charmie. How'd you tame a man like Mr. London? He's like a *rabbitus* lion."

"Rabbitus?"

"Yeah, like he's very hungry." She winks.

"Oh." I laugh. "I interviewed him for the *Overland Monthly*, a literary journal."

"Weren't you intimidated? He scares the bejesus out of me."

"Jack was a struggling author, just twenty-four, I the older, wiser editor. He'd just returned from prospecting in the Yukon."

"Like mining for gold? I would have taken him for a college man with all his book smarts."

"Whatever Jack's learned has been the hard way." I sip the earthy tea. "His mother shot herself in the forehead when he was just a baby. She survived, but authorities gave him to a freed slave who was his wet nurse. He calls her Mammy to this day."

"It's a wonder he survived at all." She presses her finger against her lips and shakes her head.

"Jack's a survivor. He sold newspapers at six years old. At thirteen he worked in a cannery. At fifteen he pirated oysters. Sixteen, arrested for vagrancy." I pause to drink.

"I'm *flibbergusted*." Bessie's chin rests on woven fingers, round eyes riveted to my face.

"At eighteen he jumped a cargo ship to Japan. When he returned, the police arrested him for Socialist agitation. But he never stopped writing. Short stories, novels, poems. He even took photographs with his Kodak 3A. Thousands of photographs: Japan, the Yukon, England, photographs for his book on poverty, *The People of the Abyss*. I became his typist, his editor, his muse."

Memories of those days now overwhelm me: the first drafts he shared, his slanted scrawl running across the pages, indecipherable and raw, his young passion that scared me and thrilled me in equal measures. I cough and turn away from Bessie, not wanting her to see my emotion.

She calls the waiter and orders pink ladies.

"Excuse me." I grab my smelling salts and inhale. Ammonia scours my sinuses. When did our relationship get so hard?

The waiter delivers frothy drinks, and Bessie toasts me. "To Charmie, the woman behind the man."

I sip the gin, willing it to dissolve my distress.

"And when did you start the hoochie-coochie?" Bessie blinks her naked eyelashes.

"Ha, another story. Jack asked me to go bicycling in the Oakland hills but broke the date."

"Why'd he do that?" She runs her tongue around the sugary edge of the martini glass.

"To marry a friend of mine." I shake my head, guilt creeping in. "Not a good friend, but still." I could never fathom why a ball of fire like Jack married boring Elizabeth.

Bessie bites into a sugar cube, engrossed. "So you didn't give up on him."

I pop a sugar cube. "Oh, but I did give up." The sweetness zings my eardrums, and I spit it into my napkin. "But my aunt Netta rode me day and night. 'Old Lady, Old Lady,' she'd taunt me. 'The one man who could save you from being a spinster and you couldn't get a first date.'"

Bessie's eyes widen. "So what'd you do?"

I smirk. "Took up with Auntie's new lover."

Bessie throws her head back and crows like a rooster at daybreak.

All the busboys turn to stare, which seems to tickle her, and she crows again. "Cock-a-doodle-doooo!"

I grab her hand. "Stop that or I won't tell you the rest."

Her mouth snaps closed.

"Jack couldn't settle down in his marriage with Elizabeth. He bought a skiff and sailed around San Francisco Bay—fishing, writing, drinking with friends."

"And you?" Bessie asked.

"I reported to his boat with my ukulele and Remington typewriter and sailed with him every chance I got. Became his first mate."

"Like a moth to a flame," Bessie says.

"Wait a minute, which one of us was the moth?"

"Still deciding." Bessie taps her chin.

"In the next couple of years, writing and playing together out there on the blue, I fell madly in love with Jack," I say. "But when I heard Elizabeth was pregnant with their second child, I broke it off with him."

"But you couldn't stay away?"

"Jack sailed to Japan for Hearst, to report on the Russo-Japanese War," I say. "He left me *The Sea-Wolf* to edit. I couldn't refuse . . ."

"It musta been torture, Charmie."

"It *was* torture while he was away. Reading his work, knowing he belonged to someone else. But Jack felt the torment, too, because when he came home, he divorced Elizabeth, and we got married."

"You betrayed your friend?" Bessie spreads her hands over her heart like a shield.

"Not something I'm proud of." She strikes my bull's-eye of guilt. Elizabeth never remarried and still holds a torch for Jack.

"But would you do it all again?" She drills her red pinky nail into her tongue.

"In a heartbeat." I hate to admit it, hard to see myself in such a harsh light.

Bessie downs her pink lady. "Two moths to the flame, then."

I've misjudged this doll. Underneath that painted face is a brain and a wit I could stand more of myself.

When I finally get back to Nob Hill, Jack is snoring. I'll tell him about the baby tomorrow.

# 6

## Oakland, California
## November 1915

*Pray do not interrupt me . . . I am smiling.*
—*Jack London,* The Sea-Wolf

Storm clouds rumble and roil above as we stand shivering in an endless line to see *The Sea Wolf*, by Bosworth Productions. Jack's first movie, showing again.

Nothing seems to go smoothly for the sweet reunion I arrange with Jack's daughters, Joan and Becky. He pours as much love and attention into them as he can, given their mother limits his time with them and strictly forbids visits to Beauty Ranch. Because I live there. Even after my nine years married to Jack, Elizabeth refuses to forgive me for stealing him away from his family.

Jack grants their every wish to assuage his guilty absence. I've learned to hold my tongue when it comes to his daughters.

"Can't you just take us to the front of the line?" Joan whines to her father. "It's your movie, and we are the Londons, after all."

"Their money is as good as ours," Jack says, distracted by the crowds at the Raven movie theater across the street, also playing

*The Sea Wolf*. The pirated version by Balboa Studios, whom Jack is suing for copyright.

"You'll win, Jack," I whisper.

He huffs, his frustration threatening to take down our day with the girls.

His lawyer bills continue to mount, adding to our financial strain. To pay for this, he's doubled his daily thousand-word writing quota. But the more prolifically Jack writes, the more debt we seem to incur. He supports four households besides Beauty Ranch: those of his children and ex-wife, his mother, his Mammy, and Aunt Netta.

"How long since we've seen you girls?" I say. "You've grown so tall."

"I'd like to see you more, but Mother says we can't." Becky clings to her father's arm, but he's looking across the street. What is she now? Thirteen? So sweet and blond, while her older sister, Joan, is dark and brooding like her mother, Elizabeth. My ex-friend.

Joan shrugs sullenly and turns away. An imperious lady of fourteen, she clamps her tender mouth tight, pulls her shoulders back in a prim dress of the previous decade. No coat. How could Elizabeth send the girls off without coats? I long to take them shopping for modern dresses and coats, teach them something about fashion. But frumpy Elizabeth forbids me from being alone with them. I can't blame her.

"You didn't come see my play." Raindrops splotch Joan's nose and cheeks.

"We were sailing the Solomon Islands," I say, "or we would have loved to come."

Jack shakes his head. "I refuse to see you on a stage, gallivanting around half-dressed, begging for attention. I can't condone such a life for my daughter."

"You rode the rails as a hobo when you were my age," Joan says, her lips curling.

"Your mother's filling your head with nonsense," he says.

Sporadic raindrops turn suddenly into hail, bouncing on the street, stinging our legs, making me curse my new calf-length skirt. Becky squeals with delight, and we run under the eaves of the movie house, breathless and giggling. I'm swept up in her childlike glee as crowds push us toward the double doors. Thank goodness Becky hasn't adopted her sister's teenage disdain.

"My hair will be ruined." Joan shields her head with her handbag, moaning.

"Mr. London, will you sign my program?" A young man hands him a pen, and Jack obliges. Several more eager fans catch on, and he's stuck signing autographs.

Finally, it's our turn, and I step up to the ticket booth and hand over a dollar for four tickets. Jack follows us into the lobby, still autographing programs and tickets.

The crack, crack, crack of the corn popper and smell of melted butter draw us to the popcorn stand, and I order two large bags, extra butter the way Jack likes it.

"Mother is picking us up after the movie." Joan primps her soggy hair. "We're going to her engagement party."

Jack reels around, turning his back to the crowd. "Elizabeth's getting married?"

The news thrills me.

"When did this happen? What sort of man is he?" Jack says.

"He took us to the carnival for my birthday." Dimples sprout on Becky's cheeks.

"Your birthday." Color drains from Jack's face. "October twentieth." He glares at me, and my stomach sinks.

"Oh my. Your birthday." How could I have forgotten? "Did your father tell you about your present?" I look at Jack, stalling.

"No, why don't you?" he says.

A thwack of thunder outside makes the lights flicker and gives me time to think.

"You asked your father for a pony, didn't you, Becky?"

The girl jumps on Jack. "You didn't, you didn't. Did you, Daddy?"

Jack smiles at me, eyes glinting. "Our mare just had a filly, and she's all yours." He bends down and kisses her cheek.

Becky hugs him. "When can we see it?"

"When you come to the ranch," he says.

"You know Mother doesn't allow us at the ranch," Joan says.

"Then we'll just have to make her change her mind, won't we?" He chucks Becky under her chin.

The usher takes our tickets, and we walk into the darkened theater. An organist plays a Wurlitzer in front of the screen.

"Let's sit up there." I take Becky's hand. "They're about to play the newsreel. We don't want to miss the beginning."

We find seats in the middle of the theater and watch a newsreel about the Great War. I wish the girls wouldn't have to see it.

Finally, the main feature starts, and Jack himself appears on the silver screen with his favorite Shire horses, Neuadd Hillside and Maid.

"There's your filly's mother, Becky," I say, and squeeze her hand. She smiles back with her new adult teeth, too big in her young mouth.

Hobart Bosworth plays Wolf Larsen as Jack wrote him: primal, animalistic, keenly intelligent, but also manipulative and bullying. I feel an empty pit in my stomach where there should be excitement. The melodramatic organ music and exaggerated silent acting cannot compare with the veracity of my husband's prose.

Jack clears his throat and coughs, a sign he feels the same way, though he'll never admit it. He's been promised thirty thousand dollars of the profits, after expenses. Money we need to pay off lawyers and the rebuilding of Wolf House.

Becky has fallen asleep on my shoulder, and I jiggle her gently.

"The movie wasn't suitable for them," Jack says, lighting an Imperial and starting up the aisle, dragging his left foot slightly. Joan follows him out.

I'd told him the story was too gruesome for teenagers, but Jack insisted.

"I liked Daddy and Neuadd Hillside best," Becky says. "Can we get ice cream now like you promised?"

"Of course, peanut." He tweaks her nose.

Nothing can be gleaned from Joan's guarded countenance. We could have just washed laundry rather than watched *The Sea-Wolf* come to life on the screen.

"What did you think of the movie, Joan?" I ask.

"I saw the other *Sea Wolf* with friends," she says.

"You went without me?" Jack sucks his Imperial.

"Mother says you must be swimming in money to have two studios making your movies."

Crouching down to her level, he blows smoke to the side. "Your mother has no idea what she's talking about. Balboa Studios stole my story, and it's costing me plenty to fight for my story rights."

Joan's mouth quirks to the side, and she pulls a paper from her purse to hand him. "Mother said to give you this."

"School uniforms fifteen dollars, bus transportation forty dollars, finishing school seventy dollars." He takes a deep drag. "I thought your mother was engaged."

"She says she will not remarry unless you increase our allowance."

"Ha. Ha. Ha." Like ice chipped off the block. "She won't allow you to visit me, yet bills me for your expenses?"

"Mother says you should support us. *We're* your family," Joan says, avoiding my eyes.

Have to admire her courage standing up to Jack. He can be formidable.

Pulling out a checkbook, he starts patting his pockets, and I reach in my purse and hand him a pen.

He whips it from my hand and writes a check. "I have two hundred and ninety-eight dollars in my account, and this check wipes out half." He studies Joan's face as if expecting her to cave, but she's stalwart.

"I warned your mother about using you girls to get what she wants." He scrawls on the check. "A spoiled colt is a ruined colt. And I do not like ruined colts."

Becky whimpers, and I pull her close, covering her ears. "Jack, you don't mean that."

Ripping out the check, he hands it to his older daughter.

Becky breaks away and runs to her mother's carriage waiting at the corner. Joan follows but halfway there, looks back.

"I liked your version of *Sea Wolf* better," she says.

"Wait here," Jack says, and stalks to the carriage. He speaks briefly to Elizabeth, then turns on his heel and walks back to me.

"What was that about?" I ask.

"Called her bluff, that's all."

"What do you mean?"

"Elizabeth didn't want to marry, she wanted to stick it to me, so I told her I don't care one whit whether she marries or not, no matter how much it costs me."

Sure enough, Elizabeth broke off the engagement. With her next check, Jack has me type a letter.

"Do you think Charmian wants to alienate my children from you?" he dictates. "No woman wants to raise another woman's children, yet Charmian is noble and willing to go the distance with me. Something you must never forget, Elizabeth, half of my work is done by Charmian. Every dollar you receive from me, Charmian has earned fifty cents of it. For every piece of bread or meat you put in your mouth, she has paid half. And yet you deny me acquaintance with my children."

I'm partly pleased that Jack defends me and partly mortified to throw our relationship in Elizabeth's face. I'm completely at sixes and sevens.

# 7

## Panama-Pacific International Exposition, San Francisco, California November 1915

*Bog-lights, vapors of mysticism, psychic Gnosticisms, veils and tissues of words, gibbering subjectivisms, gropings and maunderings, ontological fantasies, pan-psychic hallucinations—this is the stuff, the phantasms of hope, that fills your book shelves . . . Come. Your glass is empty. Fill and forget.*

—*Jack London,* John Barleycorn

Nob Hill is a world unto itself with panoramic views of the seven hills of San Francisco and beyond to the Pacific Ocean, Marin Headlands, Angel Island, Alcatraz. The Panama-Pacific International Exposition is built along the Embarcadero shoreline like a city of sandcastles, soon to be washed away.

Lying in bed at the top of Nob Hill, I hear the bright clang of cable cars and the deep, reverberating carillons of Grace Cathedral. Heavenly sounds, in my otherwise irreligious life, regale me with their jubilant noise and transform me to my beatitudes, a vision state I've been blessed with since I was a little girl. Stealing over me like the fog, the beatitudes show me a dimension beyond this earth, bringing me peace and hope, no matter my agitated state. And it doesn't hurt that Jack is enthralled by my visions and wants to record every detail when it occurs.

I let the sound suffuse my body and glide over the down comforter, billowing soft around me. There is no end or beginning as I become one with the bells, drifting in exalted cumulous clouds high in the stratosphere.

Hundreds of beings, glowing and naked, look down upon earth with loving eyes. Their light transforms my vision to their vibration, forthright and forgiving. Bells peal blissfully, and my heart sings with these heavenly beings in breathtaking harmony, louder, so much louder than my ears can take.

My body quivers with cataclysmic intensity, and I awake, panting, startled, yet invigorated. Pleasure radiates in waves through my core, through my limbs, to the very tips of my fingers and toes. I'm drenched as a babe from baptism. All my anxiety and fear has fallen away.

Still trembling from the vision, I find him hunched into the window booth in the penthouse bar. He stares desolately out on the dense fog blanketing San Francisco Bay and drains a French 75, gin and champagne. A fresh one awaits.

I see his sallow complexion, his clamped mouth, his wincing sighs, ruminating over his daughters or maybe his ex-wife's engagement or even the legal battle with Balboa Studios . . . Whatever his particular worry, it's clearly not a good time to tell him about the baby.

Jack lights an Imperial and sips his second drink, both of which the doctor advises against. Refusing to nag, I scoot across from him in the booth.

"My beatitudes visited me," I say, and his face lights.

"Tell me about it." He takes a drag from his cigarette. "Slowly. Close your eyes. Stay with the vision. Deliver me every color, every smell, every nuance."

I've broken his brooding. Happiness flushes through me, yet I'm afraid to start. What if he doesn't like my vision? What if he thinks I'm faking? I stare out at the bay. Sunlight glares off the surface like the brilliant light in my beatitudes.

I tell him what I saw in my vision, and when I'm finished, his inquisitive eyes search my face. "What else? There must be more."

So I embellish the story, swirling effortlessly from my mouth as if it happened. As long as I'm speaking, he's riveted to me. Tall, billowing clouds make rooms in the white mansion where souls live in perfect harmony. Our higher selves are loving guardians to ourselves down on earth, the part of us that knows the answers, knows no guilt or striving, only music and exalted love.

I tell him lovemaking up there is as free and simple as walking through another body and sharing that moment of time as one being. He listens carefully to that, smiles and nods.

I tell him that our worldly worries of money and fame and failed relationships and political strife are the rubbish created by the human form, that all those problems don't exist.

And when I have nothing more to tell, he leads me back to our hotel room, flush and eager. The anticipation of Jack's long legs between mine brings a delicious curl to my abdomen. Afterward, I'll tell him about the baby.

The smell of him tantalizes: Carter's ink, shirt starch, and tobacco. My fingers fumble with the key in the lock. The fob tassel swishes against my wrist and ignites a burning prickle up my arm and over my breasts. I pound the unyielding door with my fist.

Jack takes the key and opens the door. Both beds are still mussed. I hang the **Do Not Disturb** sign on the door.

Jack walks past the beds to the desk where my Remington typewriter awaits. "Let's get this down before it leaves us."

I stand here wild with desire, and he wants to write.

My abdomen cramps, and I sit down at my typewriter. He paces in front of the bay windows and repeats back my beatitudes, cunningly transformed with complex characters and a circuitous plot that amplifies my vision.

I don't really hear his voice anymore; his words move my fingers like electricity to a light bulb. The light transforms us into one.

After the writing, I get my grand lolly . . . a divine joining of our bodies, tangled together in the bedsheets.

"I've missed a period," I whisper. "Maybe two."

His eyes brighten. "Do you mean . . ."

I nod. "I know it's a boy, I can feel it," I say.

He fondles my belly and breasts in awe, and soon we're making love all over again.

He's turned away from his worries and back to our lives. My Jack has come back to me. For a moment, I feel light and giddy, until I remember Lawrence . . . and pray Jack will not.

Bessie invited us to join her for Houdini's performance at the Panama-Pacific International Exposition. So strange to think this majestic Palace of Fine Arts and ten other palaces built along the waterfront for the exhibition will soon be destroyed and forgotten.

Jack's long arm shields my back from the fog, his hand strokes my shoulder, our world transformed with the news of our baby. Layers of worry have fallen from his face, leaving him high-spirited and affectionate.

I close my eyes to savor the warmth of his arm, inhaling a mélange of smells: seaweed washed ashore, melted chocolate, pungent eucalyptus, cioppino, fresh-baked sourdough.

A foghorn blasts, and my eyes fly open. A dense haze creeps through the Roman columns, obscuring the bay, smoldering in the colored spotlights. But no one is kept away by the fog. Thousands swarm the grounds around the grand rotunda and reflecting pools.

An orchestra strikes up an ominous overture, "Asleep in the Deep," a song I've played for Jack. Mist seeps into my bones. I shiver, and Jack holds me tighter.

With all the mist, I'm glad we're tucked under the shelter of Bessie's box seats, but where is she? She stepped away for a smoke, since Houdini doesn't approve, but that was ages ago.

Half a dozen stagehands dolly in a four-by-seven tomb of plate glass framed in bolted brass and unload it center stage. The *San Francisco Chronicle* heralded the monstrosity as a Chinese water-torture tank, the newest and most dangerous of Houdini's death-defying escapes.

A siren wails, and the crowd parts for a blazing-red fire truck. Burly firemen in yellow slickers jump out, hoisting their fire hose onto the stage, and fill the oversized glass coffin with water, sloshing against the plate glass.

I lean to Jack. "Can you imagine how cold it is? The newspaper said the water's from the bay."

He snaps pictures with his Kodak, engrossed in the action.

When the firemen finish, spotlights reflect off the water chamber and a timpani drums in our ears. Houdini enters the stage, wearing a white satin boxing robe, and the crowd cheers.

I'm impressed by his hold on the audience, imperious and precise. I wonder what he sees in sweet, daffy Bessie.

"Lay-dees and gentlemen, what you are about to witness is *not* a magic show, but a dangerous escape from certain death."

His hypnotic cadence brings the audience to silence.

"You are about to experience the unfathomable." Houdini prowls the stage, commanding attention, his white robe billowing around his bare thighs in the gusty wind, giving me goose bumps.

Jack pulls me close. "Cold?"

Burrowing into his chest, I suspect my reaction has more to do with Houdini's flawless physique.

"You are about to experience what it is like to drown." His arm sweeps the rapt audience. "What it is like when you sink underwater and cannot break free. Your lungs bursting into flame. Your eyes bulging, and finally . . ." He stands perfectly still, then snaps his head to where we sit, looking straight at me. "You lose all your senses. And let go."

The lights black out, and a second later come on again. Impossibly, Houdini appears at the opposite side of the stage. Men in tailored jackets with gold epaulettes roll in an enormous clock.

"Many of you may be wondering, 'How long does it take to drown?'" He cocks his head and raises his eyebrows. "The answer? Exactly as long as you can hold your breath."

I feel a stitch in my lung.

"When I start the second hand, I want you to hold your breath with me for one minute. Everybody ready? Take a deep breath and hold." He starts the sweeping second hand, tick, tick, ticking, and I hold my breath, counting along.

Jack gives up at twenty seconds, coughing and sputtering, due to his smoke-clogged lungs, I'm sure. Most of the audience holds out for thirty seconds, then expels air like balloons. I gulp and hold in my breath, watching the second hand click toward a full minute. Then air whooshes from my lungs.

Bessie returns to our box seats, carrying three steaming mugs topped with whipped cream. "Mr. Houdini tried to teach me to hold my breath underwater." She hands Jack a mug, and he grimaces at the whipped cream. "He had this *enormous* bathtub installed and timed me with a stopwatch. Does he think I'm a goldfish? I'm not a goldfish. I'm a woman."

I take a welcome sip and cough at the taste of whiskey.

"Irish coffee." She grins impishly.

The second sip warms my insides. I wipe whipped cream off Jack's lips, and he kisses my fingers, warming me more than the drink.

The crowd applauds, and we direct our attention to the stage. Houdini whirls off his satin robe like a matador, fog caressing his robust chest and thighs. The merest of bathing suits shows off his ample attributes, yet nobody turns away in modesty. Far from it. Men and women alike ogle him shamelessly, the bawdy San Franciscans making me smile. Everything makes me smile today with Jack's arm around me and a baby on the way.

Firemen lock Houdini's ankles into stockades of heavy wood and iron. They bind his arms and chest in thick chains and attach them to a large winch. Then they crank Houdini above our heads, dangling him upside down like a chrysalis.

"Release me, gentlemen," Houdini yells.

The firemen unlatch the winch, and the spool of chain jerks and whirs. Houdini drops headfirst into the water-torture chamber, waves sloshing over the top of the tank. The audience cries out, and his head drops to the bottom of the tank. Firemen lower a heavy wooden top over him.

The clock watcher starts the second hand ticking, and I gulp in as much air as my lungs will hold.

Beside me, Bessie hums off-key and unravels a long yarn from her Irish sweater.

Tiny air bubbles cover Houdini's skin, then float to the surface. The water wavers under the lights. The fire chief grips a huge fire ax, ready to break the glass tomb should Houdini not be able to escape.

Jack murmurs he's determined to discover Houdini's scheme, scanning the stage for hidden oxygen tubes, trapdoors, or mirrors, any key to elucidate this suicidal act.

I let out a little pent-up breath.

Meanwhile, Houdini wrestles with the chains that bind his wrists and cut into his chest.

"One minute and counting," the clock watcher announces, and I gulp more air.

Bessie's box seats are too close to the stage for comfort. Houdini's plummy face bulges his appearance out of recognition, his muscles strain against the chain, leaving white marks, his chest and shoulders contort with Herculean effort.

My gut clenches with his agony.

"Two minutes and counting." The second hand ticks to the top of the clock. I let out that breath and take another.

Her sweater ruined, Bessie weaves the unraveled yarn through her tiny fingers and plays cat's cradle.

Jack pulls out his notebook and scribbles with his three-inch pencil. That scrawl will be so hard to interpret later. Sweat beads over his eyebrows, even though wet fog penetrates our bones.

I glance at the cursed clock ticking away, and soon, two and a half minutes have passed. The tender spot behind each earlobe aches. Pressure builds behind my eyes. I can't hold my breath any longer. I watch Houdini, his pain throbbing in my chest. I have to hold on.

Jack laughs at me. "Your breath won't save him, Mate-Woman."

Defiantly, I fill my lungs to bursting.

Still upside down, Houdini unlocks the final chain around his chest and yanks his feet from the iron stocks. Then, forcing his feet to the bottom of the chamber, he thrusts off the floor with his powerful thighs.

He pushes up on the wooden top and throws it to the stage floor with a crack and boom. Hoisting himself up on the glass wall with strong arms, he balances his ribs on the edge of the water chamber. Then he propels his legs up and over the edge and onto the stage, wet, shimmering, and glorious as a marlin freshly jerked from the ocean.

I gasp with the pure glory of his muscled form shivering in the shock of cold air. Liquid drips from his quaking limbs, his face still purple with blood. He slumps over and grabs his knees, carved abdomen heaving, lungs siphoning oxygen. The audience breaks its silence with cries and shouts of astonishment.

Jack studies me with a curious half smile. I don't ask why.

Houdini raises his eyes to the clearing sky and utters a few words I wish I could hear. Standing like Michelangelo's *David*, hip cocked to the left, dark curls dripping onto his forehead. Water streams from his pectorals to his chiseled abdomen, down his honed thighs, and pools at his perfect naked feet.

I feel a jolt deep in my pelvis, followed by a thick flow between my legs. "Where is a ladies' room?" I ask Bessie. Another pain makes me wince. "Emergency."

"Backstage, follow me." Shedding her unraveled sweater, she marches backstage in her red jacket with epaulettes and brass buttons, knickers, and tall, shiny boots.

Jack follows us. "What's happening? Are you all right?"

I nod, then shake my head, my mind whirring with the phenomenon we just witnessed and its startling effect on my body. I can't tell Jack what's happening because I don't even know myself. Maybe I can stop the flow and save the baby. I cross my fingers like a schoolgirl. Sometimes hope is all we have to hang on to.

Bessie stops at the door marked LADIES. "I'll be right outside if you need help." She squeezes my hand. I'm growing fond of this girl.

It takes me a while to understand what's happening. My heart is as heavy as the flow, expecting to lose my baby, my dream, my salvation . . . but soon I realize this bloody mess is no miscarriage. There is no baby. Nobody will be saved. It's only my menses, like Aunt Netta predicted, heavy, painful, bloating.

"Old Lady. Old Lady," Netta's voice nags in my head. "It's menopause."

What a desperate fool I was to believe I could have a baby at almost forty-four, with or without Lawrence to muddy the water.

Wrestling with rough paper towels and toilet paper, I'm devastated by my body's perfidy.

Jack and Bessie are waiting for me when I come out.

"Everything okay?" she asks.

My head drops, ashamed to look at Jack. "My time of the month." I was positive it was a son. It felt so different this time. A son would mean so much to Jack. To us.

Color drains from his face. "Were you trying to hoodwink me?"

"Of course not. I was positive I—"

"Are you sure?" A glimmer of hope appears on his face.

I shake my head, pressing my lips together. "No baby." Too damn old. Now what will hold Jack?

Bessie frowns, walks to the shadowy end of the hall, and sips from a flask. I could use a drink about now. My legs are shaky, and my abdomen cramps like a son of a bitch.

Houdini appears from the dark hallway, freshly splashed with wood-spice cologne. I'm grateful for his distraction.

Jack leans against the wall and lights an Imperial, propping his bad foot on a ledge, watching me—spinning his tale, I imagine. How I lied to him, tricked him, betrayed him. He clenches the cig between his lips and sucks oxygen through it as if trying to extract every molecule of air from the hallway. The tobacco flares red at the tip. He holds the smoke in his lungs, swallows it down, then lets it out in dirty bursts like a tractor expelling exhaust. Breaking off his stony stare, he turns away.

"You cheated death, Houdini." And just like that, he dismisses me and our unborn son.

Houdini leans forward, voice low. "There was never a chance of death. It's all discipline and practice."

Bessie comes over and holds my hand. Her soft touch comforts me.

"I saw life drain from your being," Jack says. "Your face went purple."

Houdini squeezes his face into strained wrinkles, eyes telescoping out, forehead rippling, veins popping from his neck. His cheeks turn red, then purple.

A hysterical laugh escapes my throat. "Stop. I truly believed you were drowning."

Jack blows a puff of smoke. "You *were* practicing death. Taunting it. Surrendering to nothingness."

"On the contrary. I'm practicing control. Using water pressure to relax my body. To be surrounded by water is as natural as floating inside your mother's womb."

My abdomen aches.

"I've felt that way," Jack says. "When I jump into the pond at the ranch, the water green and alive, sunlight filtering through the cattails. For a while I enjoy the underwater beauty. Then minnows swarm my face, leeches latch on to my thighs, and catfish nibble my feet, and I have to escape." Sweat beads his upper lip. "You were in agony up there. I saw it. Oh, it's theater of course, and you know how to milk it. But those chains bit into your neck and cut your wrists. Your body plunged in fifty-degree water. I could feel the pressure in my chest, the murky void, the force crushing my lungs." Jack grabs Houdini's bicep. "Tell me more. I need to know."

Houdini cants his head, studying Jack, then seems to make up his mind. "When I first hit the water, my calves and feet cramp, but as my body descends, I will myself to relax. I contract and move my muscles until I can loosen the chains on my arms enough to unwind them. Then I undo the locks and swim to the surface."

"Not so fast." Jack pounds the ladies' room door with his fist. "How do your lungs feel? Does acid eat through the walls of your stomach? What thoughts go through your mind? Do your eyeballs feel as if they will burst?" Jack towers over Houdini. "Does your skin shrivel or soak up the water? Does doubt paralyze your movement? Do you want to give up and let yourself drift to sleep? Tell me every detail so I may live what you lived."

Houdini's eyes shine. "While we're both entertainers, Mr. London, I choose to conceal my methods, and you illuminate them."

As the men banter, my cramps grow more violent. I feel wretched and hopeless, just like the night Baby Joy died.

Long after my baby girl was gone, my contractions and hemorrhaging persisted. They called for Jack at the movie studio in Hollywood, but no one had seen him. Lawrence came to sit by my bedside for days, consoling me through that darkest time.

Nine days later, Jack showed up, ragged, filthy, begging forgiveness when he found out Joy had died. He confessed he didn't go to Hollywood after he'd left me but had instead wandered aimlessly around Eighth Street in Oakland, where the Chinese gambling and opium dens are. There, his story blurred—whiskey, barflies, an unprovoked attack in a saloon, a battered body and bruised eye, a jail cell.

His inner demons got the best of him last time, when he wanted a son and lost a daughter instead. What can I expect him to do this time?

Bessie looks up at me. "You're white as a ghost."

Pain knifes my stomach, and I shudder. "I need a pharmacy."

Bessie marches me between the men. "I'm taking Charmie to the Palace of Flowers. We'll meet you boys at the yacht club for dinner." Not waiting for an answer, she takes me out into the fresh air.

My dream of giving Jack a son has drowned in my own blood.

Before long, I've bought aspirin and female supplies and we're walking through the Palace of Flowers. The riotous colors and overpowering perfume would thrill me any other day but now leave me trembling and weak.

"Let's stop here," Bessie says, pausing at a sidewalk café along the Embarcadero. Wrought-iron chairs and small round tables emulate the French cafés of the Champs-Élysées.

I slide into a chair, head tight and stomach churning.

Bessie unzips her carpetbag and takes out a Kewpie doll.

"You don't mind, do you?" Bessie unfurls the **Votes for Women** banner across the doll's chest. "It's just that I brought Victoria Woodhull to see San Francisco, where women can vote, and Mr. Houdini won't allow her out in public. *Excetera.*"

Bessie makes me laugh. "Is it Miss Woodhull's position on suffrage, spiritualism, or free love he objects to?" I say, feeling suddenly light-headed and giddy.

"All three, I suppose. He hates it when I march with the suffragettes." Bessie throws me a chary look and starts to stuff the doll back in her carpetbag, but I stop her.

"Glad you could join us, Victoria Woodhull."

Bessie's face lights up. "She loves chocolate. Do you think they have Ghirardelli's?"

"Wouldn't be surprised."

Bessie is ecstatic when they do. She orders hot chocolate, chocolate éclairs, and Buena Vista champagne cocktails. Just the sight of all that sugar sends my mood soaring.

I tip my coupe to her and Victoria Woodhull. "Cheers to womanhood."

"Feeling better now?" she asks.

I take a large sip of champagne. "Just that time of the month."

Bessie is quiet, puts her ear to the doll's face—listening, frowning, blue eyelids fluttering.

"Did I say something wrong?" I ask.

Bessie licks the sugary rim of her glass, her cheeks flaming. "Victoria Woodhull thinks you'd understand something . . . rather . . . delicate."

"I can try."

She lowers her chin, lips trembling. "I've never become a woman."

A laugh burbles up my throat, but seeing her pained expression, I quash it.

Bessie drinks her entire cocktail and orders another round.

"I never got my period. Never grew breasts, never got hair down there." As soon as fresh cocktails arrive, she gulps from one.

I drink mine, too, head zinging with questions. Suddenly her flat chest and boyish limbs take on new meaning.

"I *prolly* know what you're wondering. Just ask." Bessie nods at the doll. "Don't worry about her, she can be trusted with a secret."

"What about your husband?"

"I never lied to him, if that's what you are thinking." She blinks rapidly, then opens her eyes wide. "I was only a sophomore at St. Mary's Girls Academy when he came to perform for us. I sat in the first row, and he kept making eyes at me. Afterward he invited me for a soda, and it got late. Too late to go home, so we eloped. *Excetera.*" Bessie bites into an éclair, and cream oozes out the sides.

A brazenly different story than she told before.

"He introduced me to his mother after the wedding." She knocks her forehead with the heel of her hand. "She called me a shiksa. You know, a gentile woman?"

"I've heard the term."

"Well anyway, Mrs. Houdini bargained with me. If I gave her a grandson, she'd forgive that I'm Catholic. My husband would move mountains to give his mother what she wanted. Only . . . he couldn't even—I couldn't even—" She stares into her coupe, lips quivering. "I just don't have the equipment."

I look away, allowing her a moment to gather herself. The Embarcadero bustles with young families. Mothers and fathers grasp toddlers' hands, husbands push perambulators while their wives hold a parasol over the infants, young boys and fathers fly kites on the lawn near the lapping bay. A whole new generation of families is out for a stroll, and here we are, two barren women crying into our champagne.

"Mr. Houdini sent me to dozens of doctors for a cure. They poked and prodded, injected me with hemlock, forced sumac down my throat, and plastered my pelvis with poultice of earthworms and moss." She holds the éclair to Victoria Woodhull's mouth. "I am a thirty-nine-year-old adolescent."

My mind goes slack. "Then you two don't ever—"

She winks a blue-creased eyelid. "I've learned a trick or two. How else do you think I keep him in line?"

I want to ask about her methods, but leave it for another time. I raise my coupe and toast her. "To good tricks."

Three toots of an automobile horn turn our attention to the Embarcadero. A sporty automobile passes us, a real looker with an extra-long chassis, red-spoked wheels, and big brass headlights. Our eager husbands wave from behind the windshield.

"Jack's driving." I jump up. "Jack can't drive."

"Houdini loves a good apprentice." Bessie pulls me down into the bistro chair. "Why didn't you have children?" She sucks her sugar cube.

"I tried." My stomach cramps, and I'm reminded of my volatile menses. "Apparently, my womb's too damn old."

"At least you tried." Bessie slurps cream from her éclair. "Pathetic, isn't it? Marrying a man I can't—Don't get me wrong, Mr. Houdini's a good man, *excetera*. It's not his fault I am like I am." A single tear escapes the corner of her eye.

I dry it with my handkerchief. "'It is not a lack of love, but a lack of friendship that makes unhappy marriages.'"

"That's just beauteous, isn't it, Victoria Woodhull?" She touches the doll's cheek. "Did your husband write that?"

"No, darling. Nietzsche wrote that."

"Then God bless Nietzsche." She toasts my glass.

I laugh at the oxymoron. "The only problem is Nietzsche's God is dead."

"God isn't dead," Bessie says with a bewildered expression.

"Cheers to that," I toast, preferring dolls, chocolate, and champagne to Jack's harrowing philosophical discussions that never end well for anyone.

# 8

## BEAUTY RANCH, GLEN ELLEN, CALIFORNIA
## THANKSGIVING DAY 1915

*The soft summer wind stirs the redwoods, and Wild-Water ripples sweet cadences over its mossy stones. There are butterflies in the sunshine, and from everywhere arises the drowsy hum of bees. It is so quiet and peaceful, and I sit here, and ponder, and am restless. It is the quiet that makes me restless. It seems unreal. All the world is quiet, but it is the quiet before the storm. I strain my ears, and all my senses, for some betrayal of that impending storm.*

—*Jack London,* The Iron Heel

I'm setting the Thanksgiving table in the stone dining room adjoining the cottage when I hear the first guests arrive, two hours early, and we are running late.

Jack's sister, Eliza, pushes open the kitchen door with her broad hips wrapped in a white apron. She wafts a fresh-baked pie under my nose. It smells of cinnamon, raisins, and sweetmeats.

"Jack will be thrilled," I say. "It's not Thanksgiving without your mincemeat pie."

Her plump cheeks blush as she places the pie on the sideboard as gently as a fallen bird to its nest. Sweat streams down the back of her neck from working all morning in the kitchen.

"Someone is here," I say. "Come greet them with me." I need a buffer from the chin-wagging Crowd.

Eliza waddles back to the kitchen. "Oh no. I'll stay and help Manyoungi cook. I want everything to be just right for Jack." She pushes through the door.

As tough as she is, I should thank my lucky stars for Eliza. With her dedication to Jack and the ranch, she shoulders a burden that would break me if I had to go it alone.

Nakata pushes through the swinging door with a crumpled smile, maneuvering a tray of canapés.

"*Â, bikkurishita*, Miss Charmian," he says, and sets the tray on the sideboard.

"Yes, quite a surprise, Nakata. The guests weren't supposed to come until two o'clock. I'll stall them with cocktails on the front porch since the weather's nice."

I pop a canapé into my mouth, savoring the tang of goat cheese and Gravenstein apple. Catching my image in the mirror, I smooth the furrow between my brows. Autumn has been harrowing with the fire and Lawrence and my phantom baby. I would have preferred a quiet Thanksgiving alone with Jack, but he likes an audience, and an audience we'll have. I'll sneak off after dinner, when they're stuffed and quaffed and regaling each other with stories, take Maid on a ride, and clear my head.

I brush flour from my velvet riding skirt and walk out to the porch. Jack's holding Possum in his arms and greeting guests with clever remarks.

Men hitch horses to the post, fine ladies arrive by carriage, others in wagons and livery service from the train station in Glen Ellen. The triad of Netta, Edward, and Roscoe arrives in the farm truck, miraculously together again. Not surprising, I suppose. Their breakups and makeups happen so often I don't care anymore.

Chewing a hangnail, I glance at my watch, high noon. "Why is everyone so early?"

"You told me twelve," Jack says.

"I said two."

He shrugs and laughs, and I run into the front room to make cocktails. Nakata brings in a block of ice.

"Let me chop it for you." He stabs an ice pick into the block and breaks it in half.

"Go help Manyoungi. I'm sure he's having a fit."

*"Mimi ni tako ga dekiru."* I'm growing calluses in my ear.

I take the pick from him. "I'll handle this."

Jack's invited twice the number we can comfortably entertain, loving our cottage to be full of laughter, debate, and booze.

The vagabonds that smell bad I put up in the bunkhouse. The others will stay in the Wake Robin cabins and other cottages tucked in our woods. I hear a motorcar and watch the Houdinis arrive in a Dodge touring car, looking forward to seeing them again.

George Sterling corners me behind the bar, reeking of hashish. "You look luscious in velvet." He strokes the leg of my riding skirt.

I stab the pick into the block of ice. "Hang up your coat, Greek."

Sterling breathes stale air down my neck. "What did Lawrence have that I don't have?"

I refuse to let him needle me. "He didn't smell like a hashish den, for one. And he had a great accent."

"If that's all it takes, I can cop a British accent that will curl your toes." He laughs. "Perhaps you're missing your fidelity?"

"My fidelity is none of your business." I grab the ice pick at the bar and stab at the ice block.

Sterling takes the hint and slurks out to the porch with the others.

Imagine that cockroach trying to wheedle a confession from me. I hack the ice to fine chips and scoop them into my shaker with the apple cider, spiced rum, and Meyer lemon juice that Nakata has carefully prepped, and pour the concoction into glasses.

When Bessie Houdini walks in the front door, I hand her a drink.

"Charmie!" She takes the glass and kisses me on the cheek. "Now you know why you're my best friend."

I have no idea what to say. I've never had a best friend, besides Jack.

Today, she looks like an Annie Oakley postcard, with her suede fringed jacket, riding skirt, and laced boots. A horseshoe necklace dangles from her neck. Her vibrant chatter whisks away the disgust Sterling stirred up in me.

"Come see what I set up for the girls," I say.

We take our drinks over the boardwalk to the dining room. The Japanese house staff scurries around to prepare the buffet for dinner.

Just to the left of the door, I've set up a tiny table with two dolls I bought for Jack's daughters, should their mother ever allow a visit. An empty chair awaits Bessie's doll.

"Oh my goodness. Oh my goodness." She takes her doll out of her carpetbag and sits her at the table.

"May I introduce Joan and Becky," I say. Jack would disapprove of using his daughters' names as much as he disapproves of dolls.

"Victoria Woodhull is so very glad to make their acquaintance."

We join the Crowd on the front porch, their voices straining to outcheer the rest. Sterling spouts his latest poem, and I hear snippets: dreams dipped in fear, tree spirits, "our ancient and immutable domain . . ." The man's so full of horse puckey.

Jack's invited a slice of life that never ceases to amaze me: a punch-drunk boxer he met at a saloon, an Arab princess straight out of some sultan's harem, artists and poets, marauding tycoons who think we have lots of money. Jack's a soft touch when it comes to investing (i.e., gambling).

The rice farmers from Sacramento who want Jack to invest in rice paddies park themselves near the tray of cured pork from Jack's piggery. The Saint Leo church ladies seem fascinated by Edward Morrell, the San Quentin prisoner Jack immortalized in *The Star Rover*. Maybe they want to save his soul. Beautiful Blanche whispers behind her lily-white hand to Anna Strunsky, Jack's old flame who married a count.

The mayor of Sonoma, who smells of leather-tanning fluid; Luther Burbank, the botanist who encouraged investing in eucalyptus; and another handful of men crowd around Jack and Houdini, talking the Great War as if they're in charge. Armament. Weaponry. Strategy. The undercurrent of every good gathering.

Nakata rings the bell. None too soon. These folks will fall off the porch if we don't feed them shortly.

"Dinner is served, everyone." I hold my hand out to Bessie. "Follow me."

Nakata opens the heavy wood doors to the dining room, and our guests reel back and gasp. I myself can't believe the sight.

"Oh my goodness, oh my goodness." Bessie flutter claps. "It's a fairy tale."

Garlands of colorful leaves festoon the stone walls, lined with French wine barrels. Our long table, hewn from a giant redwood, stretches twenty feet into the far side of the room. Down the middle, beeswax candles in wine bottles illuminate plump, round pumpkins; gnarled gourds; and Indian corn speckled scarlet and gold. Woven palm place mats set with pewter plates and utensils flank the sides of the table, replete with four different wineglasses for Buena Vista sparkling wine, Kunde Gewürztraminer and Cabernet, and our own late-harvest Riesling. Jack says we can never have too many glasses.

"You outdid yourself, Mate." Jack pecks my cheek and welcomes our guests into the dining room.

Nakata stands behind the door, watching with dark eyes sparkling.

"How did you do all this, Nakata?" I ask.

He turns a corkscrew into a bottle of Gewürztraminer. "Even a fool has one talent." He pours the first wine for the table.

Jack holds up his glass and makes a toast. "We are the Socialists, anarchists, hoboes, chicken thieves, and undesirable citizens of the US. Notice we are not respectable. No revolutionary can possibly be respectable in these days of the reign of poverty." He drinks, and the Crowd follows suit.

He leads the buffet line, explaining his favorite dishes: ten-minute mallard, barely warm and bloody; wild turkey, quail, and venison accompanied by wild rice with forest mushrooms; baby pumpkins filled with curried pumpkin soup; Swiss chard sautéed with purple beets; chestnut gnocchi; brussels sprouts with piggery bacon.

He sits at the head of the table, with Possum at his feet and Houdini by his side. I wave to Jack. "Save seats for Bessie and me."

I find her in the corner with the dolls. Reluctantly, she bids them goodbye.

We fill our plates and join our husbands. Houdini gazes at me from across the table. My mouth gapes and shuts like a catfish, and I say the first thing that comes to mind.

"I keep seeing you underwater with your purple face and the whites of your eyes rolled back. You can't fake that."

"Oh, he's not faking." Bessie drinks her Gewürztraminer. "His head hurts for a week afterward. The doctors say he'll have a brain hemorrhage if he keeps—"

Houdini raises his hand, and she stops.

Nakata taps me on the shoulder. *"Sakana no yo ni nomimasu."* Drink like fish. "They've gone through all the white wine."

"Then pour the jeroboam of Cabernet."

He bows and leaves. I look down the table, twenty-four of us by last count. The noise level astonishes me.

"How did you two meet?" Sterling asks Bessie.

"Mr. Houdini performed at my sixteenth birthday party and stained my dress with *indivisible* ink." Bessie bats false eyelashes. "He took it home to clean it. But when he returned, he gave me a big box with a blue bow on it. Said he couldn't get the stain out and couldn't get me out of his mind. I opened the box, and there was a perfect lace wedding dress."

I laugh. "That is quite a story."

Sterling flicks the fringe of Bessie's buckskin jacket with a long fingernail, and she giggles.

Heat rises from my bodice. "Mrs. Houdini is a singer."

Bessie gulps the rest of her wine, stands, and belts out "Somebody's Sweetheart I Want to Be" better than Lillian Russell on Broadway. Her voice is crystalline, but her face contorts with sadness, and giant tears carve rivulets in her rouge.

The room falls silent. I can't stand strangers gaping at her, so I start singing with her. She smiles at me. Jack joins in, melding his deep baritone with our voices. Soon everyone is singing her heartbreaking song except Houdini, who watches with doleful eyes.

When the song ends, I lead the applause.

"If you weren't married, I'd go down on one knee," the San Quentin convict toasts Bessie.

"And if I weren't married, I might say yes!" She winks at him.

"Oh, modern women with their independence," Doc Thompson scoffs. "It's a wonder marriage survives at all in this promiscuous age."

"What is monogamy but a cage around the one you love?" Jack raises a glass. "Isn't love better coming out of desire than law?"

Oh, my stars. Is this the same Jack who's pouted for months about Lawrence?

"Absolutely right," Anna Strunsky says. "And if one enjoys extracurricular company for an afternoon or two, it simply makes your partner appreciate your affections all the more."

Blanche weaves her arm around Anna's waist and kisses her swanlike neck. "And why can't women appreciate women?"

"I agree wholeheartedly," Sterling says. "But I wonder if Count Strunsky would?"

"My husband is not here, is he?" Anna says. "Whatever I do in the wilds of Sonoma Valley is my own damn business."

Aunt Netta grabs Edward's and Roscoe's hands and thrusts them into the air. "Long live free love."

At the foot of the table, Nakata starts passing out leather-bound books to each guest, and I'm relieved for the distraction, before my Thanksgiving party turns into a California orgy.

"Which of your novels are you giving our guests?" I ask Jack.

He takes a bite of mincemeat and peers through his brows. "You'll just have to see, won't you?"

The Crowd thumbs through the pages, oohing and aahing, nodding their heads in my direction. Jack must have dedicated his novel to me.

Nakata hands me the volume, the cover gold stamped with an illustration of a boat on the ocean, clouds billowing. "*The Log of the Snark*," I read in a hushed voice. "By Charmian Kittredge London." My novel. My heart beats like a rabbit caught in a snare. Our guests stand and applaud, smiles broad and beaming. Anna Strunsky hugs me, smelling of lilacs, and kisses me on the lips. "Oh, darling girl. We've been published the same year."

Over Anna's shoulder, I see Jack clapping, eyes wild with pride.

"How? When?" I ask, too thrilled to say more.

"Macmillan published my book, too." Anna kisses me again, her ample bosom smothering mine.

"I didn't know you were writing," I say.

"Jack encouraged me, ever since we wrote *The Kempton-Wace Letters* together."

Jack's arms surround us. "So proud of you girls."

The shock hits me with double-barrels. He published Anna's book as well as mine. "I'm feeling dizzy." I pull out of the trio but get caught in the congratulating crowd. Sterling sits me at the teakwood secretary with a pile of books to autograph. One by one, I crack open the leather covers, inhaling the ink and paper.

Jack stands over me. "Is it everything you hoped?" He leans down and kisses my cheek.

"You know how I've longed for this day, Jack."

He nods and smiles, so proud of himself.

"I just never thought I'd have to share it with your first love."

After supper, guests move to the sofas and easy chairs and light up cigars and opium pipes, while Eliza and Nakata clear the table.

"How about a card trick for the Crowd?" I ask Houdini.

"I prefer the more dangerous feats of Chung Ling Soo." Jack leers cruelly, with too much drink. "Like catching a bullet with your teeth."

"Oooo." Bessie lights a hand-rolled cigarette. "Like you *preformed* with him at the Alhambra in London. You promised never to do that again."

"'Danger is dancing with death without succumbing to her charms.' Isn't that what you said, Houdini?" Jack opens his gun cabinet and takes out a French flintlock dueling pistol, as long as his forearm. "Let's dance."

"Put the gun away," I say. The set of dueling guns was a gift from another admirer of mine, claiming he'd duel Jack for me. Whenever Jack gets sozzled, he brings them out and brags.

Bowing his head to the burnished brass-and-maple pistol, Jack points it directly at the magician.

Houdini snorts. "Only if you're the shooter."

Jack glares above the barrel. "Of course. Why not?"

Sterling steps up on his chair, hand solemnly across his chest.

*"Say not, 'Why place a weapon in his hand?'*
*Say not, 'He could have written many a book*
*To render better service to his land.'*
*There comes a time when sterner things must be,*
*And all the words of Byron and of Brooke*
*Match not the stand they took for liberty."*

While Sterling rambles on, I join Jack at the gun cabinet. "Stop this cockfight before it gets out of hand."

"I thought you liked watching Houdini." Kissing me with lips tasting of port, he takes out the ammunition case, gunpowder, and scale from the cabinet.

Bessie tugs Houdini's sleeve, tilts her small, pale face up to his. "You gave me your word."

"Our host requested it," he says. "Everyone stand against that wall. You should be safe."

Bessie struts to the door, picks up Victoria Woodhull, and leaves the dining room.

Jack lights an Imperial with a smug smile.

"First rule: never smoke around gunpowder." Houdini grabs Jack's cigarette and grinds it into an ashtray. "Now, measure out one and three-quarters drams of gunpowder. Too little won't project the bullet, too much will blow your hand off."

"Black powder for muzzleloaders." Jack's shaking hand funnels gunpowder into the barrel, spilling some on the hardwood floor.

Houdini takes the pistol. "Now we just tamp the bullet down." He thrusts in the ramrod, pulls it out, then wipes the end with his handkerchief, replacing it into his breast pocket. "Now, Jack, you and I take our places at opposite ends of the room." He turns to me. "Charmian, how far would you say this is?"

"I can't let you go through with this," I say, voice wavering. "Not with Jack like . . ."

Houdini spins around and holds up his hand. "Silence." He gazes at me, and then at the Crowd. "We must have silence for this dangerous feat. One word, one outcry, could cause death."

The two men pose back-to-back, then pace to the ends of the room as the Crowd hugs the west wall, swallowing nervous giggles and snide remarks.

Houdini plants his feet wide, holds his chest high, and clacks his front teeth together three times. "Ready when you are."

Jack aims the pistol, his grip far from steady. My spine bristles like porcupine quills.

His finger pulls the trigger, and the flintlock sparks to flame. The discharge bursts from the barrel with a deafening noise and shoots across the room in a smoky trail. The acrid smell of gunpowder fills my nostrils. Possum yelps and runs to me, clawing my legs.

Houdini's body jolts, wobbles, and I gasp. His hands clutch his heart. Blanche screams and faints.

Jack runs past me to Houdini. "Charmian, call the doctor."

I nod but can't move. This isn't happening. Finally, I pry my feet off the floor and run for the telephone.

Jack embraces Houdini, holding him upright. "No, man. No. I thought you could do it or I wouldn't have—"

I'm watching them with the telephone receiver at my ear, clicking the cradle madly, trying to raise the operator. Seconds could save his life.

Jack's shoulders heave. "No, man. No, no, no."

Houdini breaks free of him and grins as wide as a Cheshire cat, with the bullet glinting between his front teeth. He stands up straight and struts in front of the Crowd, lips baring the bullet.

At first the Crowd twitters nervously, then cheers and claps. Jack is red-faced and reeling.

"Encore, encore," the convict yells from the bar. "Let me shoot the gun this time."

"Quite enough of that trick," I say, and the Crowd awaits my suggestion. Thinking quickly, I write out a clever message in the Pitman shorthand Uncle Roscoe taught me long ago.

"Whoever can guess what this coded message says wins a basket of Eliza's gingerbread cookies to take home." I walk the message around with the cookies. The Crowd loses interest, gathering around the fireplace with Sterling and Jack.

But Houdini studies the paper and draws on his open palm like a slate. "I think I've figured it out." His eyebrow arches. "One who catches bullets must possess strong teeth?"

"You read Pitman shorthand?"

"I love gingerbread." He snatches a gingerbread man and bites off the head.

Snatching the handkerchief out of his breast pocket, I find a sticky knob of beeswax. "Just as I thought. You extracted the bullet with beeswax on the ramrod."

He smiles and takes another bite of gingerbread. "My mother made cookies like these."

# 9

## Beauty Ranch, Glen Ellen, California
## Thanksgiving Day 1915

*The more he studied, the more vistas he caught of fields of knowledge yet unexplored, and the regret that days were only twenty-four hours long became a chronic complaint with him.*

*—Jack London,* Martin Eden

I scoop up Possum and go find Bessie leaning on the front railing, smoking a cigarette that smells like burning weeds.

"Your husband survived," I say.

"Mr. Houdini knows that trick scares me to death, and he doesn't care." She puts her cigarette out in a cloisonné compact and snaps it shut. "He hates when I smoke."

I slide my finger across my lips, and she smiles.

Our husbands walk out to the porch. Jack's wearing his Baden-Powell hat and carrying his rifle. I hope the fresh air will sober him up.

"Bet you've never seen a goat kid," he says to Houdini. "Ever tasted grapes right off the vine? Ever ridden horseback after a fine Thanksgiving feast?"

"I don't ride horseback," Houdini says.

Jack turns with a lopsided smile, cheeks flush with wine. "I don't drive automobiles, either, but did I let it stop me?"

"I'd like to see the fall *foilage*," Bessie says. "Besides, I wore my riding outfit." She thrusts out a hip, and the fringe on her skirt sways.

Annie Oakley, I swear.

"What about the Crowd?" I hear Sterling reciting a poem through the open door: "A Wine of Wizardry," which Jack helped him publish in *Cosmopolitan*.

Jack scoffs. "They won't even know we're gone."

"Then I get my Thanksgiving wish," I say. "A ride through the ranch with you." I tweak his Baden-Powell.

Our stableman, Luke, brings the horses around. Never a word to say, Luke's a rodeo rider who's fallen off the bull one too many times. With one bowleg shorter than the other, his trunk leans to the left. Anyone who's had a tough life plucks at Jack's heartstrings.

We saddle up, and I take Maid. Luke brings a Shetland for Bessie and a spirited black stallion named Outlaw for Houdini. Jack mounts Neuadd Hillside, his prized Shire, and leads the way. Possum scampers happily behind us.

We circle around the winery past the stone stables where the rest of the horses nibble Thanksgiving oats from burlap nose sacks. Mostly Shires from England, at least fifty by now. Black-and-white Holsteins graze in the pasture behind the barn, munching on the spineless cactus Luther Burbank convinced Jack to plant for cattle feed.

A separate barn shelters the carriages, holding half a dozen buggies, wagons, plows, fertilizer spreaders. Jack's always buying the latest new contraption. New models replace the old, driving us further into debt. Jack runs the ranch on optimism. But the promised checks never come.

Late-afternoon sunlight slants through the pines like a benediction, infusing our noses with evergreen, autumn leaves, and moss. Possum darts in and out of the vineyards, chasing rabbits.

Jumping off his horse, Jack digs in the red soil with his fingers and holds up a shiny black triangle. “Pomo Indians lived here ninety years ago.” He hands the glinting arrowhead up to Houdini on his stallion, who canters over to give it to Bessie.

She holds it in her hands like a jewel. “May I keep it?”

Jack keeps all the arrowheads we find in a Ball canning jar on his desk.

“Of course you can, Bessie,” I say, and she slips the carved stone into her fringed pocket.

Following Jack on Neuadd, we ride through the vineyard. Possum scampers to keep up. Bessie’s spunky Shetland kicks up small clouds of dust behind her, coating my nostrils with the smell of soil and overripe grapes.

“The earth is so fertile here in the Valley of the Moon.” Jack turns back to Houdini, hat shading his eyes. “Provided the Pomo Indians everything they needed. Fish in the streams, acorns from the oaks.” The pride and wistfulness in his voice make my throat ache. I love to see Jack enjoying what we have instead of yearning for what Beauty Ranch could be.

A new herd of long-haired goats grazes in the pasture below. “You had our goat cheese and pears earlier,” Jack says.

We pass the new henhouse, and I point out the exotic Andalusians, Barnevelders, and bantams that Eliza imported at great expense. They cluck and scratch the ground, unaware of their pedigree. Possum sniffs around the pen until a rooster pecks his nose. He whimpers and runs back to us.

Bessie points at eggs nestled in their empty roosts. "Looks like Easter eggs with those blue, green, and lavender."

"Easter eggs?" Jack says. "I thought you were Jewish."

"I'm Catholic." Bessie pouts. "If I was Jewish, we could be buried togeth—"

Houdini interrupts. "We don't see eggs like those in Harlem, do we, dear?"

"You've never tasted anything as delicious as Andalusian eggs," Jack says. "I'll have Manyoungi make omelets in the morning."

"Do they taste good with *mannaise*?" Bessie asks. "I eat my eggs with *mannaise*."

Jack's eyes roll under his hat brim. He can't abide women like Bessie, preferring jaded intellectual types who argue philosophy and social justice. He turns Neuadd up the hill, through a dozen acres of French prune trees. Jack points out the beehives, bristling with great purpose.

The sunlight lingers on orange-barked madrones and majestic valley oaks.

When we reach the top of the hill, Bessie squeals as loud as the swine. "It's a palace." She flutter claps once again, dropping the reins. "A pig palace." Possum runs around to the swine keeper's hut, no doubt looking for the Milk-Bones he gives him.

Though I fought the construction of Jack's piggery, I have to admit it looks like a medieval citadel. Rosy twilight bathes a fieldstone turret rising from the circle of pig huts. A kingdom of pigs. From the snorts, squeals, and grunts, it's feeding time.

Jack leads Houdini around the stone castle, explaining the unique features of his pig palace, as it may now be forever ordained in Bessie's honor. He takes Houdini up in the turret to see the view.

Bessie tries to dismount but gets her foot stuck in the stirrup.

I help her down, and she runs to the nearest hovel, where piglets gather around their protesting mother. The great sow Penelope is getting too old for this routine, little ones nipping her teats.

"Can I hold one?" Bessie says, eyes wide.

Wary of Penelope's wrath, I enter the stone pen and gently pull a piglet from her. Luckily, the sow turns her head away, unconcerned about my kidnapping. The piglet's pink skin is warm and translucent, with blue veins showing through fine white hairs. Bessie takes the baby and cradles it, cooing and stroking its skin. Houdini looks down on us from the turret and frowns when he sees Bessie.

"I miss my pig," she says.

"You kept a pig in New York?" I ask.

She shook her head. "Mr. Houdini wouldn't let me keep her. She squealed too much in bed. But we still have Bobby, a terrier like Possum; our parrots, Laura and Polly; Petie the turtle; Rudy the rabbit; and our canaries, Houdini and Bessie." She sniffs the piglet's skin. "Oh, and I almost forgot Abe Lincoln, our American eagle."

Her smile makes her cheeks round and eyes crinkle. They turn wistful when I take the piglet back to Penelope.

The men duck their heads coming out of the turret. "The circular design makes it easier to keep the troughs clean and lay fresh hay," Jack tells Houdini. "With more pigs to market and less expense, I'll make back my three-thousand-dollar investment in no time."

"Three thousand dollars for a pigpen?" Bessie says as I boost her up to the Shetland. "You coulda used *bobwire*."

"We butcher and cure our own pork," Jack tells Houdini as he mounts his stallion. "I'll send you home with a ham, best eating west of Iowa."

"I don't eat ham." Houdini clicks his heels on his stallion's haunches and trots out of the pen.

"Another Hebrew rule?" Jack snorts and canters past Houdini into a leafy tunnel of trees.

Bessie and I follow the men, with Possum weaving in and out of our wake, stopping to sniff, then running full tilt to catch up. We pass the bunkhouses and various outbuildings, the firehouse, rows of small houses for farmhands and vineyard workers, the company store, the red schoolhouse with the brass ship's bell, the little chapel.

"Are we passing through Glen Ellen now?" Bessie's black waves bounce with the Shetland's gait.

"No, we're still on Beauty Ranch."

"All these people live here with you?"

I nod. "Fifty on the payroll."

Our horses follow Jack's dust up the hill, their muscles working under our thighs. The low-angled sun is obscured by the thick canopy and sets a chill in my bones.

Once we reach the crest, we're rewarded by the sight of Jack's fish pond, a deep crevice in the granite mountain filled with a natural spring, surrounded by enormous redwoods. He's seeded it with trout from the Sacramento Delta and planted cattails for duck hunting.

The log raft floats on the glassy surface broken only by water bug trails. The same raft Lawrence and I spent hours on last summer, sunning, swimming, laughing, touching. My heart thumps in my throat. How careless of me to succumb to his charms. Squeezing my eyes closed, I swallow hard and focus on the sky painted with orange, magenta, and indigo. Mallards fly in from the north, silhouetted against the brilliant sky, and land on the pond.

Blast ka-ching, blast ka-ching. Over and over. Gunshots explode and reverberate off the granite mountainside. Houdini's stallion rears on hind legs, head high, and snorts madly.

Jack's rifle barrel smokes. Dark bodies fall from the air and splash into the water. Possum swims out to retrieve the ducks.

Jack smiles triumphantly. "Haven't lost my touch, have I, Mate?"

Bessie screams and won't quit screaming. Her hands clap over her ears, and her eyes bulge. "Not the ducks. Oh, no, no, no. Don't kill the ducks."

"Next time, warn us," I say, scolding him.

Houdini's great stallion, Outlaw, rears up in a fright, then gallops off through the woods with the magician grabbing at the reins.

"I'll take Bessie back to the ranch," I tell Jack. "You round up Houdini."

"Maid's faster than Neuadd," Jack says. "I'd never catch up to them, Mate."

Houdini's startled yells echo through the woods. "Whoa, Outlaw, whoa. Stop."

Grabbing the Shetland's reins, Jack leads Bessie toward the cottage. "Come on, Bessie, I have something to calm you down." Possum runs behind their horses, one of the ducks in his mouth.

"We won't be long," I call after them, and head out to find Houdini.

Maid trails Outlaw's dust through rows of grapevines, blood red and amber in the last light, gnarled grapevine trunks with the last leaves clinging against chill November wind. The soil changes from red to black, ancient volcanic rock.

I call out for Houdini, hearing nothing but the low rustling of a bear or a fox. Maid canters along the ridge. As we near the ruins of Wolf House, acid eats a pit in my stomach. I haven't been here, couldn't face it, since it burned down in September.

Maid approaches the outcropping of rocks where Lawrence and I watched the sun set that last night over the verdant Sonoma Valley, just as it is setting now. Golden light intensifies the brilliance of the green hills striped with rows of grapevines and patchwork orchards of apple, plum, and walnut trees.

Maid stops, snorts, and whinnies. The ruin of Wolf House rises before us like the gruesome monstrosity that it is. The burned odor suffuses my nostrils and coats my throat, making me gag. Volcanic rock and cement outline the arrogant exterior. Brick fireplaces stick up four stories high, like fists threatening the heavens. Charred beams thrust out like broken bones.

"Wolf House will last a thousand years," Jack had assured me whenever I lost sight of our goal. "A monument to everything we stand for."

I never should have brought Lawrence here that night.

Cupping my frigid hands around my mouth, I call for Houdini, then listen. Something breaks through the trees, but it's only a doe. The evening fog smothers the last rays of light over Sonoma Valley, and the temperature drops ten degrees.

A whinny startles me. Houdini rides Outlaw out from behind Wolf House, and I'm surprised how quickly he's mastered the stallion.

"Must have been quite a place." He rides toward me. "How did it burn down?"

"The sheriff claimed spontaneous combustion."

Houdini looks up at the patch of purpling sky, ringed by redwoods, and shakes his head. "Not in this redwood grove. The sun never touches the house."

I turn Maid away from the horrendous ruin. "There were plenty of theories, but authorities could never prove them. Some blamed our disgruntled foreman for the fire, since he disappeared afterward. Others claim the Socialists set it, angry at Jack's conspicuous capitalism. Our contactor blamed the painters for leaving turpentine and linseed rags lying about."

"But you know who did it," Houdini says.

I look away.

He pulls his horse up next to mine. "Who destroyed Jack's dream?"

"Jack wants to rebuild, but it's impossible. The insurance policies don't come close to covering the loss."

"I have a knack for solving mysteries," he says. "I'll investigate tomorrow in the light."

"Leave it alone. It will just rile Jack up again." I shiver. A full moon has risen orange and gigantic from the hills. "The Pomos called this the cold moon."

Jack rides Neuadd Hillside out of the woods. "Whaju doin' wid Houdini?"

No matter how much Jack drinks, he rarely sounds like this. "You're drunk, Jack. Let's go home."

"Whad's wrong, Charmian? Can't cast your spell on Houdini?" Jack sways and falls off his horse.

I jump off Maid, and we try to put Jack back on Neuadd, but we only succeed in draping him over the horse's back. Taking Neuadd's reins, we flank Jack with our horses. The cold moon lights our path.

"Charmian, Charmian, oh vexing Charmian," Jack bellows. "I have molded you out of my imagination." He holds up his head, but it lolls back onto the horse. "For better or worse, I took you, Charmian, as my Mate-Woman until the ocean swallows us whole."

Hysteria gurgles from my throat. I can't help it. Houdini must think we're both mad.

I glance over Jack's prostrate body at Houdini, who starts laughing, too. A wonderful, hearty laugh that turns the whole sad scenario around.

Then Jack joins in with a low belly laugh, which escalates to a silly giggle, which makes us laugh all the more. Like a scene from *The Three Musketeers*, our horses lead us back to the cottage and we laugh until tears stream down our faces.

I bolt upright in bed. Everything's shaking. My mirror and brush fall off the bureau. The bed frame thumps against the wall. Either the Houdinis are having a rocking-good lolly in the guest room next door or it's an earthquake. I hang on to the bedpost until the shuddering stops. Earthquakes are no lark since the big one of 1906. The Crowd will run around tearing out their hair, claiming it's the end of the world, then raid Jack's wine cellar to drown their fears in the best port their gullets can swallow.

The dawn light cracks through the curtains, illuminating a red gasoline can inside my door, a note stuffed in the handle. The sight jolts me; who would play such a nasty trick? I sprint across the cold stone floor and open the note. The writing looks like shorthand but with a twist that makes it hard to figure out, until I think to hold it up to my vanity mirror. The shorthand is mirror imaged:

"Perhaps this clue was overlooked by authorities?" the note reads. "You must have a reason to keep the secret, and that is good enough for me. Thank you for a memorable Thanksgiving."

Grateful for Houdini's discretion, I dress quickly and run the empty can to the tractor barn. The smell of gasoline brings back that horrific night all over again. A cold sweat breaks out on my neck and my chest. I risked everything in that moment of weakness.

Suddenly, all I want is Jack. I return to the house and walk down the gallery hall to his sleeping porch. Several frames along the hallway have gone crooked in the earthquake and I straighten them: original illustrations from Jack's novel covers: *The Sea-Wolf*, *White Fang*, *Call of the Wild*, *The Iron Heel* . . .

After that California wake-up, I assume that Jack will be at his desk, writing, as he always does after drinking late. Even when he writes drunk, I can usually save the work. His ideas may get trapped inside too many words and his syntax gets sloppy, but his proud purpose is as clear as a mountain stream.

But I find him still in bed, writhing and delirious, groaning with pain. An empty jug of Cabernet and dirty glasses litter the sideboard.

I ring up Doc Thompson on the telephone, and he agrees to come, though he's taken the day off. He takes an eternity to drive his buggy up from Glen Ellen, while Nakata stokes the woodstove and fills hot-water bottles from the copper kettle. Nothing works to ease Jack's pain.

"Send the Crowd home," I tell Nakata. "The party is over, the inn is closed. Tell them whatever it takes to get them out of here."

He leaves the room.

When Doc finally arrives, he's wearing dungarees, cowboy boots, and western hat, instead of his usual white coat. At least he remembered his worn leather medicine bag. Doc palpates Jack's lower back and stomach while he groans.

"No way to sugarcoat it, Jack," the doctor says through his handlebar mustache. "You have kidney stones."

Jack doubles up on his feather mattress.

"What can you do for him?" I ask.

"The only thing I can do is dull the pain until they pass." Doc flicks a long syringe with thumb and forefinger, loosening oxygen bubbles.

"What's that?"

"Morphine," Doc says, and injects the needle into Jack's backside.

"Is that really necessary?"

Jack's limbs relax, and his eyelids flutter closed.

"If you don't want him in pain." Doc leaves instructions for Jack to rest and more vials of morphine granules, which I'll be damned if I'm going to use.

I set up my Remington next to Jack's bed on a Fijian koa-wood table. The *Cosmopolitan* article has to get in the mail today. I've done the research, so I can write it myself. The sounds of Jack's heavy breathing and the chattering squirrels outside meld with the clacking of my typewriter keys.

The article is what Jack calls "colorful gully fluff," about the Panama-Pacific International Exposition, the astounding exhibits, and the impact of the Panama Canal on US trade. It's the kind of article I write for *Sunset* at a fraction of Jack's rate. Magazine articles bring in quick money compared to books and movies.

Hours later, when he wakes from his morphine coma, he reads the article and tosses the pages across the room. "Who could stomach all that flowery description? Let me have at it."

My pride deflates; he's right and I know it. "I already sent it off. *Cosmo* would cancel if we didn't meet the deadline, and we need that money."

"Quit worrying about money. Hearst will pay me a boatload for my trip to Panama." His hair is matted on one side, crimped on the other. I brush it out with a boar-bristle brush I'd traded for in Tahiti.

"You can't go to Panama alone in this health," I say.

"Hearst won't allow me to take my wife on the president's convoy."

"Let him send someone else, then."

Jack looks out his window with eyes as sullen as the November sky.

"Hearst said he needs me to smoke out the rat in Panama."

Crazy talk, like the night at Tadich's. "The last rat Hearst sent you after was a Mexican gun smuggler with chronic dysentery." He rewards me with a weak smile. I dampen a sponge with warm water and wash the fishy stench of morphine from his pores.

"Hearst thinks President Wilson's lying to the public about staying out of the Great War." Jack buckles in the middle and cries out.

"Try to relax. The pain will pass." I swab his abdomen with the warm sponge.

"He says Panama is a secret war base." He chokes on the last words and draws his knees to his chest.

I glance at the mantel clock. Way too soon for more medicine.

"Listen, Jack, you can't go to Panama with kidney stones," I say. "Let's go back to Hawaii. You're always so peaceful there. You can start a new novel."

"The Panama trip will rebuild Wolf House." Jack jolts back and roars like a mountain lion, his body distended and stiff. Then he collapses and passes out, his mouth gaping.

I grab the telephone receiver again and ring up the Glen Ellen switchboard for Doc. It rings and rings, but I hang on until he answers.

He tells me to bring Jack down the mountain to Boyes Hot Springs, where he can take the thermal waters until the stones pass. I pack a bag, and Luke takes us in the wagon. I'm looking forward to relaxing in the thermal pools. But Jack's pain worsens so much we never dip a toe in the waters. Jack doesn't even recognize me. The only thing that calms his rage is when Doc administers the morphine. My nerves are scorched with worry and exhaustion.

Finally, the stones pass and Jack resurfaces. He's jaundiced and sweaty, nose running constantly and legs twitching from the morphine. And in no shape to join the president's Panama trip. Even Jack knows that.

Then something of a miracle happens, if you believe in such things. Jack's publisher, George Brett of Macmillan, suggests he write another dog story like *White Fang*, and offers him a big advance check.

Jack shoots a telegram to Hearst: CAN'T MAKE PANAMA TRIP -stop- MRS. LONDON NEEDS ME TO MIX COCKTAILS IN HAWAII-stop-

# 10

## San Quentin Penitentiary,
## San Francisco Bay, California
## December 1915

*This time, over the previous jacket, the second jacket was put on from behind and laced up in front. "Lord, Lord, Warden, it is bitter weather," I sneered. "The frost is sharp. Wherefore I am indeed grateful for your giving me two jackets. I shall be almost comfortable."*

*"Tighter!" he urged to Al Hutchins, who was drawing the lacing. "Throw your feet into the skunk. Break his ribs . . ."*

*"A favour, Warden," I whispered faintly . . . Perforce I was nearly unconscious from the fearful constriction. "Make it a triple jacketing," I managed to continue, while the cell walls swayed and reeled about me and while I fought with all my will to hold to my consciousness that was being squeezed out of me by the jackets. "Another jacket . . . Warden . . . It . . . will . . . be . . . so . . . much . . . er . . . warmer."*

*And my whisper faded away as I ebbed down into the little death.*

—*Jack London,* The Jacket

We already dropped both our trunks and Nakata at the SS *Matsonia* bound for Hawaii, but Jack insisted we catch Houdini's show at San Quentin for the prisoners before the ship sails.

The daunting Italianate fortress constructed with two-foot-thick granite blocks and iron-lattice doors stands in stark contrast to the city of San Francisco, across the bay. December winds blow fierce and freezing. I weave my arm through Jack's to keep warm. He's focused on the tugboat headed our way, battling the waves. A powerful wind buffets the embankment and sprays me with icy seawater. Guards poke bayonets at the backs of gray-coveralled prisoners as they stumble across the dead stubble of thistle, their heavy ankle chains grinding together as they pass barbed-wire fences and electrified gates. Gunmen aim rifles at them from the watchtowers. A few prisoners gaze back across the gray whitecaps to the shining city beyond. Has anyone survived the icy ten-foot swells? The thought gives me shivers.

"The warden should be ashamed, parading prisoners out in this weather," Jack says. "A despicable display of human bondage."

The tugboat ties up at the lone dock, and Houdini steps on deck with a long black cape flapping behind him in the wind. He swaggers down the gangplank to the dock, waving to the inmates as they are marched into the prison. The prisoners cheer and wave handcuffed hands from the fenced yard. The police band strikes up a rousing Sousa march, making the whole scene more bizarre. Jack records it all in his notebook, forever putting himself inside the shoes of the afflicted and living their despair.

A guard leads us through a separate entrance. The vaulted door clanks shut behind us, the sound brittle in my bones. Our steps echo in grim hallways, my boots sticking to the floor. I don't want to know from what. Bare bulbs dangle by an electric wire, half of them burned out. There's the sweet stink of dead rats. I hold my nose and focus on Jack in front of me. Finally, we reach a vast chamber. On our left, four levels of eight-by-eight cells are stacked on each other like catacombs. On the right, floor-to-ceiling windows display a surreal San Francisco, brilliant as a gem through encroaching fog.

"What a wonderful view for the prisoners," I say.

"A sadistic reminder of what they've lost," Jack scoffs. "The loves they've left behind, the joy they'll never have again, taunting them night and day."

Jack cuts to the bone of things, and I feel shallow.

Prisoners yell profanities at each other and clang their chains against the bars. The angry racket unnerves me. Barred doors swing open with a moan; guards shove convicts in. A man wearing a straightjacket is pushed into his cell with an iron rod. Sweat rolls down Jack's forehead into his suddenly glassy eyes, chest heaving under crossed arms. At nineteen, he was jailed for vagrancy in the Erie County Penitentiary and trussed in a straightjacket so tight it made him pass out. Later, he dictated his experience to me for *The Star Rover*, entitled *The Jacket* in the UK. The book drained the life from the two of us and left him an invalid for weeks.

The warden puts a megaphone to his mouth and speaks with an Oklahoma twang. "This is not a show to entertain you." Prisoners grab the bars, straining to see the famous magician. "The governor doesn't believe San Quentin security is good enough and sent his friend Houdini to test our locks."

Prisoners jeer and rage until a guard blasts a horn.

"Why would they cheer at that?" I ask Jack.

"Anything to feel alive," he says, and again I feel dense.

Houdini swirls off his cape, and he's stripped down to a circus leotard, silhouetting every muscle and bulge of his toned body. Prisoners jeer and he humors them with a bow.

"What I am about to attempt, no man has ever accomplished." Even without the megaphone, Houdini's booming voice penetrates the chamber. "Your warden will tie me in a straightjacket and lock me in a cell. I will attempt to break out."

The warden wraps the magic man into a straightjacket, arms in stiff canvas tied behind his back. But then the warden jerks a second jacket on backward over the first.

"That wasn't part of the deal, Warden," Houdini says, though I can't be sure with the raucous noise.

"Tell the governor life isn't fair," the warden snarls, and winds chains around Houdini. Gritty chains trail down his chest and tangle between his legs and up his flanks, locking behind his neck. He buckles over with the weight of so much iron.

The prisoners caw like hyenas, growing frenzied as they watch.

Sweat springs from my neck in the clammy prison; my chest feels so tight.

"Takes your breath away, does he, Mate-Woman?" His eyebrow cants with curiosity. He's taking in every detail, not only Houdini's cruel challenge, but his physique and the shortness of my breath.

The guards lock Houdini in a cell, and the warden lifts the megaphone. "The governor dictated that I leave Houdini alone for fifteen minutes. I trust you'll watch him for me?" The guards snigger as they leave, clanging the door behind them.

"He's throwing their lack of freedom in their faces," Jack fumes.

Icy fear charges through my limbs, and I hold his arm tighter.

Houdini wastes no time, his back muscles rippling under the straightjackets. One shoulder collapses, then the other, baffling me, but before I figure out what he's doing, the inside jacket falls to his feet. Prisoners shove their faces through the bars, chanting. "Whoot. Whoot. Whoot."

But now it gets harder. Houdini falls on the cement and rolls around, straining and tensing in his vain attempt to release himself. He's groaning and screaming now, his face pinched in agony.

The convicts yell to him. "Do it. Show those monkeys who's boss."

Houdini rotates his head halfway around, and his mouth surrounds the lock. Soon the chains fall away from his neck. One arm worms across his body and pokes out. The prisoners cheer. Houdini fumbles with the chains around his groin, and slowly each one gives way. He lies back, spent and panting.

Soon, his body seems to shrivel to nothing inside the second jacket and he rips it off and jumps up to his feet. Doubled over, his back heaving, right arm limp by his side, he calls out, "Jack, can you assist me?"

Giving me his notebook, Jack says, "Don't miss anything." And he limps over to the cell. Houdini hands him a wire, which Jack jiggles into the lock, and the door springs open.

The two of them move cell to cell, Houdini touching the forehead of a convict, speaking in a monotone, and Jack unlocking the cell door and exchanging the convict with the one next to him. Within minutes they've switched all prisoners on the bottom floor.

The warden's door opens. "Hey, what's going on here?" he snarls, poking a billy club at Jack and Houdini.

"Check the cells, Warden," Houdini says. "You'll see the governor's right about San Quentin security. I'll be making a full report."

The guards search the cells, discovering the switched prisoners, who hoot in joy and derision, a deafening cacophony.

"Get them the hell out of here," the warden says to the guards, and they lead us out through dismal hallways.

"My God, that was fun," Jack says, hobbling with his gouty foot.

Houdini turns to me. "Maybe you'll write another book in Hawaii. I enjoyed *The Log of the Snark*."

"You read it?"

"I especially liked the Marquesan orgy." He smiles, making my pulse beat under my jawbone.

The guards open the heavy double doors, and we walk into the air. The fog has lifted, and the light is blindingly beautiful. So beautiful.

"Oh, good," Houdini says. "Bessie made it."

She's waiting beside our identical Dodge touring cars, dressed in sailor whites, holding Victoria Woodhull. Standing on tiptoe, she kisses my cheek, and I catch a whiff of gardenias. "Mr. Houdini told me you're sailing for Hawaii today. You know we had our wedding in Hawaii."

I smile. "I thought you married on Coney Island."

"*Irregardless*, Victoria Woodhull has never been to Hawaii." She hands me her doll.

"I couldn't. She'll be lonely without you." I try to give it back, but she refuses.

"Please take her. She's always wanted to see palm trees and hula girls." Bessie hums a Hawaiian tune and sways, floating her hands sideways in a semblance of the hula.

Our driver opens the back door of the Dodge, and Houdini gives me a tube wrapped in *M-U-M* magazine pages smelling of wood-spice cologne. "Something to keep you busy on your long voyage."

Jack snorts. "Just like you to slip my wife a love letter right in front of me."

"I assure you if it was a love letter, you'd never know." He takes my hand and kisses my knuckles. "And don't worry, the *Matsonia* will be safe."

"Like anything is safe from the Germans," Jack says.

The car takes off, and I wave at the Houdinis as they get smaller out the back window. "I wonder if we'll ever see them again."

Jack scowls at the doll. "Can't say I'll miss that crackpot Bessie."

"But you like Houdini."

"Houdini is as ephemeral as the fog, here one moment and gone the next."

"I find him charming."

"As he finds you." Jack glances out the window.

"Poppycock," I say, turning my face away so he won't see the heat in my cheeks. And there it is, undeniable. That secret spark, that forbidden desire, that I must not pursue. If nothing else, Lawrence taught me that lesson, and I've paid the price ever since. The lying that corrodes every sentence, the loss of trust that eats at the soul, the betrayal in the eyes of your beloved. Free love is never free.

My fingers itch to open Houdini's tube, but I don't dare.

When we get to the ship, I write in my journal, "Charming Houdini, I shall never forget him."

# *Part II*

## The Big Island of Hawaii

*It is life that is the reality and the mystery . . .*

*Life persists. Life is the thread of fire that persists through all the modes of matter. I know. I am life.*

*I have lived ten thousand generations. I have lived millions of years. I have possessed many bodies.*

*I, the possessor of these many bodies, have persisted. I am life. I am the unquenched spark ever flashing and astonishing the face of time, ever working my will and wreaking my passion on the cloddy aggregates of matter, called bodies, which I have transiently inhabited.*

—*Jack London,* The Star Rover

# 11

## The SS *Matsonia*
## December 1915

*Here was intellectual life, he thought, and here was beauty, warm and wonderful as he had never dreamed it could be. He forgot himself and stared at her with hungry eyes. Here was something to live for, to win, to fight for—ay, and die for. The books were true. There were such women in the world. She was one of them. She lent wings to his imagination, and great, luminous canvases spread themselves before him whereon loomed vague, gigantic figures of love and romance, and of heroic deeds for woman's sake—for a pale woman, a flower of gold.*

*—Jack London,* Martin Eden

Jack rises every morning spouting fresh ideas like the humpback whales we see migrating south to warmer waters. As soon as Nakata brings coffee to our cabin in the morning (Jack's black, mine with cream and sugar), words tumble from his mouth like he's recalling a memory, and I type them up as fast as they come.

Even though Uncle Roscoe first taught me to type, it was Netta who pushed me to type faster. It surprised us both when I reached 150 words per minute. She said I needed the skill to contribute to household finances, tighter since Roscoe started keeping a separate residence for his mistress, just as Netta entertained young men in ours.

Jack lights up an Imperial, and I glance at Bessie's doll perched on my steamer trunk. Victoria Woodhull's wide-brimmed navy straw hat frames her swept-up hairdo with tendrils at her temples. A red banner emblazons her chest: **Votes for Women.** Can't say I'm a fan of the real Victoria Woodhull, however, since the woman single-handedly botched our chance to vote by tying it to free love and spiritualism.

Jack begins his tale again, and I'm back to typing. Just when I think I know where the story's headed, he throws a whole different curve and thrills me. Macmillan will get the best-selling dog book they asked for. *Jerry of the Islands* is a tough Irish terrier sailing with his racist master on the South Seas. Jerry and his master live on a rusty old boat, buying and selling indentured labor from the islands. They outrun cannibals who want to eat them for dinner. The view of the choppy Pacific from our portholes adds veracity to the adventure we're writing.

After our session, I ask Nakata to bring sandwiches to our small alcove on the deck, far away from the dining galley. He hustles off to the kitchen in his sailor's uniform, quite overqualified for a valet, able to do anything he sets his mind to. Halfway finished with his dental course.

We've had our fill of socializing with guests at the captain's table and at Jack's lectures on Socialism, Hawaii's royal sport of surfing, and the leprosy island of Molokai. By some whim or miracle, Jack's heeding his oath to shun spirits during our sail, though he doesn't consider the ship's Madeira true spirits. Still I'm grateful for this productive, peaceful time after our calamitous autumn at Beauty Ranch.

We sit out on the deck. Soft breezes caress our cheeks, and indigo waves lap endlessly onto the horizon. Jack reads from his pile of books by Yeats, Darwin, Melville, and Jung, underlining passages for me to read. I take the chance to make notes for my new book project: *Our Hawaii*.

Half an hour passes, and my stomach growls. The kitchen must be busy.

I've been so preoccupied with our trip over the last two weeks I haven't thought much about the Houdinis. But now I look for the tube he gave me, stashed in my trunk, and tear open the *M-U-M* wrapping to find a labyrinth of shorthand. As I turn the page around, following the spiraling path, the words make no sense.

Nakata arrives with sandwiches, and I bring the labyrinth out to the deck to study. Nakata sets up lunch on a folding table between our teak lounges. *"Sakana."* Fish. He scrunches his nose.

He knows I rarely eat flesh of any sort, but vegetables are scarce when sailing. "It's all right, Nakata. I'm ravenous." I bite into the sourdough and sweet albacore. It tastes as fresh as the glimmering sea surrounding us.

Jack drinks his Madeira and looks out to sea. "Who are you to me, Charmian? And who am I to you?"

Since he's been reading Jung, I rack my brain for archetypes.

"You are my hero, and I am your mother." I'm relieved and proud of my nimble analysis.

He shakes his tousled curls, glinting auburn in the sunlight. "Dig deeper. Your answer is too simplistic."

I bite into my sandwich, stalling for time. A chunk of albacore sticks in my throat, and I wash it down with ginger ale. A school of dolphins leaps through waves beside the ship. "Look, they're still following us. You'd think they'd be tired by now." But Jack won't relent.

"Think, think, think, Mate. I can't abide a lazy mind."

My brain shuts down when he badgers me like this, but I struggle to rise to his challenge. Jack's thought process dazzles and befuddles average folks. Sometimes he allows friends to plead ignorance, but not me. He demands his woman understand his ever-expanding mind. Indeed, our relationship depends on it.

"You are the wise old man?" I guess.

His bottom lip protrudes in thought, and I think I'm home free.

"So you see me as the kind, wise father who uses his knowledge to tell stories to enlighten his audience about who they are and who they might become."

"Precisely, and I'll be your old woman."

"So we've lived everything life has to offer and now we're simply guardians of time?"

His recognition fills me with smugness. "And this is our kingdom." I wave my arm to the hazy horizon where ocean and sky become one.

He shakes his head. "Deeper yet."

"Why does life have to be such a puzzle?" I study the labyrinth.

"Let me tell you how I see it." Jack takes my hand, face glowing. "I am the anima, and you are the animus."

"And that's a good thing?" I smile, trying to lighten his mood.

"I am the anima," he says. "The unconscious feminine inner personality which dovetails perfectly with your animus, unconscious masculine personality. That's why we fit together so well, Lady-Boy. I've always tried to put my finger on it, and now I have, thanks to Jung."

"You love me for my inner man?" I ask him. "Not sure I like that."

Jack smiles at me like the winner of a spelling bee, and my tension dissolves. He can't help his beautiful mind from churning.

I take his cheeks in both hands and place a long, glorious kiss on his lips. "Anima, animus. Whatever the mystery that binds us, I love you, Jack London. And I always will."

# 12

## The Island of Hawaii
## December 1915

*They are the cyclones and tornadoes, lightning flashes and cloud-bursts, tide-rips and tidal waves, undertows and waterspouts, great whirls and sucks and eddies, earthquakes and volcanoes, surfs that thunder on rock-ribbed coasts and seas that leap aboard the largest crafts that float, crushing humans to pulp or licking them off into the sea and to death—and these insensate monsters do not know that tiny sensitive creature, all nerves and weaknesses, whom men call Jack London, and who himself thinks he is all right and quite a superior being.*

*—Jack London,* The Cruise of the Snark

After nineteen days, we are sea legged, green gilled, and overjoyed to plant our feet on the solid shores of Hawaii, our own true paradise. A rustic one-horse wagon meets us at the pier and takes us up the narrow winding road to Volcano House, just beneath the steaming rim of Kilauea. The lodge looks much as it did eight years ago, built with koa-wood logs and black porous lava rock harvested from the angry volcano belching steam and gases above us. The sulfuric fumes make me dizzy when we step out of the wagon. Nakata goes with the driver to the bunkhouse.

Blond and burly Louis Von Schram comes out to greet us in a linen shirt and khaki shorts. I rather miss the silly lederhosen he used to wear, with the waistband stretched above his paunch.

"Well, if it isn't the Wolf himself, come knocking at my door. Lock the liquor cabinets." He laughs, and his watermelon belly jiggles.

Jack steps back from our old friend, his face stony. "Von Schram, I'd have thought you'd have run back to Germany in shame, given how the mad dog is tearing up Europe."

The manager's shoulders cave. "I'm sorry, Mr. London, but you are mistaken. My name is *Van* Schram . . . from Holland."

"*Van* Schram." Jack raises an eyebrow. "So now you're Dutch?"

"Please understand, Mr. London." Von Schram's voice falters. "Since the war started, Germans are hated. People are suspicious of our loyalty." He drops his head. "But *this* is our home. It will always be our home."

Jack snorts and looks away. Given his hatred for Germany and Germans, I guess we'll have to leave.

"Thunderation!" Jack pounds the door. "Von-Van—is that what the world's come to? You're still the same man, and you're my friend." He reaches out and shakes the innkeeper's hand. "Got any jenever in that liquor cabinet?"

The lodge boasts a library with leather couches by a blazing stone fireplace. Von Schram pours Jack a jenever and a club soda for me. We sit on leather couches by the fire, burning spicy milo wood. I suppose this means Jack's dry spell is over, and I try not to mind.

"I hear the Protestants are promoting Prohibition in the States," Von Schram says. "Thank God I'm Catholic." He crosses himself and drinks.

"My position is absolute, nationwide Prohibition," Jack says.

I blurt out a laugh and cover my mouth.

"I'm serious, Charmian." He sips his jenever. "When Prohibition makes alcohol inaccessible, I shall drop drinking. And the generation of boys after me will know nothing about alcohol, save that it was a stupid vice of their savage ancestors."

He coughs and lights his tenth Imperial of the day, but I bite my tongue. Jack hates when I nag. Instead I go to the warped and out-of-tune piano once owned by Hawaii's Queen Emma, or so Von Schram claims, and play "Medley of Hawaiian Waltzes" and "Honolulu Rag," tunes I learned from the Victrola.

"Ever drink okolehao?" Von Schram pours syrupy liquid from a ceramic bottle into a shot glass and hands it to Jack. "Hawaiians distill it from ti root."

Jack takes a sip and smacks his lips. "Tastes of warm earth, pineapple, and heaven. There's something so pure and innocent about Hawaiians."

"Ha!" Von Schram slaps his knee. "Hawaiians are anything but innocent. Ever hear their creation legend?"

Jack urges him on.

"In the beginning was Mother Earth, Papahānaumoku. She indulged in perpetual intercourse with the sky god, Wākea, until their children forced them to separate. But the couple remained lovers, Mother Earth's lusty heat rising to the sky and Wākea's rain falling from heaven to fertilize her."

"Good stuff. Good stuff." Jack pours another jenever. "Charmian, are you getting this?"

Getting up from the piano, I take my notebook and pencil out of my bag and join the men.

"The couple has hundreds of children—that perpetual mating paid off, I guess." He laughs. "But trouble started when they had Ho'ohokukalani, goddess of the stars. Wākea fell in love with his daughter and had intimate relations with her."

I write all this down for my book on Hawaii. "What did Mother Earth do?"

"What could she do? Her daughter got pregnant. She had to take care of her."

"And the baby?" Jack asks.

"The baby was stillborn. Mother Earth buried the child in the warm soil, which fertilized the taro crop to feed the Hawaiian people."

"So taro is Mother Nature's revenge," Jack says, musing.

"That's why you like that native goo so much." I squeeze his hand. "What happened then?"

"The sky god, Wākea, kept impregnating his daughter until their children populated Hawaii," Von Schram said.

"That's disturbing," I say.

"It's the nature of men to want what they want regardless of how it hurts others," Jack says. "Man rarely places a proper valuation upon his womankind until deprived of them."

"Are you saying I need to leave to be appreciated?" I laugh and close my notebook. "If that's what it takes, then count me gone." I head up the staircase to turn in, hoping Jack will follow me up, but he stays up with Von Schram.

In the morning, we sip nutty Kona coffee in our room and Jack dictates *Jerry of the Islands*. The clacking of my typewriter keys mixes with the patter of rain on the tin roof and the crackling wood in the fireplace. Bessie's doll sits primly on the thatched-palm rocking chair with Houdini's mystical labyrinth on her lap. Still can't figure it out.

As soon as the heavy rain stops, I'm eager to explore Kilauea. I convince Jack to leave his reading and come with me. Von Schram outfits us with canvas ponchos to protect us from mauka showers and saddles up a couple of skittish mustangs from up-country, no match for our steady Shires at Beauty Ranch. They whinny and squirm as we mount them; they haven't been broken long.

But once we find the steep, narrow path to the craters, the horses take over and I'm relieved. They've obviously done this before. Ferns and palms lick our sides as our steeds climb eight hundred feet to a cauldron half a mile in circumference. Our dungarees soak up the moisture.

At the summit of Pu'u Huluhulu, we tie up the horses and Jack gives them water from the canteen. I set out the lunch the lodge packed us: sweet purple taro bread, smoked marlin, taro poi, and cut pineapple. We lie side by side on the rim of the crater, which is spongy with bright-green moss. Tearing off a piece of bread, I dip into the taro poi and feed it to Jack.

He closes his deep-set eyes and savors the flavor. "Ah, Mother Nature's revenge."

He offers me some, but I wave it away, laughing. "Go right ahead. I can't stand the stuff." I bite into a piece of tangy pineapple.

We eat and watch the molten earth rise and fall below us, like Mother Earth in labor. The heaving rock hisses and groans, the cracked surface spouting gases smelling like rotten eggs. Low clouds press down on us, reflecting the orange glow of the boiling wells.

Jack's hair curls in the humidity, inviting me to ruffle it. He leans into my hand, enjoying my touch. These are the moments I live to share with him, away from everybody and everything, living life, not dissecting it endlessly.

Jack leans on an elbow. "We could build a house down there with a glass roof over the crater for natural steam heat."

"No one would visit us all the way up here."

"Exactly. We'd be away from people begging handouts, away from the demands of Socialists, away from politicians suspecting my motives."

"What about the Crowd?"

"They can stay put in Carmel," Jack says. "Except the Greek. I'll invite Sterling, of course."

"What about your little wannabe actress, Blanche?"

His face hardens and I regret my words. Everything was moving along swimmingly, and I had to throw in an anchor.

"We could have been happy in Wolf House." Jack stares into the cauldron rumbling like a thunderhead.

"We're happy now."

"Are we?" He squeezes his eyes closed, and I hope sulfuric vapors caused the wetness. "Before Wolf House burned down, I believed there was nothing that could break us apart. The one woman, the one person, I could count on no matter what."

"I'm here, Jack." I put my hand on his, the earth rumbling beneath us. "I chose you, remember?"

A monstrous crack breaks open the rock, seething with red-orange liquid. A molten tide rises up like a tsunami, then falls with a scream.

We jump up. The horses stomp and snort and jerk against their reins tied to a palm. I finally manage to untie them and hand Jack his reins. But as we mount our horses, a fountain of burning orange lava shoots thirty feet in the air, falling in searing spats on the ferns and moss.

My horse bucks and rears up. "Where's the path?" I search frantically.

Jack is gone. Left me here alone. Then through the dark-green tangle of jungle, I spot the rump of his Appaloosa ahead and yell. "You're going the wrong way." But my words are lost in the rumble.

The jungle is darker than before. I try to follow him, catching only glimpses through the vines and palms. Molten rock sizzles on the cool ferns and pushes me on. The earth shudders with a mournful groan, then explodes with a frightful force. Rocks pummel my head and shoulders.

The sky flashes bright against the dark-green fernery, overexposing Jack and the Appaloosa like a colorized photograph, turning one way, then the other, bewildered, snorting, frantic. Jack should be as terrified as his steed, but his face is turned up to the raining rock and ash, watching the spewing volcano with single-minded intensity. I know he's making mental notes: sulfuric steam dampening his clothes, the feeling of rocks pelting his face, how the electric air makes the jungle quiver.

I pull the reigns of my Appaloosa closer and call out, "I'm here." The horses nuzzle each other.

He turns to me and smiles, reaches for my hand. "Isn't it magnificent?"

A low rumble shakes the ground, growing louder until the earth is roaring.

"We have to get out of here." But I've lost the path in the tangle of vines and palms.

A horrific thwack bursts my eardrums, and boiling lava shoots through the crust and erupts in a fountain of burning pumice, ash, and rock.

The orange light exposes an opening in the vines. "Follow me, Jack."

I lead us through the tropical forest, down the slippery slope, desperate to outrun the seething river of hot lava.

By the time we reach Volcano House, we're drenched to the bone, caked with ash and shivering uncontrollably. Von Schram thinks nothing of our brush with the earth's inferno.

"The volcano goddess is just showing you haoles who's boss," Von Schram says with a wink. "Pele doesn't allow white men to picnic on her volcanoes, only natives."

Jack doesn't laugh, in fact, he's not speaking at all, and his usual ruddy complexion has turned ashen. It's the stoic look he gets when his insides start churning like a paddlewheel as kidney stones knife his belly.

"We'll be leaving in the morning," I say, and help Jack up to our room.

*"Kimochi warui,"* Nakata says when he sees us. Bad feeling. "A bath is good for Mr. Jack." He hangs a copper kettle in the fire to heat and fills the wooden tub with rainwater from the water tank.

"I'll do it, Nakata. Thank you."

He bows and leaves our room.

Jack writhes and moans on his bed. When the kettle boils, I pour it into the tub and help him get in.

He looks spent and gray. "Ah, Mate-Woman. I need a drink."

I know he shouldn't have alcohol with his angry kidneys, but he's in so much pain. I pour him some sherry Von Schram left for us, kiss his cheek, and drop the phonograph needle on "Hello, Hawaii, How Are You?" He sips his drink, leans back in the tub, and closes his eyes.

I have less luck relaxing. All I see when I close my eyes is the nightmarish vision of orange lava exploding from the earth.

I sit as close as I can get to the fire, trying to warm myself and get rid of the shivers. Houdini's labyrinth is in Victoria Woodhull's arms, and I unroll it, holding it up to the light of the fire. As the page heats up, it transforms into something entirely different. Certain words turn bright red and others disappear, making a message: "Fire has always been and will always remain the most terrible of elements."

Holding the puzzle closer to the firelight, new words appear and others disappear: "I will always remain yours."

My chest hitches. The needle on the phonograph hits the last few notes of the song and bumps back, over and over. I peek at Jack, head against the rim of the tub, eyes closed, mouth open, sherry gone. His face softer and younger in this light.

I look back to the labyrinth, but the message has disappeared. No words, only streaks of color where they once were. A brilliant painting of woven color.

# 13

## Outrigger Club, Oahu, Hawaii
## January 1916

*As I write these lines I lift my eyes and look seaward. I am on the beach of Waikiki on the island of Oahu. Far, in the azure sky, the trade-wind clouds drift low over the blue-green turquoise of the deep sea. Nearer, the sea is emerald and light olive-green. Then comes the reef, where the water is all slaty purple flecked with red. Still nearer are brighter greens and tans, lying in alternate stripes and showing where sand-beds lie between the living coral banks. Through and over and out of these wonderful colours tumbles and thunders a magnificent surf.*

—*Jack London,* The Cruise of the Snark

We sail over to the Outrigger Club, where we lodged eight years before, on the white beach of Waikiki, lush with coconut palms and hibiscus. The perfumed breeze, sand beneath our feet, and nothing but brilliant blue ocean drive the nightmares of Kilauea away.

We've spent the happiest times of our marriage here, and all I want now is to recapture that happiness for us.

Our old friend and manager Mr. Baldwin finds us a traditional Hawaiian homestead called a kauhale. The grass-and-leaf hut compound has Japanese Hawaiian caretakers who live in the hale kuke, or cookhouse. Makuahine and her daughter, Kukalani, show us around the camp, the mother as wide as she is tall and Kukalani blessed with the body of a Hawaiian goddess.

Nakata's eyes trail Kukalani, a little romance in the making. Good for him. That should keep him busy, along with his correspondence dental course.

The men's hut, hale mua, is for Jack, with an annex behind for Nakata.

Hale pe'a, the menstruation hut, is mine, though I haven't seen a period since that day with the Houdinis. No hope of producing an heir for Jack, but I can still make him happy.

Makuahine offers her services as a masseuse, and Jack takes advantage of it right away, while Nakata and Kukalani unpack. They set up our writing studio under a palm lanai in an idyllic cove sheltered with date and coconut palms.

I peel off my haole clothes and don a bathing suit.

The quiet lapping of waves and intoxicating plumeria flowers are just what we need to wring the angst from our souls. Close to shore, a boulder juts out of the ocean, forcing waves to crash and spread like a peacock's tail. The beach continues north to the treacherous Ali'i Cliff, a mile up.

The Outrigger surf and canoe school lies just south of our kauhale, flaunting the tanned chiseled abdomens of Hawaiians and haoles alike. Dozens of canoes and surfboards perch against the dunes, waiting to traverse the writhing waves.

Jack and I learned to surf on our first trip here, eight years ago. He wrote "A Royal Sport: Surfing at Waikiki" for *Woman's Home Companion*, and the school's enrollment increased tenfold. You'd think he would have mentioned I surfed alongside him.

In the mornings, we sit under the lanai, and I type while Jack dictates. He tries to finish *The Little Lady of the Big House*, the novel he abandoned when Wolf House burned down. He's circling the drain, the same scenes over and over, but I edit it best I can each night. What's important is we get our thousand words a day. If we can do that, Jack is happy, Macmillan is happy. Jack's mother, his Mammy, ex-wife, and Aunt Netta get their mortgages paid. Jack's sister gets a check for the ranch, not to mention our employees. I can't even think about them—best left for Eliza to handle. My job is to type and edit Jack's thousand words. If we can do that, all is good in paradise.

Whenever I can fit it in, I'm writing my book about Hawaii, about adventures from this trip and trips past, and I'm loving every second of my work. Before sunset, I take hula lessons from my teacher, Hau'oli. All is aloha in Lani. (Heaven!)

Nakata brings Jack a lone letter that has found us somehow. He opens the blue envelope addressed with flamboyant penmanship and laughs. "From the Greek."

Papers fall out on the damp sand. I scoop them up and hand them to Jack. "The *New York Post* and the Socialist newsletter."

His jaw grinds as he reads. "Capitalists hate me because I exposed garment manufacturers for paying ninety cents for a sixty-hour workweek." His hands drop in his lap. "What about the desperate woman who strangled her infants rather than be starved?"

I read the damning article as Jack studies the newsletter, lights an Imperial, and sucks it down to the butt.

"Now Socialists hate me because I travel on first-class Pullman cars and employ a Japanese valet. If I fire Nakata, will it put food in the mouths of factory workers?" A red rash rakes up his chest. "The Socialist Party is asking me to publicly condemn the Great War as an imperialist machine that sends American workers to their death for industrialists' profit." He lights another cigarette. "They've gone soft. America must join the war. Take a letter."

When I don't jump, he snarls, "Charmian, take a letter."

I sit at my typewriter.

"Dear Comrades, I resign from the Socialist Party, due to its lack of fire and fight. Liberty, freedom, and independence are royal things that cannot be thrust upon certain races or classes. They must rise up by their own brain and brawn and wrest liberty from the world."

My fingers continue to record his resignation, though I can't believe my ears. Jack joined twenty years ago, serving the party with his campaigning, endorsements, speeches, and newspaper articles. He has been the voice of the Socialists, has been arrested for speaking out. The party sends him in like a Trojan horse whenever they need his power and charisma.

He concludes the letter: "Include the resignation of my comrade wife, Charmian K. London, with mine. Yours for the revolution, Jack London."

"Don't I have a choice in this?"

He glares. "You are either with me or against me."

"It's just that we've given so much to Socialism, fighting for human progress against predators who degrade and enslave workers."

"My dream was that my Socialist comrades were intellectually honest," he says. "My awakening is that they want power for themselves." He looks out to the ocean. "In a few years, the Socialists will forget that Jack London ever led the charge."

"If you are not Socialist, what will you call yourself?"

He ponders a moment before he answers. "I am not anything, I fear. I am utterly alone."

"Not so alone." I take his hand in mine, and we look out to the boundless ocean.

One afternoon, Jack catches a ramshackle trolley into town for a carton of cigarettes, and I decide to go down to the market in the mango grove. I'll make a romantic dinner for the two of us on the beach. On a whim, I stuff Victoria Woodhull into my tote for the outing. Getting batty as Bessie.

I get to the market just as the wahinis spread woven mats on the sand. They chant mele songs, rich and expressive, lilting as the perfumed breeze. Colorful baskets of wild yams, ohi'a'ai mountain apples, 'ōhelo berries, bulbous seaweed, delicate Hāpu'u fern sprouts prove irresistible as I fill my tote with Hawaiian delicacies Jack might enjoy.

Fishing boats pull ashore and offer their glimmering catch. I choose three bonitas for dinner, sweetest fish in the Pacific.

A sunbaked old woman raises a machete and thwacks it down, slicing through the top of a coconut. She pops a hollow reed in the opening and gives it to me with a toothless grin. The coconut milk is warm and sweet.

My totes are heavy now, and it's getting hot. I sit under a palm and sip my coconut. I wish Bessie could see the beauty of these women, their blue-black hair, cocoa-butter skin, and large swinging breasts. Right next to me, a toothless woman sells shells, dried grass, and flowers, giving me a silly idea, so I buy up her wares and carry my bulging totes back to our kauhale.

Nakata sees me coming and runs to help. *"Yokubatte mo tabe kirenaiyo."* Something about my eyes being bigger than my stomach. Truth be told, I have no idea what he's saying, but I'm grateful for assistance. He insists on preparing our evening meal, so I go down to the beach with my Kodak and materials I bought from the toothless woman.

I knot a small grass skirt for Bessie's doll and tie a scrap of calico fabric across her hard breasts, topping it off with a string of puka shells around her neck. Her severe bun won't do, so I snip a thread, and her brunette waves fall free to her waist.

"Now that's liberated," I say, posing Victoria in the wet sand with her arms outstretched in a hula. The breeze blows her grass skirt, revealing one glorious leg. I click the shutter on my Kodak and capture her freedom to send Bessie. She'll cackle like a sailor when she gets the photo. I miss her wicked laugh.

Later, I shower and smooth my skin with coconut oil. Donning a flowered island muumuu, pushed off my tanned shoulders, I wait at the trolley stop for Jack's return. I've been anticipating this moment all afternoon, and I can see my efforts from here: two koa-wood lounge chairs nestled together on the shoreline, with nothing between them but an ice bucket of Veuve Clicquot, pirated from the ocean liner.

I hear the rowdy strains of "Aloha 'Oe" before the open-air trolley rounds the Banyan tree. The bell clangs as the car slows to a stop. Jack steps off, unsteady. I run and hug him, kissing him, tasting sweet rum and pineapple.

"Hey, Mate." He breathes rum and kisses me again.

I stay close, my voice barely more than a whisper. "I have a wonderful surprise for you." Stroking the back of his head, I feel a thrill of anticipation. "Dinner on the beach." I point out the lounges. "We'll let the waves flow over our feet and watch the sun drown in the ocean."

A stream of passengers steps off the trolley and pools around him.

"Ummmm. That sounds wonderful, but—"

"I see what you mean, London. She *is* quite a woman." A beefy Hawaiian with a ukulele strapped across his hairless chest passes a bottle of rum to the man next to him.

"These folks have never seen the Outrigger Club, so I invited them—"

"Oooeee." An old sailor grabs my hand and kisses it. "You're a lucky man, Mr. London."

Jack shrinks back like a scolded hound dog. "Rain check on your plans?"

A redheaded woman dressed in flocked velvet steps off the trolley. "I'm Lydia Manning, from England," she says in heavy cockney. "Very kind of you to have us out to the club."

I glance back at my romantic setup on the beach, and a rough wave knocks over the ice bucket. The spilled ice shrinks my heart.

Jack rubs his hands together. "What's for dinner, anyway? I could eat a whale."

Defiantly, I take his arm, refusing to give up. "It's what's for dessert that counts." Together, we lead the laughing crowd passing the rum bottle between themselves.

After we pack the last pickled guest onto the trolley back to Waikiki, I walk with Jack back to our compound. Lots of canoodling and caressing of body parts, his eager touch awakening all my pent-up desires. He strokes my bottom, round and round until he's raised such lust in me I want to zig-zig-zag him right here on the path. Then I think, why not?

I pull him under a date palm and lay him down on the soft sand. Sitting astride his pelvis, I unbutton his khakis. I'm lost in the hunger of my hands, tentative at first, but becoming firmer with each stroke, until the beautiful thing throbs as hotly as my own groin.

He wriggles in the sand and groans. "Ah, Mate. I've wanted you so much."

I lift my muumuu and straddle him. Sliding his strength into me, the dry walls tear, painful, but I can't stop. I need Jack. I can change the tide against us. Our passion has sealed us together under more adverse circumstances than the monotony of matrimony. I press down, engulfing him. He moans and moves underneath me, and finally it feels good. The tension builds deliciously, and I arch back and peer at the stars through the palm leaves and thank them, every one.

But then, he goes flaccid and slips out, leaving me empty. My hands stroke and pull at him, desperate to regain momentum.

"It's no use," he says, turning away.

I roll off him, dismissed. "Did I do something wrong?"

He buttons his pants and brushes the sand off. "I'd give my right hand to know what you think of me." His voice sounds vulnerable like when I met him, not bold and blustery like he shows the world.

"I think we both could use a good night's sleep."

He pulls hair from the sides of his head. "That is *not* what you think. You tell me this, you tell me that. But close as we are, hard as we try to give ourselves to each other, you withhold your true impulsions."

"I'm doing my best here, Jack."

"It's not enough." He grabs both arms, his face searching mine. "Can't you let yourself go and let me understand the real you?"

What does he want me to say, that I am starved for the sexual man he used to be? He doesn't want the truth.

Releasing my arms, he takes a deep breath and starts anew. "According to Jung and Freud the libido is more than sexuality, more like Bergson's élan vital. The vital force of life." He throws a philosophy uppercut, and I counterpunch.

"But you can't deny the importance of sexuality on human life revealed in art, literature, poetry, and music throughout history."

He lights an Imperial. "Sexuality is but one channel of the libido, the most important channels being absolute truth and honesty." Dragging on his cigarette, waiting for my answer. The terrific strain on his mind will break him . . . or me.

I put my arm around his waist. "What about a love where two people accept and allow each other to be themselves?"

A slow smile lights his face. He walks me back to his hut, and I feel I won this round. At least we can unlace our boxing gloves for another day.

That night, he sleeps on the far edge of the bed, while I dream of my past nights of passion with Jack. I loved them so when I had them.

# 14

## Oahu, Hawaii
## February 1916

*I was jealous; therefore I loved.*

*—Jack London,* The Sea-Wolf

Jack wakes up at dawn, and Nakata brings him fresh-brewed Kona coffee on the lanai. Gauzy curtains sway in the fragrant breeze. There, in his soiled blue-butterfly kimono and swimming trunks, swollen feet digging in the sand, he dictates his story into the newfangled Ediphone I brought from the mainland so I could spend time writing *Our Hawaii*.

In the evenings, I type up his work. The tinny, scratchy cylinder recording is nothing like hearing Jack's voice, rumbling and low with emotion or running madly through the landscape created in his mind. But it's a small price to pay for my freedom to write.

*The Little Lady of the Big House* near the end, he's stymied and annoyed.

He spends the day talking into that contraption instead of joining me for a swim or horseback ride. From the water, I wave to him, lying in a hammock strung between two tall palms. His pallid arm waves back.

"Come on in. The water is so warm," I yell.

"Oh yes—no—yes. Well, no. I have all this reading to catch up on." He waves at the mounting pile. "I'm glad you asked, though. Yesterday you forgot, and I had to go in alone."

Never once have I forgotten to ask.

Nakata brings us more mail from the States. We sit in carved koa-wood chaises, Jack wears the same blue-butterfly kimono. I'm ready to burn the thing. Dividing the mail into piles, I pull out an envelope postmarked "Harlem, New York," and open it.

"A letter from Bessie and another puzzle from Houdini." Tearing open the *M-U-M* magazine wrapping, I find a hasty shorthand in black ink. I'm disappointed the cryptogram is far less remarkable than the last.

"The man loves puzzles, doesn't he?" Jack slits a carving knife through an envelope. "Ever figure out the one he gave you at San Quentin?"

I nod. "It said something like, 'Fire has always been and will always remain the most terrible of the elements.'" My cheeks burn thinking of the second message.

Jack snorts. "Does daffy Bessie write anything redeeming?"

"Not unless you're a doll enthusiast." Bessie writes as impishly as she speaks. I can almost hear her melodramatic voice telling me about her new doll, a vaudeville showgirl, and how the other dolls snub her. She received the picture of Victoria Woodhull I sent, and while she enjoyed it, she really thinks Victoria Woodhull should wear a hat to protect her porcelain skin against the harsh Hawaiian sun.

On a sadder note, Bessie complains about how Houdini left her home alone for two weeks while he performed for President

Wilson in Washington. "Here I sit teaching new words to the parrots."

Jack asks Nakata to make a pitcher of cocktails, though it's only ten o'clock. He lights an Imperial and opens a small package from Macmillan, his first copy of *The Scarlet Plague*. He inscribes a volume, blowing smoke out the side of his mouth like Charlie Chaplin in *Kid Auto Races at Venice*. We see every new Chaplin movie that makes it to Waikiki.

A dashing, unfathomable mixture of men, my Jack: adventurer, farmer, aristocrat, Bohemian, land baron, Socialist, warrior. He looks handsome to the extreme now that his kidney trouble has passed. Maybe the other trouble has passed, too, but I'm too anxious to find out. He'll come to me when he's ready. He hands me my first edition, and I read his inscription.

"My Mate-Woman: And here, in blessed Hawaii eight years after our voyage in our own *Snark*, we find ourselves, not merely again, but more bound to each other than ever."

I shudder. To think I risked Jack for a moment of pleasure with Lawrence. I look up, and he's studying my face, must see my shame.

I lean across the chaise and kiss his bristled cheek. "I look forward to reading the book again."

He opens the note enclosed from Macmillan. "Ha! I knew it. *Star Rover* is breaking all sales records. George Brett didn't believe me when I told them the public was ready for reincarnation." He hoots, and I love the sound.

"You deserve it, you really do." A wave rolls in and laps at our feet. Jack's are swollen and red, and I take them onto my chaise and rub them with coconut oil. "Does he mention how my *Log of the Snark* is selling?"

Jack scans to the end. "I don't see anything, Lady-Boy."

I hate the new name he's taken to calling me. Menacing clouds have rolled in, the ocean has turned choppy and gray. Maybe if we ignore it, this storm will blow over.

"I'd give anything to write like you." I busy myself rubbing his feet. "I'm writing *Our Hawaii* each night, rereading, reworking, adding remembered details and descriptions. Still it lacks your insight to human nature. My stories are about where we go, what it looks like, who we meet. Your stories expose the rumbling underbelly of life and death—" My throat closes.

"Charmian, listen," he says, like a patient parent who's heard it all before. "I'd rather you'd be a great swimmer than a writer. Your athletic body skimming through the waves is your masterpiece." He kisses my nose.

I focus on the sea foam beneath our lounges. "That was cruel, Jack."

"I don't mean to be." He takes my hands in his. "Can't you just enjoy life? You're always pushing, striving to be something more. Isn't your life enough? Aren't I enough?"

The haunting words of *The Star Rover* crawl through my mouth bitter as sumac, so reminiscent of one of my beatitudes. "I have been growing, developing, through incalculable myriads of millenniums." Doesn't he recognize these thoughts as mine? "All my previous selves have their voices, echoes, promptings in me. Oh, incalculable times again shall I be born."

"You sound angry." Jack swirls pineapple in his cocktail.

"You take my visions and ideas and turn them into literature that will be praised and read by generations to come." I rub my throbbing temples.

"And you resent it."

"I suppose I do, sometimes." The admission sounds childish and self-absorbed. "I tell myself it's enough to be part of your genius. But is it? Is it really?"

"So you took revenge on me with Lawrence."

"That's absurd." My ears pound like native warning drums.

"I've dedicated my life to you, Charmian."

"That's fresh." I get up off the chaise and cross my arms over my chest. "What about Anna, Blanche, and that New York journalist—what's her name . . ." Anger muddles my memory.

He huffs and smirks. "Surely you know they don't hold a candle to you."

"And how would I know that?"

"How, indeed?" He uncrosses my arm to kiss my wrist. "You liked to sail, so I built you a ship and sailed around the world. You were desperate to be a writer, so I got your book published. You deserved a grand home, so I built you Wolf House."

*And you destroyed it with your lust and carelessness.* I hear it as clearly as if he says it aloud. I still have no idea if Lawrence or Jack burned down Wolf House, but as I told Houdini, it doesn't matter. Either way it's my fault.

Nakata pours another drink for Jack. I hold my hand over my glass. "No more, Nakata." My voice is too sharp, the air too charged with undercurrent.

Jack tears open another envelope and holds up a beautiful blue ribbon topped with an impressive emblem. "The Claremont Classic. Joan must have won first prize with her horse."

"She sent you her ribbon? You should be very proud." I'm thankful to step out of the spotlight.

He holds the letter in both hands, eyes tracking the page, cheeks flushed with color.

"What else does Joan say?"

Jack's hands fall to his lap. "They've found a larger house in Berkeley, more befitting the family of Jack London."

"Joan said that?"

"Her mother's a ventriloquist."

"And they want you to pay for it."

"Of course. They have no income."

"But you just increased their allowance."

Jack's lower lip protrudes. "And private school tuition. Elizabeth insisted the girls go to Saint Mary's. Not to mention the horses and boarding stable, elocution and cotillion. The woman thinks I'm a damn golden goose."

"You should have let her remarry when she had the chance."

His face swells like a man-o'-war. "Take a letter."

I grab my journal and pen and take down his words.

"Dear Joan. Apparently, I have become nothing but a bank for my family, as I am not permitted to spend time with you, only provide money. Tell your mother she's won, on both counts. From now on I will send checks, but I do not wish to hear from any of you again. If I see you on the street, I will not acknowledge you as my own. One last piece of advice from your father, Joan. Marry for love. Your mother and I married as a philosophical statement, and look where it got us. Marry for love, for the human spirit is complicated and will not be locked in a cage of convenience." Jack gazes blankly at the ocean.

Finishing the last word, I place the page in my typing file, where it will stay until Jack calms down and changes his mind.

"Call up Baldwin and his friends." Jack tamps a cigarette on the table, turning it over and over again. "Call up Koolu and that redheaded Brit. Yes, that's it. Invite the whole Crowd." His eyes whirl. "Nakata can buy lobsters at the pier. And hire some natives to help serve. Heart of palm and papaya. Lots of cocktails." He flicks his lighter and holds the flame to his Imperial. "Charmian, if they can't come today, invite them for tomorrow and the next day. I want my table full of interesting people, remarkable people, astonishing people. The more unusual, the better."

I roll my eyes, and he glares at me.

"What? We're in paradise, aren't we? Life's short, and I want to live."

He seems to be running away from himself, filling in every moment, as if uneasy with time alone . . . or time alone with me.

Late the next morning, my feet sink into the yellow sand, my back burnished copper from the equatorial sun, my arms deliciously exhausted from paddling the canoe around the cove with the canoe boy, Kimu.

Jack's probably still sleeping since he kept the party rolling till the wee hours. New ears to listen in awe to his philosophies. Some of the guests had never set sail off the islands.

At some point last night, Jack called for a hula and insisted I join in. I held my own with the Tahitian dances, all rumbling hips and swirling torches around the bonfire.

But then toward midnight, a sliver of cloud trailed over the moon. A guitarist slid a bar over his languid strings and stopped the chatter. The other dancers peeled away, leaving young and beautiful Kukalani in the center. The crowd hushed, and their faces softened as they watched her hands swimming through the hibiscus air, her hips bending and swaying as only a Hawaiian girl's can. No one noticed when I slipped off to my hut, their hungry eyes devouring Kukalani's sensuous moves, Jack's face ablaze with the wonder of that girl . . . But Nakata was watching Jack.

I tossed and turned and at the first glimmer of dawn went to find the Maori canoe boy Kimu to take me out to find the sea turtles. The wonder of their ancient bodies swimming in the deep blue was a pleasure I won't soon forget.

Stepping around a curving date palm, I see Jack lying on a pallet under the thatched roof, Kukalani rubbing his back. Her jet hair brushes his neck as she leans near his body, her forearms gliding over his muscles. Jack moans, and the sound of his pleasure drills a hole deep into my abdomen. A man in need.

He's made no move toward my sleeping hut since our failed attempt in the sand. And he hasn't responded to my advances, his ego is as fragile as the turtle eggs Kimu and I discovered on the beach. Yet now, he is groaning with unmistakable desire with a girl young enough to be his daughter.

Wiping the sand from my feet, I step into the lanai. "I thought your mother was the masseuse."

The girl startles and jumps back, with the wild black eyes of a cornered animal.

"That's it for today, Kukalani." Jack arches an eyebrow. "Come back tomorrow, same time."

The girl's face colors, and she backs away, then turns and runs.

"Something I said?" I scoff while Jack throws on a fresh kimono.

"It's not like you to provoke a servant."

"Only those whose hands caress my husband's back." I step close and knot his sash, his smell mingling with coconut and lime. "That is where I draw the line."

"Kukalani's a good masseuse." Jack sits in a rattan chair and picks up the newspaper. "Her hands move as her ancestors' hands moved. Her hands remember more than her mind."

"Jung," I say. "Race memory."

He nods with respect. "Did you walk on the beach?"

I shake my head. "Canoeing with Kimu. He showed me where the sea turtles lay their eggs."

Nakata comes from the cooking hut with a pitcher of cocktails and bows his head as he pours two long drinks, chock full of fresh coconut and pineapple.

"Thank you, Nakata." I take the drink. "I'm parched. The surf was fierce today."

*"Jigou jitoku."* He backs into the cooking hut.

"You catch that?" Jack asks.

"Something akin to 'you reap what you sow.'"

"Is he talking about you or me?" Jack bites into pineapple.

"Nakata's sweet on Kukalani." I sip the juice.

"You must have had a good time with Kimu. I was ready to send out a search party, you were gone so long."

"He speaks little English. We communicate with our hands. But he rows like a Hawaiian god." Flashes of his chiseled arms rising high and slicing into the waves, his back rippling with strength, his easy silence. Kimu is as primal and stunning as the sea turtles themselves.

"He captures your fancy, I see." Jack opens the newspaper. "He's Maori, I guess from his tribal tattoo."

Oh, that tattoo . . . Kimu rowed in front of me, swimming trunks dangling from his hip bones. The Maori diamond began between his shoulder blades, widened at the small of his back and finished at his tailbone.

"I suppose so," I say. "I didn't know Kukalani did massage. I'm so sore." I roll my left shoulder.

Jack glances sideways. He used to massage my shoulders as I typed his manuscripts, always ending in a grand lolly.

"I see how Kimu looks at you," Jack says. "I don't blame him. You're quite the specimen, muscled and tan, eyes sparkling. How could he resist?"

I scoff. "I'm old enough to be his mother."

"What happened to the free lover that lured me away from wife and family and bewitched me with her charms?" His voice cocks like a trigger.

"You happened to me, Jack."

"Have you changed so much?"

A pineapple thorn pricks my tongue. "Is this still about Lawrence? I told you it didn't—"

"You clearly have needs that aren't fulfilled."

"What are you saying? You want me to have sex with Kimu?"

"Don't tell me you haven't thought about it." He spoons soft taro into his mouth.

"Now you can read my mind? I am my own woman, and I'll do what I want." As long as it pleases you. Oh God. It's true. I'll do anything to make it right for Jack.

Jack throws back his head and laughs. "I can still get your goat." He takes my hand. "You will always be my Mate-Woman. My soul is bound to you. It's the institution of marriage that strangles love, isn't it? We start out lusty and confident, standing together against the world." He looks out to the waves crashing on the rock only to dissipate to foam before vanishing altogether in the sand. "But over the years, the face of your beloved grows as familiar as your own." He touches my cheek with that despondent look, the look of the long sickness, then drops his head to his sternum. Once Jack slips into this deep depression, I lose him for months. My mind scrambles to think of something to stop his fall.

"What would make you happy?" My voice trembles. "You want freedom? Is that it?"

He looks up with overbright eyes.

"Who's here to condemn us? Loose tongues are tucked safely back in the States. We've promised each other our souls. What greater commitment do we need?"

"You are a marvel."

He laughs with a boyish gleam in his eyes.

Suddenly I feel giddy, lifting a palm frond to his head. "You, Jack London, are free to pursue your wildest pleasure here in the islands."

His arms pull me down on his body, and I feel his hardness on my legs. His freedom arouses him. So be it. My own limbs squirm with craving.

"One moment." I rise and pull the gauze curtains of the lanai closed.

Jack lies back in the lounge and opens his kimono. I lower myself onto him, an insatiable sensation reaching up through my body. Our quickening rhythm crashes with the waves, sending me into a cataclysmic climax I haven't felt in months.

After that release of pent-up desire, that moment of pure abandon, Jack retires to his hut.

The waves have lost their fury, the wind has died to nothing. How could I have proposed such a one-sided bargain, giving up what I want most in this world. Jack as my one and only.

# 15

## Oahu, Hawaii
## March 1916

*Show me a man with a tattoo and I'll show you a man with an interesting past.*

*—Jack London*

My insomnia persists. Some nights I wander out in my short muumuu, tiptoeing past Jack's sleeping hut, and walk along the beach as far as the rocky cliff of Ali'i, then walk back.

After my restless roaming, I sit on the sand in front of our lanai with my knees gathered up, inhaling seaweed, salt, and sea. Moonlight washes over the waves, and my weary eyes feel heavy and finally close. The ocean laps softly in my ears, and I do not hear him approach.

But then I feel him sit beside me, so close our hips are touching, knees touching, and the sweet scent of coconut oil making me quiver.

"You came," Kimu says, his eyes luminous as black pearls.

"I couldn't sleep." I watch the waves and wonder what to say. "Why are you awake at this hour?"

"I've been waiting for you to come out."

"Why, Kimu?" His coffee-colored chin sprouts a few black hairs.

"I want to take away the sadness in your eyes." He touches my temple.

"I'm not sad." I move my head away gently so not to hurt his feelings.

"I would never sleep away from you." He tosses his hair back from his shoulders with a scornful look at Jack's hut.

My laugh sounds flat. "Wait until you've been married nine years and one of you snores and the other kicks."

"You deserve more than a pickled old man." Kimu's eyes narrow. "Life is meant to be enjoyed." His brown hand runs up my calf. "Your skin shines like the moon. You swim like a dolphin, surf like Kimu, dance like Kukalani." His smile gleams in the moonlight, and I realize he's practiced this line and gotten it right.

"You flatter me, Kimu, but—" What do I say? I don't want to insult him.

He takes my arms and pulls me close, kissing me with full lips. I try to push him away, but he strengthens his hold on me.

The hut light goes on. Jack. I jump up and brush the sand from my bottom, walking toward him without any thought for Kimu.

"I see you've found a remedy for your insomnia," Jack says as I get closer.

"I was out walking; then I sat on the beach. Kimu came and sat beside me."

"Just don't lie about it. We gave permission, remember?"

"That was folly." I put my hands on his chest, and he looks away. "You are everything I need."

"I wrote Dr. Frank Lydston." He glances away. "That physician who implanted testicles into his own scrotum. I'm waiting to hear back about his progress."

"We don't need a new invention. We just have to cultivate our desire." I quote a passage he wrote in his short story "Planchette" when we were first together, when everything worked, all the time. "'All things tended to key them to an exquisite pitch—the movement of their bodies . . . the gently stimulated blood caressing the flesh through and through with vigorous health, the warm air fanning their faces, flowing over the skin with a balmy and tonic touch, permeating them and . . . bathing them in the delight that is of the spirit and is personal and holy, that is inexpressible yet communicable by the flash of an eye and the dissolving of the veils of the soul.'"

His eyes fill with tears, no trace of the arousal I'd hoped for. He turns back into his hut, leaving me alone on the beach.

Jack doesn't look up from his newspaper when I come into the lanai the next morning, tying my red silk kimono over my bathing suit.

"Your light burned very late," he says. "Another rendezvous on the beach with Kimu?"

I scoff, not taking the bait. "I stayed up late writing *Our Hawaii* and then tried to figure out Houdini's latest puzzle." I take the puzzle from my pocket to show him the concentric black squares painted on a red background. "It's impossible, but I keep trying."

"Then he succeeded." Jack grins lopsidedly.

"In making a fool of me?" I laugh and fold the puzzle in my pocket.

"In hooking your curiosity."

Nakata brings plates of raw bonita and papaya. *"Nodo kara te ga deru,"* he says to me.

Jack crumples his newspaper. "Speak English, damn it."

"He says your hand is coming out of your throat," I say. "It means you want something so badly you—"

Jack's forehead gathers like a thundercloud. "Damn straight I do." He juts his finger in Nakata's face. "I want you to stop your inscrutable insults or I'll ship you back to Japan to pull rickshaw."

Nakata's mouth drops open, and he backs away. "I am a free man, Mr. Jack." He turns and walks calmly into the cooking hut, but I know he's not.

"That's not like you," I say. "You've never raised your voice to Nakata."

"I'm in no mood for your Pollyanna this morning. My writing has been blocked for weeks, and all you can think of is your own work and seducing a boy on the beach." The long sickness hides under his rage, taunting me to stamp it out before it grabs hold.

"Take a day off, Jack. You're all keyed up. Let's go for a swim. Just you and me. Like old times." I look out to the roaring waves, fierce, but that never stopped us before.

"*The Little Lady of the Big House* is at a complete standstill."

I grab his hand. "Come float with me in the waves, and we'll brainstorm the ending together."

He snorts. "I'm the writer. You're the typist."

"I see." I turn toward the surf so he can't see how he stung me.

"It doesn't feel right lounging around the islands while Germany mows down Europe."

My sympathy snaps. "So you take your foul mood out on Nakata, who serves you so loyally?"

"Not so loyal, I think. He delivered a message from Kukalani canceling my massage today."

"I can give you a massage." Walking behind his chaise to rub his shoulders, I push my thumbs into a hard spot in his muscle. "Not even Houdini could loosen these knots," I say, trying for humor.

"Ow. That hurts." He shoos me away. "Go swimming and leave me to my misery." Taking a stopwatch from his pocket, he says, "I'll time you. See if you can break our record to Ali'i Cliff."

I notice a black shelf hanging on the horizon. "Looks like storm clouds."

"You'll be back in plenty of time," he says, his thumb on the stopper. "Get going."

"Fifty-three minutes, wasn't it?" I stuff the puzzle into my pocket and run into the ocean, letting my red kimono slip away to the sand, knowing he's watching, knowing I look good. Diving into the next big wave, I pump my arms and legs against the water.

The waves lift me and aid my swim. Good thing, because dark clouds are moving in fast. I take a breath and force my head under, the ocean water soft and buoyant, my limbs cutting through them with practiced precision.

Twenty minutes later, the clouds have moved overhead, their roiling mist flashing.

I could turn back, but I imagine the dismissive tsk of Jack's tongue when I don't meet his challenge. So I swim on, the surging waves pushing me out to the cliff. At this rate I'll easily beat our record.

My head comes up, and I cannot see the sky for the enormous ledge of water overhead. I dive under. The waves rise faster and higher than they should. My calf muscle cramps, and I reel it close to my body and kick it out. Searing pain makes me gasp, and I swallow briny ocean water. I can't afford a cramp now, I'm almost to the cliff.

As I come up again for air, the sky is black and boiling, fire rumbling in the clouds. Ali'i Cliff looms above me. A slim, bare-chested Hawaiian man blows a bull's horn, but the wind swallows the sound. From here, it looks like Kimu signaling me to come in, but high tide has already covered the beach, and giant waves batter the sheer rock wall. I'll be pulverized if I swim closer.

A bolt of lightning jags through the clouds and drowns in the furious waves. Thunder cracks in my ears. There is no way forward, no beach, only treacherous volcanic rock rising up against the ocean. My only salvation is to go back from where I came.

I flip around and swim. But the current flows against me, the undertow so strong that no matter how hard I pump, it pulls me back toward the cliff. Far down the beach, I see the Outrigger Club's burning torches. I think I spot Jack there, and I'm cheered. He came to see if I am okay.

Doubling my effort, I thrust my arms through the water. The surf crashes with crushing force on the outcropping of rocks around him. He signals me down the beach, but why?

Then I remember what he'd coached me. "Swim parallel to the beach until you're out of the current, then you can head into shore."

My strength surges, and I change course down shore. My arms ache and twinge with pain. My right calf keeps cramping, stealing any strength it has left. My left leg is not as powerful, but it's all I've got.

Torches burn bright at the Outrigger Club, but I don't see Jack anymore. My muscles feel rubbery and waterlogged, every tendon stretched tight with exhaustion.

A wave crests twelve feet high, and I ride it up. I see Jack swimming toward me, and my heart jumps. I try to swim to him, show him my fortitude, but my limbs are too weak. My head whirs like the mimeograph drum, and my breath pants quick and shallow. So dizzy. Jack's coming.

The storm clouds heave and rumble like a cauldron of lava. I'm lost in a canyon of black water.

Jack grasps my shoulders. "Lay back on my chest, Lady-Boy. You're exhausted."

His voice breaks my eggshell of courage, and I let go, sobbing. He scoops me under his arms, and I feel his heart pulsing under my back, his able arms guiding me, his legs thrusting against the current.

"Rest, Charmian. Don't fight me. Otherwise we'll never make it back."

I lay my head back on his chest, relieved. I hear only the rhythmic beating in my ears as I am cradled in his arms.

High above, the sky god, Wākea, pounds the pahu warning drum of the thunderhead. From his vantage point, I see the two of us below: insignificant specks in the vast churning ocean, the verdant Ko'olau Mountains, the waves engulfing us.

I want to ask Jack if he sees what I see, but the waves are too loud and my voice too weak.

The sky god thrusts a spear into the thundercloud—warning or blessing, I can't tell—and with a monstrous crack, the roiling clouds break open and deluge us with rain.

My body is so heavy now, an anchor falling through the depths. My nose and throat fill with water, my eyes flutter open. Jack holds me tight, my back pressed to his abdomen, my head against his chest. I realize we are sinking. The waves buffet our bodies. I try to wriggle free, but he holds tight. What's happening? Has he had a seizure? Our weight pulls us to the bottom. I breathe water into my lungs. We're going to die.

I can't rouse Jack. Squirming and fighting to free my arms and legs, I finally bite his hand as hard as I can, and he loosens his death grip. I turn to see his face, smiling serenely.

A school of angelfish swarms us. Chartreuse, indigo, orange, purple fish nibble at my toes and lash my skin with their fins. The ocean has siphoned all the oxygen from my collapsed lungs, and my vision dissolves to black.

Jack kicks hard against the water, and we ascend, both of us kicking now against the downward pull.

I break through the surface and gasp for air. Coughing and more gulps of oxygen. The clouds have moved over the mountain, leaving a sky so vibrant it hurts my eyes.

Jack comes up right next to me, choking, expunging water from his lungs.

"Did you feel that? The life breath sucked from our bodies, wringing out all the evil in the world? No deceit, no tyranny, no more struggle. Only the peace of death." He shakes his hair like Possum after a swim in the pond. "Then you brought me back. I opened my eyes from death, there was only you. My one true Mate."

My voice box rasps, soaked with salt. "You almost drowned me."

His eyebrows pop up. "I saved you, Charmian. I saved us. That's what made me come back to life, seeing you there. I want to live my life over with you."

My stomach heaves, and I vomit into the ocean.

"You're in shock. I have to get you out of here." Jack throws his arm around me and swims toward the shore. Once in the shallows, he picks me up and carries me in, laying me on the beach next to my red silk kimono and Houdini's puzzle, plastered to the sand from the rain. My teeth start to clack against each other and goose bumps ripple my skin.

"Your lips are blue." He calls for Nakata, but no one answers.

I choke up more water, my lungs burning.

"You don't really think I would drown you, do you? You have to believe me, Charmian, you are my one bribe for living. Without you, there is no reason to go on."

Laying my cheek on the warm sand, I see Houdini's puzzle has smeared blood red, the black lines turned to shorthand.

"What the eyes see and the ears hear, the mind believes."

. . . a quote from Houdini's book.

Sunlight streams through the open door of my hut and wakes me. The hibiscus-patterned easy chair is empty, the ashtray full of butts, the lamp still burning. Jack had spent all night there, watching over me with worried eyes, licking his pencil lead and writing in his notebook. I kept waking up, seeing him there . . .

My throat is parched from salt, my belly distended from gulping ocean water, my legs wobbly, but the smell of Kona coffee guides me to the lanai. I'll bring a cup back to my hut and make notes of my experience for my Hawaii book.

Jack sits by my Remington with dark swaths under his eyes, blowing a stream of blue smoke into the air. "There's my Mate-Woman. Are you feeling better? You were sleeping so soundly I didn't want to wake you."

Nakata serves me a plate of steaming malasadas, fried dough with haupia coconut milk custard. "Mahalo, Nakata. You know how I love these."

He smiles and pours my coffee.

The hot liquid soothes my throat, and creamy custard washes the salt from my mouth. The breeze is soft, the waves gentle. The storm has left everything pristine and calm.

"I've been waiting for you." Jack's voice crackles with enthusiasm. "I finally know how *The Little Lady in the Big House* ends, and I'll be damned if I'm going to tell it to this confounded machine. In fact, I refuse to speak to it ever again." He marches the Ediphone to the shoreline and hurls it against the boulder.

I gasp as the thing smashes into coils and wires and molded parts, washed away with the waves. I'm overjoyed. I never got used to listening to the staticky recording of his voice and typing words gone cold.

Jack walks back, satisfied and triumphant. "There. It's gone." He kneels beside me and takes my hands in his. "I want to tell my stories to you, Charmian. Not some box. It's the only way I can work now, don't you see?"

His honeyed words and the coconut malasada turn cloying in my mouth, yet his pleading eyes are hard to resist. Part of me wants to throw my arms around his neck and kiss his face with all this renewed attention. But after yesterday, I'm afraid. The near drowning has transformed Jack somehow, but can I trust him? And what do I want? A few minutes ago, I wanted to work on *my* book.

Jack paces the lanai. "Please, Charmian. I need to finish this novel now, or it will finish me."

I relent to his wishes, as a good muse wife does, and sit at my Remington, drumming my fingers on the keys, excited to finally finish the novel that's languished so long.

I hope Jack lets his heroine, Paula, run off with her lover, or maybe she'll decide to be faithful to her husband. Either way, I want her to be happy, she's waited long enough.

But now Jack's staring into palm trees, smoking, as if he still can't decide.

I sip my coffee patiently and look out to the glimmering water. Kimu wades into the ocean with his surfboard above his head, straight into the blazing sun.

Jack sees him, too, and frowns. "Are you ready?"

I nod, and he tells me the end of *Big House*. I can barely make my fingers type the words. When Paula can't choose between her husband and her lover, she kills herself.

Oh, Jack is clever with the story. The reader doesn't know if it is suicide or accident. Nonetheless, his heroine dies.

I finish typing the last word, my chest clenched tight. Jack lies back in his lounge chair pale and bereft. I leave the last page in the typewriter and walk out into the lapping ocean. It's safer out there.

# *16*

## Oahu, Hawaii
## April 1916

*To be able to forget means sanity.*
*—Jack London,* The Star Rover

Jack listens carefully while I read him a scene from *Our Hawaii*. "'The leper played with hands that were not hands, for where were the fingers? But play she did, and weep I did, in a corner, in sheer uncontrol of heartache at the girlish voices gone shrill and sexless and tinny like the old French piano.'" I look up, anxious. "Or something along those lines."

"Good, Mate-Woman. Don't be afraid to tell the reader how the lepers look: their gaping mouths, their noses eaten away, the yellow hue of their skin. And how they smell: the putrid stench of rotting flesh."

I can't get over the change in Jack, his attention and devotion. Yet flashes of my fateful swim still haunt me, the horror of the waves, my nostrils and belly filling with water. Sometimes at night, I imagine the stranglehold of Jack's arms and his forceful legs dragging me to the ocean floor.

I awake panicked and gasping for breath.

Talking myself back to sleep, I repaint my memory with the vibrant turquoise of the ocean, the brilliant red of the cliffs, the warmth of the yellow sand, Jack's strong arms carrying me ashore.

The truth changes with how you perceive it.

News of Jack's heroic rescue of me circles the island. The Baldwin family is throwing us a luau to honor both victim and savior. On the sandy path to the luau, Jack hugs my waist as geckos scuttle across our bare feet. His tanned face and brilliant eyes stand starkly handsome against his white linen suit, the first time he's gotten out of his kimono in a while.

I carry a woven palm tote with something special I made inside, to present to Jack tonight. Symbolic of my change of heart. The last few weeks have been like a honeymoon, and I've decided I like it this way. My white batiste dress skims my calves. I feel more the blissful bride tonight than I did at our courthouse nuptials nine years ago.

I quicken my step to keep up with Jack's brisk pace. His cheeks are flushed, and he hums an old sailor song. Catching my glance, he smiles and stops to hold me close. "When I thought I'd lost you to the ocean that day . . ." He inhales my plumeria head wreath. "I swore to myself I'd never let you out of my sight again."

I kiss him. "Better go. We're late."

In a flash of fate, Jack's aloofness has vanished, and with it his preoccupation, self-centeredness, and irritation. Now Jack follows me with his eyes wherever I go, drinking me in with unquenchable yearning. No matter who is around, he holds up his arms when I come into the room, as if he must grasp at something, someone who comes closest to understanding his need. I've come to understand it's all part of his yearning to escape from the world at large. Still, I sleep alone.

"This is a long walk." Jack grimaces playfully and starts to limp. "Call up the rickshaw next time."

We hear the mele chanting. Burning torches light up the mango grove. Tall vases hold profusions of fuchsia ginger, orange birds-of-paradise, and heart-shaped anthurium. Pineapples, papayas, hibiscus, and coconuts decorate long banquet tables under palm-thatched lanais.

Native girls swish around us in grass skirts revealing long, tanned legs and circle our necks with fragrant orchid leis. Kukalani lingers at Jack's neck with a lei, turning each orchid just so, caressing his chest. His eyes follow her graceful hands. She whispers something in his ear. A pang of jealousy riddles my stomach.

"Thank you, Kukalani." I take off Jack's lei and hand it back to her. "But Jack is allergic to orchids." Taking his hand, I lead him to the grove.

"Since when?" Jack ducks under the flowered archway.

"This is *our* night." I tweak his nose.

Mr. Baldwin and his wife, Lucille, greet us on the other side of the archway and escort us to the head table. The jangly sound of ukuleles makes my hips bounce, and Jack's hand caresses my waist. He growls in my ear, and I laugh and shake my head, dutifully following the Baldwins up to the platform.

The proper English couple we've known since our first trip to the islands came to Waikiki twenty-five years ago with the Baptist church. But Hawaiians seem to have influenced them, rather than vice versa. Mr. Baldwin wears shorts and a short-sleeve shirt embroidered with hibiscus. Lucille wears a flowered muumuu and hands me a hairy coconut with a straw. "Pineapple and coconut." She giggles. "And rum, lots of rum."

"Ready to say a few words to your admirers?" Mr. Baldwin asks Jack. He gestures to the thatched bandstand with "aloha" spelled out in flowers.

"Looks like all of Waikiki is here," Jack says.

Full tables extend deep into the mango grove. Chinese lanterns swing from the trees.

"Wait, I almost forgot something." I pull out the maile-leaf garland from my tote and drape the shiny, pungent leaves around his neck. "I made you the lei of aloha for tonight." I take a nervous breath, hoping he'll understand my new commitment to him. To us. "Aloha is being a part of all, and all being a part of me. When there is pain, it is my pain. When there is joy, it is also mine."

He takes my face in his hands. "Charmian, I—" He looks down at the sand. "I will live the rest of my days trying to deserve you."

Mr. Baldwin steps up to the microphone. "Aloha, everyone, and welcome to the Outrigger Club."

Guests applaud.

"Most of you know we were a small outfit of twenty in 1908, when a young adventurer came here to learn to surf. Mr. Jack London not only conquered the surf that year, but wrote an article for *Woman's Home Companion* that put surfing on the map. And now the Outrigger Club has twelve hundred members."

Baldwin beckons Jack to the stage. "Tonight we honor this brave man for rescuing his lovely wife from a terrible undertow."

Jack takes the microphone and holds his arm out to me. "I am so grateful my wife survived her ordeal. I'm happy to say we've buried it in the past where it belongs."

I nod, feeling my cheeks grow hot.

As he prepares to speak to the crowd, his chest rises, just one of the imperceptible movements my subconscious chronicles: how he puts his feet up on the desk when he's deep in thought or drinks whiskey from his coffee cup or locks eyes before saying something he wants you to remember. A hundred small gestures, yet how much do I really know? Was there a part of him that wanted us to drown . . . or to drown me?

Waves smash against the jutting rock, and I shiver.

Jack reads his surfing article to the club, his voice husky with emotion. "Soon we were out in deep water where the big smokers came roaring in, and I'm right there watching twenty-foot waves cresting over my head.

"It was a battle in which mighty blows were struck—a struggle between insensate force and intelligence. When a breaker curled over my head, for a swift instant I could see the light of day through its emerald body. Then would come the blow like a sandblast."

His words pummel my body with waves. Buffet me. Engulf me. Drag me down in their depths, as only his words can do.

When he's finished, fans swarm the bandstand to get his autograph, and I watch him, warily—his volatile eyes of steel and dew, sweetness and ferocity, eyes that hide profound and terrible secrets.

*"He alaka'i nui,"* someone says in my ear.

"He *is* an important leader, thank you." I turn to see who spoke.

Houdini stands close enough to make my skin tingle. My heart skips, then flitters like a butterfly. I press my hand against my chest to calm it. "Egad, what are you doing in Waikiki?"

"You were here."

His words echo from another time, like I've lived this moment before. I close my eyes and try to make sense of it, inhaling his wood-spice cologne.

"I'm still here, Charmian." Elbows fixed to his sides, forearms and palms spread out in surrender.

Mr. Baldwin claps his shoulder. "You must be Houdini. So glad you could make it."

Jack breaks away from his fans and claps him on the back. "Did you magically transport yourself here from Manhattan?"

"No, just Pearl Harbor. I performed for the troops there."

"In Pearl Harbor?" Jack's face reddens. "Aren't the army and navy fighting over that base?"

"They've finally agreed," he says.

"Is Bessie with you?" I ask.

"Bessie doesn't travel on the ocean," he says.

"What steamer did you take?" Jack asks.

"Submarine from San Francisco."

Jack grimaces. "I know all the subs out of San Francisco. Which one?"

"Classified."

A giant Chinese gong reverberates through the grove. Young men with leaf loincloths carry in steaming platters of kalua pig, coconut pudding, and poi.

Five musicians crowd into the thatched bandstand with guitars, lute, and ukulele. They play Hawaiian standards and take requests. Hula dancers interpret their songs with graceful hands and undulating bodies.

Hau'oli, my hula teacher, gestures to me, and I shake my head. The crowd's enormity keeps me in my chair.

Jack presses the small of my back. "Come on, Lady-Boy."

Houdini raises an eyebrow. "I'd love to see you hula."

Hau'oli pulls me to the bandstand, and my stomach jumps like a school of red shrimp. We dance a haunting hula, "He Kanikau Aloha No Ka Haku," a moving lament for a loved one. Focusing on the chant, I relax into the movement and sound. The dance ends too soon, and I return to our table, where Jack and Houdini are talking.

Jack immediately wraps his arms around my shoulders, and Houdini cocks his eyebrow, then disappears behind the bandstand. Taking up where they left off, these men, a battle of intellect and reflex. And what am I, the prize?

Tahitian drums begin to rumble.

"Mr. London, will you join us on the stage?" Baldwin holds his arm out to Jack.

"And now, the most famous magician on earth, the Great Houdini," Baldwin bellows into the microphone.

The magician appears on the bandstand in a shining black tuxedo, so out of place in Hawaii. "This stunt is dedicated to the brave and lovely Charmian London," he says. "Who we are all celebrating tonight." Houdini turns to Jack. "Ready, Mr. London?"

"As you are," Jack says.

"Very well." He walks Jack to the wood wall of the cookhouse. "Stand here and do not move. No matter what happens. Can you do that?"

"I can and I will." Jack raises his chin and spreads his feet in a sturdy stance.

My knees go weak and my breath shallow, all this chest beating leaves me giddy.

Houdini signals with a sharp stroke of his hand, and large drums thunder. Samoan dancers enter with bulging oiled muscles, juggling flaming knives. The dancers jump and leap around Jack, knives blazing into the ebony sky. One dancer spins and throws Houdini a fiery knife, which he miraculously catches by its handle.

I gasp and want to stop them, but Houdini hurls the knife at Jack. It zooms past his shoulder and sticks into the wall, still burning.

The crowd gasps and cheers.

The Samoan chant thrums in my ears. The fire-knife dervishes swirl and throw another knife at Houdini, who throws it at Jack's other shoulder.

Jack's eyes pop. Two knives flame at his shoulders. "Christ, Houdini. These knives are hot."

The magician flashes a smile. "He who plays with fire must have a thick skin."

"He who plays with fire gets burned." Jack looks side to side at the blaze. "Is there an end to this trick?"

"Coming right up."

"Bring it on."

Four more Samoans circle Houdini, throwing him their knives and cartwheeling offstage. Houdini throws each knife as quickly as he receives another. Two flaring knives puncture the wood at Jack's feet, two more at his waist.

The crowd groans with each flick of Houdini's wrist.

Jack's face glistens with sweat. He can't move or his clothes will catch fire.

Drums hammer my ears. "Stop," I yell, slicing my arm through the air.

Houdini holds one last burning knife like a torch, then hurls it at Jack's head.

The knife twists through steamy air slowly, ever so slowly, trailing fire and smoke on its path across the stage. As the knife thrusts into the wood above Jack's head, flames singe his hair.

I collapse into a chair, reeling and nauseous.

Houdini struts over to Jack, who is unable to move within the burning knives, and helps him out. The two of them turn to face the audience and bow to wild applause. Jack pats down his head, recovering his frazzled wits. Houdini laughs, grabs his hand, and they bow again.

I want to kill them both.

# 17

## Oahu, Hawaii
## May 1916

*There is an ecstasy that marks the summit of life, and beyond which life cannot rise. And such is the paradox of living, this ecstasy comes when one is most alive, and it comes as a complete forgetfulness that one is alive.*

*—Jack London,* The Call of the Wild

Here in Hawaii, as at home in Sonoma Valley, I have a nightly date with the moon. Now it's the full moon phase, Poepoe, as the Hawaiians call it, the treacherous moon that dredges up the bottom of the ocean and hurls it onto the land, destroying everything in its wake. Then sucks it back under again, stranding sea life in the tide pools.

Something like life with Jack.

I creep from my bed, not wanting to disturb him; he offered his own hut to Houdini. He's snoring harmonically as a chanting monk. I open the door. Bessie's doll catches my eye, begging for a moonlit walk, so I take her.

The sand is cool and gritty on my bare feet, smoothing away the rough edges, drawing me down to the lapping waves, frothing in blue light. Stars glitter in the vast cobalt sky, and I lose myself in their endless possibility.

"I thought you weren't coming." Houdini steps out from the shadow of a palm tree, moonlight silhouetting his face, shirt-sleeves and pant legs rolled up, about as Hawaiian as this New Yorker gets.

"My magic man." My. Magic. Man. I laugh to cover my excitement to see him. "You expected me?"

"You rarely sleep in the night. Like a lioness stalking prey by moonlight. You only fall asleep after you've made the kill, worked out the problem, laid a plan for the next day. Just before dawn, your heavy eyes betray you and you doze off for an hour or two."

"Am I really so transparent?"

"Quite the opposite, Charmian." Magic points to the doll. "I never took you for a doll collector."

I laugh and hand her to him. "Take her back to Bessie. She's homesick."

He runs his fingers across the doll's grass skirt with a curious expression. "Victoria Woodhull has gone native, I see."

I smile. "All women have a wild side."

His eyes darken. "You're not at all what you seem, are you, Charmian?" He searches my face for an answer, but I have nothing to say. Sometimes I have no idea what I am, except as it relates to Jack.

"Bessie told me you spent time in Germany," I say, relishing this time to get to know him. "Said you worked for the kaiser."

He chuckles. "Bessie has a vivid imagination. I performed for the kaiser's police force. They had me test their handcuffs and jail cells as I did at San Quentin."

"She also said you spied for the tsar of Russia. Advised him to take over his own army. From what I read, he listened."

Magic throws his head back and laughs. "Has Bessie ever told you the story of how we married?"

"Several stories, actually." I smile, thinking of her contrary tales.

"Then you understand." He walks on, and I follow.

"Did you like Russia?"

He peers sideways. "My mother made better borscht."

We almost reach the end of the beach, and I don't want to turn around. So nice to talk instead of argue.

Ali'i Cliff looms ahead in the moonlight, staggering and perilous. Waves sacrifice themselves on the rocky cliff, and my stomach churns remembering my swim and brush with death. Sweat breaks out between my breasts, and soon I'm shaking all over.

Magic surrounds me with his arms and holds me close. "What is it? You're trembling."

I tilt my face up and kiss him, his lips tasting of bergamot . . . then turn away. One taste, one slip of temptation. I swore I'd never go there again.

But he grabs the back of my head and draws my face close, his desire tangible and intense. He's wanted this kiss as much as I have. His lips move on mine like they'll never have enough, then move so tenderly I melt inside.

I have no idea how much time passes, but I don't want him to stop. When he does, I feel empty. When I realize he's still holding Victoria Woodhull, I laugh. Then I'm sad, because the doll is Bessie's. And so is he.

"I haven't behaved well," I say. "Not well at all."

"That makes two of us. Partners in sin. Isn't it delicious?" He puts his arm around my bare shoulders, and reluctantly, we start back. Somehow out here, suspended in a tapestry of blue, we're separate from reality.

"How are you and Jack, if you don't mind me asking?"

Ah, reality knocks. "Actually, this drowning incident transformed him somehow. He was confronted with death and walked away. Death has always been a siren for Jack. Do you understand?"

He stops walking and takes my hands. "More than you know." Moonlight washes his sculpted face, broad forehead, Roman nose, gaze as clear and mysterious as a crystal ball. He runs his fingertips over my temples and cheekbones, coming to rest on the pulse point under my jaw, and kisses me again . . . until I pull away.

When we get back, Jack is sitting by a single burning torch, painfully sober in the first dawn glow. When he sees us, he stands.

I try to relax my face, no trace of remorse.

"My wife was not included with the loan of my sleeping hut, Houdini."

Conflicted between Magic's kiss and loyalty to Jack, my feet refuse to move, my thoughts as jumbled and violent as the waves crashing behind us. Need time to think.

"I saw Charmian's footprints leading to the ocean and worried for her safety," Houdini says. "I wouldn't want anything to happen to her after what she's been through."

Jack steps closer, arms clenched. "What do you mean by that?"

Houdini glances down at the doll, then back at Jack with troubled eyes. "I came to Hawaii to tell you it's not safe here. You should come back to the States before the US joins the war."

The tension in his voice alarms me.

Jack scoffs. "The war is halfway around the world."

"Squadrons of German cruisers are swarming the Pacific. You must have heard about the German attack at the Battle of Coronel off Chile? And the Battle of the Falkland Islands?"

Jack fumbles in his pocket for cigarettes and lighter, his hand shaking.

"The Pacific Fleet is scouring the coasts to prevent German occupation in the Pacific. Hawaii is a prime target. Why do you think they've installed a long-distance radio station at Pearl Harbor to transmit messages to Washington?"

"We're joining the war?" Jack asks.

"Looks that way. President Wilson demanded a peace conference, and Germany answered with vicious attacks on Russia and France."

I clear my throat. "How much time do we have?"

"No one's saying. But once this thing starts, there'll be no travel between Hawaii and the mainland."

Jack rubs the back of his neck, inhales his cigarette. "I'll book passage." He shakes Houdini's hand. "I should thank you for this and for bringing Charmian back safely."

Houdini turns to me with brows drawn together. "I'm leaving in the morning, so this is goodbye. You'll be all right, then?"

I put my arm through Jack's. "Say hello to Bessie, won't you? And don't forget to take her the doll."

He holds up Victoria Woodhull, grass skirt and all. "She'll be thrilled to have her back."

Magic turns and walks off, his footsteps washed away with the next wave.

In the morning, I find another thin package wrapped in *M-U-M* pages slipped under my door. The special shorthand spirals counterclockwise: "The danger of love runs deep."

*Danger* is the operative word. Moonlight on his face, his touch, his lips on mine . . . Magic startles me from complacency. Awakens my dulled senses. Reminds me that I am alive and this is *my* life.

Hearing voices on the lanai brings me back to reality.

"The steamer leaves tomorrow, last one this week," Jack says.

Nakata stares blankly into the shiny surface of the coffeepot.

"You got tickets, then?" I sit down, breathing in the morning bloom of hibiscus and plumeria, trying to calm myself. "May I have some coffee, Nakata? I'll need a lot this morning."

*"Mochiron."* He pours it and hands it to me. Black. I look around for cream and sugar.

"Blech—" Jack makes a face, and puts his coffee down. "What is wrong with you, Nakata? You know I don't take cream and sugar."

Nakata steps back, looks from one to the other, then squares his narrow shoulders. "I am staying here on the island."

Jack shakes his head. "I didn't mean to yell at you. I'm all riled up about the trip."

"It's not that, Mr. Jack. I'm going to be a dentist, get married, have a family."

"What's this?" I say. His announcement shocks me.

"Of course you want a family," Jack says. "We'll find you a nice Oriental girl in Glen Ellen, won't we, Charmian?" He looks at me, and I rack my brain. What Japanese girls are there in Glen Ellen?

"I am already betrothed." Nakata's complexion glistens.

Kukalani brings a basket of malasadas from the cookhouse. I'll miss those, too.

Jack watches her put them on the table. Her eyes catch his. Sadness. Longing. I am not sorry to extract Jack from their little crush. Kukalani's hips sway with the fragrant breeze as she returns to the cookhouse. Nakata turns to follow her.

"You can't quit. I won't have it," Jack says. "You're part of our family, isn't he, Charmian?"

I'd be lying to agree. Nakata serves us well, but we've never even shared a meal.

"I am sorry, Mr. Jack. But I have made up my mind. My betrothed is *hāpai*." The poor man turns crimson.

The word takes a moment to permeate my brain, and when it does, I'm shocked all over again. "*Hāpai* is Hawaiian for 'pregnant.' Oh my, Nakata, that's wonderful news. You'll be a father. Who's the lucky wahine?"

His eyelids flutter strangely, and he stares at his feet. "Kukalani. The wahine is Kukalani."

Jack's cigarette drops to his lap, the ash smoldering on his kimono. A phlegmy cough racks his chest. He's choking. I grab my black coffee and put it to his lips.

"Drink this, Jack. It will help."

He shakes his head, but I force liquid down his throat, which triggers more coughing.

Nakata watches us with pupils as hard as obsidian. "Kukalani is a good girl."

Jack's cough dredges deep in his lungs, rough and hacking.

"Nakata, can you bring us some water?" I ask.

But he's gone.

# 18

## The Pacific Ocean
## June 1916

*Keep a notebook. Travel with it, eat with it, sleep with it. Slap into it every stray thought that flutters up into your brain. Cheap paper is less perishable than gray matter, and lead pencil markings endure longer than memory.*

*And work. Spell it in capital letters. WORK. WORK all the time. Find out about this earth, this universe; this force and matter, and the spirit that glimmers up through force and matter from the maggot to Godhead. And by all this I mean WORK for a philosophy of life. It does not hurt how wrong your philosophy of life may be, so long as you have one and have it well.*

—*Jack London,* No Mentor but Myself

Twenty-nine days from Hawaii to San Francisco Bay. Twenty-nine querulous days and sleepless nights as I plot for peace between us.

Jack's restless mind devours every philosophy book on the steamer. He chews them up and builds an arsenal of acerbic weapons with which to assault the innocent passenger who thinks it amusing to spar with Jack London.

"I assert with Hobbes that it is impossible to separate thought from the matter that thinks. I assert with Bacon that all human understanding arises from the world of sensations. I assert with Kant the mechanical origin of the universe and that creation is a natural and historical process. I assert with Laplace that there is no need of hypothesis of a creator. And finally, because of the foregoing, I assert form is ephemeral. Form passes, therefore we pass."

Celebrity chasers who pay tribute with an oft-quoted passage from *White Fang* or *The Call of the Wild*, Jack tracks like rabbits in his crosshairs. Over several rounds of drinks, he teases out their intellect, then eviscerates them with his razor-sharp tongue, leaving them ragged and breathless. I make countless excuses to retreat to our cabin, a reprieve his prey never argues. Once we are safely behind closed doors, Jack lights yet another Imperial and gloats.

"Why should I write when no one understands how to think? *Martin Eden* and *The Sea-Wolf* were protests against the philosophy of Nietzsche, following individualism to its inevitable conclusion: war against democracy and Socialism. The World War is a direct result of Nietzschean philosophy. Can't they understand that?"

"I thought you were for this war."

His head tips back and blows hot smoke to the ceiling. "This war is fought to determine whether or not men can depend upon the word, the pledge, the agreement, the contract. Civilization is going through a Pentecostal cleansing that can result only in good for mankind."

He quotes himself as often as he does his philosophers. I smile sheepishly and call the cabin man to bring our tea, missing Nakata for more than his efficient service, more than his inscrutable proverbs. He was an anchor on our stormy sea.

Sometimes I fall into a gaping pit of questions . . . Nakata, Kukalani, Houdini? Questions that beget more questions until I feel a migraine pulsing behind my eyes. I'll think about that later. Much later. Or not at all.

"What is it? Spit it out, Charmian. What are you thinking?" Jack says, tiny new veins spidering his cheeks.

The cabin boy sets tea on the table, and Jack makes a face. He wants another martini, his teetotalism long forgotten. I tip the cabin boy and lock the door.

"I am thinking that if we argue any more about the war, Doc Thompson will have my head when he takes your blood pressure next." It's reached an all-time high. Loosening his sailor-blue tie, I start to unbutton his shirt. "I'm thinking a grand lolly would blow off some steam." A quiver of anticipation. I undo more buttons.

My hands reach down, loosening his shirttails from his linen trousers. I'm growing warm, my skin tingling, longing to feel Jack's hands on me.

He leans back. "Charmian, can you take a note? You've sparked a story in me."

"Now?" Reluctantly, I grab a notepad and pencil.

"There is an ecstasy that marks the summit of life and beyond which life cannot rise." He says. "Are you getting this?"

His words devastate me. They're brilliant, but I wonder when he'll realize they come from *The Call of the Wild*.

Jack's sister stands at the end of the Sausalito ferry dock, sturdy body swathed in her calico farm dress, a straw hat shielding her eyes. When Eliza sees us, she waves her hat, and her sun-hardened skin breaks into a wide smile.

I walk down the gangplank, and she pulls me to her bountiful bosom. Sighing deeply, I listen to her steady breath, synchronizing my own with hers, and relax for the first time in months. Eliza is the missing wheel on our wheelbarrow. Jack leads the way, of course, and Eliza and I balance the load. I just hope her sunny face will lift him from his rancorous mood.

"You've lost weight, Charmian, I feel your ribs." She holds me out for a once-over.

"Missed your pot roast and apple pie." My voice breaks, and I swallow to cover it up. Her smile dissolves when she sees Jack. Bloated and jaundiced, he hobbles down the gangplank with a koa-wood cane.

Eliza hugs Jack, and color springs to his cheeks. He'll be fine now. He's always better flanked by Eliza and me to manage his overblown life. I just hope Eliza has the sense not to tell him all the ranch problems right away. I am not up to it. The journey from Hawaii has me frayed and tired. So tired.

Porters load our trunks into the back of Eliza's dilapidated ranch truck. With its worn spoke wheels and box engine, I can't believe it made it the fifty miles here. The three of us squeeze into the front seat. Eliza drives, and Jack peppers her with questions about the ranch.

Fog pours in from the Pacific and obscures my backward glance toward San Quentin . . . I almost see a tugboat landing there, Houdini emerging in his flapping cape, exchanging prisoners in their cells . . .

"The neighbors are suing us for water rights," Eliza says. "No use trying to keep it secret since there's a hearing next week."

"Ridiculous," Jack says. "The dam barely affects them, and the eucalyptus will die without that water."

"It's thick as potato soup out here." Eliza peers through the fog, trying to see the winding road, lips pressed white.

"The only property that uses that creek is Wake Robin," I say, biting my cuticle. "It's Aunt Netta, isn't it?" Her grimace tells me I'm right. "But how can she dispute riparian rights? Wake Robin is part of Beauty Ranch now."

"She's disputing that, too. She's selling Wake Robin."

A dull ache pulses at the base of my brain. Aunt Netta's ache. The ache of love with conditions. As long as I follow Netta's expectations, she's fine. Cross the line, and she demands revenge.

Eliza gives Jack a rundown on the livestock, horses, orchards, and eucalyptus while I watch the ancient redwoods of Marin give way to the green hills of Petaluma, a pointillist painting of orange poppies among the dairy cows.

As much as Netta's a thorn in my side, if it weren't for her, I wouldn't have learned to type at the speed of spoken word and play piano in a fashion that bring tears to grown men. I wouldn't have danced at cotillion and learned fine manners at finishing school. I wouldn't have become the editorial assistant at the *Overland Monthly*. And I wouldn't have stolen the young Jack London.

Aunt Netta used my inheritance to fund our household until I turned of age. When I married Jack, I was astonished to discover how adorably medieval he was in matters financial. Having been independent, I expected a separate bank account, but he insisted we merge finances under his control. By then his income so far exceeded my small inheritance it seemed silly to protest.

And we've been generous with Aunt Netta, always giving her money. When her debt got too deep, I bailed her out and transferred the deed to my name, and let Netta and Edward live there.

Now Netta wants the deed back, and knowing her, I expect she'll do whatever it takes.

My bitten cuticle is bleeding now, something she always chastised me for.

Jack takes my hand and rubs my knuckles. "Don't worry, Charmian. I'll handle Netta."

A week later I awake to Jack standing over my bed, bright sunlight streaming in my paned windows. Our new houseboy, Sekine, sets down a tray of scrambled eggs, buttered toast, and French 75 cocktails. The young man bows and backs out of the door. I have to tell him that's not necessary.

Jack hands me the drink. "We're celebrating." His face is lit with the fever of winning one of his debates. "It's done. Riparian rights are ours, as they always have been." He snorts. "Oh, Netta threw her bustle at it, the old girl made a good effort. But all her charms could not compete with the water commissioner's stamp of approval."

I sip the French 75 and make a face.

Jack drains his glass. "Ahh!"

"You shouldn't be coating your stomach with gin in the morning." My voice sounds like gravel in the rototiller.

He laughs and slaps his knee. "It's half past ten, Charmian. The hearing was at nine."

"I stayed up late editing a draft of *Our Hawaii*." I sip again and feel the champagne and gin loosen the bands of tension around my brain. "Why didn't you wake me?"

"I know how much it bothered you, so Eliza and I took care of it." He says. "Eat your eggs, they're getting cold."

"How'd you convince her?" I take a bite of eggs, suddenly starved.

Eliza comes in from the garden, wiping her boots on the rug.

He grimaces. "We paid her off."

I swallow hard. "How much?"

"Too much." Eliza clucks her tongue. "Now that you emptied our ranch account, where am I supposed to get the money to keep us afloat?"

"I guess I could do another gully-fluff serial," Jack says.

"You swore you'd never write another one of those," I say.

Eliza hangs her hat on a hook in the hallway. "Better figure something out fast. Everyone expects to be paid first of the month, and you've got construction bills from the new wine cellar, and the feed store—that's a big one this month."

"I could call Macmillan for an advance on royalties."

"We already got an advance down in Hawaii," I tell Jack. "George Brett is tired of hearing from me."

"Still time to change your mind on the state fair," Eliza said. "The quality of our Shires is unsurpassed. Neuadd Hillside would take first prize, hands down. And if we placed a steer, we could live a month on prize money alone, let alone the reputation we'd build for our cattle and horses."

"You know how I feel about going commercial." Jack purses his mouth.

"The state fair sounds fun," I say. "I haven't been since I was a girl."

"We're not showing at the state fair," he says. "Now, can we get to writing?"

# 19

## The Red Moon
## Valley of the Moon, California
## August 1916

*What did you have in you?—some childish notions, a few half-baked sentiments, a lot of undigested beauty, a great black mass of ignorance, a heart filled to bursting with love, and an ambition as big as your love and as futile as your ignorance.*

—*Jack London,* Martin Eden

Jack doesn't let finances stop him. He asks Eliza to start construction of a new stone barn for the horses and to develop plans for a school and a general store for the ranch staff. He orders more redwood logs felled and cured to raise his beloved Wolf House once again.

One night after supper, Jack settles into the parlor, lighting a cigarette and opening the top volume of his pile of books.

"I could use a hand in here," Eliza says to me, picking up the serving plates and heading to the kitchen.

"Come have a brandy with us, Eliza," I say. "Manyoungi will do that."

She throws me a withering look. "I had to let him go when Jack bought the Kohler and Frohling Ranch."

"He bought another ranch?" A frisson of shock grips my neck. "We couldn't even afford Christmas presents last year."

"Nine hundred acres." Eliza pushes open the kitchen door with her ample hip.

I grab the plates. Jack's moved green beans from one side of his plate to the other, mashed his scalloped potatoes with his fork. Ham's cold and untouched. I push through the door and dump the mess into the garbage before Eliza sees the evidence, then slip the plates into soapy water.

"He's not eating." She hands me a dish towel to dry. "You have to make him eat when he drinks."

A bitter laugh blurts from my gut. "You know there's no making Jack do anything."

She adds more boiling water to the sudsy sink, her rimless glasses steamed white. "Our Jack has not returned to us." Not bothering to clear her lenses she plunges her hands into the steaming suds and scrubs a pan. "What happened in Hawaii to get him so riled up?"

I dry a plate carefully, choosing my words. Jack's her younger brother and hero, her loyalty fierce and deep. "You know Jack. We wrote and swam. Wrote and drank. Wrote and ate taro poi, and after that . . . we wrote," I tell her. "How bad is our debt?"

"We don't need servants." She clucks her tongue. "He never needed servants with Elizabeth, she did all the work herself."

"I think our Jack has grown used to the comforts his royalties bring," I say lightly, polishing the last glass.

Eliza hands me a hot pie pan to dry, which burns my fingertips. "He only got servants because you were a society woman and he wanted to impress you."

"Where did you get that idea, Eliza? I was a secretary and editor." I put the pie pan away in the cupboard.

She hands me a glass pitcher. "Convince him to let us show the Shires at the state fair. We'll take grand prize. Then I can stud them out and make a mint." Her eyes glint behind fogged lenses. "I can show the bulls, too, and sell them off for beef. Ranchers all over the West will chomp at the bit to get their hands on Jack London's cattle."

My heart feels heavy in my chest. "Jack will never go for it."

"Then he'll lose all he holds dear in this world." Eliza's voice catches, and she leans back, eyes clamped closed, soapy knuckles gripping the kitchen sink.

It's too much for Eliza. Managing the ranch, a hundred ranch hands, vegetable fields, orchards, vineyards, winery, olive groves, cattle, horses . . . pigs, for God's sake.

The realization stuns me. We are sisters in this. Extensions of Jack. Keeping his dreams alive and thriving.

I cover her clenching fist with my hand. "When is the state fair, Eliza?"

"End of September."

"Make the arrangements. I'll handle Jack."

"We have to go to New York to find a new publisher," Jack says while I'm typing. "I deserve more money for my novels. Doubleday pays three thousand up front, and five percent on copies sold."

This new novel is called *Cherry*, a tragic tale of a Japanese girl trying to find her identity in the white world, helped by an older Caucasian man who loves her despite the color of her skin.

I get up from my chair, leaving his last sentence unfinished on the typewriter. "I'm not going to New York."

"Of course you are, Charmian. Everyone's charmed by you."

"I'm staying here. Finishing *Our Hawaii*."

He shakes his head. "I need your help in New York. It will be fun. We'll go to the Landmark Tavern, stay at the Waldorf, see the Houdinis if you want."

Houdini hasn't sent a puzzle or even a letter since Hawaii. My mind leaps back to that last night on the beach, savoring the feeling of his arms around me . . . Until I pulled away and came back to Jack.

"Pack all your most beautiful things for New York." Jack grasps my shoulders, and I see my chance.

"I'll go with you, after we go to the state fair," I bargain.

Wincing, he pours sherry from a carafe. "You've been talking to Eliza."

"She needs this. Beauty Ranch needs this. We'll sweep the state fair. Then I'll go to New York with you."

He looks out to the paddock. Luke leads Neuadd around the arena, his large feet flashing and stomping.

"Will Neuadd Hillside be any more glorious if they pin a blue ribbon on him?" he says.

I take his hand, and he withdraws it, punching me in the arm. "I'll box you for it." He grins devilishly. "I win and we go to New York. You win and we go to the state fair first." He shoves a chair out of the way with a screech.

*First*, he says. Meaning we're going to New York whether I want to or not. I put up my dukes, circling playfully. I cut an upper right to his jaw, expecting him to block me as he has in the past. But my knuckles meet his jawbone square.

I hear a pop, and a pain shoots down my arm. "Ow. Oh. Uncle! Uncle!" I hop around holding my shoulder.

Jack's denture plate dangles from his gaping mouth, his eyes dazed. His finger chalks up a mark in the air. "One for the Lady-Boy."

Eliza pokes her head in from the hallway, a dustrag in her hand. "What in the world is going on with you two?"

Jack replaces his denture and smiles endearingly. "Charmian won the boxing match. We're going to the state fair."

The three of us laugh till our stomachs ache, so damn good. We should laugh more.

# 20

## Horse Tail Moon
## Sacramento, California
## September 1916

*He was too far removed. Too many thousands of opened books yawned between them and him. He had exiled himself. He had traveled in the vast realm of intellect until he could no longer return home.*

*—Jack London,* Martin Eden

Three things should never be suffered together: Sacramento heat in September, the smell of livestock in Sacramento heat in September, and Jack's irascible mood with the smell of livestock in Sacramento heat in September.

"How much will Neuadd stud out for if he wins?" Jack strokes the stallion's broad black chest, while I help Eliza brush his white feathered ankles. George Sterling watches with unconcealed disdain, his wide-brimmed bandito hat a flagrant mockery of the ranchers.

"A few hundred, anyway." Eliza's curry hits a stubborn knot of horse hair, and she tugs through it. "Last year, the grand champion mare sold for twenty-six hundred dollars."

"I'll never sell Neuadd," Jack says.

"I'd sell my wife for twenty-six hundred," Sterling says.

Jack throws back his head in a great guffaw I could listen to all day.

"Don't give Jack any ideas," I say.

"I'd never let go of you, Mate-Woman. It was hard enough when Eliza sold a litter of piglets."

"Jeez, thanks."

Eliza points out an official-looking group of men studying horses with clipboards and pencils. "Jack, go shake hands with the judges over there. We might just sweep the field."

"I certainly will." He smiles, but his face is way too ruddy. I need to take his blood pressure.

"Now if we can only survive the heat." Eliza swipes her forehead with the back of her hand. "One hundred and ten in the shade."

"I'm trying to see the state fair as you see it, Wolf," Sterling says, surveying the fair tent. "For all your pride of soil and animals, all I see is dust and horseshit." He fans his goatee with the *Overland Monthly*. "You and I could be tucked up under the redwoods at the Bohemian Club or sipping Pinot on the Russian River."

Jack tilts his chin down and frowns. "Agriculture means more to me than any story I've written, yet you give it no credit."

Sterling sniffs. "I have no interest in agriculture."

"That's because it's real, Greek. And you live on lofty ideals and make-believe."

"Let's go check into the hotel and cool down," I say, trying to end their bickering. "See you later, Eliza. Good luck with the animals."

"Same to you, dear." She winks and pats my arm.

Sterling helps us carry bags to our second-floor room, pulsing with heat. The wall thermometer has burst from the heat, spattering silver mercury and shards of glass. Flowered wallpaper curls down at the corners. The one narrow window has been painted shut. Sterling breaks the seal with the letter opener, and together we shove the window up. I hang my head out and see the California State Fair archway below, proudly painted in yellow and red, hordes of folks going through. The sun's relentless rays bounce off the dusty ground and waver into the still air.

"Mate-Woman, help me put my feet up, will you?" Jack collapses on the brass bed, and the coils squeak and groan.

I pull off his boots, and his feet are as red and swollen as tomato pincushions. "I'll have them bring ice." I pick up the candlestick telephone, but it just rings and rings. "We'll play pinochle until the sun goes down; then we'll check back on Eliza and the animals."

"Tell them to call me a doctor." Jack groans. "I need something for my feet. They're burning like sausages on the grill."

"You're on kidney and rheumatoid medicines already." I jiggle the cradle, but still no answer. "We can't get another doctor involved. Too risky. Especially with your heart."

"What about my heart?"

I look away. Doc said that his ankles swell when his heart's not pumping like it should.

"That stench would stop anyone's heart." Sterling holds his nose.

I don't ask if he means Jack's feet or the stink of livestock below.

"Damn it all, Greek." Jack grimaces. "You didn't have to come."

"You asked me to." Sterling plants his boot on the brass footboard.

"I want you to see me as I really am."

Someone finally picks up the call.

"This is Mrs. London. Can someone bring up a big bowl of ice and a fan, please?"

"I worship at your feet, Wolf," Sterling says. "I would die to have your reputation with American readers . . ."

"I don't care about writing," Jack wails, his face red as his feet. "The difference between us is that you live to write, and I write to live."

Sterling flaps his arms like a chicken, trying to cool the armpits of his rumpled linen jacket. "You're just as spoiled as your character Martin Eden, a Socialist grown too big for his britches."

"You still don't see, Greek." Jack's lips purse, then press together, crossly working his denture plate. "Martin Eden was no Socialist. He's an individualist of the extreme Nietzschean type."

"'I see,' says the blind man." Sterling runs fingers through his long gray strands. "I thought we could mend fences here, as you farmers say. I was willing to bear witness to your agrarian dream and cheer you on with your fistful of blue ribbons. But I see you've grown too full of yourself. Too busy making movies in Hollywood, surfing in Hawaii, bedding women in every port." He snorts. "Oh, I'm sorry. Doesn't Charmian know? I forgot, the Londons don't live by the same rules as ordinary folk." He grabs his bandito hat. "You two can sizzle here in Cow Town without me."

"As if you never broke a rule or two." His exaggeration and lies irk me. "Jack's in pain. It's hot. We're all hot. Soon the ice and fan will be here, and we'll be fine."

Sterling walks toward the door.

"I'll order two fans," I say. "And martinis. Pitchers and pitchers of icy martinis." Anything to bring peace.

"Poor, pitiful Greek." Jack lights an Imperial. "The poet who struggles for his art and never makes it. Can I tell you why?"

Sterling turns around. "Educate me, oh wise one."

"You don't bleed, Greek." Jack blows smoke at him. "You piddle around the page, painting fluffy images of clouds and sunsets and call it art. It doesn't move people. Readers want to wade in the dark muck of the soul. They want the broken dreams, star-crossed lovers, suicide as a perfect ending to a meaningless life." He sucks smoke into his lungs. "You, dear Greek, are a coward. Too afraid to face the ugly truth, or too stupid to see it."

Sterling turns away, and I grab his wrist. "Jack, you don't mean that."

"Let the bastard go." He waves his cigarette like a scepter.

Sterling jerks his wrist free and walks out.

"Charmian, call for a doctor." Jack doubles over, writhing and moaning.

We never get out of the room that night or for the rest of the fair. Jack is either flat on his back or balled up in pain. But he insists I watch from the window and tell him every detail: the dust devils swirling around the tents, the apple-cheeked pride of the 4-H clubbers, the smell of roasted corn on the cob. If I'm lazy, he has me describe it again. The horseflies, the leather chaps, the searing branding iron, the scream of burning flesh.

When the fair closes, Eliza appears at our hotel room, bearing a gleaming trophy in one hand and a bouquet of ribbons in the other. I don't know how she found us, since I never had a chance to send a message, busy as I was with doctors and keeping Jack as comfortable as possible while the kidney stones pass. If there's a hell, it must feel like a kidney stone.

"What did the doctor say?" Eliza asks.

"We can't leave here until the stones pass and the swelling is down." I rub his swollen feet with eucalyptus oil.

He scrunches his nose and pushes his bed tray away. "A rabbit eats better." I set the tray of congealed scrambled eggs and bloody tomatoes out in the hallway, like I have most his meals since we came.

Eliza hands him the gleaming chalice. "Best of Show: Neuadd Hillside."

"You really did it." Jack squeezes her hand. "You said you would, and you did. I only wish I could have been there to see it."

Eliza's eyes mist over with pride. "Now you can build your grape-juice factory."

My heart jumps to my throat. "That's a good one, Eliza. You almost had me there."

"We'll make the best nonalcoholic grape juice anywhere," Jack says, beaming. "The cleanest sort of business, Mate-Woman." He runs his fingers over the ribbons, pausing to read each one with a boyish smile. Then he starts coughing, congested and heaving.

When the fit subsides, Jack is exhausted and falls asleep, wheezing strangely. I tell Eliza to take the animals back to Beauty Ranch without us. We'll join her soon as we can.

The doctor warns Jack off cigarettes and martinis, but Jack turns the tables on him: Booze or cigarettes, Doc? Not both. The doctor chooses alcohol as the worse of two evils and prescribes bedrest without cocktails.

We start writing *Hearts of Three* in the mornings, a novel based on a movie script by Charles Goddard of *Perils of Pauline* fame. Goddard writes screenplays with the ease of a short-order cook flipping hotcakes, and Jack takes his batter and cooks up an entertaining novel.

"I should never have agreed to write this bull puckey," he says. "Reduced to writing comic books, and there's not a humorous thought in my head."

He depends on me now more than ever. When I stand for a bathroom break or glass of water, his hand reaches for mine like a lost child. "I wish you knew how much you mean to me."

His neediness touches the part of me that needs him to need me. But this new level of desperation drains me. I've been here for him, haven't I? Acting the role of Saxon Roberts, the rural goddess in *The Valley of the Moon*, or the glamorous *Little Lady of the Big House* whose heart is torn in two. But who am I beyond Jack's heroines?

When I met young Jack at twenty, he spun his own image of me: suffragette, free lover, independent business woman, and heiress. Jack is the tornado, and I am the vortex that keeps him swirling. The empty eye of the storm. Nothing without Jack.

When the Sacramento hotel room heats up in the afternoons, I rub his ankles with ice, and we play pinochle or cribbage. Later, while he's napping, I brave the 115 degrees outside to find fresh fruit, apple pies, and the pralines he so loves. Anything to keep him from eating the toothsome flesh pots Doc says will kill him. Oh, and Imperials. My own lungs feel sluggish with tar.

Besides Jack's engorged feet, his joints throb with rheumatism, and kidney stones leave him shrieking with agony. When the wave of pain passes, he says, "At least if I'm crippled, I'll have more time to do all the reading I want. I'll be the happiest crippled fellow ever to come down the pike."

The Great War eats at him more than his maladies.

"Those stupid, brutal Huns." Jack tosses the *Sacramento Bee* in the corner. "They executed that nurse Edith Cavell."

"I thought Great Britain would save her." Edith Cavell harbored Allied soldiers in her home and arranged escapes to England. More than two hundred soldiers in all. "Why doesn't President Wilson step in?"

"Wilson won the election on a 'no war' platform." He lights a cigarette, bites off the tip, and spits it out. "Ahhgrg. The world is insane." He stamps out the cigarette in the ashtray and lights another.

I hand him a glass of orange juice. "It's no good getting so riled up. You can't do anything about it here."

"The hell I can't. Take this down, will you?"

I sit at my Remington and type his bitter words.

"Man devoted himself to the invention of killing devices before he discovered fire or manufactured for himself religion. And to this day, his finest creative energy and technical skill are devoted to the same old task of making better and ever better killing weapons. All his days, down all the past, have been spent in killing . . ."

We continue this wretched course for hours, as Jack funnels his anger into a new novel, *The Human Drift*. Though I hate what Jack is saying about the innate cruelty of the human race, I have to admit, it rings true.

Another scorching week passes before the doctor approves our trip home. I round up an old truck for fifty dollars and load our belongings in the back.

Since Jack's ankles still won't hold his weight, he slings his arm around my shoulders, and we struggle down two flights of stairs. When I see daylight through the front door of the hotel, I nearly faint with relief.

Jack leans against the doorjamb, huffing and sweating. He looks askance at the rusted white truck, left wheel veering off center, leather seats blistered and shredding from the sun. It seemed better when I bought it.

"Brilliant, Mate," Jack says. "We can always use another truck on the ranch." Color bursts on his cheeks like poppies in springtime. Fever or good spirits?

"Let's take her home, then," I say, and help him in the passenger side. He's never driven, save farm tractors and his joyride with Houdini at the Panama-Pacific.

I'm like a horse headed for the barn, foot heavy on the accelerator, down the dirt-and-gravel road. The truck shimmies and veers to the left, but with any luck, we'll be home for Eliza's Sunday supper.

We open the windows for the hot, dry breeze. Apple and plum orchards scent the air. Tanned field workers sing bolero and harvest fruit in wood-slatted baskets. Such a natural, simple life.

"God doesn't love the farmer." Jack shakes his head.

"What do you mean?"

"These poor devils are scrambling to pull in the crop before it's eaten by grasshoppers or rotted in the sun. They're fighting for their lives."

Now I see millions of insects hopping from the ground, flying, clinging to anything they land on. So that's the buzzing in my ears. Jack always sees the gritty detail.

"I'll book us passage on the transcontinental to New York," he says. "I have to wrangle more money from Macmillan or find another publisher. Do they take me for a dupe?"

"Macmillan has been good to you," I say. "Not like the movie studios." His trust has been ruined by their lies and shady dealings. They've paid pennies on dollars promised. Jack's films are pulling in record audiences, but unforeseen expenses always rob us of the profits, and Beauty Ranch eats through his income like a caterpillar on spring leaves.

Jack's fist hits the dashboard, and he turns away.

I grab his shirtsleeve, but he won't face me. "You don't have to work so hard." His shoulders are heaving, and I tug harder. "Not for me. Not for anyone."

"Watch out!" he yells, and jerks the steering wheel hard right into the field, but at least we miss the car that pulled out into the road. The truck's shimmy turns violent. Jack grips the wheel, holds us steady. But the wayward wheel flies into the grapevines, and the truck falls to the side. My head snaps forward and thwacks against the steering wheel. Flash of lightning. Bolts of pain. Pounding of pahu drums.

"Charmian." Jack's voice calls from the distance. He shakes my arm, and I pull away, fearful. Fearful of the dark waves, water pressing around me, Jack pulling me underwater. My drumming heartbeat.

"Charmian, stay with me." Jack pats my cheek, and my teeth clack together, chattering. My eyelids open. Pain. Too much light. Blurred with blood.

Jack and another man lift me out of the truck, now lying on its side. "You scared me for a second."

I gulp for breath. Not water, just air. "Where are we?"

"Past Vacaville."

"They think they can fix the wheel. We can rest in the saloon."

He holds me tight, and we limp to a shack on the side of the road, a backdrop of rolling hills of vineyards dotted with oaks.

The bar is packed with farmers and field hands sitting at wood tables, playing poker.

"On the house." The bartender brings us double shots of whiskey, which I push aside.

"Water, please," I rasp. My throat is so dry.

Jack downs both doubles.

"You shouldn't drink," I say.

"You were barely breathing," he says, and asks for another drink. "No matter how I tried to bring you around, you just lay there, like you were floating."

My vision blurs, and I hear only the throb of my heart. Underwater again.

Jack takes my cheek in his hand. "Yours is the only face my eyes must see. I surrender to you, you are the only one."

My eyes flutter back, stars on the ceiling.

He kisses my lips too hard. "I mean it, Mate-Woman. I would do anything for you."

I try to focus on his eyes, large and doleful. "Get the truck fixed, and let's get out of here."

"They gave us the room upstairs. We can rest and leave in the—"

I lift my head. "I. Want. To. Go. Home." I rise from the bar, steer through the men to the washroom, and splash water on my face until I'm alert. Get me home.

# 21

## Napa Valley, California
## October 1916

*I ride over my beautiful ranch. Between my legs is a beautiful horse. The air is wine. The grapes on a score of rolling hills are red with autumn flame. Across Sonoma Mountain, wisps of sea fog are stealing. The afternoon sun smolders in the drowsy sky. I have everything to make me glad I am alive.*

—*Jack London,* John Barleycorn

By the time they fix our axle, it's twilight. We climb in the truck and head out on the road. Soon Jack is snoring sweetly. I'm almost thankful for the whiskey.

As daylight fades, I lean forward, straining my eyes. I can barely make out the dirt road with the dim headlights of the truck. The undulating Mayacama Mountains trick me to following one road, then another. I turn onto a graded road, but it peters out in the middle of a vineyard. I curse under my breath, not wanting to wake Jack. The engine idles and dies. The chirp of crickets comforts me.

I look for the North Star, bright and blinking, to determine which way is west. Home.

Jack sleeps beside me, rhythmic and peaceful. I lay my head on his shoulder. His breath brushes my head, soothing as only his breath can be. His rhythm relaxes the tension in my neck and shoulders. As I marvel at the majestic sky above me, my beatitudes appear. Gentle souls drift across the stars, untethered by gravity or reality. How wonderful to roam the universe with free rein.

I wish I could share this moment with Jack. A phrase from *The Star Rover* flows through me. "I was bound on vast adventure, where, at the end, I would find all the cosmic formulae and have made clear to me the ultimate secret of the universe . . ."

A billion pinpoints of light gleam in the velvet cosmos. And Jack and I are but two specks on a planet that rotates around one of those pinpoints . . . It soothes me to think about our troubles . . . My eyelids flutter . . . Troubles are not so important compared to . . . the universe. I close my eyes and drift off.

The burning rim of sunrise lights the valley oak with its veil of Spanish moss. A bantam rooster crows. Must be about six thirty, I suppose. Sekine will be brewing coffee. The tall wood gates of Beauty Ranch welcome us, such as we are after last night.

When we'd left for the state fair in September, all the grapevines were vibrant green. Now in October they are turning bright gold and crimson. How surely time passes and things change without our notice. Hours change to days, and months to years.

I drive up to the cottage and cut the engine. Jack is propped against the truck door, snoring. I hope his binge won't set back his kidneys. The horse barn is lit up like Christmas. I let Jack sleep and go over to see what's happening.

Eliza and Sekine are kneeling over Neuadd Hillside, who is lying on the straw. Luke stands across from them, holding his hat in his hand. The stallion's ribs are barely moving.

Eliza's shoulders shake when she sees me, and I put my arm around her.

"What's wrong with Neuadd?" Jack says from the barn door and limps forward. No one answers.

"What's wrong with Neuadd?" Stumbling on straw, he roars like a bear in a trap. "Somebody tell me what's going on."

Eliza lifts her head. "Neuadd couldn't take the heat in Sacramento."

"Damn you, Eliza." Jack's eyes burn. "I told you it wasn't good to work him so hard for the fair, but you wouldn't listen." He steps toward her, and I grab his arm.

"Let's go inside, Jack. They're doing everything they can."

"Step aside, Charmian. You are not without guilt in this." He kneels beside the stallion, stroking his flank. "Get out of here. All of you. Leave me alone with my boy."

The three of them leave the barn, and I follow, turning back at the door.

Jack lays his cheek against Neuadd Hillside's chest, stroking his heaving ribs. His face trembles, then he collapses in a sobbing heap.

I once took a photograph of the two of them riding on the ridge overlooking Sonoma Valley, stallion and master, so natural and noble. That's what I want to remember.

# 22

## Beauty Ranch, Glen Ellen, California
## November 1916

*. . . He might have epitomized life as a voracious appetite, and the world as a place wherein ranged a multitude of appetites, pursuing and being pursued, hunting and being hunted, eating and being eaten, all in blindness and confusion, with violence and disorder, a chaos of gluttony and slaughter, ruled over by chance, merciless, planless, endless.*

*—Jack London,* White Fang

I get to Jack's studio early, excited about the day, our tenth anniversary. Imagine that.

A letter lies open on his ottoman by the fire. I recognize the florid penmanship on watermarked stationery. Sophie Loeb, the reporter. The woman lures Jack away every time we go to New York.

"My Dear Wolf . . ." The purple ink flows. She asks Jack to cover the World Series for her newspaper. I start to fold the letter, when the last lines catch my attention.

> "I saw a star last night—a new star—like no other yet discovered.

I will give you three guesses as to what I named it.

As ever,

Star"

My hands go numb. If he wants Sophie Loeb after all we've shared, then go. Maybe she can make Jack pant and moan like I used to.

I hear his footsteps in the hallway, and I toss the missive in the fire, burning my fingers.

This morning we're working on *The Turtles of Tasman*, which he wants to finish before we go to New York. But Jack's having trouble articulating his thoughts, which only increases his agitation.

"I'd rather sing one wild song and burst my heart with it"—he walks over to his bed—"than live a thousand years watching my digestion and being afraid of the wet."

The analogy sounds weak to me. I'll rework it later.

"Let me read you this Jung quote that kept me up last night." He pulls out a matchstick used to mark his place. "Ah, here it is. 'One should view with philosophic admiration the strange paths of the libido and should investigate the purposes of its circuitous ways.'" He thumps the book.

"Free love for all, then?" Sometimes a joke is the best I can muster when Jack launches into an intellectual tirade I don't feel up to. "Are we to be led blindly by the nose by our libido? Or do we, ourselves, decide whom to love?"

I pick up Houdini's latest puzzle, which finally arrived by post, wrapped in the usual *M-U-M* magazine pages. He hasn't forgotten me, nor I him. This puzzle is a smooth wooden cube, with no seams or cracks that my fingers can detect.

Jack furrows his brow. "Don't you see? The libido is the creative force that keeps us alive."

No doubt building a case for the affair he's planning in New York.

"Do you know what today is?" I smile the mysterious smile that indicates some deep understanding between us, though lately I don't understand anything. I'm tired.

His blue, blue eyes slide sideways. "Enlighten me."

"Our tenth anniversary." Walking behind him, I rub his shoulders. "I'm having a special dinner prepared for us." I lean down and nuzzle his neck.

He smiles, then frowns. "I didn't get you anything."

"You can make it up to me after dinner." I bought a red silk gown that will set a bonfire to his damp libido. "I thought we'd ride up Sonoma Mountain," I say. "A horseback ride to clear our lungs, Veuve Clicquot, and a shower together before dinner. I'll have Luke saddle up Rowdy for you." My words skip lightly, not wanting to bring Neuadd to mind.

"I didn't get much sleep last, staying up reading. I think I'll catch a few winks and rest up for the New York trip."

I rub a blister on my ring finger and glance at the fireplace. A corner of watermarked stationery with Sophie's purple penmanship smolders in the ashes.

I kiss his cheek. "Rest then, and I'll see you at dinner."

November is the dead month, the month when leaves of gold and orange turn brown and warm winds turn stiff and chafing. The Pomo Indians called it Kasi-Sa, cold begins.

The brisk air clears my head as I lead Maid up to the ridge. I need to look out from the bird's-eye view, where all is peaceful and clear. Squirrels scuttle under Maid's hooves, spooking her, and it's hard to keep her on the steep path.

The summit looks the same as ever when Jack and I have ridden up here for solace. I see forty miles to Mount Tamalpais, poking above the clouds over Marin. A fog bank rolls in over the bay. I can just make out the Richmond shore, a ferry navigating through patchy blue ripples.

Jack and I sailed these waters before we married. He would write while I skippered the boat, and when he finished his work, I played ukulele and sang. A bottle of gin and another of whiskey was all that filled his cupboard besides the Petaluma cheese and sourdough I brought on board. He said he'd never met a woman as game as me for adventure.

Did I think about Jack's wife, my friend Elizabeth, at home in Oakland with their family? Not as much as I should have. His brilliance and bravado mesmerized me, and I've been captive ever since.

I gaze out at the distant water and over to Sonoma Valley, golden hills blanketed with verdant oaks. I wait for peace to penetrate my heart. But none comes.

What to do about Sophie Loeb? I hug my shoulders, chin falling to my chest. Last trip to New York, Jack said he had a meeting, and I waited at the hotel. He didn't return for days. I lived through that once and swore I wouldn't do it again. His desperate grasping at straws belittles what we have together. His betrayal squeezes the air from my lungs.

When Maid and I return to the cottage, there are a couple of photographers taking pictures of Jack. He's sitting on the porch, white riding pants tucked in tall boots, red tie knotted at his neck, his Baden-Powell on his head—all dressed for riding, though he hasn't ridden a horse since Neuadd Hillside died.

"Good afternoon, gentlemen." I swing my leg around to dismount, and feisty Possum runs up to greet me. "What's all this?"

"Publicity photos for the studio," Jack says. "Come pose with me."

"You go ahead. I'll just scoot into the shower before dinner."

"Just a couple together." His fingertips draw me like a magnet.

"Of course, Mate." I stand beside him, and when he leans against me, I feel his body tremble. He's sick again but won't show it. I pull back my shoulders and smile for the cameras.

After a few shots by Jack's side, the cameraman waves me aside. "A few more of Mr. London alone. You don't mind, do you?" The photographer changes a plate of film.

I turn to Jack. "Need me to stay?" He nods.

"Ready when you are, Mr. London," the photographer prompts.

I stand back under the oaks, watching. A single lock of hair falls on Jack's forehead, wet with perspiration. His cheeks and neck are swollen with edema, his stomach distended. I'll have the doctor check him over before New York.

The photographer's flash goes off and immortalizes Jack's portrait in black and white. His body goes slack. His stare goes blank. A queer deadness sets in his expression.

"Jack, what is it?" I run to him.

He expels a stuttering breath smelling of bile. His skin is waxy and pallid.

The photographers rustle behind me.

I hold up my hand, shielding him from scrutiny. "That's it for today, gentlemen. I trust you can find your way out."

Nothing gives the illusion of youth like a red dress. The image in my cheval mirror agrees. The dress skims my toned body shamelessly. I daub lavender oil on my wrists and rub it behind my ears. Then I tuck the last of our garden roses around the crown of my head and study the effect, soft and romantic, perfect for tonight. But the lines at the outer corners of my eyes proclaim my age.

My chest whirrs with anticipation of our tenth anniversary celebration. We need this, Jack and me, a chance to enjoy each other without the tensions of other people or pressing business matters.

Sekine and I have been planning this dinner for more than a week. I miss Nakata. Oh, Sekine, with his tiny eyeglass frames over too-close pupils, is polite and attentive enough, but he never cracks a smile at my offhand jokes. He makes me feel demanding and cold.

In the parlor, Jack leans against the woven palm wallpaper and cannibal spears we brought back from Tahiti years ago. Sekine serves him a gin martini, splash of vermouth, a pimento olive. His color looks better. Sekine helped him bathe and dress in a fresh shirt and trousers.

"Don't you look the winning racehorse," I say, kissing him on the cheek and letting my mouth wander to his ear.

"Netta will be shocked by your behavior," he says, breath smelling of juniper.

I bite his earlobe with a playful snap of my teeth. "What does Aunt Netta have to do with our anniversary?"

"After she agreed to vote with us for damming the stream, I invited her to dinner."

"But not tonight." I trace his aquiline nose. "Sekine, please ring up Netta and tell her we're otherwise engaged tonight but we'd love to entertain her tomorrow."

His eyes slide to the washroom door in warning. The toilet flushes, and I feel my anniversary go down the drain.

Jack grimaces. "She says she has to speak to us about her vote. We'll hear what she has to say, then send her on her way."

He gulps the rest of the martini. "She can't reverse her vote or we'll lose the pond and the new eucalyptus grove."

"Damn the eucalyptus and damn Aunt Netta," I whisper. "It's our tenth anniversary and I've planned something." I slide my hand inside his shirt, and his broad chest rises under my touch. No matter how much he smokes and drinks, his chest still looks as if he does push-ups each morning.

He pecks my cheek. "We'll send her packing after dessert, I promise."

The juicy desire I nurtured earlier shrivels like grapes left too long on the vine. "Set an extra place, Sekine. I'll be there shortly," I say, and retreat to my sleeping porch.

Slumping on my bed, I pick up the wooden box Houdini sent, turning the solid teak over and over in my hands, trying to pull and push the side panels. Gliding my fingernails along the edges, I try to find a catch, but the box remains impenetrable. A heavy sigh escapes my lungs, and I put the box down for later. I can't give up.

I hear the Rossini opera *L'inganno Felice* on the Victrola as I walk across the front porch and down the stairs to the old field-stone winery. I resolve not to let Netta ruin our anniversary.

Dozens of candles light the moss-covered stones and heavy wood-beamed ceiling, flickering eerily on her spider-webbed face. It's freezing out here. I wrap my shawl tighter. Maybe the chill will make her leave sooner.

Netta sits ramrod straight, catty-corner from Jack, addressing him with a wagging jaw. His bobbing head follows her finger making points in the damp air, and I want to laugh. Jack's playful side sparks a frisson of desire in me.

It's been twenty-seven days since we made love, so many Xs marked on the calendar. He's been so preoccupied with the business of the ranch we've barely talked besides work. I've decided separate sleeping porches are a bad idea. If we slept together, our bodies would find each other in the night. Between the ranch, Jack's writing, and his ruminations on the Great War, our lovemaking is relegated to history. I miss his body on me, smelling of oak and horse hide; his hair falling in my face; his minty, smoky breath; his rough beard bristling on my face.

I step out of the shadows. "Good evening, Netta. How thoughtful of you to drop by on our anniversary."

Her mouth curdles. "I wouldn't have to interrupt if you weren't so selfish. How can you do this to me when I raised you as my own?"

"I thought you voted with us on the creek."

Netta flips her long tresses over her shoulder. "I want proof the creek won't run dry. In writing." She coughs, and it turns into a conniption.

Jack pours a glass of sherry and hands it to her. Pursing her lips, she siphons it up.

Sekine serves butternut squash soup in efficient silence, the smell of toasted piñons and ground nutmeg.

"The scientists didn't give me a written report." Jack takes a spoonful of soup and blows on it. "But they assured us the dam will help all of us on Sonoma Mountain in times of drought. Otherwise the water runs down to the San Francisco Bay."

Netta's hand trembles as she brings a spoon to her mouth, and it goes down the wrong pipe. As she coughs and splutters into her handkerchief, her forehead colors red. She sounds entirely congested and seems to have a hard time breathing.

After the soup, Sekine serves brook trout seared with aged Asiago, paired with the Kunde Magnolia Lane, precisely as I'd planned. Funny coincidence it's Auntie's favorite wine.

"Watch for bones," I warn Netta. She looks so frail; I want to ask about Roscoe and Edward but don't dare, since she came alone.

Sekine's pupils cross. "No bones. I pick out one by one."

"Caught fresh this afternoon from Sonoma Creek," I say, then wish I hadn't brought up the creek.

"Sekine, bring me a ten-minute mallard. I don't feel like trout," Jack says.

"Doc Thompson forbade it," I say. "No red meat, and definitely not rare."

"Sekine?" He raises a snarled eyebrow, and the servant runs to the kitchen.

Netta takes a bite, coughs again, and reaches for her wine. "Don't grow old. People turn their backs and forget you when you're old."

Her whining turns my sympathy bitter. "How could I ever forget you, Netta? Your opinions no one asked for. Criticizing my hair, my dress, my manners. Chiding me to practice piano, win the horserace, fence like a musketeer—or no man would ever love me?"

Jack claps his hand down on mine.

"What? Why squelch my words?" I notice his scowl. Ah. Worried about the water rights.

"Let's not ruin our dinner with bickering." He picks up the bottle and pours us more Magnolia Lane.

"I have to sell Wake Robin," Netta says resolutely.

"Darling Auntie," I say, trying to temper my anger. "We've been over this. I hold the deed to Wake Robin."

"Roscoe's divorcing me." She swallows more wine. "I have no other income. I need to sell."

Sekine sets Jack's bloody duck in front of him, and he tears into it.

"This argument is academic," Jack says. "Nobody can sell Wake Robin. It's mortgaged."

My cheeks flash hot. "You mortgaged Wake Robin?"

He tilts his jaw and talks through clenched teeth. "I'm sure Netta does not need to hear our financial woes."

"My Wake Robin?" My heart beats in my throat. "For what? Your grape-juice factory? Or to rebuild Wolf House? Or was it your damn piggery?"

A corner of his mouth turns up.

"You traded my Wake Robin to pay for your pig palace."

"Not traded." Jack chews his duck. "Mortgaged."

Sekine brings in Gravenstein apple Betty with ten candles blurred in the darkness.

My chair screeches against the stone floor as I push it back. "Excuse me, Aunt Netta, I've been fighting a migraine and it seems to have won."

Yanking roses from my hair, I throw them on my dressing table. Draped across the back of the chair is the silk kimono Jack bought me in Hawaii. I leave it there and change into the flannel nightgown Jack hates. Pilly and disreputable, it should be thrown away. But it's warm and comfortable and it's been an age since Jack came to my bed. Maybe I'm pilly and disreputable, too.

Rain starts to patter on the roof, a distant rumbling of thunder. Flicking on the small lamp beside my bed, I climb under the quilts, punching at the lumpy feather mattress, matted and heavy. My efforts leave it lumpier and harder than ever.

Opera music still plays from the winery. I imagine Netta and Jack finishing off the bottle of port; by now, he's probably served her his prized pear brandy. He'll charm her with his attention and wit, and she'll be forever devoted to him, as we all are. Rats to his Pied Piper.

I squeeze my eyes closed. How dare Jack mortgage my property without so much as a mention? Is nothing a woman's own in marriage? What good is it to have the vote in California if a husband has the right to do anything he wants with her property? After all Wake Robin means to me?

Before we married, Jack succumbed to the worst melancholy brought on by the hopeless struggle of the working class, the demonizing power of alcohol, and his loveless marriage. He was so despondent he could barely put two sentences together. I took him to Wake Robin to recuperate under my care. For days he buried his head under the pillow, unable to rise and write. Little by little, I introduced him to the restoring joys of the country. Waking up to a symphony of birds. The smell of a campfire. The accomplishment of riding a horse.

Then he'd sink again into his dark abyss, and nothing would bring him out of it. I truly thought I'd lost him.

I took him on one last horseback ride before he returned to his family in Oakland, up the western side of the mountain to the largest tree in the world, a thousand-year-old redwood of mythic stature and girth. Few really believed it existed and, even if they did, certainly had no idea where to find it. But when I was a young girl at Wake Robin, an old Poway Indian told me which creeks to follow and at what boulders to turn. I never took anyone but Jack.

"How did you know what I needed?" Jack had asked, head thrown back to see the top of the redwood, dark-green needles reaching up to the sky.

"Because this redwood tree has survived the world's woes longer than you have, and yet here it is, strong and serene," I said. "You can't control everything, Jack. Some things are out of your hands. Sometimes you have to trust Mother Nature."

He spread his arms wide around the trunk, his cheek flush to the gnarled bark.

My beatitudes percolated up from the deepest part of me, settling into a vibrant revelation: "You, Jack London, are the tip of the knife that cuts into the raging heart of human existence. Your novels bear pain so that others may experience without suffering themselves. You are a prophet, a forebearer, a man who lives and reflects the human condition so that future generations can understand."

"You're kidding me, right?" He turned to me with an amused grin. "All this to bring me out of the doldrums when a kiss would have done the trick?"

He pulled me down to the mossy forest bed and kissed me breathless. Then Jack made love to me under that thousand-year-old redwood tree hidden in Wake Robin.

*My* Wake Robin—now mortgaged, without mention to me.

The rain is heavier now, and so is the drubbing of my heart. I've been such a chump. I can't abide this anymore. Pulling a suitcase out from under my bed, I start to pack my warmest clothes. Sekine can send the rest. I'll go east, St. Louis first—I have cousins there—then maybe New York, to visit Bessie and Houdini. No, not such a good idea. But anywhere else, anywhere but here.

Outside my windows, the dark sky lights up, a bolt of lightning thwacks in the garden, a loud crack. The lights flicker, then go dark. Rain drums the roof tiles. I feel for matches and light a scattering of candles, and continue to stuff the suitcase—underwear, sweaters, skirts.

Creerack. Crash. The sky lights again and exposes a doe leaping away.

I'll be gone before he wakes. Already I feel the gaping cavity in my body—I have invested my soul here with Jack. What is left of me if I leave?

My eyes water with fatigue. I rub them and sit on my bed, then pick up Houdini's puzzle box, light as balsa. Through the pattering rain, I hear faint opera music playing in the winery;

they're still there. I turn the puzzle box over in my hands. What kind of man communicates through puzzles and ciphers? A man with more finesse than Jack, who stalks his desires with a club.

"She's gone." Jack startles me, slouching against the doorframe like a character from one of his movies. His skin looks magenta in the candlelight.

I study the puzzle box as if it's a gemstone.

He holds his stomach. "I'm afraid my ten-minute duck is flying the coop."

"Ptomaine poisoning. You have medicine from Dr. Porter in your medicine basket."

"Porter's a quack. Pun intended. Call Doc Thompson."

"Nothing will work until you change—exercise, no rare meat, vegetables," I scold.

He slumps into the chair by my bed. "I had to promise Netta the income from the Wake Robin cabins for the next year, but she's still on our side."

"There is no *our* side. Only *your* side. You mortgaged Wake Robin."

He groans and grabs his gut. "It's a pretty picayune world, Mate. Every person I've done anything for has thrown me down. And I've not been a pincher, have I?"

"Take the medicine," I say coolly. Does he even remember Wake Robin was mine?

"Oh, I don't mean you or Eliza." His rheumy eyes falter. "But everyone else has their hand out. The Greek insists I write reviews of his poems, that Socialist writer never acknowledged the money I sent her. And Nakata, abandoning me after all I did for him?"

"And you got Macmillan to publish my books."

"I don't begrudge *you*." He lays his cheek on my lap, and my hand hovers over his head, but I move it to the puzzle box instead.

He lies there for an eternity, groaning, gasping, belly bubbling with poison. The lights flicker on again.

"I'm not going to New York," I say, turning Houdini's box over in my hands.

"Then why did you pack your trunk?"

He misses nothing.

"I'm going to St. Louis to visit my cousins."

"Don't leave me," he says, voice raw and shaking. "You are my compass, my horn, my sounding board, my conscience." He places his hands over mine holding the box, squeezing and kneading as if he's forming rock from clay, until my hands start to prickle.

"You're hurting me, Jack."

He releases my mottled hands, and the box breaks open in two pieces.

A single monarch butterfly flitters out from the hollow center, stretching golden wings laced with black, blinking at me, hovering in a lyrical ballet. The butterfly flies around the room, the heaviness in my soul flying with it. A joyful laugh warbles up my throat.

Jack frowns. "I've lost you, haven't I, Charmian?"

I don't answer. After all, it's our tenth anniversary, and who was he thinking of? Certainly not me.

Later that night, the thunder wakes me and I peer through my windowpanes, across the stoop to Jack's side of the cottage. His lamp is still burning, a lit cigarette hangs from his mouth while he snores loudly. I throw my feet out of bed and pad across to his side, smashing his glowing cigarette butt in his overflowing ashtray. Jack mumbles something, and I bend over to hear him.

"Pray do not interrupt me. I am smiling." His eyes flutter open and closed again. A snore rattles from somewhere deep in his lungs and ends with a wheeze. Tiny droplets cover his face, neck, and chest. He'll catch his death of cold. I draw the covers up over his neck. He'll be better in the morning. He's always better in the morning.

And I'll be gone.

An empty morphine vial lies on his medicine table. Looks like he won't be feeling much pain tonight.

Jack mumbles. "To live costs overmuch, and you have refused to pay the price." A line from "To Build a Fire" . . .

I kiss my fingers and press them on his sunken cheek. "Goodbye, Jack." And I tiptoe back to my sleeping porch. The wind screams and buffets the panes of my windows. I look over at Jack's room, but the sound doesn't wake him.

Lying on my bed, first on one side, then the other, I stare at the ceiling, listening to the storm. My room lights up like noon, and not a second later the sky cracks open. A tree branch crashes near my window. I jump up and look over at Jack's room. His neck is bent over the side of his mattress, his mouth open, mouthpiece dangling, still sleeping . . .

Wish I could sleep as well; I have to try. The morning train leaves Glen Ellen at seven thirty.

I feel for the eye mask on my nightstand and slip it over my eyes, listening to rain, my heartbeat, the pahu drums . . .

# 23

## Beauty Ranch, Glen Ellen, California
## November 22, 1916

*Life is a strange thing. Why this longing for life? It is a game which no man wins. To live is to toil hard and to suffer sore, till old age creeps heavily upon us and we throw down our hands on the cold ashes of dead fires. It is hard to live. In pain the babe sucks his first breath, in pain the old man gasps his last, and all his days are full of trouble and sorrow; yet he goes down to the open arms of death, stumbling, falling, with head turned backward, fighting to the last. And death is kind. It is only life and the things of life that hurt. Yet we love life and we hate death. It is very strange.*

—*Jack London,* Tales of the North

Someone shakes me hard.

"Charmian, get up," Eliza says. "We can't rouse Jack."

I pull the eye mask from my eyes, letting in blinding light. "What time is it?"

"Ten past eight," she says.

Damn, missed the train. I throw the quilt off and set my feet on the cold wood floor.

"We thought you were with Jack, because his door was closed, but finally Sekine checked."

"Did you call Doc Thompson?" I pull on a robe against the chill and walk to Jack's porch, Eliza on my heels.

"He's delivering a baby in Sonoma."

"Then call Dr. Porter in Glen Ellen." A clod in my throat makes it hard to swallow.

Eliza wrings a dish towel in her red, chapped hands. "But Jack says Dr. Porter is wet behind the ears and—"

"Call him."

Sekine stands over Jack, pressing rhythmically on his heart.

My hand reaches out to touch his ashen face, slipping over purpled lips, chapped and clammy under my fingertips. Bending over his chest, I hear a faint rasp. That's something.

"Jack, wake up." I stroke his hair, and his head lolls back. I pick it up, his beautiful tousled waves odd against his slack gray face. "Let me try something." I seize him by the shoulders, shaking him. "Mate! Mate! You must come back! You've got to come back to me."

He comes back. Of course he comes back. Slowly, as something rising from eternity, his mouth smiles. A smirk of a smile. And I feel my unbodied soul go out to meet his.

"Help me get him up." Sekine and I lift from underneath, but he's deadweight. Using all our strength, we sit him up, swinging his flaccid legs onto the floor. His feet are grossly swollen with fluid.

Eliza returns, out of breath. "Dr. Porter is coming."

"Help us lift him. We've got to get him walking." The three of us support Jack and finally get him to a stand. We stumble around the room like tumbling bowling pins. I step on something and hear a snap. "What's that?"

Sekine peers at the carpet. "Mr. Jack's medicine."

"This isn't working. Take him back to the bed." We lay Jack down, and I pick up the broken vial. "When did he take this?"

"Mr. Jack couldn't sleep." The valet's brows press together like praying hands.

"But he took a dose earlier," I tell them. "You didn't give him more, did you?"

Sekine's head pivots right and left, his pupils blank.

"What about you, Eliza?"

"Of course not." She presses her hands to her ears. "Lord have mercy."

I sit on Jack's bed. His lips are dry and cracked. "He needs water." Pouring from a pitcher, I lift the cup to his mouth. "Cool water, Jack. Drink." The water slides down his throat, but there is no swallow. No choking. Like filling an empty vessel. "I'm drowning him." I tilt his head to the side and let it drain out. "What did you do, Jack?" I shake him softly. Then my voice turns harsh, and I shake him harder. "What did you do? What did you do?"

Eliza pulls me off him. "Get a hold of yourself. That certainly doesn't help my brother."

Her words don't penetrate. I watch for the slightest movement on his face, flicking my middle finger against his head and temple. His eyelids don't flinch. Cold morning light shines harshly on his face through his windows.

Dr. Porter arrives smelling of bacon and Ivory soap. I didn't hear his buggy. His white jacket shows the fold lines, just taken out of a package. He cracks open his gleaming leather medicine bag and pulls out a shiny stethoscope.

Wary, I watch him place the stethoscope under Jack's neck. Can't he warm it first? He moves it to Jack's chest. His actions feel slow and drawn out.

Pahu drums start pounding in my ears, my throat, my diaphragm. A gust of wind thrashes dead leaves and gravel against the windowpanes and jolts me. My teeth chatter.

"Turn up the furnace, Sekine. Jack's freezing in here."

He runs from the sleeping porch.

The young doctor lifts Jack's eyelid and shines a tiny light onto his eyeball—the white is webbed with red capillaries, muddy around the iris. All the while I hold Jack's hand, squeezing it, waiting for him to squeeze back. Waiting for his eyes to pop open. He'll admit it's one of his gags, that he's fooled us all.

Sekine returns with my big Irish sweater, his eyes focused on the floor.

"Thank you, Sekine." I lay it over Jack, clamping my teeth together to stop the chatter.

Dr. Porter returns the light to his bag and takes off the stethoscope. His peach-fuzz chin drops down as he clasps his hands behind his back. "I'm sorry, Mrs. London. There's nothing I can do."

"Make coffee, Sekine. Triple strength." I smooth Jack's hair back. "We'll revive him with coffee; then we can get him walking."

Sekine glances at the doctor, then at Eliza.

"Go," I order him.

He backs out of the room, bowing his head.

"Eliza, help me." I lift Jack's shoulder, and a burst of air expels from his mouth. "See? He's breathing. Get him up. Help me."

The young doctor's hand grips my shoulder. "Mr. London is gone. I'm sorry, he's gone."

I hold Jack in my arms. "But he's breathing. You saw him breathe—"

"Pent-up air escaping his body," the doctor says.

Taking him from my arms, Eliza lays her brother back down, all color drained from his face.

Doc Thompson's buggy pulls up outside the sleeping porches. A niggling hope springs in my chest, and for the first time this morning, I hear birds chirp and caw outside. "I came as soon as I could," he says, pushing thick pince-nez glasses up his nose and setting his crackled leather bag next to Dr. Porter's. "Delivered a thirteen-pound boy to Lettie Fisher." He chuckles. "She swears it's her last."

"Jack's in a coma," I say. "Can you revive him? The coffee should be ready by now. Could that help bring him around?"

Dr. Porter steps out of the corner. "He was gone when I got here, I'm afraid."

The old doctor leans down and listens to Jack's heart, his pointed beard tickling Jack's chest. Maybe Jack will laugh and they'll see how he teases.

Doc Thompson feels for a pulse on Jack, whose fingernails have turned purple. Doc pulls his goatee and looks at me through thick lenses.

"Bring Jack back, like you always do," I say. Pahu drums pulse in my ears.

Dr. Porter's glance falls to the broken vial on the nightstand. "Did you prescribe this? This is ten milligrams, I prescribe five."

"I cut him off long ago," Doc Thompson says.

The pahu pounds in my sternum. Drumming, drumming, drumming. "There must be an antidote."

Doc Thompson shakes his head and squeezes my shoulder. "I'm sorry, Mrs. London."

Dr. Porter hands him a parchment. "Will you sign as the second witness?"

The old doctor peers at it through his pince-nez. "This will crucify him."

I snatch the parchment away. The certificate is exacting and resolute. "Deceased. Morphine overdose."

Crumpling the paper, I thrust it in the pocket of my robe. "Mr. London did nothing of the sort."

"I cannot lie about such a thing," the young doctor sputters. "I'd lose my license."

"He's right, Charmian." Doc Thompson pulls on his goatee. "It doesn't say he did it on purpose."

"Eliza, show Dr. Porter out."

The floorboards creak under Eliza's weight. "Don't forget your coat, Doctor," she says, with a firm hand on his back. Their voices drift toward the front of the cottage.

Sitting with Jack again, I hold his hand, feel his wrist. My own pulse throbs. "Oh, Jack." The corners of his mouth are fixed in a farewell smile.

"Death is sweet," he'd said once. "Death is rest. Think of it, to rest forever! I promise you whensoever and wheresoever death comes to me, I shall greet death with a smile."

Doc Thompson sits in the captain chair, and we stay there a long while before he speaks. "I wish I'd gotten here sooner. Maybe I could have done something for him."

"You *can* do something for Jack." I turn to him. "Issue the proper death certificate."

He clears his throat to interrupt, but I don't let him.

"Jack London died of uremia," I say with dead calm. "You've been treating his kidney problems. The symptoms have been present for years—stomach problems, insomnia, melancholia, dysentery, rheumatic edema, a quickening of mental enginery." I lay my cheek on Jack's silent chest.

A crevice deepens on Doc Thompson's forehead, eyes watering beneath his pince-nez spectacles. He sighs and writes a new parchment.

He squeezes my shoulder and lays the death certificate on the bed.

The date stands out in his stark hand: November 22, 1916. Now skimming to the bottom.

"Cause of death: Uremia following renal colic. Contributor chronic interstitial nephritis."

The bleak victory settles at the base of my throat like a fist.

# 24

## Beauty Ranch, Glen Ellen, California
## November 26, 1916

*There is such a thing as anesthesia of pain, engendered by pain too exquisite to be borne.*

*—Jack London,* The Star Rover

Jack can't possibly fit in this small box, no bigger than a cradle. He's much too big a man. And after they cremate him in Oakland, he'll be nothing but ash in an urn. The pall bearers have left me in the parlor for a final moment before they load him into the hearse. Thoughtful, I'm sure, but I can't bear to see that waxy death mask again.

I can't clear a lump in my throat that hasn't budged since he died. The florid stench of flowers nauseates me, the salon packed with lilies, gardenias, jasmine. Their perfume tickles my throat, but I can't cough. Telegrams, cards, and letters from all over the world overflow the basket and litter the floor. I can't bear to read them all now, thick with sticky compliments or veiled criticism of my care of Jack. How could it happen, indeed? A forty-year-old literary genius of our time dying of martinis and ten-minute mallard.

Only Houdini seemed to guess more: "Please let us know if the shocking facts are based in truth." Worse, I want to tell him. Far worse.

I should lift the cloth to see his face one last time, but I can't move my arms. They fall by my sides.

Jack is not here.

I smell ink and hashish before I feel George Sterling looming above me, his clawing hand on my shoulder, his voice smooth and thick as he quotes one of his poems. Something about a lion and the sea.

I don't comment. He's so full of himself, yet I can't get angry. He loved Jack almost as much as I, worshipped him like a god and sparred with him like a brother. He sits down beside me, and we stare silently at the jagged silhouette of Jack's body under the cloth.

Men come in to take the coffin away, startled when they see us. I nod and follow them out to the front porch. The morning fog casts a gloomy pall on the day. As we walk down the stone steps, my boot catches my long skirt, and I falter. The Greek grabs my arm lest I fall.

"You should do a grand monument for Wolf," he says.

"Jack wanted his ashes buried on the little knoll, with a red boulder from Wolf House rolled over him."

"I am. I was. I am not. I never am," Sterling quotes Jack's words from *John Barleycorn*.

All the staff and ranch workers watch the coffin loaded into the death wagon, swaying on locked knees, faces frozen with shock. They're worried for their jobs, no doubt. What will happen to the ranch now, with all its debt, and Jack's income come to a sudden halt?

Aunt Netta and Edward climb into their truck, finally married after her divorce from Roscoe was final. I won't speak to her, can't forgive her for suing us over the creek and ruining my last dinner with Jack.

The Shires whinny and prance in place, making my eyes sting. Do they know they are carrying their master? The finality closes my throat.

"When will they read Jack's will?" Sterling asks.

"I'm sorry, Greek, he didn't leave you anything."

He shakes his head. "But I'm executor of his daughters' fortune."

I hate to tell him the ugly truth, haven't decided what to do about it myself. "Jack left his daughters twenty-five dollars a month until they get married. Their mother will have my head on a platter."

Sterling's brows knit over his beak of a nose. "Left it all to you, did he?"

"Don't worry, Sterling. There'll be nothing left by the time I pay our debt."

"At least tell me what his note said," he says.

"What note?"

He slicks back his long gray hair. "Don't be coy. Jack must have left a note. It would help me to read it."

His idea tastes bitter as sumac. "Jack died of uremia. Dr. Thompson signed the certificate."

"Yes, I heard the official version. Severe indigestion resulting in kidney failure." Sterling's nails rake my arm. "Jack did not die from his dinner. A great writer had to leave a note."

"Jack wouldn't commit suicide." Something catches in my throat, and I cough. "We just finished a new novel . . ."

"Come on, now. Wolf never planned to leave this world as a doddering old man." Sterling huffs hashish breath in my face.

"Jack had no reason to kill himself," I tell Sterling.

"A genius doesn't need a reason," Sterling says. "But if I had to guess, I'd say he killed himself when he heard about his daughter."

"Becky or Joan?"

Sterling sniggers. "Ever Jack's protector, aren't you, Charmian? It would be charming if it weren't so pathetic."

Our hired Dodge pulls up to take us to Oakland.

"Quit the guessing games," I say. "What daughter are you talking about?"

Sterling opens the door to let me in. "What's the name of the Japanese girl Nakata married in Hawaii? Kile, Kuki?"

"You mean Kukalani?"

"She had a daughter last month, and Jack sent a check."

"Of course he did, Jack loved Nakata." I lift my skirt to climb into the back seat of the car, but my foot hovers midair, then drops to the ground.

Suddenly, it's painfully obvious what Sterling is implying, like a film negative, private and dark until projected onto photographic paper for a clear and permanent record. Those shadowy questions that I pushed aside . . . Nakata, Kukalani . . . and Jack. How could I have blocked out the undeniable truth? I turn to Sterling. "What did Jack tell you?"

Sterling rolls his eyes. "Oh, Jack told me plenty about the Hawaiian girl."

"You have no right to spread your ugly rumors." I get out of the car. "I'm not going to Oakland."

"You have to. Thousands of fans are coming to pay respects," Sterling says. "The governor, the Socialists, the Bohemian Club . . . Elizabeth and the girls will be there. You have to come."

I walk up the steps to the front porch and look back.

Sterling stands by the car door, hand outstretched. "Come with me, Charmian. Jack wouldn't want you to be alone."

"If Jack didn't want me to be alone, he'd be here right now." I open the door and lock it behind me. Sterling doesn't follow. At last everyone leaves Beauty Ranch for the funeral.

Jack's sleeping porch is empty, except for Possum lying in a patch of sunlight on the bed. I pet his head, but he doesn't raise it.

Last scribbled reminders are still clothespinned to the wire above his bed. I have them memorized. "Call Burbank about spineless cactus." "Christmas goose." "Write Nakata and K about *Cherry* . . ."

Thoughts of a suicidal man?

Sekine has set everything as if the master will soon sit back in his captain's chair. I run my fingers over his leather blotter, fountain pens, sharpened pencils, cigarettes. His ashtray is clean, water carafe filled. A sunflower stares blankly from a vase by his bed, and next to his latest periodicals and books, another one is laid on his pillow.

What was he reading his last night? I open the blue binding, my editor's copy of *The Sea-Wolf*, my handwritten edits faded in red and blue. An envelope marks his place.

Inside are two tickets for the transcontinental railroad from Oakland to New York. The trip I refused Jack a few days ago now seems the only place to go.

# Part III

*His conclusion was that things were not always what they appeared to be.*

*The cub's fear of the unknown was an inherited distrust,*

*and it had now been strengthened by experience.*

*Thenceforth, in the nature of things, he would possess an abiding distrust of appearances.*

*—Jack London,* White Fang

# 25

## Grand Central Station, New York City, New York January 1917

What rare disease left New Yorkers allergic to color? The same disease must render them mute except for grunts and scowls, pushing their way through the bowels of Grand Central Station, a writhing sea of black overcoats, black scarves, black overshoes.

A young boy in a worn cap and fingerless gloves holds up the *New York Times* and barks at the crowd. "Germany launches submarine warfare. Berlin warns America not to interfere." This news would send Jack into a tailspin. I should go home, but there *is* no home now. Home was where Jack was. The clod that materialized in my throat when Jack died hasn't eased at all, a permanent obstruction making it hard to swallow.

I burrow into my thin jacket and ferret through the crowd with all my strength. I lose ground in the undertow and find myself helplessly opposite where I'd wanted to be. Par for the course since Jack died, it seemed.

At last I see the dull gray light of the street outside, and I push toward it. **Forty-Second Street,** the sign says. People funnel through a revolving door. Never liked these newfangled things, but there's no regular door, so I wait for an empty slot and jump in. The door hits me on the behind and spits me out into a blizzard of sleet. A freezing blast hits my face, whipping my eyes to tears, and within a minute, I can't move my lips.

All the way across the country in that rattling, drafty train, I daydreamed of the moment I would finally arrive in New York City and see the one person I could tell the truth. The two of us would meet on Park Avenue, me dressed in white fur like a Russian snow queen, him in long tails and top hat, snowflakes drifting around us. I conjured up the absurd fairy tale whenever thoughts of Jack buried me with him.

Jack died. His last days play in my mind, over and over, catching on a word, a touch, an expression. Did he mean to do it? Should I have known? Did I drive him to it? What about the child in Hawaii?

Thoughts stir my brain into a fever, relieved only by rage.

Jack checked out. Left me with outrageous ranch debt and movie lawsuits. He crafted his final drama to unfold after his death: his last will and testament deprived his friends and family of any last proof of his affection.

They got nothing. And left me holding the moneybag, ravaged with rat holes.

My thoughts sting white-hot as the blizzard surrounds me. An ugly laugh blurts from my mouth, and passing businessmen turn to stare, but I can't stop it. The brutal sound hacks out of me until tears freeze on my cheeks.

Jack left me.

Stepping toward the curb, I slip on the slush. I want to see Houdini, but not until I glue my fragments together. My fairy-tale plan shattered when the railroad lost my trunk and, with it, the notes I'd made for Jack's biography, the only thing that kept me sane for four days on the Transcontinental Express. I filled an entire journal: Jack's lowly birth, his world travels, his rise as the best-selling author of our time. I'll write the story like no one else could, not even Jack himself. And George Brett will finally get the Jack London biography he's been asking for.

A streetcar whooshes by, clanging its bell, people packed like penguins on a blue iceberg like I saw in Cape Horn with Jack . . .

Taxis and delivery wagons rut the streets with foot-deep crevices in crusty snow. Teams of horses clomp heavy hooves, pulling delivery wagons or elegant carriages.

Not one of them stops for a lone widow in a flimsy coat, standing on the corner, waving her hand. So different than when I came to New York with Jack, when a four-horse carriage would pick us up from Grand Central, load up our many trunks in the back and courier us to the Waldorf Astoria. Jack always took care of those things.

I wave my arm again for a cab, and it swerves past, a wave of gray slush spraying me before it stops for a man in a black coat.

What in the Sam Hill was I thinking coming to New York in January? But I had to leave Beauty Ranch; the quiet after the funeral was stultifying.

I see another taxicab up the street and step off the curb to hail it. My foot breaks through the ice and sinks up to my calf in sludge. I try to jerk it out, but my foot sticks fast. I have no choice but to reach down into the gray muck, and yank my heel out from the gutter grate.

This is all a mistake. I can still turn around and get back on that train.

But the taxi pulls over for me, and I get in. The black-haired driver turns around, snapping his chewing gum, speaking in a language I've never heard. His glass eye rolls to the right.

"Pardon me?"

With a small tug of his fisherman's cap, he repeats slowly and loudly. "Where does Lady want to go?" Without waiting for an answer, one hand grabs the wheel and pulls into the street. In the rearview mirror, I see his glass eye drift toward me.

"Waldorf Astoria, please."

"Do you have reservations?"

"No . . . I . . ."

He wags his finger back and forth. "No reservation, no room. Every hotel uptown full for big benefit at the Hippodrome. Tomorrow people will be leave." He slams both feet on the brakes. We jolt to a stop, inches from the back bumper of a Dodge touring car like the one Jack and Houdini drove at the Panama-Pacific. The knot in my throat throbs.

A brass band starts "The Star-Spangled Banner" in front of the Hippodrome. The taxicab can't move, trapped in a maze of wagons and carriages and automobiles.

"See what I mean?" He holds up his hands. "Everyone here for Houdini benefit."

My stomach jumps. I'm not ready. "Then drive downtown. You must know a hotel that can take me."

"I know a flat above a restaurant in Greenwich Village, if you have cash."

"I don't know." Too many memories. Greenwich Village always swallowed Jack whole when we came to New York—smoky speakeasies, coffeehouses, literary salons—a haven for artsy types. He never wanted to leave Greenwich.

A horn blares behind us, loud and insistent.

My empty belly groans. "Does the restaurant make good food?"

He kisses his fingertips and explodes them like dandelion seed. "Cabbage rolls like you never tasted." Swerving onto a cross street, he then makes another turn, and we're headed downtown.

Icy snow pelts people on the streets, who shelter their heads with newspapers and umbrellas, all hurrying home to someone they love.

Jack hated cabbage rolls. Will I always see life through his lens?

The rent is cheap compared to the Waldorf. I won't have to wire for more cash for a while.

Still, I wonder if this was such a smart idea as I follow Romany Marie's tapestry tunic up the murky staircase. Her pants are wide and flowy, the crown of her head bound with a scarf over long, unruly tresses.

Despite the nervous twitch in my spine, I'm intrigued. Romany Marie calmed my fears and revived my spirits with strong coffee and kreplach in her café. From the aromas coming from the kitchen, I might even gain back the ten pounds I've lost since Jack died.

Romany Marie hands me the tiny kerosene lantern she's been holding and thrusts a skeleton key in the ancient brass hole to open the door. It's even dimmer inside.

"Set the lantern over there, and I'll make a fire," she says. "There's no electricity up here."

I set it down on the low table in front of a sofa covered with beaded pillows in turquoise, purple, and scarlet.

"But we do have running water." She points to a hand pump. "You can heat it on the woodstove for a bath."

"A bath sounds heavenly right now."

She strikes a match and lights a bronze candelabra, the circle of light growing around us. Colorful chiffons billow from the ceiling like a tent from Scheherazade. Fringed velvet scarves drape overstuffed chairs. Open shelves display porcelain plates and cups painted with partridges and peacocks. In the far corner, tapestry draperies shroud a mahogany four-poster bed with a painting at the head.

"Your family came from Romania?" My foot bumps something sharp: incisors of the tiger-skin rug.

"We lived in Transylvania before it merged. The new government doesn't like gypsies." She piles more wood on the fire. "My parents started the restaurant. Papa cooked his ciorba and boiled beef, and Mama told fortunes. When Papa died, I took over. Mama never left this apartment until she passed from us."

Over the fireplace, there's a painting of a naked woman lying on the tiger skin in front of this very fireplace. I walk closer to get a better look. The brushstrokes are bold and expressive, capturing raw sensuality. Her backbone begs for the caress of each dimpled vertebra, thick waves fall over one shoulder, her enormous dark eyes hold mine.

"Nikolai Kalmakov painted my portrait in exchange for telling his fortune." She bites her knuckle, and I sense her pain, but I can't bear a sad story right now.

"I'd love to hear my fortune." Collapsing into an armchair, I slip off soggy boots and tuck my freezing feet underneath me.

Romany Marie closes her eyelids and hums a plaintive tune. She starts to sway, firelight dancing on her headscarf, dangling earrings, embroidered tunic. Resting my head against the wing of the armchair, I stare at the fire and inhale sandalwood, letting her transport me to some other dimension, as Jack's stories did. How I yearn to be somewhere else. Anywhere but in the vacuum of Jack's wake.

After a while, Romany Marie starts to whisper, low and breathy, like the wind. "Someone has hurt you."

A fist punches my throat.

Romany Marie gasps. "Oh. So sorry. I see your husband died." Firelight flickers on her frown. "Someone familiar . . . like I know . . ." Her eyes open wide. "Mr. Jack London died. This is your husband?"

I jump up. "What's going on here? What are you trying to do?"

"I'm sorry." She raises her hand with long, pointed fingernails. "Please, sit down. I can explain. Mr. London has been a long-time patron. He comes in with his publisher."

"Mr. Brett?" I gather my coat and carpetbag to leave, but where would I go?

"Weren't the two of you here before? I remember—" She studies me.

"Never." Shaking my head. "Last time I came to New York, Jack left me at the Waldorf for days without word." Showed up later with a raccoon coat as a gift for his absence.

"Your hair was longer, hennaed bright red?"

"Still not me." Jack was here with Sophie Loeb. "Maybe I should find another—"

Romany Marie holds up a pointed fingernail. "It's late." She takes the candelabra over to the bed table. "There is an extra comforter in the wardrobe if you get cold." The glow illuminates the painting over the bed.

"Oh my." My hand flies to my chest. The painting shows a younger Romany Marie lying on a red-and-gold tapestry. Her lavish breasts and defined thighs are exposed, but her eyes are half-closed in ecstasy. An enormous black swan has descended on her, iridescent body gleaming, wings passionately poised. His long orange bill reaches for her neck.

Romany blows out a breath and shakes her head. "Nikolai was quite a man." She walks toward the door, pant legs swishing between her thighs. "Breakfast and dinner are included in the rent." She opens the door and turns around. "If you're wondering if the other man has missed you . . . He has."

She leaves, and I run to flip the lock and fasten the chain, falling back against the door. The sandalwood sizzles and crackles in the fireplace. I'm alone. With the black swan.

Every time I hire a taxicab to take me to Grand Central to ask about my lost trunk, I make the cabby drive past the Hippodrome stretching an entire block on Sixth Avenue, with forged ironwork globes and flags of the world waving on the massive theater. I marvel at the huge marquee over the many entrances and look for Houdini, as if he'll be pulling a rabbit out of a hat right on the sidewalk. What holds me back from ringing them up? Wasn't that what I wanted when I boarded the train to New York? If I could just see his face, so earnest and wise and protective . . .

I go to the station one last time in search of my trunk and my notes. George Brett will be impressed with the detail I've penned, the insight I have, and he'll let me write Jack's biography. He has to.

The same Grand Central newsboy calls with his hoarse voice. "US severs ties with Germany."

I hand him a quarter and stuff the newspaper in my carpetbag to read later. "Keep the change." He grins crookedly.

My trunk has not shown up. If it weren't for my notes, I'd be glad. It's like jettisoning a part me that is finished, over. After two weeks of wearing the few clothes in my carpetbag, I force myself into Bergdorf's to buy an outfit for my meeting with George Brett.

My hand pets a glossy fur. A saleswoman with pinched nostrils and a pencil tucked behind her ear introduces herself as Edna Peabody. A good name for a character in a novel. She corrals me into a dressing room with half a dozen dresses and suits. The first dress falls to midcalf. Would be scandalous at the ranch. But I don't live there anymore, do I? The saleswoman passes judgment on each outfit, taking away the ones that make me look matronly and keeping only the ones that flatter my face and figure. Oddly, I trust her. Jack used to be my bellwether on clothes. Every outfit had to paint a dashing image. Never an ordinary pair of dungarees, always riding trousers.

The saleswoman continues to bring clothes, and I fall into an obedient trance, trying to choose a new wardrobe to fit who I am now, who I am without Jack. Even as I still wonder what he'll say about each new outfit as I study myself in the mirror. He sits there in the tufted chair behind me, smoking his Imperial, an amused glint in his eye. "Suits you, Mate," or "Mighty fine, indeed." I stand there, helpless, ears straining to hear his words.

"Are you all right, miss?" Edna Peabody asks.

My eyes fly open. "My husband will love it."

"Which ones do you want to buy?"

"All of them. He likes all of them." She glances at me strangely, then gathers the pile into her arms. I don't have much money, but I'll ask George Brett for an advance.

"What about the suit you have on? You look stunning."

Only then do I really see myself in the mirror. Ivory crepe wool, detailed with gold braided trim, the jacket hugs my waist—all the creeping fat around my middle has disappeared, my cheeks have a rosy hue from walking here from Grand Central in the snow combined with standing now in elegant Bergdorf's with blessed forced-air heat. Edna ties a jaunty scarf around my neck, which brings out the green in my eyes and makes them appear more sophisticated and intelligent than I feel. But my hair doesn't match, straggly and unkempt, mousy. That goes next.

"I'll wear this now," I say. "It's perfect for my meeting."

She smiles with a gray front tooth—then covers her mouth.

I wonder if Nakata ever became a dentist. But the fond thought brings with it the bitter betrayal of the baby.

"You can't wear that coat with this outfit," the saleswoman breaks into my shame. She disappears through the curtain and soon returns with a fox coat, tan and white fur with tinges of black. The weight of it encases me like armor; I'm immediately safe and warm. "I'll take it."

The saleswoman takes my cash without blinking and asks for my name and address to send the boxes by messenger.

"Kittredge. Charmian Kittredge." I give my maiden name, not wanting to chance sympathy just now. But then Romany Marie won't know they are mine. "Make that Charmian London." I try to say nonchalantly. "Twenty Christopher Street, Greenwich Village."

She smiles crookedly. "The package will be there by this evening." She hands me a business card. "I'd be happy to serve you again, anytime, Miss London."

I smile and walk away, grateful she doesn't make the connection. I can't face a fan right now.

Outside Bergdorf's the wind boxes my ears, and dark snow clouds threaten overhead.

Perfect weather to see George Brett, I think facetiously. But I've put it off too long as it is. What should I be afraid of? Walking six long blocks to Macmillan Publishing, I gather my thoughts, and the bustle on the streets goes unnoticed. I reach the Flatiron Building, a twenty-two-story triangle high-rise fitting into the wedge of Fifth Avenue, Broadway, and East Twenty-Second Street—the most stunning building in New York.

Macmillan is publishing my new book, *Our Hawaii*, aren't they? Why wouldn't they take my next project seriously? But niggling doubt tells me George Brett only published my work because Jack made them . . . Now that he's gone, what?

But who better to write Jack's biography? I've sailed to the Solomon Islands and around Cape Horn, ridden with him through Mexico as a war correspondent, edited his books for twelve years. I've been his nurse, his comrade in Socialism. His wife, damn it.

"Good day to you, ma'am," the elevator operator says. "Where may I take you on this bright and beautiful day?" Large ears stick out perpendicular from his brown face, and white hair coils from under his navy-blue cap; his uniform is buttoned tight around his neck, with a red polka-dot bowtie. His hand holds back the elevator door, his eyes closed.

"Macmillan." I wince and step gingerly into the elevator car. I've never gotten used to these things.

"Which floor?" he asks.

The simple question flummoxes me; I don't remember. "I'm here to see the president, George Brett."

"Penthouse, then. Twenty-second floor for the young lady." He closes the brass crosshatch, latches the safety door, then pushes the button, all with his eyes shut tight. The cables whir, and the car sways slightly. My ears pop and I hold on to the brass rail.

He takes a deep breath, and I wonder if he's scared of heights, too.

"Lavender oil," he says. "You've been here before."

"Yes."

"With Jack London." One side of his mouth turns up, one side down, eyes still closed. "Tipped me five dollars for his elevator rides."

The lump in my throat throbs.

"I'm sorry for your loss, ma'am. He was a true adventurer. My wife reads me his books at night."

The car jolts up and down again. I gasp, the knot in my throat blocking my breath. He pulls back the brass crosshatch and safety door, but I can't walk through, my knees gone wobbly.

He closes the door and flips a switch. "Take your time. I ain't in no hurry."

Jack's voice jeers in my head. "Show 'em what you're made of, Mate. Stare 'em right in the eye." Like he'd said when cannibals met our ship in Bora Bora with bones thrust through their noses. I blurt a laugh, then squelch it.

"I'm ready."

He opens the gate.

I shake his free hand, calluses on his fingertips. "Thank you, Mr.—"

"Skippy. Call me Skippy."

"Thank you, Skippy."

He reaches for the lever to close the door. "Knock 'em dead, Mrs. London."

After that no one can cow me, not even the tanker of a receptionist Jack always plied with Ghirardelli chocolates from California, with her suit of armor and bulldog chest.

"Mr. Brett is busy." She peers at the calendar on her desk.

"I'm sure he can make time to see me."

"And why would that be?" She looks over her half glasses.

"I'm sorry, Miss Johnson, how shortsighted of me." I reach to shake her meaty hand. "We've met before with my husband, Jack London."

She extricates her hand, coughs, and runs a plump finger down the days of the appointment calendar. "Well, Mr. Brett is in our London office for three weeks."

"You enjoy chocolates, I believe?" I say. "Dark chocolate with raspberry cream, am I right?"

Tongue licking the corner of her lips, she bobs down to the calendar. “Friday, February ninth, eleven forty-five.”

“Nothing until then?”

She frowns.

“February ninth, then.” I flutter my fingers at her and go back to the elevator, push the button, and wait.

“That was fast,” Skippy says.

“Mr. Brett can’t see me until next month.” Two weeks seems like an eternity with no one to see, no plans.

The elevator jerks and stops. Skippy opens the door.

“I’ll look forward to seeing you next month, Mrs. London.” He tips his hat. “It’s been a pleasure.”

I shake his hand once again. “The pleasure has been all mine.”

# 26

## Manhattan, New York City, New York
## February 1917

I step out onto Fifth Avenue. The clouds have parted, and there's not a snowflake in sight. The corridor of blue sky between imposing rows of office buildings promises a glorious afternoon. Exhilaration heats my cheeks. Jack would have adored my white fur bomber jacket and calf-length skirt. I can just hear his hum—"Eskimo princess renders Manhattan helpless with her animal magnetism." That persistent lump in my throat prevents me from laughing. Pressure builds behind my eyes. If Jack were here, he'd take my arm and hire us a carriage through Central Park. But he's not here.

By some quirk of fate, I see a poster for Houdini's show at the Hippodrome. Why have I avoided the one person I came to see?

I'll sit in the back; he won't even know I'm there. Afterward I'll call the Harlem telephone number Bessie gave me in her letters.

My ribs ache as I stand in line at the ticket booth. I think of leaving, but the line sweeps me along like a riptide. Or so I tell myself. Pressure gathers in my chest. From the buzz of excitement around me, thousands of folks are as thrilled as me to see him.

Finally, I reach the ticket booth. The girl with freckles smacks her chewing gum. Wrigley's should print manners on their gum wrappers. She places a big red sign at the front of the window: **SOLD OUT**.

I knock on the window. "Miss. Miss. I have to see the show. I traveled cross-country to see it."

She smacks her gum. "I can sell you tickets for tonight's show."

My head buzzes with adrenaline. If I don't see it now, I'll never go. I don't know how I know that, but I do.

"Now. I have to see it now."

She rolls her eyes, and I expect her to close her window on my craziness, but the hard lines around her mouth soften.

"The opening acts are already finished, but I do have a seat in the middle of the front row."

I pull three dollars out of my alligator wallet from Fiji.

"Five dollars." She says, her sympathy vanished.

"It says three."

"Front row is five." Her mouth curls up, and she points to the poster. "It's a donation to support our allies in the war, and you get a backstage pass to meet Houdini."

I pull out two more dollars and wonder if I can return the new clothes. At this rate, I'll be broke before the week is out.

Nothing could have prepared me for the vastness of the Hippodrome. Three tiers of seats house more than five thousand spectators. The stage alone could fit two enormous circus tents. Stagehands sweep the stage clean of confetti and balloons.

The crowd is restless between acts, peanut and popcorn venders loudly hawk their wares. Bags of buttery popcorn are thrown overhead. A fifteen-piece band plays a sassy tune, tinny sounding in the vast space. An usher in trousers with satin ribbons down the pant legs and a red satin vest looks at my ticket and leads me down the aisle past thirty rows while I gaze at the dome above, covered with mirrors. He hands me a program, and I squeeze through to the one lone seat in the center of the semicircular row.

I settle into my seat between a lavishly fat woman with several chins eating popcorn out of a red-striped paper bag, butter glistening on her lips, and a young boy bouncing to get his mother's attention.

Suddenly a drum rolls, and the lights go dim. Something makes me want to run, but I could never get out of these crowds. A spotlight follows Houdini, in long formal coat and trousers, onto center stage.

He looks taller, more distinguished than when I last saw him in Hawaii. His wavy black hair is slicked back from his widow's peak. I hold my chest to calm my palpitations, yet my mind insists on recalling details of our walk on Waikiki Beach, night breezes of ocean and plumeria.

The crunching of popcorn breaks the spell.

Houdini holds up his arms, palms facing the audience, fingers splayed. The audience hushes with his silent command, and I, too, fall under his thrall.

"Lay-dees and gentlemen, welcome to the Hippodrome, the largest theater in the world!" His voice somehow expands into this vast space. The audience cheers, pent-up energies gone wild. Houdini circles the stage, basking in their appreciation. "And thank you all for your generous support for our allies who are in their thousandth day of battle to maintain peace in our world.

"Some of you may have heard of the fame and accomplishments of my very special guest." He waves his arm to the right, and a spotlight appears on the red curtain at the back of the stage. The curtains part to reveal an enormous gray elephant, trunk and mouth curved up as if smiling. Five thousand people gasp and laugh, and suddenly I'm happy to be front row rather than stuck in their midst.

"Meet Jenny, the beautiful daughter of Jumbo from Barnum and Bailey," he projects. "Unlike her father, who weighed in at eighteen thousand pounds, our sweet Jenny is a demure ten thousand, and I love every ounce. Give her a hand, lay-dees and gents."

The crowd roars while a slip of a man dressed in black prances backward toward Houdini and the pachyderm follows. He whips a lead through the air like a conductor, and Jenny follows his commands. She trots across the stage, shaking the floor with each landing of her huge feet, circling Houdini, head swiveling side to side with the music. She kicks her legs out to the bass drum, her tail and trunk swinging. Houdini steps up to the elephant and holds out his arm. "May I have this dance, Miss Jenny?"

She lifts up on hind legs, and the orchestra strikes up a waltz. Houdini holds her front leg as if holding a woman's hand. They step forward, side, side, back . . . waltzing, and the crowd is mesmerized.

When the music stops, Jenny comes to a halt, lowers her front legs to the ground, and bows. Houdini swirls his hand dramatically and from nowhere produces a large bouquet of pink carnations. "I got you a little something, Jenny, for being such a good girl."

Jenny takes the bouquet with her trunk and stuffs it into her mouth, chomping them with obvious delight.

Houdini raises his arms to the audience. "Girls love their flowers."

The audience titters, and Jenny raises her trunk to trumpet, standing on her hind legs, towering over Houdini. The blast stops the audience chatter, and everyone watches to see what happens next.

Carefully, he steps out from under her and addresses the audience. "I almost hate to see this young Jenny go, but disappear she must, for that is what you came to see."

A timpani rumbles, and a team of twelve men rolls a large cage onto the stage, through the red velvet curtains.

"This is Jenny's circus cage, about eight feet square, twenty-six inches off the ground, just big enough for our Jenny."

The men open the side door and lower the ramp, and Houdini walks into the cage and points out the curtains on both sides, the solid wall at one end, and the ramp at the other end. We see stagehands through the open back curtains, standing behind the cage.

Houdini waves his cane under the cage to show that there's nothing underneath except space. He even passes his cane through to guarantee it's completely open. Once he's given us the full tour and we're convinced of its normality, he walks to Jenny and gives her a fond pat on her cheek. "Ready to go, dear?"

Jenny trumpets, and Houdini holds his hand to his ear and leans into her. "You want to hear some ragtime before you go?"

She trumpets again.

The band strikes up that new Jolson tune, "Yaaka Hula Hickey Dula," and Jenny bounces along to the beat. Her trainer marches into the cage like a bandleader, and Jenny follows him with great, lumbering steps. The cage barely fits her from trunk to tail.

Houdini signals the orchestra to stop with a flick of his hands, and the lights go black except for spotlights on the cage.

"And now for the biggest disappearing act in the world." He draws the curtains together in the back and walks around to the front.

"Say toodle-loo for now, Jenny." He pulls the front curtain closed. Her trumpet has turned to a sad growl.

"She's ready to go, men. Lock her in."

Two stagehands lift the ramp with a loud clank and insert iron pins on each side.

Sitting on the edge of my seat, I wonder how he'll pull this off. *If* he can pull this off.

Ratatatatatatat. The drum rolls. "And now if you'll count with me while I make our beautiful Jenny disappear.

"One—Two—Three."

The crowd draws in a last breath, Houdini pulls back the front curtain, and they gasp.

Ten thousand pounds of elephant—vanished. Jenny is gone.

Houdini opens the back curtain, and all we see are stagehands with hands clasped behind their backs.

Five thousand spectators jump out of their seats and scream, the sound deafening. I see only Houdini's face in the spotlight, a staged smile plastered on his face, nothing like the exaltation I'd witnessed in San Francisco after his performances. His empty eyes track the vacant cage as a dozen stagehands struggle to shove it off the stage.

Why isn't he happy with the performance? I wave bravely, now wanting him to see me. We'll go out to dinner, talk into the night. But the spotlight cuts out, leaving us in darkness before the house lights come on, and Houdini is gone.

The front row moves toward the backstage door, queuing up for a visit with Houdini. I put on my white fur jacket and pull out my Solomon Islands shell compact and redraw my lipstick. The cosmetics girl at Bergdorf's was right, berry red does make me look younger, though I can't imagine wearing lipstick at the ranch.

The ranch. A quick shot of guilt. I promised to write to Eliza and haven't picked up a pen except to re-create my notes on Jack's biography.

The line moves rapidly, and soon I'm next to duck through the door onto a platform with stairs leading a few feet below.

"Move along, Mr. Houdini has another engagement in Hoboken." A mustachioed man in suspenders keeps the line moving as Houdini shakes hands and scribbles autographs. There must be thirty of us to get through.

A magnificent creature poses on a gilded chair beside Houdini, her bejeweled hand possessively on his shoulder. She throws back her head with a low, husky laugh, and her throat shows the lines of an older woman. Instinctively, my hand covers my neck. How I hate those new rings which creep in each year like a tree.

"You're wicked," Houdini tells her. At least that's what I think I hear from the platform above him. Intimate insults.

The next man in line asks for the woman's autograph, too. Her beaded headdress winds around her waved mane and onto her high cheekbones. Gold braids bind her scarab-print dress around her ample breasts, and suddenly I recognize her—Sarah Bernhardt. Jack and I saw her in the film *Jeanne Doré*, and she tore our hearts out with the prison scene when she visits her son before execution. Not long after that, the actress contracted gangrene and had her right leg amputated. That didn't stop her bourgeoning film career.

The divine Sarah strokes Houdini's cheek flirtatiously. "Seriously, Harry, if you can make an elephant disappear, surely you can give me back my leg."

Houdini huffs. "I never claimed to have supernatural powers."

"Ah, but we all know you do, don't we?" she asks the fans, who respond with cheers and nods.

I, too, am curious. Replace her leg? Could he really do it?

"We have all seen you walk straight through brick walls and break out of jail cells shackled with chains." She signs a program and moves to the next person.

"I seen it wid my own eyes," a woman agrees.

Houdini shakes his head, but his smile belies his denial. The actress continues to charm him, and my neck steams under this fur.

"Follow this logic." She holds up a long painted fingernail to the rest of us, then turns to Houdini. "You *could* make the elephant reappear, could you not?"

He snickers. "Yes, of course."

"Then it follows you could bring my leg back. You cannot argue with reason."

Houdini laughs. I never saw him so gay. This is a different world. A rarefied world of impossible feats and famous actresses.

Now I'm the one who wants to disappear. Can I squeeze past them unnoticed?

"I'm afraid that's all the time we have," the stage manager says.

I turn around and climb the steps to leave. Those around me are grumbling, but I'm relieved. What did I hope to gain by coming here? I look back for a last glimpse of Houdini.

His eyes flash like a sunbeam waking me at dawn. I brace myself on the iron railing.

The divine Sarah takes his arm. "The driver is waiting. Help me to the car, won't you, *mi amor*?"

Houdini holds one finger up, as if gesturing me to wait, but then says, "I'll send you a letter."

Miss Bernhardt takes his arm, but he turns back at the door. "A letter within a letter." A sheepish smile and he leaves, dousing my anticipation like a taxicab spraying slush over my new outfit.

He wants to send me a letter after all we've shared?

Breakfast at Romany Marie's becomes my first order of the day. She roasts coffee beans over the fire until the nutty smell fills the restaurant. Then she grinds the beans, puts them in a percolator, and sets it on the fire grate to boil.

The new cook, a young man she brought over from Romania, presses out sweet dough and layers it with apples, raisins, cinnamon, and dark honey, which he then rolls and cuts rounds from. The scent of them baking makes my mouth water and my stomach growl with desire. When he takes them out of the oven, he slathers them with butter and serves me the first one, standing over me with questioning brown eyes.

This morning, Romany Marie slides her arm into his as I bite into the roll, my taste buds buzzing with pleasure.

"Good, huh?" she asks, and I nod, taking another bite.

Romany Marie looks up at the young man, speaks in Romanian, and he leaves, taking his mixing bowls and utensils with him.

"He's a fast learner, my cousin," Romany Marie says. "I'll be sorry to see him go."

"But he just got here," I say.

She shrugs. "He'll find a job, that one." She glances around the restaurant, but there's only a couple at a table near the front door, reading the newspaper and drinking coffee. "Three more cousins arrive next week from Romania."

I nod, starting to understand. "You're bringing them out."

"While the Romanian military wavers whether to join the Germans or Russia or the Allies, hundreds of thousands of our men have died because of our leaders' lust for blood. If our family stays in Romania, we'll have no men left. Better they come here as bakers and chefs or garbage collectors than be slaughtered without cause."

"Your family is lucky to have you."

She takes a deep breath and pats my arm. "What about you? Going out walking again today?"

She knows me well. Walking the streets of New York invigorates me. In Chinatown, I buy ginseng and marvel at plucked ducks hanging to dry. On Fifth Avenue, I see modern hemlines rise as shop girls change mannequins in the display windows. When I miss Beauty Ranch, I walk the snowy wonderland of Central Park.

In the afternoons, I write Jack's biography by the fireplace in my flat. Little-known quirks come back to me in detail more vivid than life. The pranks he played, like short-sheeting our houseguests. The diving lessons he taught neighbor children at Wake Robin, throwing key rings in the pool for them to find; hours lying together in the hammock, conjuring up ridiculous limericks. I laugh and cry reliving our lives.

And miraculously, when I hit the mattress at night, I sleep the deep healing sleep that has eluded me most of my life.

"Was there any mail yesterday?" I ask Romany Marie, as I have every day since the Hippodrome show, knowing full well Houdini has no idea how to reach me.

"Ah, yes. I almost forgot." She goes behind the counter. My heart skips. What will Houdini's letter say?

When I recognize the penmanship, my heart sinks. "It's just from Eliza, my sister-in-law."

"You're disappointed." She pats my hand. "Remember, family is good." The bell on the front door rings, and Romany Marie greets the customers.

I open Eliza's letter, hearing the hearty timbre of her voice, so like Jack's. Three pages asking guidance on things Jack used to decide; whether to rebuild a piggery wall that collapsed in an earthquake (hell no), run irrigation for the youngest eucalyptus starts, or cut down the spineless cactus he planted to feed the cattle. It grew thorns this year. She says, "Possum is lost without you and Jack." A pang stabs my gut.

Eliza's PS: Netta is worried about me and wonders where I am . . .

Romany Marie comes from behind and pours me another cup of coffee. Sipping the nutty brew, I decide to turn the page down on Netta. She's caused enough pain for one life.

That's how it's done. One decision at a time.

---

I spritz lavender on my wrists for strength and composure.

Two weeks have passed with no letter from Houdini. How could there be? He has no idea where I am staying. Our walk on the beach was thousands of miles from reality—he never thought I'd follow him home like a lost puppy. How could I think he was as taken with me as I was with him?

I shove two boxes of raspberry-cream chocolates in my carpetbag and catch a taxi uptown.

The towering Flatiron Building furrows through the sky like a field plow. Pushing back my shoulders, I march through the lobby as if I belong. At least my suit seems to, thanks to Edna at Bergdorf's. I needed an outfit that projected steely assurance, and she fitted me with a khaki military jacket and flared skirt, my armor of determination.

Despite my pumped-up courage, I'm happy to see the closed eyelids of Skippy, opening the crosshatched brass gate. "Nice to see you again, Mrs. London."

"Likewise, Skippy." I hand him a small box. "I thought you might enjoy some chocolates."

His head weaves side to side. "Um-um-um. What a treat."

This time when he opens the gate for the twenty-second floor, I don't hesitate to move forward. "Thank you, Skippy. See you on the way down." With contract in hand . . .

I check the watch Jack gave me, 11:44. Wish me luck, Jack. I walk into the office; the receptionist couldn't look more unreceptive. "Hello, Miss Johnson. Here are the raspberry creams I promised."

She takes the box, color draining from her face. "I—uh—I didn't know how to reach you, but Mr. Brett can't see you today. He's just been called away."

The elevator bell dings behind me, and I turn. A man waits, head down, drumming his fingers on the door. George Brett's hair has thinned and grayed since we last met.

"Mr. Brett." Walking toward him, I extend my hand, and he's forced to accept my firm handshake. "I wanted to thank you for the beautiful bouquet you sent for Jack's funeral."

"Mrs. London, I'm sorry I have to rush off." He shakes his head, bullets of perspiration popping on his brow. "I didn't expect you in New York. We really should let the lawyers hash out the details." He punches the button again. "Unfortunately, I have to—"

"What lawyers?"

He clears his throat, holding his finger on the button that rings shrilly. "Publishing rights to Jack's work. All quite boilerplate, I'm sure. Mrs. Johnson, give Mrs. London my lawyer's card."

His nervous rebuff irritates me, but I can't let that distract me now. "I won't take much of your time. I just came to tell you that we can fulfill Jack's biography contract."

He turned to face me. "He finished it before he—?"

"I'm writing it."

I hear the tiniest moan as Miss Johnson bites into a raspberry cream.

"You."

"Me." I tilt my head and smile—Aunt Netta's girlhood lessons.

"To be frank, Mrs. London, Macmillan took a beating publishing your book, *The Log of the Snark*." Red splotches bloom on his cheeks and neck. "And Jack insisted we publish your next book, *Our Hawaii*, which comes out this month. Let's see how that sells before we discuss Jack's biography."

"Mr. Brett, you begged for Jack's biography. Who better than me to write it?"

He pulls at his mustache. "We can't risk another failure. No one's buying books now with the Great War hanging over their heads."

I gulp, trying to dislodge the persistent lump in my throat. "I need my own source of income."

"What was Jack working on—at the end?"

"Several things—I don't know, I haven't looked at them—'The Red One,' *On the Makaloa Mat*, *Cherry* . . ."

He rolls his eyes upward. "Good. Good. Let's focus on finishing those, and you'll still get royalties from Jack's published novels, of course. As long as you grant Macmillan posthumous rights."

"Of course. Posthumous rights." The pieces fall into place.

Miss Johnson pops two more chocolates, and her cheeks bulge like a squirrel.

"Miss Johnson, quit stuffing your maw and get that card for Mrs. London." He hits the button. "Damn it, Skippy, where are you?"

She hands me a crisp white card, but the tiny type blurs in my vision.

"Perhaps Doubleday will want Jack's biography," I start tentatively, liking the sound of it and gaining momentum. "A package deal, perhaps. Jack's biography, his unpublished novels, and posthumous publishing rights." The elevator car arrives, Skippy opens the gate, and I walk in. "You know, Mr. Brett, you're right." I hold up the business card. "Let's leave this matter with the lawyers. Down, please, Skippy."

Running out of the Flatiron into the frigid air, I'm proud of my pluck. What would Jack say? The recurring question . . . What would he say, what would he do, what would he want? The echo of a man so fierce and vital that his absence speaks louder than reality.

Pulling my coat around me, I start walking to Greenwich. Thoughts of the war and Macmillan crash through my mind like an avalanche. My shoulders and lower back ache like the devil, and my boots are getting soaked from slush. Thick clouds smother the feeble sun and drop the temperature twenty degrees. I'm chilled to the bone and starving.

As much fun as it was to tell off George Brett, it probably wasn't such a good idea, given my precarious finances. He's been our publisher for fifteen years . . . Ours. There *is* no ours anymore.

# 27

## Greenwich Village, New York City, New York March 1917

Due to a boxing match between my ego and Macmillan's rejection, writer's block is named the victor. So despite the new storm, I spend all day walking New York City, exhausting my last nerve, and feeling every ache of my forty-five years in my hips and knees.

The sky has turned dark when I finally return to the alley behind Romany Marie's. The squeal of the gypsy violin and smell of goulash beckon me inside. But there's a shadowy form standing by the stairway to my flat, and I freeze.

"Who's there?"

Houdini steps into the light. He's not wearing an overcoat against the spring chill, just a black sweater and trousers. Except for the wrinkle between his brows, he appears relaxed and casual, ready for an evening at home. By contrast, I look a fright from burrowing through the snow like the horse plows on Union Square.

"Why didn't you answer my letter, Charmian?"

"Maybe you sent it to the divine Sarah?" My attempt at humor sounds childish and jealous. "How did you find me?"

He lays a finger aside his nose. "Instinct."

"Ah." I nod and feel the ache in my lower back. Why is he here now?

He smirks. "I let myself in, started the water boiling for tea."

My mouth drops open but turns into a laugh. He holds out his arm, and I take it, grateful for the help with my tired limbs.

In the dim light above the door, he points out a crevice in the brick with an envelope stuck inside. It could have been there for days, unnoticed in the dark stairway. The envelope is addressed to me in flourishing penmanship.

I reach in my bag for my key, but he opens the door first. I hang my coat next to his on the coatrack. The fireplace crackles—I hadn't had time to replace the firewood, but there's an ample supply stacked on the hearth. A new purple vase holds my favorite flowers of tuberose, heliotrope, and stargazers. The exotic perfume eases the tension in my temples. The teakettle whistles from the woodstove.

"I'll get that. Sit by the fire," he says, and walks over to the kitchenette.

The envelope in my hand makes me smile. So he did write a letter. I set it on the mantel under the Romany Marie oil painting. From the look in her eyes, she approves of my gentleman caller.

I pour a sherry from the carafe on the sideboard and almost pour one for him before I remember he doesn't drink. My knees quake with exhaustion. I'm completely undone. I take my drink over to the divan, considering the meaning of all this: flowers, a fire, tea—warm gestures that would have never crossed Jack's mind. I find myself petting the tiger rug. Curious, indeed.

He sets down a tray on the low table between the sofa and fire and pours steaming tea, smelling of bergamot.

My hands press my thawing cheeks. "I must look a wreck."

"You look like a girl after ice skating," he says, handing me a blue china cup. He sits beside me, his face softened by the firelight, so different from the alert performer I'd seen on the stage.

"I don't suppose you'd care to tell me how you made Jenny disappear."

He smiles mysteriously and blows on his tea.

"I thought not." I laugh. "As remarkable as that was, I couldn't help missing the derring-do of your escapes."

His bottom lip pushes up. "Bess couldn't take the pressure. Too many injuries, too many close calls." He sips his tea. "She's always been a nervous type, but it got too much for her."

"Is she all right now?" I drink the tea.

"As long as I don't perform escapes." He stares at his teacup, his mouth set in a grim line.

"So you're back to performing magic."

He snaps his fingers, his fingertips flame, and he lights the candelabra. "All of life is mystery and magic." His fist clenches, and the flames go out.

Despite the impressive showmanship, I know I've hit a sore point. He misses escapes.

"My mother used to make lebkuchen." He offers me cookies smelling of allspice, citrus, and nuts. "She would have liked you, Charmian."

Taken aback by his comment, I chew the spicy-sweet lebkuchen.

"*I* like you, Charmian." He traces my jawbone with his thumb, and a scintillating current flows through my face.

"I like *you*, Magic," I say glibly, trying not to assume too much. Our breath mingles, black tea, bergamot, cinnamon.

His eyes close halfway as if mulling something over, then he kneels in front of me. But he simply unbuttons my boots and sets them by the fire. Slips off wet stockings and garters, making me shiver.

"Your feet are like icebergs." He rubs them with warm hands, strong and dexterous. It seems odd to have him rubbing my feet, but right now it's the best thing in the world, his knuckles rotating on my soles, his fingers twisting my toes. I lie back and relax. A low moan escapes my throat.

The next thing I know, he's carrying me to the bed encircled with tapestry curtains. The comforter has been folded back, and he lays me on the horsehair mattress, lumpy and unforgiving, a punishment to my aching muscles.

His lips brush my cheek with a slight shock, breath spicy like the cookies. "Your suit is wet. May I help you?"

Then he's unbuttoning the bone buttons and peeling me out of my jacket and blouse, down to my ivory satin camisole. Carefully, he hangs them in the wardrobe. Desire warms my abdomen.

I push the thought away and start to unbutton my skirt.

"Let me," he says, and slides it off.

The way he caresses my legs with such tender concern, his eyes following their path. I moan and twist my legs, aching for his touch.

"This mattress must be hell."

"Like losing a prizefight. There's a feather bed in the cupboard." I start to get up.

"Lay back and relax." His hands hover over the length of me.

I close my eyes and try to unwind. My breath slows, my heartbeat slows, and soon the lumpy mattress fades away. In fact, I feel nothing beneath me but cool air.

I open my eyes. His hands still hover above me, then slide beneath me in the empty inches between me and the mattress.

"What are you doing?" I laugh.

"Don't talk. Enjoy," he says, and I drift higher, maybe a foot off the mattress. "Keep breathing and remain calm. Would you like to sleep this way?"

"I don't think so."

He pulls the feather bed out of the cupboard and spreads it underneath my floating body. "That should be more comfortable."

He raises his hands once again and lowers my body onto the thick cushion of feathers. It feels divine. My whole body feels renewed. I groan with pleasure.

He throws a comforter over me, folding it down at the top. When he tucks me in, my breath hitches with disappointment.

"Charmian, tell me to leave." A small smile plays on his sculpted lips.

I draw his head down to mine and kiss him.

Houdini stays.

First light brushes my eyelids, and I reach for him, a single tuberose left on the feather bed in his place. The sizzle of the stoked fire chases the morning chill from the flat, the delicious smell of boiling coffee tempts me. He must be at the stove. My eyes sweep the room, but it's vacant, save for fresh bagels, cured salmon, and cream cheese set in front of the fire.

I lie back on the feather bed, remembering our closeness last night. We never parted, as our hunger for each other never sated. And now he's gone, and I have no way to reach him unless I go back to the Hippodrome and fight the crowds—or worse, call at his brownstone in the tony Harlem neighborhood where he lives with Bessie.

Bessie.

I haven't allowed myself to think about her. It's been a year and a half since I met her, yet the memory of her vivid personality still fizzes in my mind like pink champagne. She told me they weren't intimate, didn't she? Or am I twisting facts to suit my purpose?

This new guilt angers me. I should be free to love as I wish . . . But sweet, quirky Bessie bubbles up.

I wrap a Japanese kimono around me, a gift from Jack. What would he think to see me now? There it is again, wondering about Jack. I imagine him winking or scowling, egging me forward, pouting petulantly. I will not, cannot, let his disparate signals confuse me even now, after his death.

I pour a cup of coffee and settle into the divan with the egg bagel my magic man left me. What do I do now? Wait until he shows up at my doorstep again?

The envelope Houdini left me from that first show is still on the mantel. I open it, and a ticket to his Hippodrome show falls onto my lap. Inside are two pages, a smaller one tucked within the other. A letter within a letter. In formal penmanship, he writes about the Statue of Liberty, our great symbol of freedom, the broken chain around her feet, reminding us that shackles others impose cannot bind us. He signs it simply, "Magic."

Is he confessing his own obsession with freedom? Or saying that Jack's death has set me free?

And the smaller page, written in the Pitman shorthand: "Meet me tonight at the Hippodrome. We have waited too long."

So he had contacted me after all.

Romany Marie fills her hammered bronze bird feeder on the back porch of the restaurant. Sparrows, starlings, and laughing gulls come to eat from the feeder.

"Taking a trip?" Her dark eyes flash shrewdly.

I can't stop the smile on my face, though I know I should be discreet. "Just overnight."

"Well, from the look of the roses in your cheeks and the muscles on your suitor, I'd say you are in good hands."

"You met him?"

She smiles with painted burgundy lips. "How else would he find bagels in Greenwich?"

My laugh is hopelessly giddy.

Romany's dark eyes narrow. "Don't break his heart."

Breath huffs out of my nose. "I have no such intention. We are very good friends."

"Even though you have not yet discovered it, you are at the stage of life to get what you want. Perhaps he is not." Her black eyebrow arches. "But he likes Romanian food. Bring him around Thursday for stuffed peppers. His mother used to make them."

Waving goodbye—I'm not about to discuss the complexity of our relationship—I high-step my way through the fresh milk bottles in the narrow alleyway. My heel catches on one and tips it over, spilled milk.

Unseasonably warm winds buffet the avenues, bringing the hope of spring. Suddenly the tea dress I'm wearing doesn't feel as silly as it did when I first put it on. He said to come tonight, but I thought I'd catch his matinee.

Pedestrians stride purposefully in front of the Hippodrome, collars open, smiles on their faces, like actors in a Hollywood movie depicting spring in New York. It's early, but no one's lined up for tickets to the show yet. A hasty sign in front of the ticket office says, **Matinees Canceled Until Further Notice.**

My chest tightens. Now what? I jerk at a door—locked. I try another and another in the bank of eight, my frustration growing. He's not here. No one is here. The last door opens, and adrenaline surges through me. Yes. I slip through the door. The enormous lobby echoes with the closing of the door, and I stand still, heart racing.

Not a soul around, yet a commanding voice drifts in from the auditorium. I walk toward the doors in my heels—I try to walk softly, but the click, clack, click on the marble floors sounds like a flamenco dancer.

I open the door a crack and peer in.

No ushers, no orchestra, no spotlights. Just Houdini on the stage, wearing the same black sweater and trousers from last night. A couple hundred men are wearing military uniforms—marines, army, navy in separate sections. The audience sits ramrod straight in their theater seats, not a smile or utterance from their lips.

I slip into a back-row seat and sit low.

A bugle begins to play taps, and the soldiers stand at attention while the American flag rises into the air. When the plaintive tune finishes, the soldiers throw up their hats and catch them again. Houdini punches the air with his fist. "Huzzah! Huzzah!"

"As president of the Society of American Magicians, I've dedicated our membership to the service of the American military. The foremost magicians in the country are working with the military on camouflage, cryptography, counterintelligence, and escape techniques, which we'll focus on today."

He takes a deep breath. "Remember one thing and one thing only. The Germans cannot hold you captive if you tell yourself this one thing." He taps his temple with his forefinger. "My brain is the tool that sets me free."

He said something like that at Tadich Grill in San Francisco—a lifetime ago.

"The Germans are arrogant, and that arrogance is their own worst enemy. They think their jail cells and handcuffs are second to none, but they're child's play if you keep calm and carry a small wire—say a woman's hairpin or tailor pin."

He holds up a thin sliver, glinting in the light.

"My assistants are passing tailor pins out to you now. I suggest you conceal that pin in the inside seam of your undershorts, not too close to the crotch, if you catch my drift."

The soldiers chuckle.

He holds handcuffs above his head.

"Practice, practice, practice with the handcuffs my staff is passing out. You cannot go to Europe without knowing with certainty you can unlock any handcuff."

He demonstrates different types of handcuffs and how to unlock each one. Locking himself in a cage, he instructs them how to use the tailor pin to gain freedom from any prison cell.

He explains his inventions for espionage: hollow heels to conceal tools, cameras that work only once, ink that vanishes upon opening the envelope. Secrets he's never revealed before. No matter who pleads with him, I've never seen him expose how a trick is done.

When does a master reveal his secrets? When there is no other choice. He's preparing them for the Great War. As he ends his presentation and the soldiers are leaving, he notices me and grimaces.

I shouldn't be here. As I run out through the lobby, into the biting air, my chest is heavy.

Houdini follows me. "You weren't supposed to see that. No one can see that. Not yet."

"Your note said—I thought you wanted me to meet—" I glance down at my carpetbag, in which I'd tucked a new negligee and a change of clothes, just in case.

"Ah, remember? I wrote the letter within a letter weeks ago, and you never came." He grabs my hand, looking right and left. "They can't know you were here." He signals a Winton Six limousine parked on the street. The chauffeur opens the back door, and I get in, carpetbag on my lap. Houdini slips in after me. The chauffeur starts up the limousine, slides the window closed between us, and pulls into traffic.

"You want to come with me?"

"Where are we going?" I ask.

"Long Island," he says, and I laugh.

"Where Coney Island is?"

"Ah, Bessie's stories of how we met . . ." He looks wistful.

"Which one is true?" I ask.

"Whichever one she's telling at the time."

It's not right, gossiping about her.

He takes my chin in forefinger and thumb. "Hey, hey . . . don't worry about Bessie. She's queen bee, my Bessie, running two households exactly as she sees fit—the Brooklyn house with my brothers and their wives and the Harlem brownstone with her mother and sister and a menagerie of birds, dogs, rabbits, by last count." His eyebrows pinch together. "I love Bessie and would never want to hurt her, it's just—"

I put my hand on his. "She told me about her condition."

His eyes open wide. "She never tells a soul, she must trust you." He squeezes my hand, puts it down, and looks out the car window. "Anyway, she's a peach of a girl . . ."

I should go back to Greenwich.

I expect the Coney Island Boardwalk—sun, sand, and ocean—but instead we go a couple miles southeast of Mineola to a field overtaken by frenetic activity. At the gate, workmen are taking down a small sign that says **Hempstead Plains Aerodrome** and replacing it with a larger sign: **Hazelhurst Field**. Two military guards stand armed and at attention at the gate. One approaches the limousine, and Houdini lowers his window.

"Good afternoon. I should be on your list. Ehrich Weiss and my guest, Mrs. London."

The guard nods and checks the roster, then salutes. "Hangar Three, sir."

"Ehrich Weiss?" I ask.

"My given name." He takes my hand, eyes sparkling with mischief.

The limousine drives past rows of barracks under construction and another tower, the frame already higher than the old ones. Thirty or so biplanes stand ready in the field. One is taking off, and another awaiting its turn. The roar of the engines is deafening.

Houdini's mouth moves, but I can't hear. "What?"

The limousine pulls into Hangar Three, and it's quieter there. Mechanics are working on half a dozen planes.

"I said, don't worry, I have earmuffs in the plane," he says.

My stomach flip-flops. "You can't be serious. I've never flown."

His forefinger touches the side of his nose. "Don't worry, we have a good pilot."

Bessie said he quit flying after his crash. I wonder if he would take it up again, now with Germany attacking every country within reach.

The limousine stops in front of a sturdy-looking biplane painted dull gray, nothing as exciting as the showy plane to the side, with its red, white, and blue–striped tail and red propeller.

Our chauffeur lets us out and opens the trunk, producing two small duffels. Houdini hands him a twenty-dollar bill. "We'll be back tomorrow evening, about seven."

"Yessir, Mr. Weiss, sir." The chauffer salutes, gets back in the limousine, and drives out of the hangar.

A small, swarthy man in a gray jumpsuit strides over from the colorful plane, wiping his greasy hands on a rag. Houdini shakes his hand.

"Charmian London meet Antonio Brassac, ace pilot and airplane mechanic."

"That's a beauty." I nod my head toward the plane he's working on.

"A millionaire's toy," he scoffs.

Houdini nods and pats the gray plane. "Nothing like the Jenny."

"You seem to have a thing for girls named Jenny," I tease.

"Curtiss JN-4, nicknamed the Jenny, ma'am," the pilot says. His confidence takes the edge off my jitters. At least we'll have someone trustworthy behind the wheel.

Walking around the plane, Houdini tests the upper and lower wings on each side, the wheels, the propeller, the fuel pumping into the tank.

"She's clean, boss. Checked her over myself, nothing to worry about," Antonio says.

Houdini hands me one of the duffels. "You can change over there." He points to a restroom.

My nerves shoot like fireworks. I should feel great anticipation, like I did when Jack and I boarded the *Snark* for our world sail. But that was so long ago, when my spirit was young and alive . . .

Or was it only Jack who teased out my spirit? And I'm colorless on my own. The thought makes me mad. I rip open the duffel and pull on the olive-drab jodhpurs and long-sleeved shirt, which fit me to a tee. Studying myself in the mirror, I realize I haven't seen the spark in my eyes for too long. What could possibly be bad about feeling alive again?

I laugh at my feet. Heels don't do a thing for the outfit.

When I walk out to the plane, Houdini is wearing an identical outfit, except with tall boots. He grins and hands me a box. "Size five?"

Inside, there's a pair of shiny brown boots that reach up to my knees. It feels so girlish and silly, but they thrill me just the same.

We fit goggles and tight caps over our heads, making me feel like a turtle in its shell. He holds the ladder, and I climb up into the plane, taking the seat behind the pilot. Just enough room for my small body. Where's Houdini's seat?

Right in front of me, he fastens himself into the cockpit, Antonio watching from below.

I start to hiccup, my diaphragm flopping around like a fish on a hot skillet.

Houdini checks and rechecks the instruments, then salutes Antonio and starts the engine. The Jenny moves out of the hangar and onto a long asphalt runway.

Houdini guns the engine, and we sail down the runway at frightening speed, my fingernails implanted in his shoulder blades. Where did my guts go? The airplane struggles to lift off. Houdini pulls up the steering wheel. The plane peels off the runway, then bounces back. We are nearing the end. He'll have to stop. But he lays his entire body back, and the nose pulls up as if under his will. My stomach soars with the plane.

Air roars past my ears, the ground recedes below us. Houdini gives me a thumbs-up, and I squeeze his shoulders. We're flying!

The Atlantic Ocean below laps at the beaches as we head down the coast. Pure exhilaration comes back to roost. Jack would have loved this.

Never thought to ask where we were flying. I didn't care. As we fly, I watch the coastline change from broad beaches to dense forests, then rocky cliffs. I watch the sun's long arc overhead, traveling west over America. I had initially imagined a joyride, but this is getting long for that. The engine and propeller noise is much too loud to ask any questions, so I sit back and enjoy the ride.

Four hours due south, we are still flying. A full moon rises from the dusky eastern horizon. Below, a city looks surreal in the late sun. The Capitol's dome shines bright as a beacon, and Houdini begins our descent.

It is one thing to be flying through the air without a care, quite another feeling entirely when the nose of the plane brings the earth closer and closer.

But Houdini sets the plane down on the runway as smoothly as apple butter on bread. My heart pounds my rib cage, and my ears buzz so loudly I can't hear a thing. On the runway, Houdini talks to three army officers; I have no idea their rank, but they sport innumerable ribbons and bars and badges. He doesn't introduce me, and I'm glad since I still can't hear a thing. I spy a restroom and take the moment to change out of my gear and back into my dress.

Apparently Houdini did the same, because he's in a new suit. A sight I'm not used to. I only think of him in skintight swimsuits or sleek tuxedos, performing on a stage. A normal suit seems unfitting for my magic man.

Another limousine drives us through rows and rows of budding cherry trees.

"Where are we going?" My voice is too loud, and I point to my ears. "Sorry, my ears are plugged."

"Ever stay at the Willard hotel?" He squeezes my hand.

The electric streetlights of Washington, DC, highlight his strong cheekbones and Roman nose. I'd keep staring if he weren't watching. But since he is, I sit back and focus on the Capitol, gleaming and stately like a grand wedding cake. In a few short blocks, we pass the White House, quiet and surreal, guards pacing the grounds.

The limousine pulls into the Willard hotel's circular drive, and doormen in red cutaway jackets and top hats open our doors simultaneously.

A blond man greets Houdini, clasps both his hands and shakes them with great enthusiasm. A meticulous mustache forms a pristine outline around his top lip. A name tag pinned to his pinstriped tailored suit says, **Mr. Fitzgerald, Manager**. He can't seem to let go of Houdini's hands, shaking them, grinning under his blond mustache.

Houdini leans to him and says something I can't hear.

The manager nods vigorously. "Of course, of course, Mr. Houdini. Not a word." He walks behind the reception desk.

Women in ball gowns and fur coats commandeer the arms of men in formal suits, on their way to dinner, I suppose, and my stomach rumbles. I haven't eaten since this morning.

Persian tapestry sofas and gilded chairs are filled with overfed, self-important politicians and their wives. No Socialists here, from the looks of things. Such man-made opulence seems a poor substitute for nature in my eyes.

Chinese porcelain urns are planted with the same kinds of tropical palm trees I've seen growing in Hawaii or Fiji or Mexico. Roman columns soar to arched ceilings painted with clouds and cherubs.

My knees go wobbly from the long flight, and I lean on a chair.

"You must be exhausted. Mr. Fitzgerald won't be long, and we can go to our room," Magic says.

His caring words hit my ears like a foreign language. Our room. A rush of guilt charges through my body; for Bessie or Jack, I'm not sure.

"I prefer my own," I blurt, and regret it when Magic's eyes dim.

"Of course." He walks to the desk and has a word with the manager.

What a perfect fraud I am. Living my life under the banner of liberated women, and now faced with the opportunity to prove it, I react like an innocent virgin.

The manager comes back with Houdini. "Can the bellman bring your bags?"

"I'll take them." Magic grabs my carpetbag and his oversized valise.

"Oh no, allow me." The manager reaches out, but Houdini swings his bag away.

"This bag never leaves my hands." He wipes his glistening forehead with a handkerchief, collects himself, and smiles. "But you can carry this one if you like." He hands the manager my bag.

"Of course, my apologies." He walks us to the grand staircase leading to the mezzanine. Ivory-enameled hallways glimmer with gilded cornices and sconces. Houdini's walking so closely, his hip brushes mine. My fingers graze his.

"The Willard is so proud to have you here, Mr. Houdini."

I barely hear the manager's patter, so attuned am I to Magic's scent of wood spice and fresh air, the clip of his polished wingtips on the marble floor, the soft rustling of wool between his powerful thighs.

"The newspapers have stirred everyone to a frenzy about tomorrow," Fitzgerald says.

"What's tomorrow?" I ask.

"Houdini's jump from the *Washington Times* building," he says matter-of-factly, as he turns left down a gracious hallway.

I grab Magic's hand and whisper, "I thought you gave up dangerous feats."

"I can't pull rabbits from a hat forever." He smirks.

"You won't do anything foolish, will you?"

"For thirty years, I've escaped death, and maybe one day it'll catch me. But not tomorrow. I wanted you to be here."

Mr. Fitzgerald stops at a doorway and inserts a key with an elaborate gold tassel. "I think you'll be pleased." He opens the door and gestures for us to go in. "The princess of Sweden stayed here last week."

Mr. Fitzgerald turns on the electric lamps, each with its own ruffled shade, and the room springs alive in an abundance of floral chintz, like an overgrown garden.

He prattles on about the periods of the furniture and a particular English designer—William Morris, he says.

There are pink roses on the dresser in a white hobnail vase, snapdragons on the nightstand. Ruffles and frills and florals mix like a cocktail of too many ingredients. Feeling woozy, I sit on the bed, unstable in this glossy world. Missing riding horseback, shooting skeet, exchanging cigarettes for beads with headhunters. Missing Jack.

The manager must ask me something I don't catch, because he's looking at me expectantly.

"It's lovely," I say, longing to close my eyes.

Houdini pats my hand. "Take your time freshening up, and we'll go down for dinner."

"Dinner is good," I say.

As soon as the men leave, I lie back on the bed, and my eyes close . . . The bed is so soft and warm . . .

. . . a woodpecker knocks on the side of our cottage, interrupting Jack's story as I type. The woodpecker so insistent . . .

I bolt upright. The knocking comes from the double doors on the far side of my room. I open them, and Houdini is there, smiling roguishly. Adjoining rooms.

"I must have dozed off. Give me a minute." My step has a surprising spring to it as I walk to my bathroom, slip out of my dress and into the shower, sudsing my body with castile soap. Every nerve ending tingles with pleasure.

Stepping from the shower into a thick Turkish towel, I look into the mirror surrounded by round bulbs. Flourishing complexion, bright eyes, chest drumming with excitement, a delicious curling deep in my belly. I deserve this.

Walking to the double doors between our suites, I slide my arm up the doorframe, mimicking a femme-fatale pose I saw in a movie. Magic's back is turned to me, resplendent in plum velvet.

I slip a bare leg out of my towel, a swimmer's best feature. "Let's dine in, shall we?"

He turns, holding a burning match, the flame reflecting in his irises of aqua and moss. "You read my mind." A purple silk ascot tucks loosely into a velvet shawl-collar jacket with nothing underneath. Smooth pectorals gleam in the light of the candles on the dining table, set with crystal goblets, silver domes over plates.

I go to him and blow out the match. His hair feels soft on my fingers. For a moment I stare at his earnest face, tracing his broad forehead with my fingers, down the ridge of his cheekbones, to his aquiline nose, the slight bow in the center of his upper lip. The full pout of his lower lip makes me bite it.

"You're hungry," he says, and lifts me up. My towel falls to the floor. He lays me out on the bed, holding my arms above my head. He gazes at my breasts, my white arms, my newly concave belly, and draws a shuddering breath. "I want to feed you."

Normally, I'd laugh at a corny comment like this, but I want to see what he has in mind.

Holding my wrists with onc hand, he pulls the purple ascot from his neck and wraps it across my eyes, behind my head, then laces it around my arms and wrists. Fear frizzles through me like an electric filament. I try to ease my qualms. I trust him, don't I? He's tying the ends of the silk to something—the headboard, I think. My arms are pressed against my ears . . . I squirm a little.

Hearing a slight ding of metal, I soon feel his warmth above me. A sweet smell, then his mouth plunges onto mine, taste bursting on my tongue. Boysenberries. The berries rupture with tartness along my tongue, sending a zinging sensation to my eardrums. He feeds me berry after berry with his teeth, explores my tongue, licks juice from my lips, our mouths mingling in delicious tartness.

He leaves me, and I miss the taste of his tongue. A dollop of cold fluff plops between my breasts and another on my belly. I allow his sensual gift to unfold without a word as he moves the cream around my chest and stomach in leisurely circles.

A tingling builds in my center, and I rock side to side as best I can with my arms tied above, wanting him.

"Tonight is your night," he says.

I arch to him, begging. "I need you, Magic."

"You will get everything you need."

Writhing and reaching for him. I never got all I needed with Jack. Despite my gasps and groans, Houdini doesn't stop. His fingers persist until wave after wave crashes over me over me over me . . . Every tension in my body released, years of hidden grief.

Unbinding my arms and eyes, he kisses me, soft as a zephyr. I pull his arm, anxious to feel him on top of me.

He shakes his head. "That will have to wait until after I perform tomorrow. I need all my strength."

Disappointment cuts like chipped ice through my veins; Jack has turned me away so often. When Houdini gets up to turn off the lights, I make a break for my room, chest heaving, unwanted hot tears flowing down my cheeks.

Houdini grabs my waist from behind. "Don't leave. Please sleep with me. I need you in my bed, Charmian."

All the nights I waited for Jack to say that.

"Please stay." He kisses my neck, smelling warm and spicy.

I let him take me back to bed, where he curls around me. We lie like this together in darkness and silence, his breath brushing past my ear, slow and hypnotic. I'm almost asleep when he murmurs, "Don't worry, darling. We'll have plenty of time . . ."

He's wrong. There's never enough time. Time runs out no matter how enduring it seems in the moment. The scents of plumeria and sea salt. The triumph of a shiny trophy. Sea spray pelting our cheeks. And words. True words, poetic words, provocative words rendered in ink and blood on the printed page.

Then it's cut short. Loose ends fraying. Things that need saying. Hurts that need healing. Love that lingers unreciprocated. Never enough time.

# 28

## Willard Hotel, Washington, DC
## March 1917

Someone knocks on the door, brittle and insistent. The curtains glow with pale light. Magic unwinds himself from my body, puts on a robe, and unlocks the door. Nothing special. Nothing magic. I smile. Sometimes he is just a man unlocking a door.

The hallway light illuminates across the Oriental carpets, and I'm happy the bed is far from its path.

"Gentlemen, may I help you?" he says.

A pause, then a clipped voice, low but determined. "Sir, we have orders to escort you at oh-six-hundred hours, sir."

Houdini steps out into the hallway and closes the door behind him. I catch only a few words. "How long? Why wasn't I told? My wife . . ."

His wife. Bessie. I sit up, searching for my nightgown on the floor before I remember it's still in my carpetbag—in my room. If I run for it, they may open the door and catch my shameful flee. So I pull the covers up under my chin and wait. Did Bessie hire them?

Houdini comes in, and I catch a glimpse of two men in army uniforms. He closes the door on them and leans against it, eyes fixed on his black bag.

"I'm afraid I have to go. It can't be helped. I'm sorry." He picks up the bag and takes it into the bathroom, closing the door. The water runs.

My mind scurries like mice in an attic. I run for my room. My bag is on the luggage rack untouched. I should get dressed.

Hearing Houdini come out of the bathroom, I grab the terry bathrobe hanging in the wardrobe.

He opens my door, already dressed in a dark suit and white shirt, his black valise in his hand.

"You're leaving." I run my hand through my hair, imagining its odd angles.

He watches my movement with the focus he'd give a new card trick. "It seems I have a meeting I wasn't aware of."

"Who schedules a meeting for six o'clock in the morning?"

"A very busy man." He entwines his fingers in mine, gazes at my face. "Are you real? What are you doing to me?"

"What did I hear about your wife?"

He takes my chin between his forefinger and thumb and kisses me. "I told them they should apologize for waking my wife." He kisses me again and walks to the door. "I'll come back for you at ten."

When I open the door at eleven, it's a soldier, bald as a newborn.

He salutes. "Lieutenant Dorry, under General Stratten."

A small bandage sticks at an angle above his lip.

"Mr. Houdini has been detained and asked that I bring you to the *Washington Times* building."

"Detained by whom?" I ask.

"I'm not at liberty to say, ma'am," he says. "We should go, ma'am. There is quite a crowd already."

He leads me through the lobby and helps me into the back seat of a black sedan, an American flag fluttering from its hood. He sits in front with a private who drives us through back alleyways of Washington, DC. He has another bandage at his neck. The man needs to sharpen his razor. Nakata prided himself with his Japanese razor, which could slice a hair in two. The memory leads down a rabbit hole I refuse to follow this morning.

The black sedan stops at the back entrance of the *Washington Times* building. The lieutenant takes me to an Otis elevator. My stomach tosses and turns—I'm glad I didn't eat breakfast. We rise four stories, and the lieutenant leads me out onto a large open floor with rows and rows of desks. Telephones and typewriters are abandoned by their operators, who are pressed against the front windows.

"There's room over there," he says.

I position myself close to the window and look onto a sea of people, a hundred thousand or so, like a school of fish. Someone bellows over a microphone, but I hear only echoes from here. A brass band plays "Pomp and Circumstance."

I look for him on the small platform in the midst of the crowds. Muscular men crank a thick cable in fits and spurts around a winch. I follow the cable up.

Houdini hangs upside down like a chrysalis from the arm of a crane. His upper body and arms are trussed in a leather straightjacket, buckled in the back, his feet manacled with chains and locks.

My heart thrusts up my throat, throbbing in the glands under my jawbone.

The clock on the cathedral chimes twelve, and Houdini begins to twist and squirm in his straightjacket. Even from my vantage point, I can see his neck tendons bulge and turn red with fury. He bends and brings his head up to his waist, over and over as though suffering an epileptic fit. He jerks down. The rope spins him around. He forces his encased arms over his head and works at the buckles in the back. He frees the strap connecting the sleeves of the jacket, flipping his feet up through the strap, then he pushes his feet down. How his arm sockets remain intact, I have no idea. He flexes his body like a bow and arrow and shucks the jacket off, howling with pain. Something is wrong, but he drops the jacket to the ground, right arm flailing at the wrong angle.

The crowd roars their support.

Workmen below start to crank the winch and lower him down . . . but the ropes tangle and the winch stops moving. A wind sways Houdini outward, then momentum thrashes him against the building with a horrific thwack. His head hits the brick with a mushy thud.

Blood spurts from his forehead. The wind shoves him against the building again, and he tries to push away with his left arm, right arm still dangling.

The workmen pull at the winch, and the rope drops Houdini two floors down and stops short. Jerks him up again.

I scream, lost in the shouts and shrieks of the rest of the spectators.

Panicked now, I watch the men on the ground untangle the cable and slowly unwind it. Houdini swings upside down as they lower him. Eight minutes to get him down. Eight minutes of manacles cutting into his ankles. Eight minutes of blood throbbing in his head.

"He needs me." I run to the elevator, but by the time we reach the ground, they've driven him away, no one knows where. The lieutenant takes me back to the Willard, an hour and a half to travel the few blocks in the crowds. My mind skitters with worry.

He must have broken bones, must have a concussion . . . Bessie was right to worry. He could have been killed. I feel sick.

A newsboy hollers outside the hotel. "Extra! Extra! Houdini escapes death at *Washington Times*." I hand him a nickel and buy the thin edition.

"Don't worry," the lieutenant says when he lets me off. "The president will get him the best care."

"The president," I say.

He bites his lip. "You didn't hear that from me."

When we enter the elevator, the lieutenant salutes an army guard and another when we get off on our floor. Two more guards stand at our doors. "These officers will stay right outside your door if you or Mr. Houdini need anything."

A prisoner in my own room.

The lieutenant turns on his heel and walks to the elevator, leaving me in the hallway.

The suite door opens, and a man with a black satchel and top hat is leaving, buttoning his overcoat, and wrapping a tattersall scarf around his neck. "You must be Mrs. Houdini, so glad you're back." He shakes my hand. "Dr. Peterson, from the White House. Your husband is in grave condition, I'm afraid."

A warning from another time, the same knot at the base of my throat.

"He'll have to stop these antics, or they'll kill him," the doctor says.

"Why didn't they take him to the hospital?" I ask.

He glances at the army guard, then back at me. "Orders." He clears his throat. "Keep him quiet. He has a concussion, dislocated shoulder, three cracked ribs. The worst of it is his punctured lung. Gave him morphine, so he'll have no pain tonight."

The hallway sways, the electric lights too bright. Jack's death rushes back.

"I wish I could stay, but I have another call. Walk with me, and I'll tell you what you need to do for our patient." The doctor takes my arm and walks toward the elevator, speaking loudly. "Make sure he takes the pills I left every two hours to control the pain." Lowering his voice, he adds, "Someone cut Houdini's rope."

I draw a quick breath, and he squeezes my arm until it hurts.

"Telephone if you need me." He hands me his card and steps into the elevator; the attendant closes the brass gate.

I rush back to see him. The guards let me into our suite.

His breath whistles, chest laboring to breathe. The tapestry draperies have been drawn.

He lies flat on his back, bags of ice under his ankles, bruised and swollen to twice their size, skin raw. Bandages are wound around his chest and head. A sling holds his right arm close to his chest.

I sit in the chair by the bed and watch his eyelids jump wildly, his chest shudder up and down. He's sleeping, but not peacefully.

Should I telephone Bessie? Let her know what's happened? What good would it do to break her heart twice?

I watch him sleep, my magic man, ruined by his desire to break through life's boundaries.

Like another man I loved.

In the morning, the doctor returns, checks him over. Houdini won't take the morphine granules he offers. I order a big breakfast, but he only eats the eggs—no toast, no coffee. I sense he wants silence, and I comply to his wishes.

He lies completely still. Closes his eyes halfway and breathes deeply, not speaking, not moving for two days, except to eat salmon and spinach from room service.

Finally, his purple bruises broaden, turn to smudges. The contusions around his ankles where iron cuffs sliced into his skin start to lose the angry swell.

On the third day, he feels well enough to relieve the guards and telephone the doctor not to come. He sends Bessie a telegram: NEWSPAPERS EXAGGERATED -stop- PUBLICITY STUNT -stop- HOME NEXT WEEK -stop-

Then he unplugs Alexander Graham Bell and hangs a **Do Not Disturb** sign on the brass doorknob of our room.

Magic lies naked with me in our bed, passing the hours as if there's nothing else going on in the world. No magic show. No war. No Bessie.

At least for him. My mind drifts to her goofy laugh and baby-blue eye shadow.

The man the world knows for his unwavering focus is now focused on me. *Unnerving* is an understatement.

His fingers reach under my arm and trail slowly down to my waist, grabbing it lustily. "You are such a *woman*, Charmian." He leans to kiss my belly, hands caressing my hips. "You are unreal to me."

His fingers roam sensuously on the neglected parts of my body, the undersides of my arms and knees, the tender skin on the inside of my thighs. He descends on me like the swan in Kalmakov's painting, his chest and abdomen rippling on my skin. Electricity needling me with pleasure.

My body is overwhelmed with sensation: a vast river rushing into a drowning whirlpool. Lost in the deep.

When my consciousness returns, I slip out of bed. My legs are shaking so much I'm barely able to walk to the bathroom. I sit on the side of the cold porcelain tub and turn on the hot water, pouring fragrant bubble bath from the Willard's crystal pitcher on the counter. Watching the bubbles rise to the top and burst.

Lowering myself into hot water, my throat aches with emotion. But why now? Jack hated hysteria in women. And by hysteria, he meant any emotion that included tears.

My body looks the same through water and foam, but I know better. Every secret crook and cove has been discovered and conquered. When my body recovers, I'll crave this all over again, like drinking water in a desert, drunk too fast and too much, it makes one ill.

I slide the castile soap over my body until my limbs stop shaking and tears stop running down my cheeks.

Drying off, I pull on the soft terry-cloth robe and hear a strange voice from the adjoining suite. Magic's voice, but commanding and crisp.

"Rolfe will never wait a month, hire another technician to process the film. Hire two."

Feeling ridiculous lurking behind the door, I pad in quietly. He's pulled open the curtains to our elegant nest. Queen Anne chairs with curvy cabriolet legs, Tiffany dragonfly lamps, cornflower-and-goldenrod wallpaper.

He sits at the desk in his white shirt and trousers, his back to me, looking out to the snowy street, holding the telephone receiver to his ear. "We can't get a reputation for being slow. Hire men now so they're up to speed before the next film." His injured shoulder hikes up. I go to massage it, but it's so tight my fingers can't penetrate. My hands knead his shoulder by rote muscle memory. Another man, another time. Disturbed, I drop my hands to my side.

"I know young men are enlisting." His voice strains. "So hire older men. Anyone can work a crank." He reaches for my hand. "I won't lose this job. Make it happen." He hangs up the handset.

"Trouble with your film company?"

He pulls me around to stand between his thighs. "Nothing for you to worry about."

It should be refreshing not to be embroiled in his business as I was with Jack, so why do I feel shut out?

My hands dive into his wavy hair. "Is it about the *Master Mystery* series you're planning to make?"

"How'd you know?"

"I read *Variety*." I sit down on his lap, hand rubbing his neck, fingers hungry for the feel of his skin. "Tell me about it."

His brows pinch together. "Nothing much to tell."

"Come on, tell me."

"I'll play an undercover agent for the Secret Service."

"Art mimicking life?" I laugh.

"Let's go to Ebbitt's Grill, a great saloon around the corner, best rabbit on the East Coast."

"Magic, talk to me."

He stands, and I have to get up. He crosses to the mirror, ties his bowtie, difficult with his injured arm. But something about his stiff jaw keeps me from helping him.

"The doctor told me escapes will kill me. Maybe a movie career is not so bad."

I stand behind him, our two faces reflected in the mirror.

"What are you doing with the Secret Service?" My voice rises in spite of myself. ". . . and the president, for pity's sake?"

Houdini grabs his top hat. "How about that rabbit?"

Over the next week, Houdini often leaves me for two or three hours. He never tells me where he's been, and I don't ask. When he returns, he takes me to bed, ravenous for me. He loves me in a way I've always longed to be loved. As a woman. Not a comrade, not a muse, not a confidant. Purely as a woman.

I'm swimming too deep.

# 29

## Greenwich Village, New York City, New York April 1917

A blizzard has blown over New York, killing all the tree blossoms in Central Park. The Hudson has frozen over again.

Taking care to be very quiet, lest Houdini wake, I light the woodstove to take the morning chill off the flat and start the percolator for coffee. I tiptoe out of my flat and downstairs, where Romany Marie has my order ready. Gogosi and a cheese-and-mushroom strudel. No bacon. I carry it upstairs, excited about the day. But by the time I return, my plan has gone awry. Magic is in the bath already, and I've missed bringing him breakfast in bed.

I set breakfast on the table, smelling the tuberose he brought me yesterday and thinking how he'll love what I've planned. I turn on the Victrola radio I bought him for his birthday and set it to the station he likes, playing the Original Dixieland Jass Band.

"This program is interrupted with an important announcement." The radio crackles with static and a blaring siren. Houdini steps from the washroom, bare chested, a towel wrapped around him. Soap suds cover half his face.

"President Woodrow Wilson has declared war against Germany. The president cited Germany's refusal to suspend submarine warfare in the Atlantic and the Mediterranean, as well as attempts to entice Mexico into an alliance against the United States . . ."

Our eyes lock until the broadcaster stops talking. "The president did it," Magic says. "He finally did it." Magic's chest expands, and he returns to the bathroom.

My head buzzes with the news. What will it mean? I pour coffee from the percolator.

A couple of minutes later, he reappears, dressed in suit and tie, one side of his face shaven and the other stubbled but wiped clean. He bolts to the door, then turns back.

He kisses me on the cheek. "I have to enlist; then I can start."

"Start what?"

"The plan." He walks to the door. "I'll be in touch."

Macmillan has finally published *Our Hawaii*. George Brett scheduled a book signing for me on Fourth Avenue's Book Row, even as America joins the war, like it hasn't sunk in. This is the zenith of everything I ever hoped for.

When I walk in, Mr. Brett looks twice, and I'm glad I turned over my book tour wardrobe to the fashionable hands of Edna at Bergdorf's, though I'd worried that the pleated handkerchief skirt seemed too avant-garde. Mr. Brett shakes my gloved hand as if we've never fought. "Jack would have been so proud of you today."

I blink and huff before I realize it. Jack.

"The readers will be thrilled to meet you," he says, backpedaling.

He means they'll be thrilled to meet Jack London's widow, and by the number of folks lined up outside, he's right.

"I brought in Kona coffee and coconut malasada like you suggested. The customers will love it." He takes me to meet the owner. "Mr. Cohen, this is Jack London's wife, Charmian."

Half my age. The young man shakes my hand with the dry palm of a bookseller. Antique coins fasten the French cuffs of his crisp white shirt and button his smart vest, and he has long sideburns. "We are proud to launch your book tour, Mrs. London. I've been reading *Our Hawaii* aloud to my wife and daughters at night. We're just at the old palace with Queen Lili-Lula—" His face colors.

"Queen Liliuokalani. Yes, that was wild. But keep reading. The next bit is about carnival at Diamond Head. Spear throwing, pa'u riders, fire goddesses, paniolo steer roping."

"What a life you led," he says.

"I'd like to think there's another chapter. Shall we get started?"

He shows me the table and chair with stacks of *Our Hawaii* and Jack's other novels. Part of the deal, I suppose, promoting Jack's books as his widow. I paste a smile on my face, take out my fountain pen, and they open the doors.

All the fans offer condolences, then ask their burning questions.

"Was he an adventurer or a philosopher?"

"Politician or entrepreneur?"

"Farmer or writer?"

And no matter the question, my answers sound the same: It's impossible to contain Jack London in one word. He was all this and more.

Talking to readers about life with Jack is like talking about a different woman altogether: spearing dolphins, dancing hula, and horseback riding to Kilauea volcano before dawn. Memories of Jack are painted with riotous colors—a scorching orange sun rising from the purple ocean, misty rainbows streaming from cerulean heavens.

Afterward, I'm exhausted, but Mr. Brett has arranged a private interview with a reporter from the *New York Times*. The tiny bespectacled man seems truly moved by my story of the leper colony on Molokai. Being an avid Jack London fan, he asks about the theme behind *On the Makaloa Mat*.

I quote my favorite passage about a woman choosing love over money. "'But oh, all the Pierce-Arrows and all the incomes in the world compared with a lover—the one lover, the one mate, to be married to, to toil beside and suffer and joy beside, the one male man lover husband.'"

The reporter thanks me profusely. The review will be in Sunday's newspaper.

"You had him eating out of your hand," Mr. Brett says.

"We did seem to get on," I say. "Does it matter so much?"

"Your writing career depends on it," he says. "From the looks of things, you should get started on Jack's biography."

"Make an offer, and I'll compare it with Doubleday's." Make him squirm.

I walk home with my paper sack of malasada through Washington Square Park, cherry trees blooming, a father flying a kite with his son, a poet reading aloud under the triumphant arch dedicated to art. A new sense of pride fills my chest. I belong under this arch now, a published author, with two books in print and another in the offing. Would Jack be proud? Here he is again, overwhelming my thoughts.

I tear off small pieces of a malasada and throw them into the pond for ducklings following their mother. They fight over the bits.

Tears dam up behind my eyes. Why? I've found the lover of my dreams, and I'm crying over a man who'd "rather be ashes than dust," as Jack often said. Not a day passes, not an hour, without this terrible emptiness. Like I'm waiting for Jack to come back from a trip, like he'll be home for dinner, anxious to share a new philosophy or explain a new ranch project. Beaming his handsome grin at a joke. His brimstone eyes, fired up about politics. Fifteen years together.

I throw the rest of the malasada in the water, and the mother duck steals it from her scrambling brood, gulping it down with a swallow.

I find the path, my footsteps heavy and lumbering over the cherry blossoms littering the sidewalks.

"How did it go?" Romany Marie puts red candles into Chianti wine bottles on a dozen tables, adding a new color to layers of dripped wax. She looks fresh in her embroidered peasant blouse and circle skirt, flat leather shoes laced around her ankles.

"Sold ninety-five books." The smoky-spicy smell of paprika and sautéed beef makes me dizzy with hunger.

"I'll get you some goulash, and you can tell me all about it." Romany Marie pushes the kitchen door open, and I sit in my favorite corner, where I've watched patrons arrive: musicians, poets, actors, painters, singers. Aunt Netta would be agog at this place. Grudgingly, I wonder how she's doing, whether Edward stayed with her.

Romany Marie brings a crock of steaming goulash, black bread, and sweet butter. *"Mananca bine."* Eat well.

It smells so delicious I dig right in, taking a bite, so hot it scalds my tongue. My hand flies up to my mouth, waving madly. Blowing in and out.

She pours Chianti into flat glasses and clinks hers to mine. "To all your dreams coming true."

I nod and sip the wine to cool my mouth, my throat too constricted with emotion to talk. Looking down at the goulash, I avoid her gaze. Get a grip on myself. I dip a spoon into the stew and stir.

She watches me as she drinks her wine. The fiddle player comes in with a wave of his hand and sets up by the bar. I take another bite.

"Charmian, how do you feel?"

"I should feel good. I have my second book published, and Macmillan is chomping at the bit for another."

She takes my hand and turns it over. "But something's not right."

I tug it back, but she holds firm, tracing the lines.

"You're wasting your breath on me, Romany Marie. I don't go in for that type of thing."

Her finger draws a crease down the fleshy side of my palm. "Your intuition line is very pronounced." Her dark eyes flash in the candlelight. "But see here? Your marriage line cuts it off."

I hold my hand up to see what she's talking about, my thumb rubbing the sharp indentation where the lines cross.

"You have one marriage." Her earrings jangle. "But see how the line feathers at the end? You enjoy many lovers later in life."

I stuff my hand in my pocket. "I think I'll turn in. I have another book signing tomorrow."

Romany Marie's long fingernails graze my arm. "You cannot hide from what is written."

Magic hasn't been back in almost two weeks.

I spend time with Romany Marie in the restaurant, listening to the radio for any war news. Paying customers have stopped coming, but artists never leave, huddling in corners of the restaurant, painting odd still lifes in dull colors. War changes everything.

"Why don't you go to the theater to find out if he's okay?" Romany Marie says.

"I'm sure he's busy." I rip off a hangnail.

She takes my hands in hers, my cuticles torn and bleeding.

I pull my hands away. "If he wants to see me, he'll come here."

"That doesn't sound like you." Her dark eyes watch my face.

"He obviously moved back home." Home. That word again. "He doesn't need me to gum up the works."

I squeeze her hand and slide off the stool, go for a long walk.

There's a new marquee at the Hippodrome. The flashing bulbs of the sign announce that the Great Houdini has raised five hundred thousand dollars so far in war bonds from his new *Cheer Up* revue. Today's show must be almost over. The ticket booth is closed. No one is in the lobby. I open the theater door and slip in.

Two spotlights cross in the middle of the stage, highlighting the Great Houdini unlocking chains from around a trunk . . . the illusion they called Metamorphosis, which Houdini and Bess first performed together on Coney Island and made them famous touring the world.

Houdini undoes the locks and unwinds the chains from the trunk and opens it. Sweet Bessie pops out, her arms bound with knots. Knots I once tied. The impish pixie from whom I've stolen a husband. Houdini unties her, and Bessie bows in her courtly velvet costume, looking like a royal page of England.

Houdini sees me and gives a slight wave.

Later that night, Houdini shows up at my flat, apologizing profusely for his absence; he's been organizing the magician union to raise money for the war. There is nothing to forgive, I say, but he makes it up to me anyway. In his arms, I don't think, just enjoy.

In the morning, he's going out to Yonkers to start filming his *Master Mystery* movie series. He seems concerned to leave me alone again; I tell him I have my book signings to keep me busy.

Macmillan scheduled me at a bookstore on Fifty-Ninth Street, midtown Manhattan, to promote *Our Hawaii* and Jack's other books. Hours into the signing, I squirm in my chair to revive my sleeping bum. I can't see the end of the line wrapped around the store.

So this is what I agreed to: people paying the price of a book to touch the last piece of Jack London. Me.

I'm so mired in pitying myself I don't recognize the reek of gardenia until she steps up in her zebra-striped suit and ostrich-feather hat.

Bessie.

She leans across the desk and plants gooey pink lips on my cheek.

My mind freezes.

"When do you finish here?" she says. "I'll wait for you."

For the next two hours, she watches from the balcony, smoking skinny brown rollups from a Bakelite cigarette holder and wiggling fuchsia fingertips at me.

She has waited so long I can't muster an excuse not to accompany her in the taxicab back to their brownstone off Central Park North.

"I've been meaning to telephone," I say in the cab. "But with the book tour, I just haven't had time."

She smiles sweetly with those tiny yellow teeth. "Mr. Houdini's in Yonkers, as I guess you know."

She knows.

We get out at 278 West 113th Street, their four-story brownstone of dark-red brick. Bessie inserts a key into the front door.

"Who's there? Who's there?" I hear from the dark foyer.

"It's only me, Laura," Bessie says, switching on the chandelier and sticking her finger in a large gilded birdcage.

"Only me, only me," the parrot says.

"Squawk!" the other parrot screeches.

"No need to get jealous, Polly. Come give Mama love." She pours birdseed into the feeder, and the parrots peck at it.

"Gimama love," they say. "Gimama love."

My eyes adjust to the dim light. The birch-and-maple paneled foyer is a museum of everything Houdini. Engraved trophies, movie posters, wands from master magicians, a curio cabinet of hundreds of handcuffs, a bronze bust of Houdini, a statue of Sarah Bernhardt.

"The jeweled cup is from the Grand Duke Sergei of Russia, the ebony wand from the king of Belgium." Bessie holds out her hand. "May I take your jacket?" She hangs it on a row of hooks under the staircase. From behind her, there's a whirring noise, clicking and huffing, a glint of metal and glowing eyes.

I jump back. "Who's there?"

Bessie cackles like a witch. "Meet Automan, the evil robot. He kills you with electric rays from his fingertips."

My hand presses my chest. "You scared the bejesus out of me." On closer look, the robot makes me laugh with its ping-pong-ball eyes, paint-bucket head, stove-pipe limbs, and biscuit-tin feet.

"Mr. Houdini created him for *Master Mystery*. That stairwell below leads to his workroom and gymnasium." She turns Automan off. "The door at the front was Leopold's medical office until he stole Sadie from my other brother-in-law, Nat. Now it's just me, my sister, and mother who live here."

"Family can be tricky." Sad to think I count family on three fingers: Jack, Eliza, and Netta. Where does Houdini fit in?

A fox terrier with a missing front leg scoots backward down the steps and jumps on me. Makes me lonesome for Possum.

"Bobby likes you." She takes a dog biscuit from an urn, and the terrier circles on hind legs. "Good boy, Bobby." Dropping the biscuit into his mouth, Bessie starts to climb the stairs with her tiny red-and-black spats boots. Bobby scampers ahead.

On the second floor, several hallways branch off a round peacock-blue carpet emblazoned with a gold dragon. Bessie leads me to the corner of the house, puts her ear to a closed door, one finger to her mouth. "This is my gallery," she whispers. "Only my very best friends are allowed." She opens the door and steps inside, her eyes keen with appreciation.

Eight hundred or so dolls greet us with porcelain faces and glassy stares from every surface.

"Introduce yourself to the girls, and I'll stir up some pink ladies." She struts across the rose carpet to the bar, pours gin and grenadine in a shaker, and plays it like a maraca.

The parlor is pretty in pink: a bloodwood pianola stands near a fuchsia silk window shade, two mauve sofas face each other in the center, rose tapestry chairs flank the ornate silver radiator, a magenta velvet settee sits in front of the bar. I wander around the room, examining dolls of Russian, French, German, and English origin, a bassinet of baby dolls, even Indian dolls. When I find Victoria Woodhull, back in her blue-striped dress and **Votes for Women** banner, I take her in my hand like an old friend.

Bessie sets pink ladies down on the mirrored glass table. "There's room for us on this divan."

Dolls sit in the corners, so I nestle next to the Russian redhead wearing a fur coat and ice skates.

Bessie drops a red paper roll into the pianola. "Mr. Houdini bought this to keep me company while he's gone. He's always gone."

The piano keys and even the pedals start to play "Don't Bite the Hand That's Feeding You." Bessie sings along in a vibrant soprano.

"You have a gorgeous voice." I gulp my pink lady to calm my cheating heart, a jury of dolls judging every move. Only Victoria Woodhull seems sympathetic.

Bessie flounces down next to me. "So good to finally talk to somebody." She raises her glass to the dolls. "Besides them, I mean. They've heard it all before." She giggles and takes a long drink. "I had a fight with Mr. Houdini."

Gin goes down the wrong pipe and sends me into a coughing fit.

Bessie dashes behind the bar, turns on a faucet. "We had a giant row about him being gone so long in Washington . . . then, poof! The president declares war, and he goes to Yonkers on business. Shady business, if you ask me." She hands me a glass of water.

The three-legged fox terrier jumps on my lap, licking my face.

"Air kisses, Bobby—you know better." From a jeweled box on the table, she takes out a brown rollup, smells it, and smiles. Then she fits it into her Bakelite cigarette holder and flicks a flame from an exotic Aladdin's lamp.

She holds the smoke in her lungs, speaking in a strained voice. "Then he telephoned me since the *Master Mystery* bigwigs are here; he's staging a publicity stunt and a party afterward at the Houdini Picture Corporation." She blows smoke between us. "Bringing his leading lady, Ruth Stonehouse." The smoke clears, and she's watching me.

"Sounds glamorous," I say glibly, sipping my cherry gin, while the pianola plays "Jelly Roll Blues."

"*Variety* ran front-page pictures of her hanging on Mr. Houdini at Coney Island."

A flickering behind my retina. A beautiful actress on Magic's arm. "I'm sure it was just for publicity."

"That's what *he* said." Her bottom lip quivers. "I know I've never been enough for him. But why do I have to see them *together*?" She takes another sickening drag, eyelids quivering.

I take her free hand, clammy and cold. "Oh, Bessie. You're dreaming up things."

"He wants *me* to throw the party." Her breaths come fast and shallow. "A highfalutin Hollywood party for his highfalutin friends." Her fingers flutter in front of her face. "Directors, producers, movie stars . . . Ruth Stonehouse . . ." She falls back into the dolls, her eyeballs rolling to milky white.

Bobby licks her face, and she doesn't react. I put the terrier down on the floor, then feel for her breath. There is none, so I slap her cheek.

Her eyes fly open, and she whimpers, "Help me, Charmie."

I take her hand. "What do you need?"

"Help me throw the party, I can't face it alone."

Looking at this sweet painted cherub whom I've betrayed, I say, "I can do that."

Bessie squeals and kisses me smack on the lips.

# 30

## Greenwich Village, New York City, New York May 1917

Troubled times call for sweet fried dough.

Romany Marie serves up sweet Romanian gogosi while I explain the mess I got myself in with Bessie.

"The party is Saturday." I take a bite. "I'll greet the guests and duck out when they watch Houdini's film clips."

Romany Marie points her finger up, toward my flat. "He's waiting for you."

I take the gogosi and head out. "Why didn't you tell me?"

"You were hungry."

I make a face at her and run up the back stairs.

Magic is in the claw-foot tub, up to his chin in ice cubes, reading the *New York Post*.

"Come join me, the water's fine," he says, voice quivering.

"What are you doing?" From the look of melting ice, he's been there quite some time.

"Never know when you might get caught in an ice storm." His teeth are chattering.

"I assume you're in there for a reason?" I pull over a chair.

"I'm jumping into New York Harbor on Saturday to publicize *Master Mystery*."

"Sounds ambitious." I offer him a gogosi, and he refuses.

"The police have devised some inescapable handcuffs that took the blacksmith five years to make. And Acme Shipping will pack me in their heavyweight export crate drilled full of holes."

"More like a death wish. I thought you gave up escapes that could kill you."

He smirks and drops his newspaper to the floor. "Can't let Jenny do my work for me the rest of my life." His blue lips quiver, and his teeth clamp together to keep from chattering.

"Why are you in ice? It's May."

"The harbor was thirty-two degrees yesterday. The body survives seven minutes until it passes out."

"How long will it take you?"

He shrugs. "I've never seen those handcuffs."

I pick up the newspaper off the floor and read aloud. "*Houdini's last jump!* 'Saturday's jump will be Mr. Houdini's last,' said the dainty one-hundred-pound Mrs. Houdini. 'Our daughter is having a baby, so naturally we'll want to be with our grandchildren.'" I lower the paper. "I didn't know you had a daughter, let alone a grandchild on the way."

"Bessie." He snorts and shuffles his bright-red toes to the top of the tub, ice overflowing to the floor.

"Have you ever stopped to consider why she makes up stories?" I say. "Maybe she feels neglected."

"Hooey." He grimaces. "She's flexing her muscles, showing me who's boss."

I don't like him dismissing her. "Bessie is a pussycat."

"With the claws of a tiger," he says.

I feel the mercury rise and burst from the top of my head like the thermometer in Sacramento. "She's fighting for attention. Can't you see?" I push back my chair. "Is marriage a game to you men? A toss of the dice, an arrow to a bull's-eye, so many pawns and rooks captured until you checkmate? Why stay in a marriage if you're not in love? It's demeaning and cruel . . . and . . . just plain heartless."

He pushes himself up to a stand, his nude body mottled white and red, goose pimples covering arms and legs, genitals hard and shrunken. He steps out and wraps a towel around himself.

"Hey. Hey." He tries to grab me, but I walk away.

Wrapping his arms around me from behind, his body cold and hard against my back, he buries his face in my neck. "This is no game, Charmian. I'm in love with you."

I turn around and kiss him and let the whole damn mess happen all over again.

Bessie and I have decorated Houdini Picture Corporation with giant *Master Mystery* posters, spotlighted from above. Bessie brushes Houdini's red velvet theater chairs so not a speck mars them. She insists on a second sweeping of the floors. The popcorn maker has been popping all morning, and red-striped bags stand ready to fill at the last minute, so they don't get soggy with butter. Bottles of soda pop are stuck in a copper trough of ice. Oversized candy bars and licorice await bigwig sweet teeth. A film reel of Houdini's escapes is threaded into the film projector.

"He'll love it. He'll *ab-silly-loot-dilly* love it." Bessie flaps her arms like a hummingbird. I do love this girl.

"We should be going. They toss him into the river at noon." I can't bear to say his name in Bessie's presence.

"You should talk him out of this jump," Bessie says, sipping from her pink flask.

"I have no power over your husband." I toss buttery popcorn in my mouth.

"We both know that isn't true." One painted eyebrow arches high.

My day of reckoning has come, and I feel strangely ready. "Bessie, I—"

She puts two fingers on my lips. "Let me say this. I wanted to the other night and lost my nerve. Before you, Mr. Houdini had accepted getting older, going back to magic, making movies. Then you come into our lives, and he's hitching submarines to Pearl Harbor, flying planes to Washington, and dangling from skyscrapers."

"Bessie, I never meant—"

"It's not so awful when you think about it. I know Mr. Houdini loves me, and I love him. And you and I love each other, don't we? Didn't your aunt make it work?"

The triad. "You don't really feel that way."

"I don't want to lose him, Charmie. We can't lose him." She hugs me close, and I stroke her short hair, wispy and fine as a dandelion wand. Her gardenia perfume clears my head like smelling salts.

"We'll discuss this after the party."

She smiles up at me, and I kiss her forehead.

"You're a very special woman, Bessie."

The sky is the color of pewter, and it's foggy and frigid for a May day. Not exactly the balmy weather we'd hoped for. Governors Island is packed with spectators as I shoulder my way through the crowds, Bessie under my arm. "Stand aside. This is Mrs. Houdini. Stand aside, please."

We make it to the pier where photographers are snapping pictures of the *Master Mystery* stars, Ruth Stonehouse in her mink stole and Houdini in his sleek swimming suit defining every muscle.

"Why don't they put him with someone his own age for a change," Bessie whines.

The starlet looks so young, while Houdini is graying at the temples, tense and distracted, peering into the murky waves.

New York City Police put the handcuffs on him and shackle chains around his swimming trunks, through his legs, securing the chains with locks, then throwing the keys far out into the choppy river.

Magic lifts his head and looks around at the spectators, searching.

"Over here, darling." Bessie waves and blows him kisses.

He smiles, sees us together and frowns, pauses, then waves. He steps into the shipping crate and takes one last look at us before they close it up. Men pound in iron coffin nails with a sledgehammer. The crate is perforated with round holes—is that better or worse for Magic in the cold water?

"Oh my goodness, oh my goodness." Bessie flutters her hands. "I hate this. He wanted to kiss me this morning, and I just gave him my cheek."

Burly workmen truss the crate with ropes, knotting them repeatedly. Then, without warning, they push the crate over the pier into the gray water with a tremendous splash.

My stomach drops with his falling body. Pushing our way to the end of the pier, I look down, but the crate has disappeared in the dark water. Only bubbles rise to the surface and burst. I've seen him in so many escapes, why should I feel so petrified now?

Beside me, Bessie starts humming like a whirring beehive, digging her pointed nails into my palm, until I swear they'll break the skin.

Soon the chief of police calls out, "One minute." And the crowd cheers.

Then Bessie starts singing in high vibrato . . . "Good Luck, Good Bye, God Bless You."

The chief of police interrupts the second verse, "Two minutes."

"How long is it supposed to take?" I ask him.

"Mr. Houdini expected to be up by now, but he can't last more than three minutes, ma'am."

Bessie sings "At the End of a Beautiful Day."

"Three minutes," the chief yells.

"Shouldn't you do something?" I say. "It's past time."

"He told us not to interfere, no matter what happens," the chief says, and stares into the water.

I tug on Bessie's sleeve. "Make them pull him up. It's past three minutes."

"You don't understand, do you, Charmie? It's his way out. He thinks he has to decide between us, and he can't." She starts singing a damn hymn this time, round eyes riveted on the sky. People are panicked all around us, and she just keeps on singing.

I confront the chief. "We demand you bring him up immediately. He can't survive this long."

"Stand back, ma'am. There's nothing we can do." He looks at his stopwatch. "Four minutes."

I shake Bessie's shoulders. "You want him to die? We have to save him."

Her blue eyes grow large and wise. "You can't save him, Charmian."

I back away, confused. Horrified. She'll let her husband die down there.

"There he is!" someone yells. "Way out there." The crowd cheers, and I look in the direction they're pointing.

Three hundred yards out, he's swimming toward the pier, his powerful arms thrusting forward. The current must have dragged him out.

I grab Bessie up in my arms and whirl her around and around, laughing and crying at the same time.

Burning through the morning fog, the sun gleams on his strong shoulders, making the final strokes. Bessie bounces on her toes. Movie-studio tycoons in double-breasted suits and striped ties move in front of us to congratulate Houdini in front of newspaper photographers. Bessie is pushed behind just as Houdini reaches the pier, waving me over. I want to rush to him, hug him to me . . . so glad he is alive.

But Bessie calls, and I have to choose.

"Charmie, help." Her small gloved hand waves from behind some spectators.

Unable to resist, I wend my arm through the crush of bodies and pull her through, handing her over to the chief of police. "Make sure Mrs. Houdini gets to see her husband before anyone else." Including me.

He nods his chin.

Bessie turns to me. "Stay with me. He'll want to see you, too."

I back away. "Someone has to bag up the popcorn."

She smiles and turns back to where policemen hoist Magic out of the river, soaked and shivering. Bessie slams her tiny body into his, and he wraps his arms around her. The crowd shouts and whistles, goes crazy with enthusiasm. Houdini raises his fists high and roars in triumph.

I struggle out through the jostling crowd, all trying to get a look at the Great Houdini. I glance back. Bessie and Houdini kiss. That juicy plum kiss I wanted for my own.

I walk down the pier, through cheering crowds. At the street, I turn back for a last look. Bess and Houdini are silhouetted at the end of the pier, still holding each other tightly.

But I don't return to Houdini Picture Corporation, I take a taxi to Greenwich.

Romany Marie kisses me on both cheeks and hands me my carpetbag. "I'll send all your fancy clothes to the ranch."

"Keep them," I say, looking around the restaurant. "I have no idea where I'm going."

"I put some gogosi in your bag," she says, and the taxi honks his horn outside. "Men! Always in a hurry to go nowhere."

"If Magic comes looking for me, tell him something, will you?"

"Of course. What?"

"The magic is in the memory."

I kiss her on both cheeks and get into the taxicab to the train station.

The transcontinental is empty save for an older matron, whom I help with her bag. She asks where I'm from, and I answer, California. She says she knew it because she saw me in one of Chaplin's motion pictures. I smile and nod and look for my seat at the back of the train car.

Here I can watch the passengers get on and off at each stop. People who have somewhere to go. Unlike me. Eliza gave up writing long ago when I didn't answer her letters. She doesn't deserve that, but I had no idea what to write . . . "Dear Eliza, I'm having an affair with my best friend's husband, and we're planning to elope"?

That would go over well.

One thing is clear: this free-love thing is for the birds.

By the time we reach Amish Country, I've eaten all the gogosi and feel nauseous. The cornrows pass by my window like the end of a film strip flickering through the projector. After the hero kisses the heroine, after the swell of the orchestra, after "The End," after the credits roll through . . . The film strip just flaps and flaps through the projector, to the rhythmic clack of the railroad tracks, until the screen goes white and the lights go up.

The conductor finally makes his way back to me, a young man in his twenties, hair slicked back. I reach in my carpetbag for my one-way ticket and hand it to him. He punches it and hands it back with a sad smile, like I remind him of someone, maybe his mother.

Stuffing the ticket back in my bag, my hand lights on a package wrapped in pages of *M-U-M* magazine. It smells like woodspice cologne.

Maybe I should throw it away, toss it out into the cornrows without looking. I can't dwell on what could have been.

I tear open a corner of the wrapping. It's a book. Two inches thick, deckle-edged pages with an ivory leather cover engraved in gold across the bottom: "*Charmian Kittredge London.*" The first page is blank, and the second and third. I thumb through the blank pages and laugh.

# *Afterword*

*The Secret Life of Mrs. London* is a work of fiction. The characters of Jack and Charmian London, Harry and Bess Houdini, and most of the other characters, while based on real people, are fictionalized. While the story events coincide with actual events in the Londons' and Houdinis' lives, they are all fictionalized, and some are entirely from imagination. I have sometimes quoted dialogue from the Londons' works and letters. For the purpose of the story, I condensed the historical events into two years, whereas they span five. More lore about the characters of this novel can be found on my website at www.rebecca-rosenberg.com.

# *Acknowledgments*

I want to acknowledge Charmian London for her biography *Jack London*. Within those pages, she bares her soul to tell their story from her perspective. I want to thank my many readers and authors for their encouragement and candor: Malena Watrous, Maryann Sheppard, Ralph Smith, Anne McMillan, Kirsten Lind, Robin Boord, Peggy Cramer, Jim Cramer, Jayne Ehrens, Diane Rosenberg, Pam Schlossberg, Lori Fantozzi, Jim Fisher, Paulette Fisher, Kathleen Fitzgerald, Beth Mink, and Diane Brown. Each of you have my sincere gratitude. Thank you, Gary Rosenberg, for listening to the same story over and over again with rapt attention. Thank you to my agent, Sasha Raskin; my team at Lake Union; and my editors, Danielle Marshall, Miriam Juskowicz, Amara Holstein, Christopher Werner, Laura Petrella, and Jessica Gardner for bringing this novel to fruition.

# *Reading Group Guide*

1. Charmian and Jack London box together for fun and fitness. How does their boxing reflect on their marriage? What is Charmian's role in their relationship? How often does she win?
2. Charmian was raised by her aunt Netta in a household of free love, which was associated with women's rights at the turn of the century. What does Charmian think about free love? How does it influence how she sees Jack London? What attracts Charmian to Jack even through his self-absorption? What does Charmian crave most from Jack?
3. Charmian tells Bess Houdini about Jack's childhood: Jack sold newspapers at six years old . . . At thirteen, he worked in the cannery. At fifteen, he pirated oysters, sixteen—arrested for vagrancy . . . At eighteen, he jumped a cargo ship to Japan. When he returned, the police arrested him for Socialist agitation. Through all that, he never stopped writing. Short stories, novels, poems . . . She became his typist, his editor, his agent. How does Jack's poor, working background affect his work ethic and politics?

4. Jack London was the president of the Socialist Party. Yet Charmian and Jack fought about how expanding Beauty Ranch goes against Socialist ideals. Charmian says, "Surely you see that continuing to expand the ranch is against Socialist principles. We don't need more land, and we don't have the money, besides." To this Jack replies, "I've neglected your reading, Charmian. We are beyond those ideas now." What new philosophy is driving Jack to expand Beauty Ranch? Does Charmian buy it?
5. Bess Houdini and Charmian couldn't be more different women. What do they like about each other?
6. Bess Houdini suffered a condition called primary amenorrhea, in which a woman never goes through puberty, has a period, or develops breasts or other sexual characteristics. How does this affect her as a woman? How does it affect her relationship with Harry Houdini?
7. In November 1915, World War I had been raging for a year and half, yet the United States did not join the war until April 1917. How do Houdini and London differ in their opinions about World War I, and does that change through the novel?
8. What is it that attracts Jack London and Houdini to each other? How are they alike, and how do they differ physically, mentally, emotionally?
9. Who burned down Wolf House is a mystery to the present day. Who does Houdini think burned it down? Why? Who does Charmian think burned it down? Why? What did Wolf House's burning mean to Jack?

10. What meaning does Hawaii hold for Jack and Charmian? What issues follow them there?
11. How is the Jack London we meet through Charmian London's viewpoint in *The Secret Life of Mrs. London* different than the public persona of Jack London? What aspects surprise you?
12. What are some of the turning points in Charmian and Jack's marriage?
13. What brings Charmian and Houdini together? Why don't they stay together?
14. After Jack dies, what does Charmian need? How does that change in New York? How has Charmian changed from the beginning of the novel to the end?

# *About the Author*

California native Rebecca Rosenberg lives on a lavender farm with her family in Sonoma, the Valley of the Moon, where she and her husband founded the largest lavender-product company in America. A longtime student of Jack London's work and an avid fan of his daring wife, Charmian, Rosenberg is a graduate of the Stanford Writing Certificate Program. *The Secret Life of Mrs. London* is her first novel.